"James d[illegible]
plot twis[illegible]
—John Ti[illegible]

Every Crooked Path

"True to James's style, the plot is full of secrets and mind games that are entertaining and thought-provoking."

—*RT Book Reviews*

Checkmate

"High tension all the way . . . Fast, sharp, and believable. Put it at the top of your list."

—John Lutz, Edgar Award–winning author of *Single White Female* and *Slaughter*

The King

"His tightly woven, adrenaline-laced plots leave readers breathless." —The Suspense Zone

"Steven James offers yet another slam dunk in the Bowers Files series!" —*Suspense Magazine*

Opening Moves

"A mesmerizing read . . . My conclusion: I need to read more of Steven James."

—Michael Connelly, *New York Times* bestselling author of *The Wrong Side of Goodbye*

"Steven James has created a fast-moving thriller with psychological depth and gripping action. *Opening Moves* is a smart, taut, intense novel of suspense that reads like a cross between Michael Connelly and Thomas Harris . . . a blisteringly fast and riveting read."

—Mark Greaney, *New York Times* bestselling author of *Gunmetal Gray*

continued . . .

"Prepare yourself for a horror-of-a-ride, edge-of-your-seat thriller of thrillers." —Fresh Fiction

"[A] fast-moving, intense thriller that has as many demented twists and turns as the crimes themselves."

—Examiner.com

The Pawn

"Riveting." —*Publishers Weekly*

"[An] exceptional psychological thriller."

—Armchair Reviews

THE BOWERS FILES

Opening Moves
The Pawn
The Rook
The Knight
The Bishop
The Queen
The King
Checkmate
Every Crooked Path
Every Deadly Kiss

EVERY DEADLY KISS

THE BOWERS FILES

STEVEN JAMES

BERKLEY
New York

BERKLEY
An imprint of Penguin Random House LLC
375 Hudson Street, New York, New York 10014

ISBN: 9781101991572

First Edition: July 2017

Printed in the United States of America
1 3 5 7 9 10 8 6 4 2

Cover art: Hooded man © Beto Chagas/Shutterstock Images;
Church © Kevin Keys/Shutterstock Images
Cover design by Jae Song

To Jim, David, Bec, and Trinity.
Cancer could not conquer your joy.

PART 1

“You Too.”

Although typically transmitted through aerosol means after six to eight days, with recent advances in synthetic biology, in time the *variola* virus could also, theoretically, be modified to transfer well before the patient is symptomatic.

—FROM AN INTERVIEW WITH DR. VLADISLAV KUZNETSOV IN THE *ANNALS OF ENDEMIC AND INFECTIOUS DISEASE*, APRIL 2002, PAGE 133.

At the root of many of the mythical tales, according to some writers, one finds the never-ending battle between light and darkness, the former being usually symbolized by a hero, and the latter by a monster.

—FROM *BLUEBEARD: AN ACCOUNT OF COMORRE THE CURSED AND GILLES DE RAIS, WITH SUMMARIES OF VARIOUS TALES AND TRADITIONS* BY ERNEST ALFRED VIZETELLY, 1902, PAGE 12.

1

Saturday, May 5
Aspen Cove Lake, Minnesota
10:32 P.M.

He watched her stir the Manhattan he'd just mixed for her. He didn't want to be too forward, so rather than sit beside her on the couch, he chose the chair facing her. The cabin's living room window, black with the night, stared at him over her shoulder.

"So," she said playfully. "How about a little game?"

"What kind of game?"

"It's about secrets." She set her drink next to his wineglass on the rustic coffee table resting between them. "I'll tell you one of mine and then you get to tell me one of yours."

"I noticed how you phrased that: I *get* to tell you one."

"Uh-huh. But it has to be something you've never told anyone else before."

"Alright."

"I mean, *never*. Not *anyone*."

"Okay."

"Promise?"

He lifted his glass as if he were toasting the idea. "Promise."

"Alright." She took a sip of her drink. "I once saw a guy die and I didn't do anything to help him."

He blinked in disbelief. "What happened?"

"It was back when I was in college and I was at this frat party, right? And people were shooting up, getting high, drinking—all that. It was a little out of hand and I'd had too many shots of tequila. I should've just gone back to my dorm, but I let this cute guy take me upstairs to one of the bedrooms. You know."

"Sure."

She repositioned herself. "He wanted to do these lines of heroin and we were gonna do them together, but he went first and overdid it. OD'd. I could have probably helped him or called 911 or something, but I was too scared and I just watched him collapse and have this seizure and this gross vomit came foaming out of his mouth and then he was just super still—except his arms and legs kept shaking. But finally they stopped moving too. It was like you see in the movies: he wasn't breathing or anything. I was terrified that something bad would happen to me if I told anyone I'd been with him in that room—that I might be accused of killing him or go to jail, or whatever—so I snuck into the hall again, pretended I was just looking for the bathroom, made my way past all those other people at the party, and ran back to my dorm as fast as I could. I couldn't sleep for the rest of the night. The next day I heard his body had been found. They just called it an OD. No one ever came and talked to me. But I saw him die. I was there."

"And you could have helped."

"Yes."

He was quiet.

"Okay." She leaned forward. "Your turn."

"I'm not really sure what to say."

"Something no one else knows," she reminded him. "Something you've never told *anyone* before."

"I can trust you?"

She held up her right hand in a noble salute. "Scout's honor."

He grinned slightly. "You were never a scout, were you?"

"I slept with a guy once who used to be one."

"Ah. Gotcha."

"Taught me all his knots."

"I'm sure I didn't need to hear that."

"So, tell me your secret." She poured him more wine and slid his glass toward him.

"Are you trying to get me drunk?"

"I can't tell you *all* my secrets." She waited until he'd taken a drink. "So. Tell me."

"Well . . ." He took a long breath. "Then I'd say the toughest thing of all for me is when they promise they won't tell."

"What do you mean?"

"After I handcuff them to the bed, before I really get started. Most of the time they promise they won't say anything if only I'll let them go. They just keep going on and on like that. It's not nearly so bad when they just beg me to stop or they scream, or even pray. But those ardent, desperate vows of silence—those are the hardest to listen to."

She stared at him coolly. "It's not even funny to joke about stuff like that."

"I've never told anyone that before."

"I know, but in this game, in my game, whatever you tell me, the secret, it's gotta be true."

She glanced toward her purse on the dining room table, where he'd set it for her earlier, and for a moment he had the sense that she might go for it, but instead, she just said in a hushed voice, hardly louder than a whisper, "You said, 'they.'"

"They?"

"You said sometimes 'they' promise. 'They' beg you. Who is 'they'?"

"The women I bring home. The last one, I actually believed her. I let her go. But I shouldn't have. She lied to me. She told. They weren't able to pin any of the previous deaths on me so, with good behavior, I ended up serving fifteen years. But—"

"You're a sick bastard." She rose, strode to the table, and snatched up her purse.

He couldn't quite tell if she believed him or was just upset by what he'd said.

She hurried out the door.

He followed. "I didn't mean for you to leave."

"Screw you."

At the doorway, he stood watching her by the car.

Brisk. Cool. Even though it was spring, this far north, a tinge of winter still lingered in the forest.

The light from the porch reached far enough for him to see her fumbling through her purse for the keys, which he'd taken out earlier when he placed it on the table for her.

Both her keys and her phone.

He tapped the button on the key fob and the doors beeped, unlocked. "Does that help?"

She gasped and faced him, then somewhat clumsily

kicked off her heels so she could run faster, and took off into the dark woods surrounding the lake.

It did not take him long to catch her.

Though she struggled more than any of the others had, he managed to get her back to the cabin.

To the bedroom.

To the bed.

After he'd cuffed one of her wrists, it was much easier to get the other one secured to the bedpost as well. It always was.

"When I said I didn't mean for you to leave, I was telling the truth. When I said I don't like hearing their promises, I was telling the truth too."

As he stepped back, she yanked uselessly to get free. It'd been so long since he'd heard the sound of handcuffs rattling in that way that he'd forgotten how much he liked it, how familiar it had been to him.

Before.

"I'll scream. I swear to God!"

"This is the only cabin on this end of the lake so I don't believe it'll help, but I won't stop you if you'd like to give it a try."

She did, and while she did, he tilted the television to face the bed. This far out in the country, without cable, he needed to use a DVD instead of streaming the video. But he'd brought one. It wasn't a problem.

He wanted everything positioned just like it'd been with Scarlett. He wanted it to be just right.

After he'd pressed play, he removed the box cutter from the dresser drawer.

Early on, he'd experimented with a number of different

methods, but he preferred this one, had ever since he was a boy.

"What do you want from me!" The terror that rose in her voice was already tinged with desperation.

"I want you to be honest." He sat beside her and slid out the blade. Locked it in place. "No secrets. Just like before."

"Listen. Seriously." The words came in quick, hurried gulps. "You need to let me go."

"Why?"

"I lied at the bar. You have no idea who I am. You don't know how much I'm worth. I'll pay you whatever you want. Just please let me go."

"And you won't tell?"

"No, I promise I—"

But before she could finish her avowal of silence, he jammed the blade through her right cheek, clipping a tooth and burying the tip into her jaw. One swift, firm movement. One sweep of his arm. "Do not make such promises!"

She cried out in obvious pain, but then made a valiant attempt to collect herself. "I'm . . . I'm . . ."

He removed the blade. There wasn't much blood.

But there was some.

She spit it at him.

"I know who you are, Simone." He wiped the bloody saliva from his chin. "And I know how much you're worth. Tell me where Scarlett is."

"What?"

"Scarlett Farrow. You used to model with her back when you two were teenagers. The same agency. Brenning Talent Associates. In L.A."

"Scarlett? What are you talking about?"

"I think you know where she is."

"I haven't seen her in years."

He held up her phone and scrolled through the apps until he came to an alias on TypeKnot. He showed her the screen. "Snowball4? Who is that?"

"I don't know."

"Snowball was the name of the stuffed animal in the movie. Her rabbit."

"It's anonymous. I don't know if it's really her."

"Where does she live?"

And then sudden resolve. A steely gaze. "I'm not telling you."

And so he began to carve.

He used the box cutter until he had what he needed from her. She did tell. Eventually, yes, she did.

When at last he stood, the cuts were many, but they were not all deep.

"Don't worry. You're not going to die from those."

He heard screams from the television and glanced at the screen. The scene from the lake. Yes, it was a pivotal one, vital to all that was to follow in the bedroom. The closet. The church.

With Simone's phone, he sent a text to the person with the screen name Snowball4, then snapped a photo of Simone for himself.

The last one.

In a way, the photograph reminded him of the famous picture of Regina Kay Walters taken by Robert Ben Rhoades after he'd abducted her, cut her hair, and made her wear that black dress and those heels in the barn before killing her. It was one of the most memorable final photographs taken by killers that was floating around the Internet.

For all the world to see.

And now, here it was: the last picture anyone would ever take of the ex–swimsuit model—until the crime scene was eventually processed and her remains were photographed for the case files.

He walked out the bedroom door.

"Where are you going?" Simone gasped. Again, he heard the clang of the handcuffs as she tried futilely to pull free.

"I think that, considering what you did to that young man back when you were in college," he called through the doorway, "you being here is a form of justice. It's poetic, in a sense. Things coming full circle."

"No, don't—"

He returned, carrying his duffel bag. "You could have helped him. Instead, you just stood by and let him die. If you hadn't told me that story, I might have ended this for you quickly with the box cutter, but I think I'll let you choose how things play out, give you ample time to contemplate what you did—"

"Time?" She caught on. "No, no, no. Don't go." More rattling. "Don't leave me here!"

"Justice for what happened in the past. Isn't that what matters most?"

He opened the duffel bag and removed the grenade.

"What is that?" she asked, but he suspected she already knew.

"This one has a time delay. The striker lever, here, it's held in place by this pin. When I pull the pin, as long as that lever is still depressed, we're fine. But after it's released, with this type of grenade, we'll have four, maybe five seconds to get to safety." He gestured toward the cuffs. "And that'll be a bit easier for me than for you."

Being prudent not to release the striker lever, he pulled the pin.

"Open up now."

"That's not real. You'd never blow up your cabin."

"Secret number two: this is not my cabin."

In her surprise, she instinctively opened her mouth, but when he attempted to insert the grenade, she clenched her teeth in an act of intransigent defiance. Rather than fight her, he pried the fingers of her right hand back, then placed the grenade into it with the striker lever secure against her palm.

Wrapped her fingers around it.

"Careful now." He let go of her and stepped back. "As I said, I'll leave the end of the story up to you. When you're ready for this to be over, just open your hand. You'll have five seconds to make peace, to ask for forgiveness for your sins. Five seconds to find redemption. The couple who owns this cabin will be out of the country for another two weeks. If you manage to survive that long, you deserve to live and you'll have earned the right to tell the authorities about me. Good luck."

Just as he always did with the women, he leaned in and placed a tender kiss on her cheek, even as she tried in vain to twist her head away.

After collecting his things, he stepped outside into the chilly Minnesota night.

Finally, he had a city.

At last, a place to start.

Detroit.

He climbed into the car and pulled onto the long, winding drive that led to the edge of the property.

After parking just beyond the swinging gate to the county road, he walked back to padlock it shut.

As he was snapping the lock, he heard the scream, bright and shrill and slicing like a long, narrow blade through the night. A moment later, the explosion from the cabin rocked the forest, its echo reverberating restively across the lonely, black waters of the lake.

And so, Lady Justice had found her way through the years and placed her feet firmly in the present. Just as she was supposed to do.

With thoughts of Scarlett and all that was to come, he drove south through the star-sprinkled darkness.

Toward Motor City.

2

Wednesday, August 1
17 miles outside New York City
1:01 P.M.

Given the opportunity, my friend Special Agent Ralph Hawkins never passed up a chance to kick in a door.

And today, for tactical reasons, FBI SWAT Commander Torres was offering it to him.

Four members of Torres's team surrounded us. Normally, they would use the Halligan bar to breach the door and gain access to the house. Today we had Ralph's boot.

That would be enough.

Faster than the bar.

Through his headset mic, Torres confirmed that the snipers were in position, then said, "On my count."

Ralph readied himself. A former Ranger and knuckle-tough, when he entered a room, the other alpha males would take one look at him, then quietly find their seats, fold their hands in their laps, and wait for instructions.

I don't mind the rush of adrenaline myself, and in another life I might have even signed onto Torres's team, but in this one I would let these guys go in first.

"Three . . ." Torres whispered.

I'd track the offenders for them instead. One team. Different roles. Different cogs.

"Two . . ."

If Blake really was in this house, they were better trained to deal with him than I was. Now, a dynamic entry to—

But before Torres could say, "One," Ralph shouted "FBI!" and kicked the door brutally open, shattering the lock and sending the panel smacking with wood-splintering ferocity against the interior wall.

Torres and his men curled in from both sides of the doorway, buttonhook formation, and disappeared into the darkened home.

Assistant Director DeYoung had been clear: agents Ralph Hawkins and Patrick Bowers could be present but we had to let the SWAT team clear the residence. So, for the moment, we stayed outside. I wasn't thrilled by the idea, and knew Ralph wasn't either.

We stood to the sides of the doorway to get out of what law enforcement personnel call the "fatal funnel." Offenders shoot through doors, not so often through walls.

"You really Hawkinsed that door," I told him.

"You made my name into a verb?" His rumbling voice was just short of a growl—but it wasn't harsh. All authority.

"Your life is a verb."

"You could have used my first name."

"Probably better to say you 'Hawkinsed' it than you 'Ralphed' it."

"You might have a point," he acknowledged.

The team called out as they moved through the home: "Clear."

"And once again," I said to Ralph, "you didn't wait for 'one.'"

"Two's the loneliest number."

From inside the house: "Clear."

"I thought one was?"

"Naw. Everyone always counts down to one. It's the default climax. Two was feeling slighted."

"So you didn't want to diss two."

"No, I did not."

Another affirmative shout from one of the SWAT guys.

"That enough for you?" Ralph asked me.

"Plenty."

We entered, weapons in low ready position.

These days, policy dictates that agents carry Glocks so I'd had to jump through some hoops and fill out a mountain of paperwork, but in the end I was able to keep the .357 SIG P229 that'd served me so well in the past.

Sometimes efficacy requires you to extend the leash of protocol.

All of the lightbulbs in the windowless room had been removed, so apart from the smudge of light that filtered through the doorway behind us, the lancing beams of our flashlights were all that intruded on the darkness.

I last saw Blake in June in a warehouse near Jamaica Bay, and I'd been tracking him ever since. He and his mountainous bodyguard, a guy who looked big enough to give even Ralph a run for his money in a fight, actually helped save the lives of an NYPD detective and a Port Authority officer.

Despite their assistance, however, because of their connection with organized crime and their links to violent extremists and the human trafficking of minors, we weren't about to make any deals. They were the kind of people you have nightmares about. Terrorists come in many forms, and sometimes they look just like the guy next door.

And so it was with Blake. Early fifties. European descent. A distinguished yet unpretentious demeanor. Clear, calm eyes.

Because of his size, his associate was a bit more obtrusive.

We were going to bring these guys in and they were never going to see the light of day again.

I still didn't know why they hadn't let the officers die that night, but if they hadn't acted, neither Tobin nor Naomi would have made it. And I might not have survived the night either.

Afterward, Blake and his human tank slipped away.

Our latest intel placed them here at this house, and DeYoung gave us the green light to move in.

Although no subjects were in the living room, stationary figures populated the room, standing all around us.

Nine female mannequins, all wearing lacy lingerie.

"What the . . . ?" one of the SWAT guys muttered. "What is this about?"

"The silent ladies," I said. "It's Blake's deal. The first time I met him, he had mannequins just like these in his office. Then later, there were more at that warehouse the night he got away."

Blank faces. Unblinking eyes. A solid gaze that somehow bore the ghostly vestige of intelligence.

The mannequins left the impression that there'd been a striptease cocktail party and all the women had suddenly been transformed into identical, expressionless mimes before being frozen permanently in place.

"It's a little disturbing." The guy was eyeing them suspiciously, as if they might suddenly come to life.

"I second that," Ralph said.

"So he was here?"

"Or someone wants us to think he was," Ralph replied, echoing my thoughts.

Since 9/11, the FBI's primary mission has shifted from law enforcement to counterterrorism, so anything dealing with domestic terrorist threats falls under our auspices. However, in this case, because of Blake's involvement in drug smuggling, the DEA was involved in the investigation as well.

The human trafficking brought ICE into the mix.

NYPD was involved because of the location.

It was a classic example of jurisdictional overlap and, although in instances like this the agencies do their best to work together, it's not always easy to delineate who's in charge of what. Toes get stepped on. Egos get wounded. Communication isn't all that it should be. And worst of all, vital details have a way of slipping through the cracks.

Ralph was here to make sure that didn't happen.

Typically, he and his team at the FBI's National Center for the Analysis of Violent Crime only provided investigative consultation, profiling, and case analysis, but he got things done and he wasn't afraid to get his hands dirty.

Which is why DeYoung assigned him to this case.

Torres appeared in the hallway. "We've got a body in the garage."

"Blake?" I asked.

"Not unless he's aged twenty years in the last two months. It's this way."

3

Ralph knew how I felt about this part of my job, so as we followed Torres, he shot me a quick glance.

I gave him a nod: *All good. I'm fine. Don't worry.*

It wasn't queasiness.

It wasn't uneasiness.

It went deeper, coming from a place that the woman I was currently dating referred to as "the cursed blessing of empathy."

I've certainly seen my share of the dead during my last eight years in the Bureau—and the six before that working homicide for the Milwaukee Police Department—yet seeing corpses still wrenches up deep emotions for me every time I go through it.

However, I was thankful that working these cases had never become simply routine or mundane. I wanted the pain to be fresh and tender and real. It helped me remember why I do what I do. To dispassionately view evil without emotion is a sign of psychopathy, not professional impartiality.

Anger and justice were in my blood.

And that was okay by me.

Maybe it all stemmed from the first time I saw a corpse, back in high school, when I found the body of an eleven-year-old girl who'd been abducted on her way home from school. The killer had sexually molested Mindy before strangling her and leaving her body in an old tree house beside a marsh near our town.

It was a rainy autumn day when I found her.

Cold, gray tears in the air.

Dead, drenched leaves underfoot.

The isolated location and tracks on the dirt road nearby had led me to believe she might be in the tree house. At the top of the ladder, I paused momentarily, then crawled through the tree house's entrance.

And saw her.

Mindy's body was propped against the wall. Motionless. Facing me.

Death was no longer just something out there distant and amorphous that other people had to cope with. It was something I could see just ahead of me on the trail, peering back over its shoulder with a grin that was all teeth and restless hunger. And yet, somehow at the same time, it'd found a way to sneak up on me from behind. A panting beast, never content and always on the prowl, coming at me from both sides at once.

At us all.

In the hallway, Torres said, "By the way, Pat, aren't you supposed to be on a plane to Detroit?"

"Flight doesn't leave for another four hours."

Then he turned to Ralph. "You didn't wait for 'one.' Again."

"Pat already pointed that out."

"And?"

"Two was feeling slighted," I said.

"Huh." Torres pressed open the door to the garage.

We followed him inside.

A man's body hung from a taut, yellow, braided nylon rope tied to the rafters. Though the noose had grooved into his skin when it tightened, it was still visible. A kicked-out chair lay on the floor near his feet.

The man's pasty, cyanotic face left no question about whether he was alive.

And so the feeling came. Sorrow tainted with rage.

There's nothing beautiful or lovely or elegant about death, and the more of it you see, the more you know this is true. No matter how you spin things, there's no Hollywood glamor to a corpse. We don't just pass away. As soon as we stop breathing, as soon as the blood stops feeding the brain, we begin to rot.

Meat on bones. Dreams of eternity wrapped in a sloughing cloth of skin.

Gaviola, one of Torres's team members, and the one who'd been the first in the garage, nudged the dead man's leg with the tip of his MP5 to turn him so that we could more clearly see his face, but I stepped in and pressed the gun barrel aside out of respect for the deceased.

"Would you treat him that way if he was your dad?" I said.

"I . . . Sorry."

I repositioned myself so I could see the victim more clearly.

Caucasian. Gaunt. Six foot, maybe six-one. Early to mid-seventies.

"You know him?" Torres asked.

"No." I shook my head. "Never seen him before."

A faded tattoo of an alphanumeric code marked the back of his left hand.

Ralph gestured toward it. "Russian. That upside-down *h* and backward *R*? I've seen this kind of identification before. The Soviets used it to differentiate their scientists who worked in their bioweapons programs and germ warfare units back in the Cold War. No names. Just numbers and letters. For anonymity."

"A bioweapons scientist," Torres muttered. "That cannot be good."

The other SWAT members arrived as I studied the garage.

Two more mannequins were poised nearby. One had a whiskey glass in her hand. "When the ERT gets here," I told Torres, "have them check under the victim's fingernails."

"For DNA? In case he might have scratched someone?"

I walked toward the mannequin. "For fragments of rope. In suicide by hanging with this type of rope we almost always find tiny filaments of it caught beneath the person's fingernails."

"Instinct," Ralph noted. "Self-preservation. People claw at life even if they've decided they want to die. They can't help it. If the fingernails are clear, that's usually an indicator that—"

"It might not have been a suicide." Torres finished his thought for him.

"Exactly."

I examined the whiskey in the glass. Three unmelted ice cubes glistened in it. No moisture on the outside of the glass.

"This ice is still square," I told them. "No air-conditioning out here. In this heat that ice wouldn't take long to melt. And the glass isn't even sweating yet."

"He was just here," Gaviola exclaimed.

"He's close," Torres announced to his team. "Check every house on this block. Go!"

As one, in swift, well-coordinated crisscross formation, they swept out, and a moment later Ralph and I stood alone in the garage.

I wanted to check the ice, but at this point, since it had at least been in the whiskey since the SWAT guys entered the house, I doubted that any prints on it would still be identifiable. However, it was possible.

"Ralph, check the freezer in the house." I scoured the drawers beneath the workbench for pliers. "See if there are any ice trays."

He went inside, then called back. "No trays."

Huh.

"You thinking prints?" he asked when he returned.

"Possibly."

I recalled one case involving the homicide of an elderly woman who'd been beaten to death in her apartment. She lived alone, and although a female caregiver would visit twice a week to assist her, that was it as far as visitors. When we investigated the scene, I noticed that the toilet seat was up and I thought: *Why would a woman who lives by herself tilt the toilet seat up?*

Sure enough, we dusted under the lid and found partials from the forefinger and middle finger of a guy in the system with a rap sheet for half a dozen previous assaults.

He confessed, and would now get to spend the rest of his life in prison thinking about how he'd been caught because he tipped up the lid, used the toilet, and without thinking, left that lid up.

No one thinks of everything, and if you study those fault

lines between intent and action long enough, you'll find the truth.

I spent a lot of my life analyzing fault lines.

In the bottom drawer, I located a pair of vise grips that I figured would do the trick.

"Where are you going with this?" Ralph asked me.

"Someone might have touched this ice before dropping it into the glass."

"DNA?"

"Or prints."

I used the vise grips to transfer the ice to the freezer in the hopes of preserving any fingerprints that might have still been present. Then, as I stepped into the garage again, I found myself evaluating the layout of the house in relationship to the size of the garage.

"No," I muttered. "That's not right. It's not long enough."

"Long enough?" Ralph said.

"This garage." I leaned into the house to have another look. "Based on the size of the rooms we passed through to get here. It looks like it's maybe two meters too short."

"There you go with meters again," he grumbled.

Back in the garage, I studied its dimensions. "We need to catch up with the rest of the world."

"We're America. They can catch up to us, or at least try to—but you're saying the garage length? You took note of the house's floor plan? What? When we were outside?"

"Yes."

"Because everything matters."

"Yes." I was combing the wall for some sort of entryway. "Give me a hand here."

It took some searching, but at last we located a false back to a shelving unit.

Ralph knelt and steadied his weapon as I flung the panel aside.

He went in first, then a moment later called for me to join him.

No one inside.

A cluttered desk, a dated computer, and a folding chair were crammed into the narrow sliver of a room.

Dozens of papers were pinned to one wall. Charts, graphs, memos. All handwritten in a nearly indecipherable script that looked Russian.

The other wall had the photographs of victims—chemical burns, lesions, boils, febrile rashes, pitted and gangrenous limbs. Many of the pictures were black-and-white. Some were faded Polaroids that might have been taken years or even decades ago. Most of the recent ones appeared to be of teenage girls.

A number of the victims were clearly deceased when the photos were taken.

Many were not.

Ralph cursed under his breath.

"Germ warfare?" I knew that from Ralph's military background he had more expertise in this area than I did. "Biological weapons?"

"Yeah. And more than one kind."

Based on what we knew so far, I was glad there were no vials or chemicals in the room.

Ralph's Russian was suspect and mine wasn't even rudimentary, so we weren't able to make much of the scribbled notes. The Evidence Response Team must have already been en route because they arrived soon after we'd begun examining the room for anything not written in Russian.

We came up short on that, except for locating the torn corner of a shipping manifest to a Great Lakes port.

The ERT took over processing the scene, and after sweeping the house and finding no sign of any contagions or bioweapons—thankfully—they cleared us to leave. However, as Ralph and I spoke outside, I was still a bit torn between taking off and lingering a few minutes longer.

He glanced at his diving watch, the Reactor Trident that his wife, Brineesha, had given him recently for their ten-year anniversary. "You should probably get to the airport, bro. Do you have your stuff with you?"

"I left it at Christie's place this morning."

He gave me a knowing smile.

"The couch, Ralph. I was sleeping on the couch."

"Right."

"I'm afraid things on that front are not exactly where they could be."

"Ah. Her religion."

"She puts a high value on marriage, on the implications of intimacy. I have no problem with that."

"But it hasn't been easy, though, huh? The couch, I mean?"

"True enough," I admitted. "But last night, that wasn't the issue."

"Go on."

"We had a . . . well, a slightly heated discussion."

"From my experience, discussions like those are never 'slightly heated.' They're either served ice-cold or burned to a crisp."

"This one was kind of crispy."

"And?"

"We'll work it out. Don't you have a flight too?"

"No. I was gonna speak at that symposium in Chicago, but I pulled out so I could focus on this case. Keep me posted on things in Detroit."

"I will."

"Now get your ass moving. The last thing I need is Assistant Director DeYoung on my case for you missing your flight."

4

Blake checked the screen of his ringing phone.

The number of the man he knew as Fayed Raabi'ah Bashir came up—or at least the cell number the jihadist was using today.

A terrorist.

A freedom fighter.

Depending on how you looked at things.

"What's the status?" Fayed asked as soon as Blake answered.

Blake had never met him, didn't know what he looked like. There were rumors he'd studied in the States. Whatever his background, he was nearly as fluent in English as he was in his native Arabic.

"All taken care of. The FBI doesn't know what they're looking for. And even if they did, they're searching in the wrong place. The ice should be enough to keep them occupied. I haven't heard from you about Maria. Is she still alive?"

"My people are editing the video. It's nearly complete. You will have a copy of it tomorrow."

"That's not what I asked."

"She served us well. I called to tell you that the first half of your payment has been transferred. Where are we with—"

"She wasn't supposed to serve you well, you were supposed to serve me well. When I delivered her to you, you made me certain assurances. Have those been kept?"

"We will have more information for you soon," Fayed reiterated, still avoiding a direct answer.

After a brief internal debate, Blake decided to let the topic of Maria's condition be for the time being. After watching the video, he would take whatever action the circumstances called for. And the more time passed, the more definitive a response he expected he would have to give. "Are we still on schedule?"

"Ali is flying in tonight. He should get to Detroit by eleven. The rest of the money will be wired to your account on Friday after the first responders arrive."

"And the events up in Michigan with—"

"It's all been arranged."

Then Fayed ended the call and Blake slowly lowered the phone, thinking about Maria, about why he'd taken the measures he had, why he'd handed her over to the former Muslim Brotherhood member who'd started The Brigade of the Prophet's Sword three years ago.

A group that was responsible for at least a dozen terror attacks since then.

For Blake, dealing with Maria was business.

But it was also personal.

Sometimes it's just not possible to separate the two.

He'd known her for twelve years, ever since first meeting her in L.A. back when he was still a deep undercover narcotics cop and she was getting her feet wet with her new role as an Office of Professional Responsibility lawyer with the FBI's L.A. Field Office.

They shared certain tastes and proclivities, and their

friendship had extended into territory that neither of them had anticipated. Sometimes friends become more than friends and lovers become less. Over the years, they'd found themselves on both ends of that continuum.

But recently, Patrick Bowers had been poking around in corners where he didn't need to be looking and she'd failed to cover her tracks as well as she should have.

Blake knew that if Bowers found her out, he might find him out. And so, he'd made the necessary, albeit painful, decision to end his relationship with Maria. Fayed agreed to provide him with a service regarding her that his own feelings toward her had precluded him from personally carrying out.

Still, he had no malice toward her, no desire to see her suffer, and so he had required Fayed's word about making her death swift and painless.

But over the past few days, based on what Fayed had told him—and what he had not—Blake had started having profound doubts that the Islamist had honored his promises.

Now, seated at the table nearby, Mannie was typing, his meaty fingers somehow flying nimbly across his computer's keyboard with amazing precision, almost never double-punching any keys or accidentally pressing the wrong one. Born in The Gambia, Mannie's skin was luxuriously black. His eyes, sharp and knowing.

"I might have something," he said in his gravel-pit voice.

"Where?"

"Minnesota, a couple months ago, not long after he was released. Someone used a grenade. Killed a woman in a cabin near a remote lake close to the Canadian border. She used to be a model. Says she'd been cuffed to the bed."

This did not involve Fayed, at least not in a way Blake knew of.

But it did involve him and someone close to him.

"A model?"

"From L.A. Represented by Brenning Talent Associates."

"That's him."

"Do we go to Minnesota?"

Blake evaluated the situation. "Not if it was several months ago. It's likely that an isolated rural community would be close-knit. If people started going missing, it would attract too much attention. He'll likely have moved on." He indicated the computer. "Keep looking. Anything else with grenades."

"Or with the movie?"

"Yes. Or with the movie."

5

I left Christie's apartment, toting my computer bag and rolling the carry-on suitcase behind me toward the elevator. She walked quietly by my side. Her fifteen-year-old daughter, Tessa, trailed behind us.

Christie was a single mom. Understatedly pretty. Though deeply grounded in her conservative fundamentalist Christian faith, she had a soft, alluring mischievousness in her eyes. We'd hit it off right from the start, meeting in the rain, sharing an umbrella. It was, as she put it, "maddeningly romantic," just like that original "Bus Stop" song by the Hollies back in the sixties.

Sharing an umbrella.

And then more.

But now, we'd barely spoken since last night when we'd said all those things we hadn't meant.

Fire and blame and barbed words. We'd both apologized, but arguments can leave open sores that apologies aren't always able to heal. Sometimes the passage of time provides you with a stronger salve. Sometimes it doesn't.

A text came in from Ralph and I passed the handle of the suitcase to Christie so I could check the message. Blunt and direct: No sign of Blake. No ID on the victim. Ice too melted for prints.

I texted back: Check for prints on the freezer door handle and the cabinet where he kept his whiskey glasses.

"So then, as far as the guy I was telling you about," Tessa said, picking up a story she'd started sharing about a guy she'd met at her favorite bookstore, the Mystorium. The place specialized in rare and out-of-print crime novels and she couldn't seem to get enough of them—or of the college guys who liked to hang out there. "I'm like, 'What do you do?' And he's all, 'I'm between jobs.'"

"And how old was he again?" Christie asked.

"I don't know, whatever, a couple years older than me. Twenty. Twenty-five."

"Twenty-five is ten years, Tessa. Not a couple."

"Alright, so a couple of a couple. Of a couple."

The girl was brilliant, moody, opinionated, and needy in ways she wasn't even aware of. She wore a torn long-sleeve T-shirt that read I'LL STOP PROCRASTINATING TOMORROW and a slightly too-short black skirt over fishnet tights, despite the summer heat.

She moved up to walk beside her mom. "So I said to him, 'Between jobs? Seriously? Who do you think you're fooling?' I mean how many employers are out there saying, 'Oh wow. Look at this guy. He's not *unemployed*, he's just *between jobs*.' Anyone who claims he's between jobs should automatically be disqualified from applying for anything that requires a modicum of intelligence or integrity for being either too much of an idiot to realize he's really just unemployed, or too much of a coward to admit it."

"That's a little harsh," Christie chided her.

"Harsh is the new nice."

"I see."

We arrived at the elevator and before I could press the

down button, Tessa punched it somewhat aggressively. "I mean, people don't do that with anything else: 'Don't worry, I'm not an alcoholic, I'm just between drinks . . .' 'I'm not really divorced, I'm just between marriages . . .' 'I'm not making a pig out of myself with these buffalo wings, I'm just between diets.'"

The doors opened.

She let out an irritated sigh. "Stupid people annoy me."

And in this, we had something in common.

We entered and I tapped the button for the ground floor.

As the doors glided shut, Tessa gestured toward my bag. "You travel light, Patrick."

"It's just until the weekend. I should be back Saturday night."

"So, by that time, I'll no longer be a virgin babysitter."

"Excuse me?"

"My daughter might have put that a bit more delicately," Christie offered. "She's just explaining that she's going to babysit for the first time tomorrow night."

"Ah. Nice. Who's it for?"

"My friend Rachel will be out of town. I suggested Tessa watch her two kids."

"Yeah, thanks for that, Mom. For sentencing me."

"Volunteering you."

"Right. I mean, really—Patrick, can you picture me babysitting?"

Hmm . . . Not exactly, I thought.

"Sure," I told her.

"Yeah. Like I believe that."

"It's just two kids—a baby and a five-year-old," Christie reassured her. "You'll do fine."

"If 'fine' means everyone surviving the night and not

burning down the house while boiling milk for the baby, then we can only hope. I just better not have to change any diapers."

"That usually goes with the territory. And you don't need to actually boil the milk."

"Oh. Right. Too hot. Gotcha."

Tessa's biological father had never been part of her upbringing. Christie didn't talk much about him so I didn't know the whole story, but I did know that after she became pregnant back when she was still in college, her relationship with him had ended. She raised Tessa alone.

It'd been a rough journey for her—for both of them—I knew that too.

Christie's choice not to put Tessa up for adoption fifteen years ago had meant tight finances and long hours working two jobs ever since. Only recently did a promotion allow her to cut back to just the management position at the graphic design studio.

Once we were outside the building, I asked Tessa to give us a second and she walked over to hail a cab, mumbling something about ride sharing and why hadn't I entered the twenty-first century yet.

When Christie and I were alone, I said softly, "Listen, last night. I know we—"

"Both said things we didn't mean. I'm sorry."

"Me too. I feel like we've been missing each other lately."

"Ships passing in the night."

"Are we at least heading toward the same shore?"

"I think so. We'll talk it through when you get back."

A cab drove past without slowing down. Tessa flipped off the driver.

"I don't want to leave knowing things aren't okay between us," I told Christie. "Are we good for now?"

"We're good."

"Alright."

"I love you," she said.

"You too," I replied instinctively, but then immediately backpedaled. "I mean I—"

"No, it's okay. Don't worry. It's fine."

This was actually one of the issues that'd come up between us. Last week she'd offhandedly noted that I used those two words a lot.

"Which words?" I'd asked her.

"When I tell you 'I love you,' you say 'You too.'"

"And I do. I . . ." But then it hit me. "You're saying there's a big difference between telling someone 'I love you' and saying 'You too.'"

"I don't want you to feel pressured into saying anything, into making any kind of promise or commitment you're not ready to make. I . . . I didn't—I don't ever want to do that."

"Don't worry. You're not." And although I knew she wanted to hear me say those three words outright, for some reason I hadn't been able to yet.

"I love you."

"You too."

That last sentence is just so much easier to tell someone than the first.

And it speaks just as clearly about where your heart is.

Tessa flagged a second cab and as it pulled to the curb I leaned close to Christie. "I know there's a lot for us to talk about, I know that we need to—"

But she placed a soft finger to my lips. "You need to go. Call me when you get there."

"I will."

For a fleeting moment I wondered if I should say anything about the person who'd requested my help in Detroit, but immediately recognized that now was definitely not the right time for that.

Special Agent Sharyn Weist and I had dated eight years ago while we were at the Academy together in Quantico. It was against their policies for New Agent Trainees to pursue romantic relationships, but the chemistry between us had been strong from the start and we'd chanced it, skirting along the precipice of getting caught and expelled.

Thankfully, neither of those things happened. I broke things off right before we graduated, and Sharyn and I hadn't been in touch since then. A month ago I'd told Christie about dating a woman back when I was at the Academy, but I couldn't see how mentioning the fact that I'd be working with her in Detroit now was going to help matters between us.

Openness and honesty aren't the same thing. A lot of pain can come when you confuse them.

Honesty is usually for the good of the other person. Openness, on the other hand, is often only for the benefit of ourselves.

Most of the time when someone says, "Hey, I was just being honest," he wasn't—he was just being *open* and it probably wasn't intended to help you out, but instead to make himself feel important. I wasn't about to lie to Christie, but I didn't need to share something that might drive a shiv deeper between us.

Eight years is a long time. I was only going to Detroit to consult on this case for a few days. Nothing more.

The cab driver got out and popped the trunk.

"I left something for you in your bag," Christie told me quietly.

"What is it?"

"I'm not telling." A sly smile. "You'll have to wait and see."

"I look forward to it."

I used my imagination. I liked what I saw.

We said good-bye, but when I kissed her, her daughter scoffed. "Seriously? You're gonna give her a 1950s-I'm-on-my-way-to-work-dear-Ward-Cleaver kiss? You can do better than that. You *better* do better than that."

True enough.

So I did.

Christie didn't seem to mind.

"Have a safe trip," she told me.

"I will."

I stowed my luggage and slipped into the backseat.

"Where to?" the driver asked me in a thick Persian accent.

"JFK."

As we pulled into traffic, it took me a few seconds to dig the seat belt's end out from where it was jammed down by the door, and when I glanced back at Christie and Tessa, they were both watching the cab drive away.

Tessa had one hand raised in a statuesque good-bye, but then I realized she was simply holding it up to the light and studying where the shadow slid across her wrist.

I was rolling down the window to wave back to Christie when we turned the corner and the edge of the apartment building cut both her and her daughter off from view.

6

When I boarded the plane, it didn't appear full, so even though I'd been assigned 18C, I found an empty seat near the back of the cabin where I could study the digital case files Sharyn had sent me without other passengers inadvertently seeing them.

The text was probably too small to read from another seat, but the photos were all too easy to make out, and I definitely didn't want anyone to see those.

Feral dogs had gotten to two of the corpses before they were discovered, and the dogs had not been discriminating in the parts of the bodies they chose to gnaw off.

Thankfully, only about half of the seats were taken and no one ended up beside me.

Once we were in the air and on our way to Detroit, I opened the files on my laptop.

In the last decade, a third of all properties, both commercial and residential, in Detroit have been foreclosed, including more than eighty-five thousand homes, Sharyn had written in the assistance request she'd sent to Assistant Director DeYoung. *Nearly all of them remain abandoned, so these four bodies might be just the tip of the iceberg.*

Three female victims, one male. Different ethnicities and socioeconomic backgrounds. All from different neighborhoods of the metro area. Even the cause of death varied: one was shot, two were stabbed, and one was beaten to death, most likely with a baseball bat, based on the nature of the wounds.

Each had been found in an upstairs bedroom closet, positioned seated, facing the room, a letter carved into his or her forehead. The lab was able to determine that the cuts had been made twenty to twenty-six hours after the time of death.

So, someone was returning to the bodies to mutilate them.

W carved into the first victim. Then *O*, then *R*, then another *R*.

The *R*s were carved backward.

Which now made me think of the code on the back of the dead scientist's hand.

Simply based on the limited number of words that might spell—basically all forms of *worry* or *worried*—the working theory was that the next letter would be a *Y* or *I*.

Worrit means to "tease." Maybe he was doing this to tease, to mock, the police.

Forensics wasn't sure of the type of blade used, but they were working from the hypothesis that it was a razor blade of some type.

The crimes showed a high degree of callousness and brutality.

Coldhearted.

Calculating.

It left me with a chill.

Though no physical evidence connected them, the victims' positioning and the carved letters were enough to link them.

"I want you there," Assistant Director DeYoung told

me. "If there really is a serial killer stalking the streets of Detroit and he kills again—and we might've had the resources to stop him—well, that's the worst kind of bad on any number of fronts. Spend a couple days. Work up the geoprofile. See what you can do."

With the Bureau trying to establish itself firmly in the twenty-first century, DeYoung wanted to do all he could to show the public—as well as the Congressional Budget Office—that we were fully embracing relevant emerging technology. Geoprofiling and the type of crime scene analysis that I specialize in were high on that list.

Since I was an environmental criminologist and the lead geospatial investigator in the Bureau, it was becoming more and more common for me to consult with other Field Offices and law enforcement agencies throughout the country.

In a nutshell, my approach had to do with studying the timing, location, and progression of serial offenses rather than looking for means, motive, and opportunity. The process grew out of research dealing with how people perceive and process their surroundings and then make rational choices that lead them to engage in criminal acts.

I don't believe crime is random. It's the result of decisions made by people who want something that's out of bounds—either legally or ethically. We want to do something we're not supposed to do, or to have something we're not allowed to have. We covet. We act. We pursue.

Desire precipitates action, whether we're cognizant of it or not. And that desire involves pursuing pleasure or relief.

And throughout the process, we instinctively try to save time, money, and effort, and avoid apprehension. This affects the location and timing of crimes, and, by working through FALCON, the Federal Aerospace Locator and Covert Operation Network, I can narrow down the geographic area the offender would most likely be using as his home base.

So, I don't profile behavior. I don't psychoanalyze people. Instead, I look at the footprints the offender left as he moved through time and space, and then try to let his trail through the past lead me to his location in the present.

The airplane jolted as we hit a pocket of air.

One of the flight attendants came on the PA system requesting that we put on our seat belts, and reminding us to wear them "low and tight across your lap"—whatever that was supposed to mean.

Really, is there any way to wear a seat belt *high* across your lap?

Her instructions sounded like something Tessa would start riffing on or rolling her eyes about. I just ended up shaking my head.

Turning to the files again, I tried to get a clearer sense of where the crime scenes were in relationship to each other.

Although I'd had layovers at the Detroit airport, I'd never had the chance to venture into the city itself and wasn't very familiar with it.

However, I did know that Detroit was a city of fighters and overcomers. It'd been on the cutting edge of the music scene more than once, from Motown to street rap. And its theater district was second only to New York City's. However, the city's population had been in decline for decades.

The information Sharyn had sent noted that, at just over six hundred thousand residents, its population was a quarter of what it'd once been, and it was continuing to drop each year as more people continued to move out than move in. Fifty thousand stray dogs roamed the streets. Detroit had both one of the highest crime rates of any city in the country and one of the lowest clearance rates. More crimes. Fewer solved. Not a good combination.

The city's average police response time was currently at fifty-four minutes, compared to the eleven-minute national average.

Thousands of squatters lived in the empty houses that were on sale for as little as $500 apiece—and weren't attracting buyers even at that price. Scrappers removed metal and sold it by the ton.

They call copper "Detroit gold," Sharyn wrote. *For a while, the scrapping was so bad that the scrappers would go into the restrooms at restaurants, use hacksaws to remove the pipes, and then leave with the pipes hidden in their clothes. And the scrap metal dealers weren't helping matters. We finally had to crack down and outlaw them from accepting manhole covers stamped with the words* City of Detroit.

It was crazy.

It was Detroit.

She noted the trend of killers from neighboring states, including gangs from Chicago, using Detroit's abandoned homes as dumping sites for corpses. However, since the four victims in the current case were all from southeastern Michigan and had no known gang affiliations, that didn't appear to be the case here.

In investigations like this, when you're looking for more needles in a haystack, you have to start somewhere, and typically that means looking in the pockets of those who've found the previous needles.

But all the bodies had been reported through the DPD's

anonymous online crime reporting program—which left no one to interview, and an awfully big field of haystacks scattered throughout the city to search through on our own.

According to the Detroit medical examiner's office, the victims had all been dead for between forty and forty-eight hours when the anonymous tips came in.

The positions of the bodies and timing of the tips clearly indicated more than a coincidental connection—but I don't believe in coincidence anyway.

If you burrow far enough into the facts, you'll find that there's always a pattern. Cause and effect lie buried in the soil of apparent happenstance. Sometimes they're buried deep, but they're there.

The key is timing and location.

Trying to establish motive is a losing battle because it's a conclusion you can never unequivocally confirm.

Why does someone kill? Who knows. But why *then*? Why *there*? What does the fact that the bodies were left in those particular houses, in those rooms, at those times, on those days tell you about the offender's habits and travel patterns? And, in this case, what did the timing of the anonymous tips tell us about the nature of the criminal events or the tipster's connection to the crimes?

I immersed myself in the research and lost track of time until the pilot announced that he would be turning on the seat belt sign again because of turbulence and that there was a lot of traffic at the airport but he was still confident we would make our "on-time arrival at 7:31 P.M."

7

18470 Runyon Street
Detroit, Michigan

"You got the pills?"

"Yeah," Erik replied. "My mom never counts 'em."

"And there's enough for all four of us?"

"There's like half a bottle." Erik shook the bottle to prove to his friend Canyon that there were plenty.

Ever since the two of them had gotten their driver's licenses last spring—first him, then two weeks later, Canyon—they'd been driving in from Grosse Pointe whenever they could to explore the parts of Detroit their parents never ventured into. And never would've given them permission to visit, either.

Erik had been in abandoned homes all over the city—nearly everyone he knew had. Sure, it was *officially* trespassing, but with so many empty buildings everywhere, what were the cops going to do about it? They didn't care. There were too many other *actual* crimes to solve.

However, Erik had never been to this block before and he wasn't super thrilled to be here. There were a couple crack houses close by—he knew that much. But from what he'd heard, the stuff here on this street went deeper. Weird. Way out there. Twisted.

"You sure it's okay if we go in here?"

"It's fine, I told you." Canyon sounded frustrated as he led him toward the lawn. "Igazi comes here all the time. He told me the cops never bother anyone on this end of the precinct."

It wasn't the cops that Erik was worried about, but he didn't want to seem scared, so he didn't bring that up.

Fast-food wrappers from Popeyes, two drained forty-ounce malt liquor bottles, and a discarded child's tricycle with a missing wheel littered the yard around them.

"And the girls?" he asked Canyon.

"They're waiting for us inside."

"Mimi and her friend."

"Gwen."

"Yeah, Gwen." Erik repeated the name skeptically.

"She's cool. Don't worry, man. I've met her. You'll like her."

"You still haven't told me what she looks like."

"I'm telling you, it's all good. Now, c'mon, I don't want to keep 'em waiting."

Erik followed Canyon toward the porch.

He'd always thought his friend's name was a little odd, but sorta cool too. "What kind of name is Canyon, anyway?" he'd asked him once.

"Before my dad went to medical school, my parents were into hiking and they named us after outdoor stuff. My sister—the one who died in the car accident—was named Arête. Has to do with rock climbing. I guess she was the high point. I was the low one."

++++

Just a few minutes ago, Erik had parked two blocks away and left his car in a neighborhood that had a vehicle in nearly every driveway.

That's the way it was in Detroit. You might have an entire street that's abandoned, but a few blocks away every house is occupied. There wasn't really any pattern. It all depended on when the people decided to bail, cut their losses, and escape the city.

Urban blight, they called it.

Blight—a word he'd learned in English class. Meant *decayed, deteriorated, destroyed*. The three *D*s.

Never a good thing.

Not what you want your city to be known for.

Erik studied the outside of the house as they neared the porch.

Usually, no one took time to board up the windows of the buildings once they were deserted, but this one was different—at least on the first floor. All of its windows were boarded up, leaving only the broken second-story windows uncovered.

The front door had been left wide open, so the house seemed to be giving two contradictory messages: one from the plywood-covered living room windows: "Stay out," and one from the invitingly open door: "Explore my secrets."

Explore my blight.

Erik still didn't like the fact that Canyon hadn't told him what Gwen looked like. Okay, so Mimi was hot—no question about that—and he took that as a good sign that her friend would be too, but who knows? It was always possible that Canyon and Mimi were playing a trick on him and had invited some girl they knew he would never like.

He seriously hoped that wasn't the deal. He didn't like turning people down and he really didn't want to hurt the feelings of some girl he'd never met.

Canyon peered in through the front door. "Mimi?" he called. "Gwen?"

Neither one of them replied.

The two boys walked inside.

The boarded-over windows sealed out most of the sunlight, but just enough of it slid in between the plywood sheets to allow them to see without having to use the flashlights on their phones or the actual flashlight Canyon had brought along.

The sofa was one of those sleeper kinds, and was popped open. One of the metal support legs was bent, making the whole thing slope down toward that corner. The tangled sheets on top of the mattress were raggy and faded and Erik didn't even want to know what the spotty yellow stains were from.

The two reclining chairs had been knifed open and the white cushiony stuff inside them was spewing out. He'd been deer hunting with his uncle a bunch of times in the Upper Peninsula and the chair's wounds reminded him of what happened with the guts of a deer when you slit its belly open to field-dress it.

Not the best memory.

He looked away. "So, where are they?"

"Lemme text Mimi."

Graffiti was spray-painted on the walls, symbols Erik had never seen in any of the houses he'd been in before: upside-down crosses, goat heads. Pentagrams. He didn't know a lot about what they meant, but he knew enough. "Man, once we find 'em let's go to a different house. I don't like this."

"You don't like what?"

"Being here. This place. There's something about it."

"You're being a pussy."

"No, that's not it."

"Alright then, shut up and come on. Let's go find the girls."

As Canyon tapped at the screen of his cell to text his girlfriend, Erik noticed a phone on the kitchen table blinking to life. "Hey, it's in there." He stepped over a mess of filthy clothes that might have been left there by a squatter and walked to the kitchen table.

Canyon looked up from his phone. "What do you mean?"

Erik held it up so his friend could see. "This is Mimi's, right?"

"Yeah, it is." Canyon sounded a little uneasy. "Something's not right." He called for the girls again, and this time Erik heard muffled noises coming from the end of the hallway, from somewhere beyond a door that was slightly open. By the look on his friend's face, Canyon heard them too.

A splattering of red dotted the wall where the refrigerator would have stood. It didn't look like paint.

Canyon turned on his flashlight. "Mimi?" As he called her name there was a catch in his voice.

No reply. Just more muffled sounds.

"Come on." Canyon jabbed the beam of light through the shadowy hallway and the boys crossed it toward the door. When Canyon eased the door open, Erik saw the basement steps leading downward.

Faint light curled up through the darkness.

Candlelight.

"Mimi?" Canyon called. "Gwen? You down there?"

The indistinguishable sounds grew more urgent.

Erik wanted to run, to get as far away from this house and this basement and those symbols on the wall as he could. Get out, get out, get back to the car—but the girls were here. And there was no way he was gonna leave without them, especially if they were hurt.

Canyon flicked out the switchblade he always carried and started down the rough wooden staircase.

As Erik followed him, he wished that he had a knife too.

About halfway down, an old wood furnace came into view, along with a looming pile of boxes, a workbench, and a shelf cluttered with mildew-covered books.

Cement-block walls.

A dirt floor.

More of a cellar, really, than a basement.

Erik was a few steps behind Canyon, and as his friend reached the bottom, Erik saw her.

A dark-haired girl he didn't recognize.

She was seated against a thick metal support pole at the far end of the cellar, gagged. From this angle, Erik could tell that her wrists were tied behind her, around the other side of the pole. Her ankles were tied together too.

That has to be Mimi's friend. That has to be Gwen.

A dozen or so candles were scattered throughout the basement, their flames licking and hissing faintly at the darkness like the tongues of angry snakes.

Mimi was lying on her back, motionless, near her friend. Her eyes were closed. She might have been asleep. It looked like she'd put on fresh lipstick, and it glistened wet and ready in the eerie flickering candlelight.

"Mimi?" Canyon's voice quivered as he called to her. "You okay?"

Gwen tugged at the ropes, struggling to get free, eyes

wide and frantic. She tried to say something, but because of the gag, Erik couldn't make out what it was.

Canyon's eyes were still on Mimi, but he hadn't started walking toward her. It was like he'd become frozen in place, or maybe he was trying to decide if he should take another step forward at all, or go back up the stairs instead.

If he's not gonna do anything, you need to!

Erik held out his hand. "Give me the knife."

"What? Why?"

"I'm gonna cut Gwen free. Go see if Mimi's okay. Go on!"

Carrying the knife, Erik hurried to Gwen's side, then knelt beside her and slid the gag out of her mouth.

"You okay?"

"Untie me," she gasped. "Get me out of here. Hurry! Before he comes back!"

Out of the corner of his eye, Erik could see Canyon on his knees next to Mimi, who still hadn't moved.

Erik worked at the rope, but even though the blade was sharp, the rope was thick and wound so tightly around Gwen's wrists that he had to be careful not to cut her skin along with the rope.

Movement caught his attention and he glanced toward Canyon again. His friend was urgently patting Mimi's cheek. "Wake up. Come on, wake up, wake up."

Gwen squirmed again, but that just made it harder for Erik to keep from slicing her wrist as he sawed through the bindings. "Hold still, okay? I'll get it. I don't want to cut you. Relax. Hang on. I'll get it."

As she moved, so did he, and the blade nicked her.

"Sorry!"

But she was anxiously scanning the cellar behind him and didn't even seem to notice.

Finally, the rope's frayed ends dropped away and her hands were free. The rope around her ankles went a lot faster and as soon as he'd cut through it, he used his free hand to help Gwen up. However, just as she got to her feet, she screeched, "Behind you!"

Erik whipped around as Canyon lunged at him, grabbing his shoulders and shouting, "Gotcha!"

The two girls squealed in delight.

They were messing with you! All this! They set everything up just to scare you!

The girls laughed hysterically, and Mimi, who was standing up by then too, said, "Erik, you shoulda seen your face. That was *awesome*!"

At first Canyon laughed too. But then the laughter faded. His smile faded too.

He looked down.

Erik's eyes followed his friend's.

Down.

To the knife that he'd used only moments ago to free Gwen. The knife he'd still been holding when she yelled and he spun around and Canyon leapt at him. The knife that was now buried all the way to the grip in the stomach of his best friend.

"No, no, no," Erik said.

Canyon still had his hands on Erik's shoulders and his grip tightened as he tried to steady himself. "Dude," Canyon mumbled. "Is that . . . ?"

Erik wanted to undo everything, to make it better, to make it right.

He drew the knife back toward him as if that might help, like starting over in a video game, make it so that none of this had ever happened.

Do-over.

Redo. Redo. Redo.

Hands trembling, he dropped the knife and for some reason noticed that the blood on the blade picked up dirt as it hit the ground and rolled to the side. Dusty earth, stained dark with blood.

Dark.

With.

Blood.

Canyon's knees gave way.

Erik tried to support him, but ended up just helping ease him to the ground.

Now the girls were beside them. Gwen was screaming and Mimi was saying over and over, "Oh my God . . . Oh my God . . . Oh my God."

"You stabbed me, bro," Canyon muttered. Erik expected cursing, blame, fury, but it was only surprise in his friend's voice. Just deep and terrible surprise.

"It was an accident," Erik said desperately. "I didn't mean to. I . . ." But then he stopped. It seemed like no matter what he said, it would never be enough.

Canyon had his hand pressed against the place where the blade had gone in, but despite that, a lot of blood was coming out, and had already covered half of his shirt.

A widening circle of red.

It kept coming, oozing between his fingers.

Erik fumbled for his phone to call 911 as Mimi bent beside her boyfriend and begged him, begged him to be okay.

Redo. Redo.

Start over.

Now.

8

As soon as we touched down on the tarmac, I checked my phone and found a message from Sharyn: Got another body. I'm waiting curbside. Sky blue Yaris. They're holding the scene for us.

I replied that I would be right there.

After entering the terminal, I hastened through the crowd, tugging my suitcase behind me. Sharyn's choice of words in her text struck me. Most people might've just written *blue hatchback* or *light blue car*, but with her, the car wasn't just blue, it was the color of the sky.

I made my way outside and it took me only a moment to locate her Yaris about twenty meters farther up the curb, in front of the baggage claim area's exit.

She stood beside the car door, scanning the crowd, but evidently hadn't seen me yet.

Brunette. A touch of exotic beauty that she got from her Brazilian mother. At five-eleven, she was nearly tall enough to look me in the eye back in those days when we were together and she wore heels on our under-the-radar excursions to D.C.

As I approached her, I could see that she was as fit as ever. With her slim figure and model-worthy looks, she might have stepped right off the cover of a women's fashion magazine.

In truth, Sharyn had been a model while she was a teenager, after hitting childhood stardom in Hollywood when she was ten. But her parents were as bad at managing her career as they were at getting along with each other, and after their bitter divorce right around her seventeenth birthday, they hadn't left her with much.

She used most of that to pay her lawyers, agents, and managers, and then to cover her college tuition: a bachelor's degree in criminal justice and a master's in criminology from the University of Maryland–College Park.

She graduated debt-free, changed her name, and started a new life, leaving the Hollywood starlet life behind her. No social media. No interviews. No glamor or hype or paparazzi. In a rare move, the Bureau had helped her bury her old identity so it wouldn't become a distraction from her work.

I'd heard rumors that she'd had a stalker and that he was part of the reason, but I wasn't sure. She'd never brought it up, and out of respect for her privacy, I'd never asked.

Scarlett Farrow was gone forever.

And, like a phoenix, Special Agent Sharyn Weist had risen from the ashes.

Now, she glanced in my direction. "Aha. Trying to sneak up on me, huh, Pat? You need to work on your spycraft."

"I'll keep that in mind. It's good to see you."

"Ditto." She lifted the Yaris's hatch and then appraised me briefly. "You're looking good."

"So are you." The words just came out, a compliment for a compliment. Completely innocent.

"Thank you."

"Your text," I said, pivoting to the case. "They found another body?"

"Yes. I'll tell you what we know on the way." She nodded toward my suitcase and computer bag. "That it?"

"That's it." I set them in her car next to a Barbie doll backpack and a clutter of coloring books.

Sharyn read the look on my face. "Olivia is seven," she explained. "She's at her dad's this week. We alternate. Long story."

It didn't take a lot of calculating to figure out that Sharyn must have gotten pregnant soon after we dated.

Very soon, actually.

While she was closing the hatch, an SUV pulled up uncomfortably close behind us and we had to brush past each other as we shuffled toward our respective sides of the Yaris.

As she was squeezing by, she hesitated briefly, then gave me a soft hug.

I took it as her way of acknowledging that we were friends, that we'd been close.

I hugged her back. Based on our history, a handshake wouldn't have been enough. But I kept the hug light and brief so it wouldn't communicate more than it needed to.

When I eased back from her, she touched a wisp of hair away from her eye, then nodded once in a truncated, professional manner, and said simply, "Okay."

"Let's get to the scene," I said.

"Let's."

9

A trickle of sweat ran down the back of Ali Mahmoud Saleem's neck as he stood in the passport control line at the Hartsfield–Jackson Atlanta International Airport.

Relax. Be easy. No one must know why you are here.

He was twenty-four. A Muslim, yes, but not from the Middle East, not an Arab—which was one of the reasons he'd been chosen. Less of a chance of being profiled or appearing on a watch list.

There were more than a hundred and thirty ethnic groups in his home country of Kazakhstan, but Russians, Uzbeks, and Kazakhs made up the majority of the population. As a Kazakh, he looked more Mongolian than Middle Eastern, with the distinctively wider eyes, rounder face, and stockier frame than his Chinese neighbors across the border, not far to the southeast of where he and his sister lived.

Though his heritage was Muslim, he hadn't grown up as a devout follower of Allah and the stubble on his face could barely be called a beard. His tan slacks and white oxford were more than a little crumpled and wrinkled now, after his flights from Ust-Kamenogorsk to Almaty, and then to Frankfurt, where he transferred to a direct flight to Atlanta.

Too many hours in the air.

Now, just one more leg of the trip: the final connection to Detroit.

The queue in front of the passport checkpoint was long and hadn't been moving at all for the last ten minutes. Something had happened, some sort of security crackdown, and it looked like it might be a couple of hours—which would likely cause him to miss his flight.

Deal with that when it happens, Ali. Do not cause yourself distress by worrying about that over which you have no control.

Movement near the ceiling caught his attention.

Somehow, a bird had gotten into the terminal and was searching for a way out.

Its frantic, erratic flight reminded Ali of what he was doing here, of the possessors of the elephant, of the besieged city, of the decreed stones.

And those birds, all those birds, crossing the desert toward the Holy City.

That old story from fourteen centuries ago was still relevant today—maybe more so now than at any other time in history.

The airport's displaced bird hovered overhead after momentarily lighting on a sign above one of the border agents' booths.

Ali remembered his training, the soldier with the scimitar, the tests Fayed put him through, and the man kneeling there in the sand beside them, his wrists zip-tied together behind his back, the black hood over his head.

No, Ali. Do not think of such things.

The rejecter's cries for mercy; his frantic, stuttered prayers.

No, do not!

The glint of that wicked blade in the sun.

Ali distracted himself by quietly reciting verses of the Qur'an, anything rather than allow himself to dwell on that day in Yemen when Fayed finally let him out of the room and started his training.

The sand. The sweeping arc of that sword.

Breathe.

Relax.

The wet, spurting sounds in the desert.

All will be well.

As long as he remained vigilant and alert and avoided calling any attention to himself, his sister would be safe. He tried to reassure himself with that thought, tried to quell his intractable hesitation to go through with things as planned.

Faatina, the woman watching his sister, Azaliya, would hear if anything went wrong.

He could not let that happen.

The bird finally flitted to a sign not far from him instructing passengers to have their passports ready for inspection. This time, however, one of the border agents managed to flop a light jacket over the top of it, capturing it before it could take flight again.

A few of the people in line clapped, but most did not. Perhaps, if nothing else, they selfishly wanted that bird to remain trapped in the terminal simply to provide them with a distraction during their intrepid wait.

As the agent carried the bird away, Ali could hear its muffled cries. And to him, they seemed like those of the hooded man forced to his knees: those terrified, desperate pleas for help in the dark.

10

Three teens—two girls and one boy—were huddled together outside the dilapidated house on Runyon Street when we pulled to the curb.

Dispatch had given us their names and I'd checked their DMV records on our drive from the airport, so I knew that the girl with the walnut-colored hair was Gwen Hurst. Sixteen.

Mimi Bianchi stood beside her. Seventeen. Blond.

The boy, Erik Carter, looked flushed. All three kids should've probably had paramedics monitoring their condition or attending to them for shock, but instead of EMTs, two stern-looking Detroit Police Department officers flanked them.

When we'd learned the other boy's name was Canyon Robbins, Sharyn had said softly, "The medical examiner is Dr. Robbins. I wonder if they're related."

Three cruisers were parked in front of the house. Crime scene tape stretched only across the porch. They didn't even bother with the rest of the house. Why waste the tape? Why, when you're dealing with more murders per year than every other city in the country except Chicago and New York City?

A cluster of thirteen bystanders had gathered across the

street and most of the people had their phones out, filming everything. With the current friction between law enforcement officers and the residents of low-income urban areas, there wasn't anything necessarily surprising about the citizens recording things, but considering the number of vacant houses on this block, there were more people here than I would've expected.

Maybe they suspected, as we did, that this crime was linked to several previous homicides.

And, of course, to the public, a serial killer's crimes are a lot more interesting than just another random murder.

As Sharyn and I crossed the scraggly, unkempt lawn to speak with the teens, I assessed the neighborhood.

Wildly overgrown.

Weed-infested.

Two homes across the street had burned down, and the blackened beams of their remains looked like splintered, charred bones jutting up from the earth. A nearby empty lot still retained the concrete footprint of a small house that must have been demolished before its debris was cleared away.

The block's remaining homes were in various states of disrepair. Sagging roofs and porches. Missing doors. Shattered, jagged glass, or boarded-up windows.

None of the houses appeared to be currently occupied—unless squatters were residing in them under the radar.

The neighborhood looked like a war zone.

A deserted high school crouched at the end of the street, with no fence surrounding it to keep out trespassers. Based on the extent of weather damage and graffiti, it appeared that the school had been closed for years.

Halfway up what was apparently the outer wall of the

gymnasium, someone had spray-painted an elaborate panther that peered out across the neighborhood as if it were searching its own private urban jungle for prey.

From my experience rock climbing over the years, I instinctively picked out a route up the side of the building that the artist might have ascended to tag the wall—just stem up using that brick ridge along the corner, then undercling the window with one hand while painting with the other.

Tricky, but doable.

Having a sense of the neighborhood, I focused on the teens again, who were now only a few steps away beneath the branches of a sprawling red oak tree.

Tear stains streaked the girls' makeup.

"Is he gonna be okay?" Mimi called out to us, apparently assuming that we'd come with an update about their friend.

"The doctors are with him right now," I answered. "They're helping him."

I avoided saying, *They're doing all they can*, since, even though that phrase has the *intent* of being good news, it almost always comes across sounding like bad news.

During the drive, we'd checked with the hospital and learned that Canyon Robbins, the boy who'd been stabbed, was in critical condition.

He wasn't the victim Sharyn had texted me about.

And he wasn't the one we were here to investigate.

"But if they're helping him, then he's gonna be okay, right?" Mimi pressed, looking for any reassurance she could get.

"He's in surgery now," Sharyn replied, prudently avoiding any speculation or giving any unwarranted assurances about his condition or chances.

We'd both learned this at the Academy: state the facts, avoid making promises regarding outcomes over which you have no control.

Sometimes context and compassion require you to temper what you say.

Honesty but not always openness.

All at once, Mimi turned and snapped at Erik. "You stabbed him!" Stifling back a sob, she lifted an accusatory finger. "You probably *killed* him!"

"It was an accident. You were right there. He jumped at me and I—"

"He's gonna die and it's all your fault!" The pent-up emotion got the best of her, and she shoved him. The boy stumbled back, his ankle caught on the bottom step of the porch, and he tumbled to the ground, an uncoordinated flailing of arms and legs.

The officer to her left intervened, grabbing her arm more roughly than the slight scuffle called for, and yanked her back.

"Quiet!" he demanded. His nametag read *Kramer*. "Both of you. I've had enough. Stop it or I'm cuffing you."

Typically, in situations like this you don't want to undermine the authority of other law enforcement officers or authority figures, but if this guy ended up getting any harsher with them, I would have to step in and take him to task.

Erik climbed somewhat clumsily to his feet and brushed himself off.

I didn't want to intimidate the kids or make them defensive, but I did need to identify myself, so I tipped open my credentials and said, "I'm Patrick Bowers. I'm with the FBI. Agent Weist here and I are trying to sort out what happened in the house. While we wait to hear more about how Canyon is doing, can you tell me what you know about the woman who was found upstairs?"

"You mean the *body* that was found up there," Gwen corrected me. "I can't believe there was a *dead person* up there, right up above us the whole time!" She shivered with revulsion. "I promise, we didn't have anything to do with it. I'm serious!"

"Alright. Help me understand what happened. Why did you come here?"

"It was Igazi's idea," Gwen said.

"Igazi?"

"Canyon's friend," Erik explained.

"Where can we find Igazi?" Sharyn asked.

"I don't know. I don't even know if that's his real name or not. It's what people call him. 'Igazi' means 'blood' in Zulu—or, I don't know, that's what Canyon told me. He's a street artist."

"Graffiti?" Sharyn said.

"Yeah."

"Okay." I made a note to follow up on that. "Why did you choose this particular house?"

"Just to be alone," Mimi answered.

I gestured toward the other homes on the street. "But why not one of those? Some of them are tucked back pretty far from the road. They might've offered a little more privacy."

"This is where Igazi said we should come," she reiterated.

Igazi again.

"So, agents." Kramer heaved an impatient sigh. "Are we good here? We're supposed to take 'em in."

Any additional questions could wait. Right now I figured it was more important to get these three to a doctor to make sure they were okay.

Sharyn glanced my way and I nodded.

"Yes," she told Kramer. "You taking them to the DDC?"

"Yeah. Their parents are gonna meet us there."

Sharyn assured the three teens that we would pass along any updates about their friend, gave them each a business card with her cell number in case they thought of anything else, and then Kramer and his partner led them to a couple of nearby cruisers.

When they were gone, I asked Sharyn, "DDC?"

"Detroit Detention Center. Booking isn't done at each precinct any longer. It's all centralized."

Even though, from all we knew, Canyon's stab wound was accidental, the police would still need statements from each of the teens before determining if any charges were going to be filed.

She went on, "A couple years ago, word spread that if the cops arrested you and you claimed to be hurt or were in need of medical attention, they were required to take you to the hospital. Asthma, a bruise—really anything at all."

"And suspects would do that to postpone getting booked, and also to get to a place where there was less security, more of an opportunity to slip away."

"Exactly." She donned exam gloves and I did the same. "It wasted a lot of time and resources—neither of which the police department in this city has enough of anyway."

"The DDC has medical staff on-site?"

A nod. "It's your one-stop shop for processing suspects and keeping them alive at the same time. I know the place all too well. My ex is a doctor. He helps out there sometimes."

We ducked beneath the crime scene tape while the bystanders on the other side of the street continued to film us.

One person's tragedy is another person's entertainment. It's been that way from antiquity—the Internet just adds more seats to the arena, just makes it easier to watch the games unfold.

For all I knew, Sharyn and I were already starring on someone's YouTube channel.

The two of us passed through the open door and entered the house.

11

I scanned the living room.

Most graffiti artists have a distinctive style, and the satanic symbols on the walls appeared to have been painted by someone a lot less skilled than whoever had tagged the panther on the high school down the street.

Igazi?

Maybe.

We would find out.

A sleeper sofa, two sliced-open reclining chairs, and a few floor lamps cluttered the cramped room. A scattering of dried autumn leaves lay beneath the boarded-up windows. Discarded clothes, junk mail, and unrecognizable debris lay strewn haphazardly across the floor.

In an abandoned building like this, dirt and grime eventually collect everywhere and now lay wherever I looked.

The Second Law of Thermodynamics at work.

No, the universe isn't thrumming on into complexity, but continually descending into cold and final chaos. In the end, everything deteriorates—galaxies, solar systems, planets, cities. Living rooms in Detroit.

A universe ruled by the god of decay.

In this job, the God of grace is a lot harder to see.

The fine mist of blood spatter on the kitchen wall

matched the nature of blowback from a chest GSW at close range, which we'd learned during our drive was the preliminary assessment of the method of death.

If you work in this job long enough, you learn to read the blood even if spatter analysis isn't your specialty, and the pattern here was consistent with the shooter standing about a meter from the victim.

After finishing in the kitchen and surveying the remaining rooms on the ground floor, we headed toward the steps to view the woman who'd been left in the master bedroom upstairs.

I asked Sharyn, "What's your sense of things? Do you anticipate any jurisdictional hurdles here? The Bureau assisting with a serial homicide investigation?"

"Actually, the DPD kicked it into our lane. They reached out to us. Their funding comes from the local tax base, which has been gutted over the last few decades as the city's population has bottomed out. Detroit has fewer officers now than they've had since the 1920s. Lieutenant Sproul is only too happy to have more eyes on things, especially with a high-profile case like this."

"So we're going to have to do the heavy lifting."

"Yes, we are."

The layer of dirt on the steps had only been disturbed on the right side by the officers who'd prudently kept over there to minimize the impact to the scene.

Second floor.

Top of the stairs.

A DPD officer who barely looked old enough to get into an R-rated movie, let alone work a scene like this, stood sentry beside a door near the end of the hall.

He was biting his lip uneasily as we approached. I wondered if this might be his first homicide.

In a way, I hoped so—because that would mean fewer nightmares, fewer memories to haunt him.

In a way, I hoped not—because then he might've gotten used to it. But that was its own kind of nightmare.

After Sharyn and I had identified ourselves, he said, "Schwartz and Julianne are in there now."

Sharyn looked at him curiously. "I didn't think they'd arrived yet."

"Showed up pretty much right away. Told me to wait out here."

"Okay."

She must have noticed how flushed he looked because she patted his arm and read his name badge. "It's okay, Officer Springman. You'll be alright."

"Yes, ma'am. It's just, I've never . . . That's my first dead body in there."

"You'll get used to it," she said.

Or maybe not, I thought.

I paused momentarily at the doorway and drew in a breath, hoping to center myself in preparation for seeing my second body of the day.

Then I let it out.

Didn't help.

Never does.

I stepped into the room.

12

A wedge of dreary evening sunlight slanted through the jagged glass of the single window on the north wall, illuminating the bedroom.

A slim woman in her late twenties wearing a CSI cap and an elegant wedding ring was recording the body's temperature and checking the amount of lividity. I noticed that her left arm hadn't developed properly. Meromelia. She seemed to manage well enough with just the one functioning arm.

The prematurely graying man beside her looked only a couple years older than me, maybe forty or so. His eyes were set just a little too far apart, leaving the impression that he would be able to see what was happening off to each side of him as well as in the front. He'd emptied the victim's pockets and was bagging the items, placing them on the impeccably made bed.

Incongruities are often clues—and the clean, neat sheets in a home like this was incongruous, to say the least. We would definitely check the sheets for DNA from whoever might have straightened them.

Sharyn already knew both officers and when she introduced us, I learned that the young CSI tech was named Julianne Springman. The man with her, Detective Ted Schwartz.

The officer outside the door had referred to Schwartz by his last name, but showed a higher degree of familiarity by calling Julianne by her first name. Since the two shared the same last name, I guessed that they were related.

He wore no wedding band. Brother and sister? Exes?

I'd ask Sharyn later.

The victim's body was positioned on the floor, seated with its back against the bed, unlike the other victims who'd all been found in the closets. Her hands were folded in repose on her lap. The killer had intertwined her fingers and there was a measure of dignity to that. She could almost have been praying. However, any mood of tranquility was ruined by her head hanging limply forward. Her eyes were open and her skin was cyanotic and claylike with the mask of death.

If a homicide victim's eyes are closed, you can almost convince yourself that the person is simply asleep or has entered some form of eternal rest. But when her eyes are open like this, it's not quite so easy to get yourself to believe that things are in any way okay.

The bloodstains on her shirt were consistent with the spatter in the kitchen.

A gunshot to the chest.

Considering the location of the wound, I suspected death came quickly and that she didn't suffer much.

A small blessing. But a blessing nonetheless.

"She was posed," Ted observed. "Just like the others."

Not exactly, because she wasn't in the closet, but I said nothing.

To stage a scene is to alter it so that it appears to be a different type of crime. To pose a victim means leaving her in a position that carries some meaning or significance to the offender.

Both reveal intention in their own way. Staging is a redirect. Posing is often a middle finger raised against the victim or the authorities. Sometimes the posing contains a very intimate, very personal message.

So the posing here indicated that he'd left her like this for a reason, although it was too early to discern what that might have been.

Why here? Why the room and not the closet?

A different killer?

I knelt by her side.

Early twenties. African-American. Slight frame. By the way she was seated, it was difficult to determine her height, but I posited between five foot and five-three. She wore a pair of cuffed skinny jeans and a loose-fitting, pearly white long-sleeve blouse, unblemished save for the bloodstains. And the bullet hole.

No sign of a struggle.

I used my Mini Maglite to search beneath the bed, but its beam only revealed undisturbed clods of dust and a dated children's picture book, also covered with thick dust.

The other scenes I'd evaluated on my flight here often had a jumble of trash in the rooms—in most cases, more than this one did: piles of broken record albums, picture frames, children's Halloween costumes, discarded Atari games, laundry detergent bottles, just about every type of litter imaginable. All left behind when the homeowners moved out.

There was no anonymous tip this time and no letter carved into her forehead.

Is this crime even linked to the others?

Every anomaly is an arrow pointing to the truth.

"Why up here?" Ted said.

"Up here?" Julianne asked.

"This room. If the killer was just trying to dispose of her body, he'd most likely leave it on the first level or perhaps drag her into the basement." It sounded like Ted was thinking aloud. "Why would he go through all the trouble of dragging her up the stairs after she was dead?"

"She was carried," I said.

"How do you know that?"

I ran my finger along the floorboard for approximately ten centimeters beside the victim's feet and then showed the dirt on my finger and the track on the floor. "No drag marks here or on the stairs."

Then I noted the clean cuffs on her pants and pointed out the pristine, unblemished sleeves of her shirt. "No dirt. No scuff marks. Nothing on her hands or sleeves. With this much grime in the room and on the stairs—"

"Hmm, yeah," he said. "So she *wasn't* dragged."

"To carry a body up a flight of stairs shows commitment," Sharyn noted.

"It speaks to relationship," Ted observed. "Plus, there wasn't any effort to dehumanize the body. Very controlled. Very deliberate. This guy is ruthless and careful."

"Five victims." Sharyn's eyes were on a headless doll on the floor near the window. She seemed to shiver, then looked away. "Five different homes. No obvious connections between the victims. What's he trying to tell us? How's he choosing his victims?"

I had no answers.

"Have we been able to identify her?" I asked Ted and Julianne. "Do we have a name?"

"No," Ted replied. "Not yet. No one's been reported missing."

As I inspected the body, I considered the sight lines in the room. All of the previous victims had been carefully positioned as well without any effort at concealment or obfuscation, just as Ted had noted.

But this woman wasn't staring out of the closet.

I eyed the place on the wall where, if the victim had been alive and able to lift her head, she would have been looking.

Though the paint was old and faded, one rectangular area about a foot wide and maybe eighteen inches high was less faded than the rest. A 4d nail was centered near the top of it.

Taken in connection with the other crimes, I decided it was at least possible that she was left here to draw attention to what was missing on the wall.

I placed my hand beside the faded area and photographed it for perspective.

Ted was watching me. "A painting maybe?" he suggested.

"Maybe." I tapped the wall. "But I want to know for sure what was hanging here."

"How are we supposed to find that out?"

"Start with whoever used to live in this house. Based on the faded paint and considering the lack of direct sunlight that would reach this wall because of its orientation to the window, whatever was hanging here was here for a while. Let's find the former residents and ask them. Whoever they were, they moved out before last autumn, but only later did someone board up the windows, so—"

"Wait. How do you know that?"

"The dried leaves beneath the living room windows.

Someone boarded up the windows after they blew in from the tree out front—red oak leaves."

I examined the victim's personal items that had been bagged and labeled on the bed: a set of Lexus car keys, a crumpled wad of bills, a phone.

"No purse?" I asked.

"No," Ted replied.

Pointing to the bag with the set of car keys in it, I said, "Do we have someone searching for the car?"

"There's an officer driving around the neighborhood."

This woman has no letter carved into her forehead. Maybe the killer didn't have the chance yet to return to the body.

Julianne had been studying the body when I entered the room. "Are you able to determine the time of death?" I asked her.

"I'll need to do some more tests to nail it down."

"Ballpark it for me."

"Well, based on lividity and the lack of abdominal putrefaction stains, I'd say we're looking at eighteen to twenty-four hours ago—but that's just an initial estimate."

"Okay."

Half as long as any of the previous victims when the tips were sent in.

An incongruity.

A fault line.

Just what we needed.

"I can't believe she's the fifth one we've found," Ted muttered.

"Actually, she's the first one we've found," Sharyn corrected him.

"How do you figure?"

"The location of the previous four victims was given to

us. The tips told us exactly where they would be. In this case, however, when Canyon was stabbed, the officers who responded searched the house and found this woman here. No anonymous tip."

It was a good point. The differentiation was significant.

I picked up the bagged mobile phone. "Do we know if this is her cell?"

"It was in her pocket," Ted told me.

"I already dusted it," Julianne said. "It's been wiped clean—I mean, the outside of it has. Not the data."

"You were able to access it to check?"

"Well, no. I just mean I know the outside is clean. No fingerprints."

"You're sure there aren't any on the home button?"

"Yes. Why?"

Solving a crime often depends on reconstructing who last spoke with or saw the victim, or who might've been present when she died. That often involves determining if she was planning on meeting someone close to the time of death. If the phone wasn't locked or encrypted, and we were able to get into it, selfies, text messages, microblogs, calendars, and reminders—any of those things could offer valuable leads.

Because of that, as soon as we can, we attempt to access a victim's phone or mobile device. If possible, even before leaving the scene.

Sometimes a phone is the best witness of all.

I opened the bag.

"I know you want to get into that cell, but if you enter the wrong password, it might wipe the data," Ted cautioned.

Our Cyber Division was making strides accessing locked

iPhones through NAND mirroring, but that process was tedious and time-consuming and I wouldn't be able to do it here.

However.

"If I'm right about what kind of phone this is," I said, "I won't need a password."

I went to the body and, noting the bracelet activity tracker on the woman's left wrist, I guessed she was right-handed.

"Do you have the photos you need?" I asked them.

"Yes," Julianne said.

"Is it alright if I move her hand?"

"Yes."

I'd never tried this before and I didn't know if it would work, but I figured it was worth a shot.

I lifted the woman's right thumb. Fingerprint scanners don't work well with cold fingers, so I slowly exhaled warm air onto its tip, being careful not to leave too much moisture behind.

Carefully, I laid it against the home button.

It took a few tries, but at last the screen unlocked when I tried her right index finger instead.

"Let's find out what your name is," I said to her softly.

13

Once I was in the phone, it didn't take long to discover that the victim was a twenty-two-year-old accountant named Jamika Karon.

After we pulled up her address, Ted called dispatch to get a unit to her home, which was about fifteen miles southwest of the city.

Holding the phone by the corners just in case there might have been any prints that Julianne missed, I checked to see which apps were still open.

Seven were: a web browser, YouTube—she was halfway through a cat video—a texting app, the actual phone app, a messaging app called TypeKnot, a dating one called Hook'dup, and a breaking news application that was currently trending with a story about an unidentified woman who'd been found in an abandoned house on Runyon Street.

A tragic twist of irony: while her body sat here, her phone was streaming the story of her death.

The news app had been updated most recently with a video of Officer Kramer and his partner leading the three teens to his car. The camera angle told me that it'd been filmed by someone in that crowd across the street.

Going to the window, I studied them.

Sixteen people.

Three more than when Sharyn and I had arrived.

No one was acting suspiciously.

I accessed Jamika's texts and email.

She had nine unopened emoticon-rich texts from late last night and today. They came from "Sis," "Hank," and "Bennie"—names we would look into. By the informal way they addressed her, it was apparent that they all had a close relationship with her.

The last text that'd been replied to came from a number that didn't correspond to any names in her contact lists or address book. She'd written, "See you there!" in reply to a message that simply read, "Well?"

The exchange had happened last night between ten twenty-one and ten thirty-four, which coincided with the time of death Julianne had postulated.

Sharyn, who'd been scrutinizing Jamika's personal effects, asked, "What are you thinking, Pat?"

"The best way to find out who she was meeting is simply to ask."

"Ask who?"

"The person who texted her."

I laid down Jamika's cell, opened an app on my own phone to record the audio of the call, and then tapped in the number.

At the window again, I saw that the sun had dipped behind the school's hulking shell, leaving long, angular shadows cutting across the neighborhood.

As the call began ringing, one of the men in the crowd turned his phone to look at its screen.

Okay.

That got my attention.

He wore a black hoodie that shrouded his face, but I could see the back of his hands and tell that he was light-skinned.

He toyed with one of the ends of the hoodie's draw-strings as he studied his phone while the one in my hand continued to ring.

At last he tapped his screen and I heard a male voice in my ear: "Who is this?"

I gestured urgently for Sharyn and Ted to join me at the window.

"I know about last night." I wanted to see if I could get a reaction and establish without a doubt that it wasn't simply chance that the man outside had answered his phone at the same time someone had picked up the call I'd put through. "About what happened after she texted you. We need to meet."

He glanced around the neighborhood. "Who the—?" But he never finished his sentence. Instead he abruptly ended the call and eased back from the crowd before bolting through a nearby yard toward the school.

That was definitely a reaction.

I didn't want to turn my back on him for a second, so rather than taking the stairs back to the first floor, I smashed out the rest of the window's glass, grabbed the drainpipe outside, and half slid, half leapt to the ground. My landing wasn't perfect, my left leg buckled, and as I rose to my feet, I called for Sharyn to detain the onlookers and set up roadblocks. "Two blocks. Every direction!"

Ignoring the pinching tightness in my ankle, I sprinted through the deepening shadows, pursuing the subject toward the school.

14

I shouted for him to stop, but he disappeared into the building.

They never stop.

Neither do I.

SIG and Maglite out, I whipped through the doorway and entered a hallway that stretched the length of the school.

Dim. Illuminated only by the light that leaked in through the open classroom doors. Most of the baffled ceiling panels had fallen down and lay trampled on the floor, likely by the scrappers who'd removed the lockers that had once lined these walls.

No sign of the suspect.

"FBI!" I moved forward cautiously. "Step out with your hands up!"

He could have fled through the neighborhood. Instead, he came here.

He's comfortable here. He knows this place.

No sounds—but the baffles on the floor could be muffling his footsteps as they were doing to mine.

I swept my light in front of me.

A girls' bathroom door stood open to my left. I ducked in for a visual sweep, making sure to avoid stepping on the strips of asbestos that must have been ripped off the pipes before they were removed.

The bathroom's metal stalls were gone, but the toilets were still there. Three had been sledgehammered, and the remaining one served as a repository for spent spray cans.

Empty.

Back in the hall, I heard urgent steps far ahead of me and rushed toward them, passing a trophy case that still held a collection of trophies from the days when the high school was still being used. No one had bothered to remove them.

And then to the library, where the footsteps led.

Inside, rows of shelves stood in quiet formation, all devoid of books.

Words came to me, but I didn't know where I'd heard them before: *Wooden skeletons stripped of their paper flesh.*

No windows. No natural light.

I passed my light through the line of shelves and once again clearly identified myself as a federal agent. The words bounced around the library like solid objects. I called out again for the suspect to step out and put his hands up, but there was no response.

Gun ready, I quickly swept around the edge of each shelving unit in turn, clearing the rows.

I was half done when the thudding began.

The echo of impact.

Shelf against shelf.

Giant dominoes, colliding heavily against each other, toppling in a line toward me.

Scrambling for safety, I leapt to the side, barely managing to get out of the way before the shelf smashed down where I'd been only seconds before. As it landed, a cloud of choking dust billowed up around me.

Coughing, I crossed the library, edged through the door that the suspect would've needed to pass through to flee, and found myself in a hall that terminated at the gymnasium.

Detective Schwartz must have followed me because he appeared at the other end of the hallway just as I was about to enter the gym. I sent him to check the boys' locker room down the hall.

The gym floor was severely warped, as if it were a wooden wave pool frozen in midripple. In some areas, the floorboards were bowed knee-high, waterlogged and swollen from the weather coming in through the shattered windows or the leaking roof overhead.

The boards flexed underfoot as I crossed them, creating an odd sensation of me not having my footing even though I was walking across the floor.

Ten meters above me, metal beams and girders spanned the length of the gym. Above those, broad strips of ceiling tiles had rotted away as they let in the water that'd bowed this floor.

The missing tiles revealed an attic ventilation area above the gymnasium. As I scanned the area, a light sprinkle of detritus filtered down through one of the openings, telegraphing movement above me.

He'd already made it up there.

This guy was fast.

Scary fast.

Unless there's more than one person.

Wary of a second subject, I located the access ladder near the stage at the far end of the gym and ascended it, wondering why the suspect would have gone up here rather than fleeing into the night.

Why trap yourself in the attic?

To hide? Thinking no one would think to look up there? To wait things out?

The faint sound of police sirens cycled into the gymnasium. Backup was still a ways out.

I had to duck through the attic's low entrance, but found that I could easily stand once I was on the other side and balancing on one of the narrow, swinging catwalks above the gym.

Hot, staid air, despite the late time of day.

Dust particles that'd been kicked up by recent movement migrated through my flashlight's beam. Tiny specks of the rotting past. Chaos. The god of decay.

A few glimpses of strangled light found their way through slits in the roof joists above me, creating a strange patchwork of light and shadow.

The network of wooden plank catwalks crisscrossed the ventilation area, supported by unsubstantial-looking cables attached to the roof's rotting support beams.

The gym's faux ceiling hung about two meters below the catwalks, and beyond that were the girders and narrow supports. Through the sections of caved-in tiles, the warped floor was visible three stories down.

A dormant ventilation fan nearly as tall as I was stood four meters from me, its dust-encased metal blades imposing, but stationary.

As I moved forward, the catwalk creaked and swayed underfoot and I wasn't sure how much I trusted those narrow cables or the exposed, weather-weakened beams they were bolted to.

Holding the SIG in one hand and flashlight in the other, I couldn't grasp the cables to steady myself. Normally, my balance wasn't too bad, but I was no gymnast or balance beam walker, so as I edged forward, I did so with careful, hesitant steps so I wouldn't slip off and crash through to the gym floor.

A figure stood at the far end of the catwalk, facing me, but his head was lowered and I couldn't make out his face. His height and build appeared similar to the man I'd chased into the school, but I wasn't able to identify if it was him.

He was holding something in his left hand.

"Drop the weapon!" I leveled my gun at him. "Now!"

But as I was angling my light toward him, he clicked on the hefty flashlight he was holding and tipped its fierce beam into my eyes, momentarily blinding me.

It caught me off guard and I blinked and squinted, trying to see again. I heard him running toward me.

I shouted for him to stop, but he kept coming, each step causing the catwalk to rock enough to distract me, enough to force me to focus on staying upright rather than on addressing the threat he was posing to me.

He might have a weapon.

"Stop!" I shouted again.

But he raced forward, using that light to keep me from seeing his face.

"I will shoot!"

Fire, Pat!

No! He might be unarmed. You can't shoot without the clear indication of—

You have to. He's a threat and—

He leapt at me with a fierce crescent kick that connected with my hand and sent the Maglite flying away from me and twirling across the attic, tossing curls of uncertain light and shadow behind it in its wake. It bounced off the boards and landed on one of the remaining ceiling tiles, casting its angular cone of light across the attic, but in the wrong direction for me to make out my assailant's face.

Somehow, the guy kept his balance as he landed on the catwalk.

He swung his flashlight at my right hand, smacking violently into my wrist, but I held on to my weapon. Then, for some reason, he tossed the light aside and it dropped through the paneling beneath us.

He kicked at me again.

I knew enough about fighting to know that in martial arts with every move you're setting up for the next one. So, a punch might set up for a kick; a kick might set up for a punch. Kick, kick, punch. Usually, combinations have two, three, or four moves. And this guy liked his combinations.

This time I was able to block his foot, but he quickly followed up with a hook that I wasn't expecting. His fist caught me in the jaw and the force of the blow sent me spiraling backward. I lost my balance and fell onto the catwalk, crashing onto my side.

Immediately, he was on me, going for the gun.

I had no leverage, and if he got the SIG, I would have no chance of stopping him. So, rather than risk letting him get it, I flicked it aside. It dropped onto the fragile paneling, smashed through, and plummeted to the gym floor.

He stood, poised and ready to attack me again.

Both hands free now, I grabbed a cable, and swung up to my feet.

I didn't like this at all.

Fighting this guy on his terms was not going to work. His balance was far better than mine and if I wasn't careful, I was going to end up next to my SIG on the floor of the gym.

The rafter above me was out of reach, but I could snag it with a high enough jump.

Okay, so that was a possibility.

"Hands up where I can see them," I ordered him, though I had no weapon to back me up.

He didn't reply and he didn't move, but rather just stood there, backlit by the Maglite's beam jutting up from where it now lay, out of reach. Then all at once, he swept in at me, closing the space between us in one fluid motion, sending another kick flying at me, this time toward my face.

I ducked, but his heel grazed the top of my head on its way past.

The catwalk pendulumed to the side as he landed, but again the movement didn't seem to bother him.

Maybe that's why he came up here. His balance. Because he knew he'd have the advantage.

"I'm a federal agent," I said. "Stand down!"

No response.

This man wasn't going to fall on his own.

Alright then, I would help him.

I crouched, then leapt, going for the beam above me, but with the tweaked ankle I didn't get the height I was hoping for. Although I stuck it with my right hand, my left hand slipped off. But my right hand's grip was firm enough for me to do a pull-up and plant my left as well. I swung my legs up and kicked him hard in the chest with one foot and directly in the face with the other, knocking him backward.

He teetered on the edge of the boards, waving his arms urgently to regain his balance, but then tipped back into the darkness and crashed through the ceiling tiles, dropping to the gym floor without uttering a sound.

From this angle I couldn't see him land, but only heard the groan of the floorboards as they flexed under the impact.

I let go of the beam, dropped back onto the catwalk, and peered into the gym, trying to make out his face, but only saw his motionless form shrouded in the day's long shadows.

Catching my breath, I hurried back through the attic's entrance to the ladder that led to the gym.

On the way down, I kept wondering why he hadn't fled when I was in the library, why he'd gone to the attic in the first place.

With the flex in the floor, I doubted that he had been killed, and I figured that after I cuffed him I could ask him why he ran.

Or there might've been another person here in the building the whole time. Maybe you were fighting the wrong guy.

But he was dressed the same as the man outside the house.

That means nothing. There could've easily been two people wearing the same outfit.

When I emerged in the gym, he was gone.

I rushed to the hall.

No one.

Nothing.

Ted flew out of the library, where he must have decided to check after finishing up in the locker room. "I heard something," he called to me. "You alright?"

"Yeah. Check out front—the door he came in. I'll head around back."

I passed through the gym, tossed the exit door open, and scanned the area outside the school.

No one fleeing on foot.

Blue and red lights pulsed through the neighborhood from the DPD cars that'd arrived, but I didn't see any people. Using my phone for a light, I scoured the nearby underbrush, but, apart from a rabbit that I startled and sent scampering into the night, there was no movement.

When I returned to the gym, I heard the shouts of officers in other parts of the building, and as I was reaching for my identification, Springman, the young officer who'd been guarding the crime scene appeared, gun drawn, shouting for me to *put my hands up!* But a second later when he recognized who I was he lowered his weapon.

"Our guy is close," I told them. "Likely injured. Find him. Go."

He took off.

No one else in the gymnasium.

No body on the floor.

No flashlight.

And no gun.

Wherever the suspect was, he now had my SIG.

15

Atlanta, Georgia

The border agent was finishing up with a short, stout, Eastern European woman who'd been on Ali's flight. Just one more person—a businessman in a finely tailored suit—stood between Ali and the agent.

Be obedient.

Do nothing to raise suspicion.

He drew his computer bag closer to his side.

"They can refuse you entry for 'undeclared reasons,'" Fayed had told him. *"Which means they can do so for veritably any reason they choose. And according to the laws of the infidels, they have no legal responsibility to tell you what that reason is."*

The agent handed the passport back to the woman, who nodded graciously and ambled forward as the man in the designer suit approached the agent's booth.

You're next. Just get through.

Ali moved forward and waited dutifully behind the strict yellow line painted on the tiling.

To make it easier for the agent, he tucked his boarding pass and declaration form into the pages of the passport, using them to bookmark where his photo was.

Less than a minute later, the agent finished with the business executive. No hassles, no problem.

He waved him on.

Be at ease, Ali.

Breathe.

With a disinterested glance above his glasses, the border agent signaled with two fingers for Ali to come forward.

Good eye contact. Let him trust you. This is just a slight inconvenience that you must go through, that all visitors must go through, before entering the United States of America. You haven't done anything wrong. You're simply here to visit relatives in Michigan.

The agent was staring absently at his computer screen as he held out his hand to receive Ali's passport.

When he handed it over, the agent, whose nameplate read *T. Snelling*, studied the photo, then thumbed through the pages that'd been stamped from Ali's slew of trips from Kazakhstan to Germany and England over the past two years. Work as a translator often required travel, which was another reason he'd been chosen for this mission.

However, his trip to Yemen for his training had no stamp. That one had been privately arranged by people who knew exactly who to bribe.

"This your first visit to the United States?" Agent Snelling asked.

"Yes."

"Purpose of your trip?"

"I'm visiting relatives in Dearborn, Michigan."

Immediately he berated himself: *No, no, no, Ali. You didn't need to tell him all that. It sounds too prepared. Just the state, you just needed to mention the state.*

Snelling was studying Ali's face now, carefully comparing it to the passport photo. "How long will you be staying?"

"A week. Well, just over a week. Eight days."

The agent set the passport facedown on the glass face of a scanner. "Names?"

"Names?"

"Your relatives in Michigan. In Dearborn. What are their names?"

"Gregor and Tatiana."

"And you're named Ali Mahmoud Saleem."

"Yes." Ali couldn't tell if it was a typical line of questioning or if he'd already raised some sort of suspicion. "I'm a Muslim," he explained, before being asked. "I took a new name. It is all on my passport. My name is."

"I see that. But the names of your—how are you related to Gregor and Tatiana?"

Ali felt a slight tremor in his throat.

"They are my cousins."

"When was the last time you saw them?"

"Two years ago in Germany when my uncle got remarried."

"Is there another one now?"

"Another—?"

"Wedding. Here. In the States." The agent's voice had taken on a sharper edge. "Is that why you came?"

You're provoking him.

"No." Ali stumbled for the right words. "No wedding."

"Then why now? Why fly all the way over here for eight days to see them?"

Ali had been eyeing the scanner and suddenly realized that Agent Snelling was looking directly at him.

"Tatiana is starting a new business."

"What kind of business?"

"A restaurant," he said too quickly. "She is starting a bakery."

"Which?"

"Which?"

"A restaurant or a bakery?"

"They bake bread as well as pizza, serve it."

"Uh-huh. And you flew all the way over for that? For a pizza?"

"I came to see them."

Agent Snelling lifted the passport but didn't return it to him. He was scrutinizing the screen of his computer instead. From the way the monitor was positioned, Ali couldn't see what was on it.

"We have a few additional questions for you," Snelling said at last. "I'll need you to go with Agents Wilder and Dartmoor for a secondary screening."

He motioned for two of his associates who were standing nearby to come over. He gave them Ali's passport and they led him to an interrogation room after taking his bags from him, even though he told them he was fine carrying them himself.

++++

No luck.

We searched throughout the school, down the street, and in the abandoned buildings nearby, but found no sign of the man I'd chased from the crime scene.

With the gymnasium's bowed floorboards, I could certainly understand how he'd survived the fall, but afterward he'd just disappeared—and with the number of officers we had sweeping the area, that was no easy task.

One team interviewed the bystanders who'd gathered near the house, but no one could—or would—give us a description of the man who'd been standing there beside them filming.

There's a stigma in many urban areas about "snitching," and that dynamic might've been at work here. Often, people fear retribution when the police leave—which is understandable but doesn't help our job any.

In addition, sometimes friends and relatives of the victim want to take justice into their own hands.

And justice on the streets rarely looks like it does in the courts.

While the DPD expanded the perimeter, shut down the surrounding streets, and went door to door, I returned to the house to finish assessing the scene so the medical examiner could have the body transported to the morgue for an autopsy tomorrow.

16

Ali found himself in a small room, not much larger than the one-bedroom apartment in Ust-Kamenogorsk that he shared with his fourteen-year-old sister, Azaliya.

For the last two years he'd done his best to raise her now that their parents were gone, leaving to start a new life and find work somewhere else in the country. And never even sending word about where they were or what they were doing.

Gone.

It had been hard on Azaliya.

With the recent worldwide downturn in oil prices, uncertainty of the global financial markets, and the divestment of two of the Russian billionaires who owned much of the land in the area, the economy of Ali's city—which depended almost solely on income from the nearby oil fields—had been decimated.

Many families had lost everything.

At least he and his sister had a place to stay.

A number of geopolitical forces came into play to make things in the region even more unstable, all stemming from unrest in the Middle East: the civil war in Syria, the tightening of coalition forces against insurgents in Iraq and

Afghanistan, and the military offenses of countries such as Turkey against Muslims considered to be "extremists."

Those factors meant that it had become more difficult for the leaders of the groups Westerners called Islamists, or jihadists, to recruit new members from the Middle East.

Even though oil money gave the groups significant revenue, their casualties were drastically cutting into their numbers.

Consequently, they'd ventured farther east, into Kazakhstan, to recruit fighters and to enlist those willing to make the ultimate sacrifice for their cause. They made the appeal to other Muslims, primarily ethnic Kazakhs: jobs, money to send back to family members, a vital role in fighting the infidels. Their duty as Muslims.

"What is there for you here? Come and fight with your Muslim brothers," they would say. "You'll make more money than you could ever imagine that you can send back to support your family, and then you'll receive immeasurable riches in paradise."

After, of course, a martyr's death.

Fayed had waited until the end of Ali's training to tell him what his mission would be.

His men had taught him how to wear a suicide vest so that it wouldn't be noticeable, where to position himself in the crowd, and when to detonate it to produce the most efficacious results.

He'd been expecting additional instructions on how to pack it with nails, or how to wire it himself, but instead they just gave him the inhaler and told him how long it would be, after he used it, before he became symptomatic and contagious.

"But what is it?"

"It is retribution for the Crusades. It is the will of Allah. It is the birds flying in over the desert clutching the sacred stones in their beaks and in their claws."

"The birds?"

"Surah Al-Fil."

"Of the Elephant?"

"Yes. All that you need to know will be explained in due time."

Then they explained the virus's progression.

"After the symptoms start," Ali had asked, "what happens then?"

"Then your sister will be safe and cared for. And you will receive your reward."

But in truth, the bestowal of pleasures in the afterlife held less appeal to Ali than the knowledge that Azaliya would be safe in this one.

Now, here in this cramped room at the airport, one of the agents stayed with him while the other took his bags to an adjoining room, visible through a metal mesh-reinforced window spanning the length of one wall.

"I'm going to pat you down," Agent Wilder told him. "Is there anything in your pockets that could harm me? Any needles or sharp objects?"

"I have done nothing wrong."

"Is there anything in your pockets, Mr. Saleem?"

"No. I don't understand why you are doing this."

"Hold your arms out to the sides, please."

No, no, no. It can't happen like this. What if they find it? What if—

Suddenly, he felt totally unprepared for any of this. He was just a translator. He wasn't a terrorist. He was—

Think of your sister.

Do as he says.

After the pat-down, the agent said, "Have a seat, sir."

As Ali did, all of his senses seemed to sharpen simultaneously.

It'd happened to him once before, two years earlier when he was having chest pains and went to see a physician.

After the examination, the doctor told him to wait in the room, then went to consult with another physician.

While he awaited his doctor's return, he heard a nearby faucet dripping distinctly and clearly, above the faint blip and hum of a machine somewhere down the hall. He noticed the acrid, bleachy smell of the cleaning agent they'd used in the room. He realized how skin-colored the walls were and he couldn't shake the feeling that he was inside a diseased body with a heart pulsing, that he himself was a dying man surrounded by the drip and hum of blood.

And now it was happening again.

The drip and the hum.

His senses sharpened. All attuned.

The pulsing of blood.

He sensed the damp rub of his shirt's fabric under his left arm, the sweaty pressure on his legs as he shifted in his seat. On the wall, the hands of a circular clock ticked their way around the face, each second clacking louder than it should have.

Tick.

And tock.

And tick again.

The agent had used cologne, a fresh and wind-brushed scent that seemed out of place in this stifling, cramped room.

Tock.

"Sir," Ali said, "I don't understand what—"

Tick.

On the other side of the glass, Agent Dartmoor wiped down his bag, doing an explosive trace detection. Ali knew about ETDs. Part of his training. Back in Yemen. Back when—

Agent Wilder interrupted his thoughts, "Please explain to me your reason for coming to the United States."

"I told the other man, out there in the booth."

"Yes. Now tell me."

17

While examining the rest of the house, I paid particular attention to the blood spatter in the kitchen and the cellar where Canyon Robbins had been stabbed, but found nothing else of note.

Sharyn tried to find out who'd uploaded the video to the news app site, but the links and postings were all anonymous.

I searched online for the name "Igazi" but couldn't identify anyone living nearby with that name, leaving the likelihood that it was a street name or nickname.

I relayed to the team how the fight in the attic had gone down and how the assailant had used his light to blind me as he came toward me.

"You could have justified taking the shot," Ted said.

"Maybe."

But I didn't want to justify anything. I wanted to be right in the first place.

"That guy could fight," I told them. "Spin kicks at my head, and each time he would land on the catwalk again. Gymnast-like balance. Someone that good has spent serious time honing his skills."

"Martial arts or close-quarters combat?" Sharyn offered, half as a question, half as a conclusion.

"Likely. Yes."

Ted spoke up. "With the neatly made bed beside Jamika, a military background might be a possibility."

Officer Eddie Springman, who I found out from Sharyn was indeed Julianne's brother, told us that he'd taken Taekwondo classes, knew some of the local dojos, and agreed to look into martial arts studios in the area. "I'll see which instructors or students have served in the military, or know of someone named Igazi."

Since we hadn't mentioned the name to him, I looked at him curiously. "Why do you say that? About Igazi?"

"I spoke with Kramer on the radio while you were in the school. He told me the name of the guy you suspect."

"He's not a suspect yet," I clarified.

"Sure. No, right. I get that."

"TypeKnot," Ted said to Springman. "That's your generation. What can you tell us about it?"

"You can chat, share videos, post photos, whatever. Face swap."

"Do you use it?"

"No, but, I mean, I have it installed on my phone. I just never— It's not my thing."

"And it's one of those apps that deletes your posts after a few seconds?"

"Depends on the settings, but yeah. Unless you screenshot it. Nothing's private for long online." He laughed as if he'd just told a joke.

As Ralph had commented to me one time, *"The Internet makes stupid cling to you forever."*

I tried contacting Angela Knight at the Bureau's Cyber Division to see if she could trace the number I'd found on Jamika's phone, but she'd left for the day and her associate wasn't able to come up with a lead. Additionally, when he tried to analyze the audio recording I'd made of the call, the voice sample was too brief to determine anything substantive.

As it turned out, the medical examiner was indeed Canyon's father, so he sent his assistant to transport the body while he went to be with his son at the hospital. Julianne's CSI team finished processing the scene, and it was finally time to leave for my motel.

As Sharyn drove, she asked if I'd had a chance to get dinner on my flight.

"Not unless a packet of peanuts counts. I'm afraid I wasn't in first class."

"We're both tired. Hungry. It's been a long day. How about we grab a bite? I know a Mexican place that's not too far. They make a mean chicken fajita. You still like chicken fajitas?"

"Well, yes."

"Is that a yes to dinner or to liking fajitas?"

"Just the fajitas. Maybe tomorrow on dinner. I need to get settled in here."

"Sure. Okay."

She was quiet until we pulled into the motel's parking lot, but then offered to wait for me if I'd like. "For supper, I mean—if you just need a few minutes? I'm just making sure."

"Rain check. Good night, Sharyn."

"Alright." As I opened the car door, she added, "You're going to need a way to get around Detroit. I arranged for a car. I'll have a couple of officers deliver it here in the morning. Seven thirty work?"

"Perfect. Thanks. And there's one more thing I'll be needing."

"That is?"

"A gun to use until I get my SIG back."

"Got it. A car and a gun. I'm sure we'll have a briefing tomorrow, but I don't know the schedule. I'll call you in the morning around eight thirty or so, give you the plan for the day. In the meantime, you have my cell number. Let me know if you need anything. Anything at all."

18

As Ali hurriedly related his cover story again, he watched Agent Dartmoor in the adjoining room wipe down the zippers on his suitcase and begin inspecting the items inside it, one at a time.

His socks, his underwear, and then—

"That is my prayer mat," he told Wilder.

"You're Muslim."

"Yes, yes, I told the other man this. What does that matter?" Sometimes he spoke in a stilted manner when he was nervous, and found himself doing that now. "This is the country of freedoms, yes? Of freedom of religion?"

"Yes. We are the country of freedoms."

Dartmoor lifted the plastic bag containing his pill bottles and held it up to the window to show to Wilder.

"What kind of medicine is that?" he asked Ali.

"For my heart. It is for my heart. I have a weak heart."

Then his shaving kit.

Flipping it open and dumping out the contents and evaluating them.

You must do it now. Before it is too late.

Finally, she emptied his computer bag and picked up the inhaler.

Now, Ali!

He let himself start breathing quickly, short shallow breaths. His nervousness helped, but it was more than nerves, it was—

"Relax, Mr. Saleem."

"My inhaler. I need my inhaler."

"We'll get it to you in a minute. Now, I need you to tell me—"

Ali began to hyperventilate, bent forward, and leaned one hand against the table to steady himself.

Wilder hesitated for a moment, then signaled for Dartmoor to come in.

As Ali feigned gasping for air, he found himself actually struggling to breathe for real. It was no longer just an act.

She appeared in the doorway.

"Let him have the inhaler," Wilder told her.

At first she hesitated, but when she saw how distressed Ali was, she handed it to him.

Hastily, he held the mouthpiece to his lips, pushed down the release mechanism, and took a long, deep puff. Then another. He coughed slightly, then began to breathe easier.

He took one final puff, just to make sure.

And so.

It was done.

"Are you alright?" Wilder asked him.

"Yes."

There was no turning back.

The virus was not designed to be contagious yet, wouldn't be until after interacting with his specific DNA, and then only after forty-plus hours. It was amazing what synthetic biology could do. But afterward, oh yes, it would spread.

The two agents finished testing and analyzing all of the

items Ali had with him. He answered the rest of their questions calmly and carefully, knowing all too well that if he was denied entry, if he was sent back to Kazakhstan, he would never see Azaliya again, and the subsequent suffering she would go through and the abuse she would be forced to endure would all be his fault.

More will die.

Like the man in Yemen.

That Rafidah, one who rejects, kneeling in the sand.

By the time the agents finally released him, his flight to Detroit had already departed. They told him he could speak with "a representative" to request a voucher to stay at a hotel that night and receive assistance in rebooking his flight, but he declined.

Though to some extent he was relieved that he had carried out this aspect of his mission, he'd been instructed not to use the inhaler until he was in Michigan.

He didn't know the full extent of the plan, but from what he did know, the timing was vital in order to see things through to the end.

Now, all of that had been put at risk.

From piecing together the little he'd been told and what he'd inferred from the conversations he'd overheard, the genetic modifications altered the properties of the virus, increasing its virulence, but only after the contagious stage of the disease had ensued.

In other words, the victim would remain out of bed and asymptomatic while the virus was contagious so that it would be "more widely disseminated."

Contagious at forty-two to forty-four hours.

But not symptomatic until sixty-eight to seventy-two.

And by the end of the week he would be dead—unless

he was one of the extremely rare exceptions. But with a mortality rate of nearly ninety-seven percent, that was not very likely.

With the help of a Russian scientist, Fayed's group had confirmed the virulence of the disease using some of the schoolgirls that Boko Haram had most recently abducted in Nigeria and converted to Islam, turning them into martyrs.

Eighty-eight of the ninety-one girls that had been tested died within six days. All now in the arms of Allah.

Or so Fayed had assured him.

Of the three that survived, two had committed suicide when they saw how disfigured they'd become. The final girl was stoned to death after she admitted that she'd secretly remained a Christian all along and had never truly converted to Islam.

You need to get to Dearborn. You need to meet with Fayed.

After the border agents returned his luggage to him, Ali walked as casually as he could to a bathroom, where the airport wouldn't have any video or audio surveillance.

Only when he was alone and locked in an empty stall did he check his mobile phone.

A text from Fayed's number was waiting for him: All set, brother?

Ali replied: Call me.

Less than ten seconds later his phone rang.

In a hurried and hushed voice, Ali summarized what had happened at the border checkpoint.

The whole time Fayed Raabi'ah Bashir listened silently. No questions, no response, until at last Ali finished by saying, "What should I do? I have missed my flight. The next one doesn't leave until morning."

After only a slight pause, Fayed told him to use the credit card and documentation he'd been given to rent a car and stay at a hotel for the night. "I will text you which rental car company to use and which hotel to stay at. Once you are there, I want you to wait until you receive further instructions. Do you understand?"

"Yes. I'm sorry, I had no choice, I—"

"How are you feeling?"

"I'm fine. There won't be any symptoms for another couple days."

Fayed didn't respond to that, but instead said, "I will get you the information regarding the car and hotel. Be brave, my brother."

"Yes."

"Allahu Akbar."

"Allahu Akbar."

After the call, Ali deposited the inhaler in the bathroom's locked sharps container for needles and bio waste, where it would soon be expeditiously destroyed without any scrutiny or inspection.

As he rode the underground train to the main terminal, he noted that there were nine other people with him in the car. All breathing in the same air.

Inhale.

Exhale.

Tick.

And tock.

Life was separated from death by only the thinnest of membranes. That diaphanous film of a passing moment. The cessation of a single heartbeat.

Tick.

There.

Tock.

That was it.

Nothing more to come.

Just like with that man with that hood over his head.

But his death was not so clean and sterile.

With all that spurting blood.

There, in the dark and dampened sand.

There, with the high desert sun, the unblinking eye that watched over all, just as it had been doing since 570 BCE when the birds flew to Mecca to destroy those who had laid siege to the Holy City.

During the ride toward baggage claim and ground transportation, Ali turned toward the corner of the train car so that no one would see, raised his hands upward toward his chest, cupping them slightly, and surreptitiously prayed to Allah, the God he wasn't even sure existed, that none of this would put his sister in any more danger, and that somehow, if at all possible, no more innocent people would die.

19

After dropping off my bags in my room, I decided I needed to at least eat something, so I found a nearby gas station, where I picked up a can of V8, a Snickers bar, and the sole remaining leathery-skinned apple that was left in the wooden basket near the checkout counter.

I also snabbed a new Mini Maglite.

Christie had made up that word "snabbed" one morning when I was leaving for work: "Can you snab some yogurt on your way home?"

"'Snab'? I've heard of 'grab,' 'snatch,' 'snag,' 'nab.' But 'snab'?"

"It's nouveau."

"You made it up."

"Maybe." A tiny smile. "But it's a good word, right? As soon as you hear it you immediately know what it means. No dictionary needed, and it's fun to say."

"So, I can snab an object. Can a person be snabbed?"

"Oh, yes. But you wouldn't want that."

"Doesn't it matter who's doing the snabbing?"

"Well." She straightened my collar for me. "I suppose if you were snabbing me, that I could deal with."

On the way back to the motel, I noticed that all of the storefronts on this street except for a seedy-looking marijuana shop called Puff and Blow were shuttered, dead, and dilapidated.

Someone had written JUST MARRIED on the back window of the car parked in front of the cannabis store, but the *i* had worn off.

Okay, that's awkward.

A late-model Lincoln sedan with darkened windows prowled the street, slowing as it approached me, the driver perhaps on the hunt for a drug deal or a mark for a robbery, but I waited it out, watching it stoically as I slowly finished the V8 and began working my way into the Snickers. Eventually it moved on.

From my limited familiarity with Detroit, I knew that the city administrators were promoting urban gardens, and even farms, within the city limits with the goal of creating a smaller, greener city.

But the renaissance that the city had been shooting for over the last three decades had been slow in coming.

How do you retool a city of this size? How do you alter an infrastructure that was built to support a metropolis of three million people and downsize it to be appropriate for a fifth of that? How do you find the time and money to demolish a hundred thousand homes, businesses, churches, schools, or warehouses when your city is already bankrupt? Who pays for it? Doing one a day, every day, would take nearly two hundred and seventy-five years. And what do you do with the patchwork tracts of vacant land?

No easy answers.

That's where my mentor came in.

The mayor had called on my old professor and advisor for my doctoral studies at Simon Fraser University, Calvin Werjonic, PhD, JD, to consult with the city council. Since he was the world's foremost expert in environmental criminology, there was no one better qualified than he was to help.

From keeping up with him online, I knew that during his consultancy he had exhaustively studied and analyzed the demographics and layout of the city.

It might be a good idea to pick his brain at some point as we moved forward with this case.

++++

Using the password he'd gotten from his contact in the New York City FBI Field Office, Blake logged into the Federal Digital Database and reviewed the information regarding the woman who'd been killed in northern Minnesota at Aspen Cove Lake.

Simone Tee.

Thirty-three years old.

According to the case files, a patron at a nearby bar remembered her leaving with a man who fit the description of the person Blake suspected was responsible for her murder. And, taking into account the connection with the modeling agency, Blake also believed he knew who the killer's ultimate target was. However, he wasn't sure where she would be these days or even where to begin looking for her.

That man had been obsessed with her ever since first seeing the movie, ever since taking her home from that nightclub more than fifteen years ago.

Blake had always found obsessions to be, somehow, at the same time both difficult to understand and also quite easy.

We all want a "why."

But often there is no "why."

What leads to an obsession?

Who knows?

Obsessions aren't something to make sense of, but instead they grow from any desire that remains unchecked by logic or unbridled by conscience.

No, there's never a satisfactory explanation that justifies an obsession. If a reasonable person could find justification for that action, it wouldn't be an obsession. Just like phobias. If you're afraid of a cobra, that's justified. If you're afraid of a garter snake, that's not. And fear of buttons? The number thirteen? Or perhaps linonophobia, the fear of string? Or one of the strangest of all phobias, one that oddly enough even has a name: anatidaephobia, the fear that wherever you go, somehow a duck is watching you? Irrational. Unjustifiable. But real.

And so, with the man who went by so many names, the obsession was what it was: present, impossible to understand, yet all-consuming in its power over him.

Find her and you'll find him. Then you can stop him. You have an obligation. The day he went to prison you promised yourself you'd do it if the day ever arrived. You know what he'll do if he's free. He'll kill until he's killed. You can't let that happen.

Blake spent thirty minutes scouring the Federal Digital Database for the name "Scarlett Farrow" and any iterations of it but came up empty.

Trying a different approach, he examined Mannie's research, looking at other crimes in which a grenade had been used. Mannie had found nineteen instances worldwide since April, but some were suicide attacks. Blake decided that the crime in Detroit merited the most attention. Someone had thrown a grenade through the front door of one of the precinct's stations, but it had failed to go off.

Blake hadn't heard about it before, but in a city with this much violence it was hardly newsworthy, especially since it hadn't gone off.

Taking into account the background of the man in question, the grenade made sense.

He'd always shown an interest in them, even when he was a boy.

Those and the blades.

"Grenades and blades. Grenades and blades. Grenades and blades, blades, blades."

The rhyme of death that he'd started chanting when he was only seven.

Blake still had the scar on his arm where the boy had used the box cutter on him.

"All in fun," he'd said. *"Just a game. Just a game, game, game."*

Though Mannie tipped the scales at over three hundred fifty pounds, he moved as deftly and quietly as a lynx and Blake didn't realize he'd even entered the room until the light shifted and his friend's behemoth shadow draped over the desk from behind him.

"What are you thinking?" Mannie asked.

"Considering Fayed's connections to Dearborn and this recent unsuccessful grenade attack in Detroit, it might be time to pack our things. Perhaps we can kill two birds with one stone."

"Fayed and Dylan."

"Yes."

"But not *kill*."

"Not Dylan. No."

Blake and Mannie's fake identities were good, but still, to avoid unwanted encounters, they only used public transportation when absolutely necessary. Otherwise, they took the Cessna Citation Sovereign. It'd been registered in Canada, a common technique for avoiding some of the FAA's oversight. It also made those occasionally necessary border crossings less obtrusive.

"Should I contact the pilot?" Mannie asked.

"Yes. Tell him we leave first thing in the morning."

20

Back in my motel room, I checked to see if I'd received any messages from dispatch or any updates on Canyon's condition.

Nothing.

I hoped that tonight, at least for the boy, no news was good news.

As it turned out, Jamika's Lexus was parked three blocks down from Runyon Street in an abandoned garage. Both the house and car were being processed. Officers were speaking with the three people who had texted her last: "Sis," "Hank," and "Bennie." Although, as it turned out, none were relatives.

Ralph sent me a note that NSA had identified a text from someone tipping off Blake that we were going to raid that house this morning. That's what'd allowed him to slip away while the task force's focus was on that specific neighborhood. No word yet on who'd tipped him off, though only the Joint Task Force members and DeYoung knew when we were going to be there. Gaviola, who'd gotten the original intel, was working with Torres to pinpoint who it might have come from.

I texted Ralph back: Anything more on the Russian bioweapons scientist?

He replied: Still checking. This guy's identity is buried deep and they're having a tough time translating his handwriting. He used some sort of code or shorthand. We've been able to make out a connection to Boko Haram and a reference to a date when they abducted some schoolgirls. Looking into it.

While setting the phone down, I noticed that the previous text had been that one from Sharyn right after I arrived in Detroit: her message informing me that another body had been found.

Seeing her again today had been tougher than I thought it would be and, considering the recent bumps in the road Christie and I had been experiencing, it made me ask those "what if" questions.

What if I hadn't broken things off all those years ago?

What if life hadn't waited so long to bring us together again?

What if . . . ?

Our brief hug when she first met me at the airport spoke volumes, even though we hadn't exchanged a word.

I loved being with Christie, but the fact that she had a teenage daughter made things complicated. I'd never been a dad, didn't exactly see myself as a father figure, and, since it'd just been the two of them for so long, I wasn't really sure how I would fit into their lives moving forward from here.

The future was a topic that Christie and I hadn't talked through nearly as much as we should have. And now, Sharyn had reappeared from my past and stepped right into the middle of all that uncertainty.

Sometimes the passage of time makes it hard to reestablish the same degree of closeness or trust with our friends from the past. Interests change. Habits shift. Religious beliefs, political views—they all evolve. Most friendships are for a time. I think that's natural.

But some relationships seem impervious to time. Even if years pass between your encounters with each other, somehow you're able to pick up right where you left off.

Same level of trust.

Same familiarity. Same intimacy.

And here, with Sharyn, that's already how it felt.

The decision to break up hadn't been mutual.

It'd all been my choice.

Eight years ago I'd anticipated that after we left the Academy, life would take us in different directions, and I'd wanted to make that transition easier for us both.

As it turned out, it hadn't necessarily made things easier, but it had certainly made them simpler.

For a while.

A long while.

Until today.

Truthfully, I'd been hoping that more of an awkwardness would have crept in between us—maybe the weight of the years, or the festering of old wounds, or the avalanching consequences of misunderstandings, those phantoms from the past that follow us everywhere.

But we had no old wounds that I knew of, and any misunderstandings—at least from my end—had evaporated, and were, by now, long forgotten.

No lurking grudges.

No lingering regrets for things unsaid.

But didn't you say yes to coming here at least partly because you wanted to see her? Wasn't that a factor, even just a little bit?

Probing for motives.

Never a good idea.

To keep my thoughts from drifting toward her, I busied myself with unpacking, and when I came to the bottom of the suitcase, I found what Christie had left for me wrapped up in my favorite Marquette University T-shirt.

A small, compact, folded-up umbrella.

A reminder of the day we met.

There in the gentle rain. There on that all-too-busy, all-too-lonely sidewalk of Sixth Avenue in New York City.

Tonight, with all the activity and distraction after I landed, with the foot pursuit and the subsequent analysis of the crime scene, I'd forgotten to call and tell her that I'd arrived in Detroit. I could have smacked myself in the forehead.

I checked the time.

Already after eleven.

Since she typically went to bed early, I texted instead of chancing waking her up with a call.

I apologized and explained that the case had consumed me right off the bat, that the night had gotten away from me, and that I would talk with her in the morning. I ended by writing, I found the umbrella. Thanks :)

Within a few minutes she responded, texting that she understood, and wishing me sweet dreams.

You too, I replied, hitting enter before I realized what I'd written.

Scarlett Farrow—I

The Lake

Scarlett liked being ten—well, actually, ten *and a half.*

She'd practiced this scene a ton of times—but that didn't really make it any easier.

It was still kind of scary.

And sad too.

She shivered and wrapped the towel tighter around her shoulders. The lake was chilly, actually, *cold*. And she'd had to spend like an hour in it because this was the scene where Millie's dad drowned when he was trying to save her, and he got his foot caught in that fishing line, tangled up around the posts under the pier.

So she had to pretend to drown.

They'd had to reshoot it a bunch of times.

Of course, she knew that none of this was real, that no one had actually died. It was only a movie. She was just playing a part.

She knew those things in her head, but sometimes on the set when they were filming, or when she was sinking beneath the surface and gagging on all that gross lake water acting like she was drowning, it was hard to remember them. Because even when you're just acting, those things are still happening to you. You can't change it so they're not.

They always *are*.

Now, her mom fussed over her, making sure her wet hair was right, so it would "look good for the camera." Scarlett could smell the wine she'd been drinking all morning when she thought no one was looking. All the while, her dad stood over by the pier, joking with one of the actresses—the one he'd been spending a lot of time joking with lately.

Then they all took their places.

Before starting a scene, Scarlett always tried to remind herself of what'd just happened in the scene before. She thought of two things—why her character was sad, and what she would be doing to try to be happy again. She wasn't sure if this was what you were *supposed* to do, but it seemed to help her get into the action better and to feel more of what Millie would've been feeling.

Millie Evans was only eight, but the director told Scarlett that it was normal for actors to play the role of people who were younger than them. "Especially with kids," he said. "Happens all the time."

Now in this scene, Millie's dad had drowned in the lake behind their house, near where he did baptisms for the church where he was a pastor, and afterward the neighbors helped drag his body to the shore.

To make herself cry like she thought Millie would have, Scarlett thought about that day last year when her cat got hit by the truck out in front of their house. She thought about how she'd been there when it happened and how Mr. Whiskers was alive and running toward her one second and then dead the next, how he became just a tangled mat of messy fur smeared with blood and squishy guts and white bones sticking out in all sorts of weird, scary ways. And she thought about how much she wanted to hug him, but how she knew that she couldn't even go near him or she would start bawling or puking all over the place.

So now, Scarlett thought of Mr. Whiskers and what it felt like to want to love and touch and hold someone, but also, at the same time, to want to run away, far away, to go as fast as you could to a safe place. And she thought of how Millie would feel all those things at once: love and fear and terrible, terrible sadness.

For the scene, they used this sort of giant doll that looked just like the man in the movie who was playing Millie's dad—except the doll was all pale and dead-looking. After they pulled it out of the water, she was supposed to walk over and touch its hand and then run away and start to cry and find her stuffed bunny and hug her tight.

Millie's dad's sandals had come off in the water and his feet jutted up ugly and thick and still.

His rubbery skin really *did* look like it was on someone who was dead, and it scared her.

While they were shooting the scene, she kept reaching out but couldn't get herself to actually touch it and they had to refilm it, until her dad—her *real* dad—got mad and asked the director to give him a minute with her.

He knelt beside her and told her firmly that she was wasting everyone's time.

"I don't want to do this anymore," she told him.

"Well, you have to finish the scene."

She folded her arms. "But I don't want to."

"Afterward we'll get some ice cream. How does that sound?"

She was cold and wet from all the filming and it was like he didn't even realize it. The last thing she wanted was ice cream. "No."

"Candy then."

The other people nearby had turned away and were talking quietly with each other and acting like they weren't paying attention to her and her dad.

She didn't like that. She wished they would stop him or at least make him listen to her.

"I don't want to do this anymore," she repeated, this time loud enough for everyone there to hear.

"We don't always get what we want," her dad said in her ear, in that hot angry way he talked sometimes.

"*You* do," she said, "'cause of all the money I make for you."

There. She'd said it. What she'd been thinking.

He took her hand and tugged her toward the human doll.

No one stopped him.

"No!" she gasped.

"Stop being a baby."

"I'm not!"

And he made her touch its arm, not just its arm, but its face. She tried to make a fist but her dad forced her fingers to touch that cold, wet cheek.

"Daddy, please—"

"When they start filming again . . ." His voice reminded her of a snake, of something hissing and mean and ready to bite. "If you don't touch it, I'll make you kiss it."

She started crying. "Daddy!"

"You understand me?"

At last she nodded.

He patted her on the shoulder like nothing bad had happened and stepped back, telling everyone that things were fine and that they could start filming again.

By then she was crying and when the director saw that, he quickly signaled for his cameraman to start rolling.

No one helped her.

Maybe they'd just wanted to make her cry for real all along.

Maybe that's what they were trying to do.

Scarlett's fingers were trembling as she touched the hand of the doll, and then she quickly ran away and cried and cried, thinking of Mr. Whiskers and what her dad had just done.

As she held Snowball, and the nice lady who was playing her mom—well, actually *Millie's* mom—came and hugged them both, Scarlett let the tears, the real ones, squeeze from her eyes while those people with the cameras filmed it all and the director gave her a thumbs-up to tell her how good she was doing.

Bones and fur and blood and the staring cold eyes of that giant dead doll.

Her hand on its slimy, rubbery cheek.

No, you can't just separate what's happening around you from what you're feeling. No matter how much you tell yourself it isn't real, in a way it *is* real—because you're really there and those things really are happening. So, as Scarlett cried there at the lake, the tears weren't all pretend.

Cold and dark.

The church wasn't very big, more of a *chapel*, as the grown-ups called it, but it had a tall steeple that left a shadow on the ground that made everything seem even colder and darker than it already was.

And after that day, dolls just made her way too sad because they made her think of Mr. Whiskers in the road. And more scared too, from remembering her dad yanking her over, closer to that thing, and making her touch its rubbery, wet skin.

So she never played with a doll again, whether life-size or small enough to cradle like a baby in your arms. No. Not at all. Not ever again.

PART 2

Gas on the Flames

Sometime between 1993 and 1995 the *variola* samples that had been stored in Moscow's Research Institute for Viral Preparations since 1980 were transferred to the State Research Center of Virology and Biotechnology, alternately known as the Vector Institute, outside of Novosibirsk. My sources have confirmed that in time, however, in the aftermath of the fall of the Soviet Union, systemic breaches in security resulted in over half of the samples being reported "lost" or "missing," which, for all intents and purposes, means they could currently be anywhere in the world being studied or utilized by extremist groups or hostile nation states.

—FROM *THE NEXT GREAT THREAT* BY SALVADOR TIEGEN, 2007, PAGE 291.

21

Thursday, August 2

I rose early to slip in some exercise before the officers delivered the car to me at seven thirty.

No fitness center at the motel, so before leaving for my run, I checked with the hospital to see how Canyon was doing. Beyond the fact that he was out of surgery and recovering, they didn't have any specifics.

At least he'd survived the night.

One step at a time.

Taking my phone with me to monitor any updates from Sharyn or the hospital, I ran past that stretch of closed businesses and the marijuana shop I'd seen last night. At first, my ankle plagued me from that less-than-graceful landing outside the house on Runyon Street when I improvised a way of exiting that second-story window, but it started to loosen up as I ran.

Two blocks farther down, I caught sight of a park and headed toward it.

Though already layered with humidity, because of Detroit's proximity to Lake Erie and Lake St. Clair, the air was still relatively cool. Midsixties.

A rickety, paint-flecked playground rising from the weeds had managed to stay intact through the years and seemed bonelike now, a somber, skeletal reminder of recesses and summer vacation, though it didn't look like children had played here in a long time.

After testing the strength of a rusted bar to make sure it could hold my weight, I started a max set of pull-ups.

But I was wrong about the bar.

Without warning, on number twenty-eight, it tore loose and I thudded to the ground, managing to tweak that same ankle again.

With pull-ups out of the question, and not exactly thrilled about the prospect of running laps around the park on a nagging ankle, I settled for push-ups, ab work, and air squats.

I went all at it.

An intense workout usually helps me clear my head, and today was no different. The facts of the cases and the questions they birthed—both from the investigation in New York and the one here in Detroit—began to line up before me.

In New York, we had Blake on the move and a dead bioweapons scientist. A source had tipped Gaviola off that Blake would be at the house, so was it bad intel? If not, who warned him we were coming? What was the Russian scientist's name and connection to Blake? Had it been a homicide, or a suicide, as it appeared?

In Detroit: five bodies and almost no clues.

I ran through the specifics again: One male victim, four females. Age range from early twenties to early forties. Two African-Americans, three Caucasians. Mechanism of death—GSW, blunt force trauma, and the stab wounds to the chest that two of the victims died from.

No trace evidence left behind.

The victims were from disparate neighborhoods and had vastly different income levels: from below the poverty line with the first one, Maxine Nachmanoff, to nearly a quarter of a million a year, with the fourth, Dr. Meredith Getz.

By all accounts the offender didn't appear to be choosing his victims based on gender, race, age, geography, or socioeconomic class.

So then, what?

We were tipped off about the first four bodies approximately forty-eight hours after the time of death. However, the latest victim, Jamika Karon, was found after twenty or so. In that difference, in that incongruity, lay the relevance. The discovery of the body appeared to be happenstance, but was that really all it was?

What was the killer trying to communicate by posing the bodies as he had and carving those letters in the foreheads of the earlier victims?

Did those four teens or Igazi, the street artist, have anything to do with Jamika's death?

And how did the suspect get out of the neighborhood last night after falling to that gym floor?

All fault lines to explore.

On my way back to the motel, as I passed that strip of failed businesses, I couldn't help but think of the dead dreams that each one represented. And, for some reason, it brought to mind that trophy case that I'd seen yesterday in the abandoned high school.

All those trophies left behind. Even when the school closed, none of them meant enough for anyone to keep or even just throw away. Not even the scrappers were able to come up with any use for the trophies. And so they left them, and even now, years later, they still sat there gathering dust, testaments to accomplishments that meant nothing in the end.

There really is a fleeting impermanence to everything we do, and what seems so important at the moment, often in hindsight doesn't turn out to be really that important after all.

Failure and detours and dead ends.

On our way to a destination we can't even be sure exists.

With that, my thoughts switched back to Blake again.

Dead ends.

Detours.

Dead end number one: When I was reassigned from a case last month, I did some checking and found that, oddly enough, the order had originated in the Office of Professional Responsibility before DeYoung signed off on it.

Dead end number two: Some of the information regarding leads on Blake's past had been buried in an almost insurmountable pile of red tape, and all of my repeated attempts to get clearance for it were denied.

Dead end number three: From what I'd seen, Blake had access to the Federal Digital Database. A confidential informant that I was supposed to meet with one night never showed. He was later found dead, killed execution-style. Computer forensics tracked down his laptop and found evidence that he had the password for the FDD that had been active in the week of June when I first ran into Blake.

But now it struck me that it was also the week I first met Maria Aguirre, an OPR lawyer who'd recently transferred to New York City from L.A.

Huh.

Timing.

Location.

At first she seemed like she might be a stickler for protocol, but not long after we met, she asked me to falsify the details in a report, making it clear that she valued expediency over the truth.

Which didn't jibe with the tortuous red tape that was coming out of her office in regard to the search for Blake.

And the last time I saw her, she'd mentioned something about Blake's silent ladies, and now it occurred to me that it was a term he'd used in a conversation with me, but I couldn't recall ever mentioning it to Maria or specifically delineating it in the case files.

That comment, along with the Federal Digital Database access and the confluence of timing and circumstance, left me unable to shake the thought that there was more going on than met the eye regarding the connection between Maria and our unsuccessful search for Blake.

Maybe it was enough, maybe not, but it certainly justified a discussion.

In this job you learn that sometimes an investigative route might not seem to lead anywhere, but when two or more of those dead ends converge on the same location, it's a clue in itself—because that doesn't usually happen unless someone has taken specific steps to cover his tracks.

His fault lines.

Or hers.

And here, a few too many of the dead ends I'd run into so far in the Blake investigation ended at Maria's office.

I hadn't seen her around for the last week or so, but it appeared that there were enough dots connected for me to text a request to her secretary to set up a meeting on Monday when I was back home.

So I paused by the gas station and sent it in.

If she agreed to meet, that promised to be an interesting meeting.

To say the least.

++++

As Blake and his associate were on their way to meet their pilot at New Jersey's Teterboro Airport, he heard from Fayed that there'd been a slight problem last night in Atlanta with his man, and that he would be driving up rather than flying.

"What kind of problem?" Blake asked.

"One that need not concern you. He is through border control. He will be in Michigan tonight. We have reorganized the schedule. It's all in place. And so is our cell."

"The oxygen tanks? The respirators?"

"They will be taken care of before dawn."

Before beginning on this project, he and Mannie had been vaccinated, so being in the area would be safe, at least for a couple days.

And after that, because of the virulence of the virus and how contagious it was, after its dispersal, it wouldn't matter where you went. If you weren't vaccinated, there really wouldn't be any safe place at all. Anywhere.

22

I arrived at the motel parking lot right before seven, both worn-out and rejuvenated at the same time in the way that good workouts make you feel.

A cruiser and a white, decade-old, unmarked Crown Victoria were waiting out front.

An officer I hadn't met stood beside the squad, absently swiping across his phone's screen. He was the man who'd been standing beside Kramer and the three teens last night.

As I crossed the lot, Kramer emerged from the motel lobby balancing a stack of sweet rolls and two cups of coffee in his arms.

"Hey," he called to me, his mouth full. "Bowers, right?"

"Yes."

"Got your car here. You try these sweet rolls yet? Killer. There's coffee in there too."

Over the years I've developed a, well . . . a bit of a discerning taste when it comes to coffee, and I didn't have overwhelmingly high expectations about the quality of beans that a chain motel on this end of the price range would offer. "Thanks. I'll have to check that out." I tapped my watch. "You guys are early."

"Didn't want to make you wait." That might have been

sarcasm, but I couldn't tell for sure and I gave him the benefit of the doubt.

"I appreciate that," I said.

At his car, Kramer handed the coffee and pastries to his partner, then dug a set of keys out of his pocket and tossed them to me. "Enjoy Detroit, Agent Bowers. It's a city with, oh, so much to offer." This time the sarcasm was clear.

"Yeah." His partner spoke up. "If you like feral dogs and drug deals and gun crime. And grenades."

"Grenades?" I said.

"Detroit is the carcass of a once-great city," he replied glumly, but also with a touch of poetic introspection. "You ever see someone get treated for gangrene? You gotta excise all the parts of the body that are rotting. Hurts to cut 'em out, but if you don't, she won't last long. Pain is her only hope of survival."

I couldn't see his badge.

I decided he would be called Officer Sunshine.

"What does that look like with a city this size?" I asked.

"Huh," he said derisively. "You deal with crime with kid gloves and you get kid-size results. Deal with it like a man, maybe you'll make some progress." He spit on the parking lot, then smeared the saliva back and forth harshly with the sole of his boot.

Okay.

"Have a good day, Agent Bowers." Kramer swung open the driver's door of the cruiser. "See you at the briefing."

"When is it?"

"Haven't heard yet. Sometime this morning. Lieutenant Sproul is gonna send out word."

"By the way," I said, "did Agent Weist requisition a firearm for me as well?"

"I don't know anything about that."

"Alright. Thanks."

They pulled out of the lot. And, as if in a blatant attempt to propagate the stereotype, by the time they reached the street, Kramer was already making his way through another pastry.

Grenades?

Seriously?

In the lobby: four of the sweet rolls Kramer was raving about awaited me, still in their $1.99-per-dozen grocery store box.

Pass.

Three overripe, darkening bananas on the counter.

Pass.

Coffee: instant. Decaf.

Ouch. Pass.

Three for three.

On the way down the hall, I snabbed some ice.

Back in my room, I took some ibuprofen and had just positioned myself on the bed to ice that ankle when my phone buzzed with an incoming text from Christie's daughter: Call me as soon as you can.

Tessa was on summer vacation and when she didn't have to get up for school, this girl didn't typically even make her way out of bed until at least ten o'clock, let alone manage to be awake and coherent enough to string a sentence together before seven thirty.

Also, like so many teens these days, she wasn't much of a phone talker—more of a texter, so clearly something was up.

I speed-dialed her.

She answered. "'Bout time."

"Tessa, your text came through fifteen seconds ago."

"Yeah?" She said that as if it proved her point. "And?"

"What's going on? Is something wrong?"

"Only if you count Mom crying herself to sleep last night."

"What are you talking about?"

"What did you say to her? Did you two argue or something?"

"No. Tell me what happened."

"All I know is what I heard from the other side of her door. It was like eleven thirty or so and I had to pee, so I walked to the bathroom, and then on my way back past her room, I heard her crying—muffled, though, like she was trying to hide it. It went on for a while. Tell me what's up with that."

"I don't know why she would have been crying."

The lateness of my text exchange with Christie last night came to mind—that, and the fact that I'd forgotten to call when I first arrived in Detroit. But she wasn't petty or overly sensitive to those types of things and I doubted that either of them would have brought her to tears.

Tessa said, "You two have been fighting."

"That's not true."

"Um. Yes. It is. I heard you two nights ago. I'm not deaf."

"We've just been trying to sort through some things."

"Yeah. Loudly. And angrily. That might count as fighting to some people."

"Listen, I can't think of anything that would have troubled her that much."

"Uh-huh. Well, then you better talk to her and see what's going on. Because *something's* eating at her. And it's making her super upset."

I doubted our recent disagreement would have affected her that deeply and wracked my brain trying to figure out what else might've happened. Since Jodie, one of my co-workers from the Field Office, was sharing the apartment with them, I wondered if there might've been some sort of misunderstanding on that front. "Is Jodie around? Has she been—"

"Jodie's been at work. Basically, always at work. We hardly ever see her—she's gone when I get up, and pretty much keeps to herself. Besides, they get along fine."

"Okay, I'll give your mom a call. Is she up yet?"

"I haven't heard her moving. Besides, I didn't mean *call her this second*. Wait so it's not too weird with you calling too early." Tessa yawned dramatically. "You know, it just hit me. Literally, there are two kinds of people in the world: morning people—who are *beyond* irritating, by the way, and oughta be shipped off to their own chipper little continent somewhere where they can all be perky and affirming together. Or their own planet. Even better."

"And I suppose the second group isn't evening people—it's sane people."

"Huh. Wow. That's actually better than what I had. I was just gonna say *anti-morning* people. Anyway. I know which group I'm in." Another yawn. "I'm going back to bed. But I'm telling you, Patrick, I'm worried about Mom. Don't break her heart. She deserves better than that."

Then without another word, she hung up.

I made a mental note to call Christie at nine thirty—not too early, not too late. But then, acknowledging the very real possibility that I could become busy or distracted, I also set a reminder alarm on my phone.

Then I finished icing my ankle, hit the shower, and sorted through what I needed to do this morning regarding analyzing this case's data to start developing a geoprofile for these crimes.

23

7:34 A.M.

Dispersal in 31 hours

Last night, out of an abundance of caution, Ali had closed his hotel room's shades before climbing into bed, and now, despite the time, only a faint smear of sunlight had managed to ooze in.

He hadn't fallen asleep until nearly three o'clock in the morning, and even then sleep had only come fitfully, until five or so when he finally dozed off for good into the disorienting, surreal world of dreams.

A mixture of memories and imagination and longing, smearing themselves across the craggy dreamscape of the subconscious.

Dreams.

Thousands of soldiers dying outside the sixth-century Arabian city, the black sores covering them like rough, obsidian pebbles stuck to their skin.

Bodies in the sand.

A decimated army.

Rotting in the sun.

Then the birds that had flown in, that'd brought death

to this army of Abyssinians, now swooped down en masse to pick clean the corpses.

Then the dream tore loose from the past and spun forward into the future as those splintered images of the desert merged with Ali's dread of what was to come.

Fear that would not stay caged.

Thousands more of the dead and dying, scattered across sidewalks and parks, decomposing in office lobbies and high-rise hallways and cruelly stained hospital beds.

At last, with the dark descent of a thousand thousand birds into the landscape of a modern skyscrapered city, the dream ended without any closure, but just the unsettling portent of suffering to come to the waking world, a destination pregnant with screams and pain.

Ali had been told enough about the progression of the virus to know that insomnia and troubling dreams were symptoms, but it was far too early for him to be symptomatic. It must have just been stress.

"You will have general malaise after three days or so," the Russian doctor had told him. "Fever. Muscle aches. Flu-like symptoms. Those will precede the rash."

So common. So inconspicuous.

Which is why the disease had so often gone undiagnosed throughout history, untreated until it was too late. But then again, the treatments wouldn't have mattered much, since there was no known cure for smallpox.

Nearly half a billion people killed by it since the beginning of recorded history.

Ali rolled over and tried once more to sleep, but could not.

He needed to know what step to take next, and just hoped he hadn't compromised the mission by using the inhaler last night.

He rubbed a drowsy hand across his eyes, then checked his phone.

No messages.

Scrolling to the airline's website, he found that the first flight to Detroit had already departed.

Do not worry. Fayed will tell you what you need to do when the time is right. It is all in Allah's hands.

He unrolled his prayer mat, directed it toward the Kaaba in Mecca, washed his face for the partial ablution, raised his palms close to his ears, pronounced the opening exaltation, and then began to recite the Surat El-Fatiha.

++++

I toweled off, threw on some clothes, and updated my files with the information we knew regarding the times of the homicides.

However, my thoughts kept gravitating back to Christie.

I've never really understood women all that well, so I decided that before contacting her, it might be smart to pick the brain of someone with more experience than I did at making things work with the opposite sex.

Ralph and Brineesha had been a couple for nearly twelve years and had weathered lots of ups and downs together. Also, Ralph had met Christie and knew me better than just about anyone did.

I shot him a text asking him to give me a call when he had a chance, then got back to the analysis of the crimes. Although this appeared to be a serial killer, it didn't appear that he was abducting the victims, but rather encountering them at those sites.

Is he luring them? If so, how?

And what significance do those times and locations hold for him?

11:02 P.M., June 10, Maxine Nachmanoff. 3741 St. Clair Street. With the letter *W* cut into her forehead.

12:35 P.M., July 6, Gideon Flello. 168 Worcester Place. The letter *O*.

6:14 P.M., July 9, Dakota Sawatzy. 6347 Walton Street. The letter *R*.

And finally, Meredith Getz, 10:22 P.M. on July 21 in a house on 14156 Montrose Street. The letter *R*.

Jamika, no letter at all. Time of death—close to that of Dr. Getz.

Lunchtime. Lunchtime. After work. Then the last two, later at night.

I was processing the times in relation to the locations of the crimes when Sharyn called at just after eight.

After a quick "good morning," she got right to it. "Listen, I know this is earlier than I said I'd contact you, but I just got word: Canyon Robbins, the boy who was stabbed last night, he's recovering. He's awake."

"We need to talk to him, see what he can tell us about Igazi—who he is, how he's involved in all this."

"I figured you'd say that, but here's the thing: Lieutenant Sproul scheduled a briefing for the Joint Task Force at nine. The precinct is pretty much across town from Grandshore Medical Center, the hospital where Canyon is."

"Nine?" I checked the time. "No, that's no good. I don't want to be rushed with this kid."

"And also, if I recall correctly, briefings are right up there somewhere next to root canals and camel spit on your list of favorite things."

"I didn't know I had a list."

"I pieced it together. Induction."

"Camel spit? Really?"

"I'm just saying."

"Alright. Well, talking to Canyon is the priority right now. Maybe someone at the meeting can bullet-point things for us, fill us in over lunch."

"That, or I'll see if Sproul can postpone it a couple hours. With traffic at this time of day, I'm guessing Grandshore Medical Center is a good twenty-five minutes from your motel. Did Kramer get you a car?"

"A trusty old Crown Victoria."

"Ah. Classic. A Vickie. So very stealthy. No one will see you coming in that."

"This one's been around since back when I was a cop, probably be around for another decade after I retire. He didn't have a gun for me, though."

"Oh, don't worry, I stopped by the armory. I've got you covered."

"I see what you did there—got you covered."

"Right."

"I'll meet you at the hospital."

"See you in a few."

24

Ali's prayers did not bring him peace, and he could not help but wonder if perhaps his lack of faith had nullified them.

He rolled up the mat and packed it in his suitcase.

The digital clock beside the bed blinked red with the time: 8:11.

For some reason it struck him that it was just one digit off from 9/11.

But in this case, the result would be many, many times worse.

How much did the Almighty, the Creator, the Knower of All, really become involved in the affairs of men? How much did He let things play out in the universe based on natural law, in contrast to inserting His will into orchestrating those events toward a certain end?

Do not ask such questions. Submit. This is your duty. This alone.

Truthfully, this week it seemed as if things were resting solely in his hands and not in God's at all.

After all, he was the one who had to see things through to the end; he was the one who had to give up his life, not Allah.

Do not think such things!

Though still anxious about what step to take next, Ali knew better than to initiate any communication with Fayed. It was his job simply to listen and obey.

This, he had learned explicitly.

This, he had learned well.

During his training, when he'd first arrived at the compound in Yemen, he'd been taken to a room and told to sit on the cot and wait for further instructions. Then Fayed and the two soldiers who'd brought him there left him alone.

An hour passed. No one came.

Two hours. Then three. Five.

Six hours ticked by. They'd left him with his watch—perhaps just so he could chart the tedious passage of time.

When dusk stretched over the desert, he began to believe that they indeed had forgotten about him. He was tempted to walk outside, to find the men, to politely remind them that he was still here, still awaiting his orders.

But he did not.

After all, even if they had forgotten about him, they would not appreciate being reminded of that fact, of their failure.

He did his best to remain faithful in his prayers but obeyed the dictates of the brothers who had left him here and he did not leave the bed.

Night passed.

No one came.

Morning.

He waited.

Without air-conditioning or a ceiling fan, the room was stifling.

The airless vent on the wall offered no relief and its presence simply served to mock his situation.

Two days.

At times, he heard shouts and screams outside.

At times, the spray of gunfire or the single sharp report of a gunshot followed by a stretch of blank silence before another gunshot rang out, but he did not move from the cot. He did not let his curiosity get the best of him, did not even slide over to peer out the window.

Three days.

No food, no water, no toilet.

He made do.

Finally, as the oppressive sun baked that room on his fourth day there, Ali's thirst was almost unbearable. He felt dizzy and delirious and nearly certain that they truly had forgotten he was there.

Cramped, weak, repulsed from sitting in his own filth, he finally decided to leave, to walk out the door and go back home and be done with all of this.

Yes.

Leave.

Whatever the consequence of that choice turned out to be.

Outside the building, he would tell the first person he met that he'd been waiting for these four days without food or water, that there must have been some kind of mistake, that—

The sound of voices outside his room filtered in through the door.

Two men. Possibly more.

One was laughing.

After a quick deliberation, instead of rising from the cot, Ali stayed there and eyed the door apprehensively.

If they walked past, he would go and find them and explain everything, but if they came in, he would take the—

The door swung open and Fayed entered, sipping from a sweating and crinkled plastic water bottle. The soldier who followed close behind him wore fatigues and a black ski mask and carried an automatic rifle. Even more unsettling, however, was the imposing curved sword that hung from the thick leather belt encircling his waist.

Ali recognized that type of sword from the recruitment videos he'd seen while he was still in Kazakhstan: a scimitar.

It was the sword of choice for the beheadings carried out by The Brigade of the Prophet's Sword.

The man's fatigues were flecked with dark splotches of dried blood.

But not all of it was dry.

No, no, no. Please—

"Ali," Fayed said. "We've been watching you." He gestured toward the door, which still stood open. "This has been unlocked the entire time and yet you have not left your room. In fact, you have not even moved from that cot to look out the window. Not for four days, brother. Were you not curious?"

Ali had suspected that they might have a camera hidden in the dead vent above the bed, and Fayed's words made that seem even more likely.

"I was not brought here to be curious." Ali hadn't spoken since being left alone, and his voice didn't sound anything like he remembered it.

"And why *were* you brought there?"

To protect my sister, he thought. *To save her from people like you.*

"To serve Allah," he replied. "To receive orders. To carry them out. To establish the worldwide Caliphate."

Fayed exchanged a glance with the soldier who bore the scimitar.

Ali's pulse quickened.

Perhaps he hadn't answered properly. Perhaps they could see through his words and read the doubt in his heart.

Duplicity.

Lies.

Fayed strode toward Ali and he thought it was over.

He knows, he must know. It is—

But instead of slapping him or binding him or shooting him in the head, Fayed handed him the bottle of water. "Drink up, my brother. Stand. Stretch. You have passed your first test."

Ali guzzled the cool water.

And water had never tasted.

So.

Good.

Before.

He tried to stand, but when he pushed himself to his feet, the stiff, abeyant muscles in his legs refused to accept his weight and he collapsed.

"Here," Fayed offered. "Let me help you."

With his assistance, Ali rose and stretched his legs slowly until his circulation got moving again.

After allowing him to wash himself and change, Fayed said, "Ten were brought here. All have failed. All. Apart from you."

"The gunshots?"

"We could not have them leaving and betraying us by disclosing our location or our methods. You understand, yes?"

All the other men are dead? All the ones you arrived with?

"Yes," Ali replied. "I understand."

Dead.

All in the name of Allah.

All for the cause of the Caliphate.

Fayed led him outside into the blazing, unyielding desert sun.

Ali's eyes weren't used to the brightness and he had to shield them against the stabbing light. However, the soldier with the scimitar was prepared and handed him a pair of dark sunglasses from a pocket in his fatigues.

"We want people who will await orders however long that might be," Fayed explained. "An hour, a day, a year, a decade—and will then carry them out without question, without hesitation, without reservation or restraint. Are you ready to learn the ways of true Islam?"

"Yes."

Fayed led him around to the back of the building, where a man knelt on the ground, his wrists bound behind him, guarded by two other fighters with the distinctive insignia of The Brigade of the Prophet's Sword sewn onto their sleeves and over their hearts.

After handing off the rifle, the ski-masked soldier drew his scimitar and approached the kneeling man.

And then it happened.

Everything changed when that sword came down.

Now, here in the hotel room, Ali felt a shiver of revulsion, and despite his disquieting doubts about God, Ali prayed for those memories to become mist, for Allah to blow them away with the wind of His mercy.

You must not get distracted, he rebuked himself. *You must not be ruled by the past. You must think only of what lies ahead and not what lies behind.*

After he'd dressed, he placed his phone beside him and then sat on the bed just as he had done on the cot at that compound in the desert—awaiting his orders so that he could carry them out without question, without hesitation, without reservation or restraint, just like a faithful follower of Allah would do.

25

Sharyn was waiting for me in Grandshore Medical Center's well-appointed lobby.

In contrast to the rest of the neighborhood, the hospital looked newly renovated and impeccably maintained. Clearly, someone had poured some real money into this place—maybe before the streets surrounding it became hollowed out in the wake of so many people fleeing the city—or maybe afterward, in an attempt to draw residents back to this part of Detroit.

To accent her trim, stylish blazer, Sharyn had on a pair of elegant aqua blue earrings and a matching necklace that I recognized right away.

They'd been a gift from me back when we were together.

"Sleep alright?" she asked.

"Yes." I didn't comment on the jewelry. "You?"

"Like a rock. Your loaner Glock is in my car. I'll get it for you when we leave. You just need to sign your life away with a few dozen forms."

"What would work in the Bureau be without paperwork?"

"Part-time."

"I think you might be right."

"The Glock was the best I could do on short notice," she said. "I know you prefer a SIG."

"You do know me pretty well, Sharyn."

"Well, I guess . . . I mean, I used to." An uncomfortable and slightly flirtatious stillness drifted between us. "Sorry about that," she said. "I didn't mean to . . ."

"Don't worry. It's alright."

"Okay." She lowered her eyes demurely for a moment to gather herself, then at last looked up and pointed down the hallway. "Main admitting is this way."

As we navigated past the lobby's chairs and end tables, I said, "This hospital still has that new-car smell to it."

"Less than two years old. The Ferilex Corporation has made a huge investment in this community."

"Ferilex?"

"A multinational firm. I'm not even sure what they're all into. They make medical supplies, do some work with GMO food, trying to help produce more crops in Africa. They were recently granted a government contract to provide emergency medical equipment here in the state. That's about all I know. They have a distribution center here in Detroit."

"A medical supply company put money toward the hospital?"

"Well, officially their foundation did—and I wouldn't say they exactly 'put money toward' it. They paid for nearly the whole thing from the ground up. Including the region's finest autopsy facility."

"Huh."

"I know: it might have raised some eyebrows elsewhere, but in Detroit when that much money meets this much need, well . . ."

"Money talks."

"Yes. The hospital is part of a growth initiative to revitalize the city to try to lure people back to the— Oh, that reminds me. You were right about the timing. I checked into it: the family who owned the house where Jamika Karon's body was found moved out in April and never came back. I spoke with the wife. They never boarded up those windows."

"Have the evidence techs look for prints on the edges of the boards where they might have been handled. Who knows. It's a long shot but it might be worth a look. Were you able to find out anything about the picture that would've been on the wall in front of Jamika?"

"An old painting of Jesus. The woman I spoke with said it wasn't worth anything. It'd been there for years. They left it behind. Left almost everything behind. No idea how long it might have been gone or why anyone would have taken it."

The receptionist greeted us with a pleasant smile and directed us to Canyon's room. "One fifty-three," she said chirpily, in true morning-person fashion that would've certainly annoyed Christie's daughter. "Just go down the hall past the café. It's right across from the fountain."

"Café and fountain?" I said. "Nice."

"Uh-huh." She tilted her head effusively when she smiled, as if she were auditioning for the Morning Person of the Year Award.

Her landline rang and she wished us a glorious day as she reached for the receiver.

That incoming call got me thinking, and when Sharyn and I were about halfway to the café, she said, "I can see the wheels turning. What's going on in that noggin of yours?"

"The victims' phones. In each case they were found not just at the scene, but in the victims' pockets. That tells us a couple things."

"Hmm." She reflected on that. "If the victims realized they were in danger, they would've likely taken out their cells to call for help. And in the case of Jamika, there was that text to the person you ended up chasing. It hadn't been erased."

"Right. There's no record that any of the victims tried to call 911. If the killer was messaging them, he certainly would've been aware that there would be evidence on the phones that could lead us back to him."

"So, either the victims weren't worried enough to try calling for help, or the killer placed the phones in there after he . . . well, afterward."

"And either way, he wasn't concerned about us finding them—and perhaps even wanted us to."

"He hasn't left any prints or DNA," she noted. "But yet he leaves the phones. Why?"

"I don't know, but I think we take a closer look at the contents of each of those phones, what apps the victims had downloaded—photos, contacts, texts—and which ones were open when the phones were recovered. That might be the link we're looking for."

"You think he's toying with us?"

"Let's hope so."

"Why's that? Wait, let me guess: more of a chance of him making a mistake."

"Exactly. As soon as offenders stop simply trying to get away with their crimes and start trying to rub it in our faces, they typically show their hand."

"I like how you approach things, Pat. I think I would have enjoyed working with you over the years."

"Yeah," I said without really thinking. "You too."

You too.

"Me too," I corrected myself.

She contacted Detective Schwartz to have his team get started on analyzing the phone apps. As we passed the café, the aroma of freshly roasted coffee, *good* coffee, along with the smell of eggs and bacon drifted through the hall.

Which only served to remind me that breakfast was still on my agenda.

We arrived at room 153 just as a tousled-haired, medium-frame doctor was exiting it, easing the door gently shut behind him. He appeared to be about my age. Lean. A brisk intensity about him. Tom Cruise–ish features. Almost as much scruff as I had.

"Kevin?" Sharyn gasped. "What are you doing here?"

"I know the boy's parents. His dad's the ME." He appraised her, then me. "I heard about what happened and pulled some strings so I could be the attending physician. I didn't know you were working this case."

"And I didn't know you were on call today. Where's Olivia?"

"She's at that Princess Ballerina Camp. Ballet for seven-year-olds every morning this week. We talked about it."

"Yes. And we agreed that if she went, you would stay close to the studio in case she needed anything."

"She's fine, Sharyn."

Even without introductions, it was pretty clear this guy was Olivia's father, Sharyn's ex.

"I'm Patrick Bowers." I extended a hand to him. "I'm working with Sharyn."

"*The* Patrick Bowers?"

The question caught me off guard and I wasn't really sure how to answer it. "Well, I'm . . ."

"The one who used to date Sharyn?"

"Kevin," she said. "That's not an appropriate thing to—"

"I'm just trying to establish who I'm talking with here."

"Yes." I lowered my hand. "That's who I am. And yes, we used to date."

"Well, I'm Dr. Gordon and I used to be her husband."

"Okay."

"Before our divorce."

"Kevin!" Sharyn protested. "Enough."

If his last name was Gordon, Sharyn must have kept—or gone back to—her own name.

Now it was his turn to offer a handshake.

I accepted.

His grip was knuckle-crunchingly firm, so I reciprocated with just as much pressure.

It's all part of the unspoken code of the handshake: too limp a grip and you'll appear weak, but squeeze too hard and you'll come across as desperate to prove yourself.

However, in Kevin's case, I got the impression that he was used to being the guy in charge, and used to letting other people know it.

By my grip I let him know that that was no longer the case here.

I let go.

"I heard about the homicide," he said, addressing Sharyn now, rather than me. "You don't really think Canyon had something to do with it?"

"You know I can't discuss the details of an ongoing investigation with you, Kevin."

When he responded, his words turned icier, his way of reiterating that although we might be FBI agents, here at the hospital we were on his turf. "Canyon shouldn't be seeing visitors yet."

"Well, then." Sharyn edged in and took hold of the door handle. "We'll be sure to pass that along if anyone shows up while we're in there."

He'd thrown down the gauntlet.

She'd picked it up.

Kevin worked his jaw back and forth stiffly a couple of times before backing up. "Don't upset him, Sharyn. He's been through a lot. That boy doesn't need any more trauma."

He gave me a stern glance. "Bowers."

"It was good to meet you too, Doctor," I told him.

After consulting his clipboard briefly, he strode down the hall toward the café. Sharyn just shook her head and gave an aggravated sigh, then edged the door open and the two of us stepped into the muted light of Canyon Robbins's hospital room.

26

Canyon lay propped up in bed, scrolling on his phone. "Whatcha need *now*?" he said impatiently, without looking our way. He must not have heard our conversation outside the door and thought his doctor had returned.

"Canyon, I'm Agent Bowers with the FBI," I said. "This is Agent Weist. We have a few questions regarding what happened in the house on Runyon Street."

The eye contact he made with me was brief and fleeting, but once his eyes locked onto Sharyn, his attention became quite focused indeed.

Back in the days when we were dating, I'd sometimes wondered if Sharyn had any idea how much power she had over men. Her work as a model had taught her how to catch someone's eye and hold his gaze with a quiet confidence, an air of mystery, and a touch of seduction. That, combined with her stunning natural beauty, was a pretty potent combination for guys, at least the straight ones.

It didn't matter that Canyon was half her age. Beauty is beauty.

He laid down the phone on the pivoting shelf in front of him and swung it to the side. Then he shifted slightly, trying to scootch himself up a little more, but almost immediately grimaced, stopped, and closed his eyes, drawing in a long, tight breath.

"Are you alright?" I asked, realizing immediately that, given the circumstances, it could be construed as a rather ludicrous question.

"Yeah."

"Do you need us to get you anything?" Sharyn offered.

"No." He opened his eyes. Peered at her. "I'm good."

"Sure?" she said.

"Yes."

"Well, you look like you're recovering remarkably well. From what I was told, that was quite a serious wound."

"Yeah, no kidding. They told me I coulda died."

"I'm glad you're doing better."

"Me too."

She took out a pen and a flip notepad, but I knew how good her memory was. The notebook was just for show.

"Canyon," I said, "your friends told us that Igazi suggested you use that particular house."

"Uh-huh."

"Before yesterday, had you ever been in it before?"

He shook his head. "Uh-uh. He just said it'd be a good place."

"For?"

"Pranking Erik."

Sharyn jotted something down. "Do you know why he thought it would be good for that?"

"I guess just 'cause it's empty and has a creepy basement. Not too many cops visit that block. I don't know. They found a body upstairs, though, right? A woman?"

"What do you know about that?"

"I mean, nothin'. I didn't even hear about it 'til I read Mimi's texts this morning." He hushed his voice. "How'd she die? What happened?"

"We're still determining that," I said.

"I heard she was shot."

"Did Mimi tell you that?"

"I read it online. There's this forum."

"What forum?"

"One of the threads from TypeKnot."

I gestured toward his phone. "Show me the site."

"Um. Okay."

Sharyn handed him his cell. "Who left the graffiti in the living room?"

"I don't know." He was scrolling to the forum. "That was on the wall when I got there."

"You mean when you arrived last night with Erik?"

"No. I went there earlier, just by myself." He found the site and passed the phone to me, but as he continued his explanation he was looking at Sharyn. "You know, to check out the place before the girls showed up."

"I need to look up a few things on your phone," I said. "Your contacts and messages. Do you give me permission to do that?"

"I guess. Yeah. Sure."

I studied the TypeKnot thread as Sharyn asked him, "Did you check out the upstairs too?"

"Uh-uh. Just the basement. When Mimi and Gwen came in, they lit the candles, set everything up. We were just messing with Erik, you know. We thought it'd be funny. He didn't mean to stab me. I know he didn't."

"I understand."

"Is he gonna get in trouble? I don't want him to go to jail. I didn't . . . It was just an accident."

"That's all still being sorted out," she replied. "Today, we're here to learn what we can about the woman who was found upstairs. Does the name 'Jamika Karon' mean anything to you?"

"Is that . . . was that her name?"

"Yes."

"Man, I didn't know her. I swear."

While I scrolled through the forum, I located an exchange where people voted on how they thought the victim had been killed. Right now, 51% had voted for shot, 28% strangled, 12% stabbed, 9% other.

Under "other," quite a few graphic suggestions were given.

I forwarded the link to my phone.

"Let's get back to Igazi for a second," Sharyn said to Canyon. "Is that his real name?"

"It's what he goes by. I've never heard him use any other name."

"How do you know him?"

"We hang out a little. That's it. That's all."

"Describe him for me. Is he Black? White? Chaldean?"

Her question about Igazi being Chaldean would've taken me by surprise if I hadn't read in the case files that there was a sizable Arab population living in the Detroit area. Chaldeans were a subgroup of Arabs who were ethnically Christian rather than Muslim—if you can really be any religion just by birth and culture rather than commitment and will, something that I personally doubted.

"He's white and old. Like maybe a little younger than you. Wait—I didn't mean you're, like, *old* old."

"I understand. Facial hair? Tattoos? Scars?"

"No beard or anything. Black hair. I don't know about scars or tattoos. I never saw any." His demeanor had changed—longer pauses, less eye contact, more fidgeting, and I wondered if he was really giving us the truth.

"What about height?"

"Not as big as me, but he's tough. Looks like he works out a lot. Yeah. Kinda skinny, but super strong. Does parkour."

The parkour angle could explain the agility of the suspect yesterday and how he was able to walk away after falling to the gym floor. And a medium-framed, wiry, athletic man did fit the description of the person I'd fought in the attic.

The guy who now had my gun.

"Where can we find him?" I asked.

"I don't know."

"How do you get in touch with him when you want to hang out?"

"Mostly through TypeKnot. It keeps the numbers private."

Though I'd seen Tessa using the app, I'd never downloaded it myself. It was one of the newer social networking apps that was particularly popular with teens.

I opened Canyon's TypeKnot app. "What's his screen name?"

"Bloodbrother13."

I found it, took a screenshot of the image, then sent it, along with the user's profile, to my phone.

"Have you heard from him since yesterday?"

"Uh-uh."

I checked Canyon's contacts as well as his recent text and email messages and social networking apps but found no mention of Igazi's name. His texts were deleted. At the moment I didn't have a way to clone Canyon's phone, but I was able to upload the links, profile pages, and even the address book to mine.

"Do you have his picture?" I asked Canyon.

"No."

Thinking I might have missed something, I held up his cell. "Is his contact info on here anywhere?"

The boy shook his head.

"Just through TypeKnot."

"I understand he's a street artist."

"Graffiti? Sure, yeah, he does some tagging." Canyon was rubbing his thumb and forefinger together worriedly. "Look, we didn't do nothin'. I didn't kill anyone. None of us did. We didn't even know anyone was dead. We never would've gone in that house if we knew she was there."

When Sharyn replied, she found a way to be compassionate but firm. "No one is accusing you or your friends of killing anyone. We just want answers. Over the past few months there've been a number of other bodies found in abandoned houses like that one on Runyon Street. Maybe you've heard about them on the news?"

He shrugged noncommittally.

"Canyon, do you know anything about those murders?"

I noticed that she went for the more provocative term—"murders" rather than "crimes"—perhaps to gauge his response.

"No," he told her.

"Are you the one who reported those bodies to the police?"

"What? No way!"

"Do you have any idea who might have? Maybe Igazi? Could he have known about them and told the police?"

"No. Uh-uh," he emphasized. "I'm telling you, seriously, it wasn't any of us."

I asked him, "Do you know of any reason why Igazi would have suggested that you use that house last night in particular?"

"Actually, we were gonna go today, but Gwen couldn't 'cause of a swim club meet or something. That's why we switched it to last night."

Hmm.

"When did you change your plans?"

"I don't know. At like five, right before we headed to the house."

"And did Igazi know?"

He shook his head. "I never told him."

Interesting.

I finished with his phone and laid it on the shelf by the bed. "Did you see anyone else around that house while you were there either time?"

"Uh-uh. I never saw anyone."

I had nothing more at the moment.

Sharyn closed things up by saying, "Canyon, can you think of anything else that you might've seen or heard that could help us learn what happened to that woman?"

"No. Seriously. I wish I could help you more."

"Alright. Thank you." She put her notepad away and took out a business card. She scribbled her phone number on the back of it and handed it to him, just as she'd done with the other kids last night. "If you think of anything else, call me, alright? That's my cell number."

"Okay. I will."

++++

Canyon Robbins waited for them to leave his hospital room, waited until the sound of their footsteps began to get soft as they walked down the hall, then went to TypeKnot and sent the message to the person who'd told him about the house: They know.

The reply came almost immediately: Who? Cops?

FBI. They're asking about last night.

What'd you tell em?

Nothin.

You sure?

Yah! What should I do if they come back?

Don't do anything. Don't say anything. I'll look into it.

I'm done. I'm out.

Canyon waited, but when no reply came through, he sent another message: Seriously. I'm not gonna go to jail over a few drugs.

Then the reply: Jail is not what you need to be worrying about right now.

What's that supposed to mean?

He waited, staring anxiously at the screen, his hands trembling slightly, but nothing more came through.

This person was not someone Canyon wanted to screw with or get on the wrong side of.

No.

Not at all.

Not considering what the person had done—and was capable of doing.

After reading that last message about what he should or should not be afraid of, Canyon wanted to run, to hide, and he would have, except he was stuck here because of the stab wound.

Which, come to think of it, really was starting to hurt.

For a moment, he thought about calling that hot FBI agent, or even contacting his dad for help, but then he remembered what the person who'd shown him the house and sold him the Oxycodone had said would happen to his father and mother if he told.

Canyon deleted TypeKnot and removed all the data files associated with it from his phone.

Then he did something he hadn't done since he was a kid and his dad took him to Sunday school at the Mormon church where he was an elder. Canyon Robbins prayed.

27

As we passed through the hall, I asked Sharyn what she thought about our interview with Canyon.

"That boy knows more than he's telling us," she said.

"I agree. His baseline shifted when he started sharing things we couldn't have verified."

"Also, the timing of when Igazi sent those other kids to that house is just too convenient. We really need to find him."

"You just read my mind, Sharyn."

"I'm glad I haven't lost it after all these years."

From what we knew, it certainly seemed as if Igazi was trying to set up those kids to be present at the house at the very time when the anonymous tip about the body's location would've been sent in.

But they went a day early.

The guy came back to carve into Jamika's forehead. That's why he was there at the site of the crime.

"There weren't any texts on Canyon's phone," I said. "But he mentioned he'd received texts from Mimi this morning."

"A teenager who has deleted all of his texts? Why would you do that unless you had something to hide?"

"I think we might want to contact Mimi and get a copy of that exchange."

"I'll get an officer on it."

"And also parkour runners that fit Igazi's description. It's probably a relatively small group."

She put a call through, then said, "Hey, Pat, listen, I'm sorry about what happened when we first got to Canyon's room. With Kevin, I mean. I had no idea he was going to be here today."

"It's not a problem."

"It put you in an awkward spot."

"No need to apologize. Really."

"Okay." It seemed like she might want to say something more regarding the topic, but she held back and instead asked, "Did you get what you needed from Canyon's phone?"

"I think so. I forwarded his address list and TypeKnot contacts to Cyber for a meta-analysis. Maybe they can compare it to the data in the contents of the other victims' phones and identify who Bloodbrother13 or Igazi is in real life."

"That's—" She stopped midsentence, drew out her phone, and checked an incoming text. "Ah. Good news—well, that is, depending on how you look at it."

"What's that?"

"Our briefing has been shifted back to one thirty—so you won't have to miss it after all."

Oh.

Wonderful.

"Hang on," I said. "With everything that's going on, doesn't that seem a little much to you? Postponing it four and a half hours?"

"Scheduling issues, I guess. Looks like it was Lieutenant Sproul's call. He just transferred in a couple months ago.

I've only worked with him once before, but . . . How shall I say this: I wasn't exactly sure where he was coming from."

"That was carefully worded."

"How about this: the man's raft is on the water but it isn't quite inflated."

"Ah. And yet he made lieutenant."

"Sometimes it's not the cream that rises to the top, it's the foam."

"True enough."

As we neared the café she said, "Listen, I didn't get a chance to eat breakfast earlier. I was on the phone with my lawyer. Custody issues—which only made seeing Kevin here this morning even more, well . . ."

She let her voice trail off. Her words carried a lot of emotion, but I wasn't sure if it was just frustration or anger.

I tried to think of an appropriate response. "It's been rough, huh?"

"I just hate that Olivia is caught in the middle of this. Anyway . . ." She swiped her hand definitively through the air as if she were pushing the topic aside—out of sight, out of mind. "With the briefing pushed back, it looks like we have time for a quick breakfast. What do you think?"

"I could eat."

++++

Ten minutes after their plane lifted off from Teterboro for Detroit, Blake used the Sovereign's Wi-Fi to download the video that Fayed had sent him. The one of Maria's death.

As he watched what happened to her, his stomach churned with a surge of nausea that he was barely able to hold in check—even after all the things he had seen over the years, even after all the things he had done—still, he was disturbed by what he saw.

He'd heard about the virus's hemorrhagic presentation, read about it, but seeing it like that, seeing a real person decline so dramatically, that was a whole different matter. And then there was the end. With her hands.

Why did Fayed even send this to you? Is he that presumptuous? Wouldn't he know that he's signing his own death warrant?

"I'm calling Fayed," he told Mannie, not even trying to quell the antipathy in his voice. "While I'm on the line, I want you to trace it."

"You think he's still in Michigan?"

"Let's find out."

"It'll be encrypted."

"Do what you can."

It took them a few minutes to calibrate the program on Mannie's laptop to sync with Blake's phone, but finally when the frequency was identified and they'd logged in to the tracking program, Blake put the call through.

Fayed Raabi'ah Bashir answered. "Why are you—?"

"I watched the video," Blake said bluntly. "I saw what you did to her. When I agreed to deliver her, you made me a promise. You assured me that she—"

"As it turned out, she had valuable information for us."

"You gave me your word, Fayed. You said you would make it quick."

"We determined that this course of action was necessary."

"Five days is not quick."

"She was able to provide passwords and access credentials that would have taken our cyber team weeks to obtain on their own."

"Passwords and credentials weren't part of the deal. And both of her hands?"

"That was her decision," Fayed's tone had stiffened. "We offered her the choice."

Mannie tapped his computer screen twice and gave Blake a thumbs-up: he had the location.

As Fayed went on, he spoke condescendingly and used Blake's real last name. "Mr. Neeson, this is not the time for the timid or the fainthearted." Blake guessed that it was a tactic to show that he'd done his homework, or perhaps to prove that Maria truly had given him the information he was looking for. "Sometimes," Fayed said, "sacrifices must be made. This is the time for resolve. For lions, not cubs."

"Yes. You are right, Fayed. And when I find you, I'm going to show you just how resolved I can be. Blood for blood. Your life for hers. Five days for five days. Sounds about right."

The jihadist scoffed. "The United States government has been trying to find me for more than three years. Will you really do what they cannot?"

"Actually, that's my specialty."

End call.

"He gazed at Mannie. "Michigan?"

"Dearborn."

"Well, it looks like Fate might just be smiling on us today."

"We should enjoy the warmth of her smile while we can," Mannie said reflectively.

"Earlier, Fayed mentioned that his man ran into some trouble in Atlanta last night, but that he'd made it past security. Can you or any of your black hat friends get into the airport's security cameras?"

"Not Hartsfield–Jackson." Mannie shook his head. "No. I'm not that good, and neither are the guys I know. Maybe if we had a week. But even then . . . I don't think so."

Blake mentally flipped through the hundreds of contacts in his mind from over the years, the names, the phone numbers, all stored in his memory, that one place that could not be hacked, and came up with one.

"I might know of someone. Name's Terry Manoji—or Wilson—he's been known to go by either name. He's with the NSA."

"I don't think I know him."

"It's from before your time, before we met. I did a job for him. He owes me a favor." Blake unpocketed his phone. "And I believe this just might be a good time to collect."

28

The hospital's café looked a lot more like a Starbucks than any hospital cafeteria I'd ever been in. Ambient lighting. Teak tables and countertops. Lounge seating. Light jazz playing through Bose speakers.

An orderly lounged on the leather couch, typing leisurely on his laptop. Two women dressed in scrubs sat across from each other talking in hushed tones at the table closest to the multi-armed brushed satin floor lamp.

We placed our order.

"This is not your grandma's cafeteria," I said.

"Gotta keep up with the times. All Ferilex money. Word is, the CEO is a real coffee aficionado. Small batch. Fair trade. Shade grown. Organic. You know."

"Sounds like a real stand-up guy."

"Ah, that's right. You and your predilection for overpriced java. Folgers would do it for me."

"Ouch. That's painful to hear."

"You'd probably get along well with Idris. If you could ever find him."

"What do you mean?"

"Idris Kourye. The CEO. He mostly keeps to himself. Pretty reclusive. They say he travels a lot. Charity work. He's an Arab-American. So, to avoid making it appear that

Muslims are being singled out or targeted for scrutiny, the media hasn't really probed too deeply into the Islamic charities he works with—but some are a bit questionable. If you ask me, they've given him a bit of a pass. There are over thirty thousand Arabs in Dearborn—in a way he's the best known and also the least known at the same time. Sure gives a lot of money to the city, though. Can't begrudge him that."

"Well, maybe we'll meet and be able to compare notes on coffee roasting. Who knows."

"Sounds scintillating," she said, with a slight touch of sarcasm.

"Someday I'll convert you, Folgers Girl."

"Good luck with that."

Though I offered to pay for our breakfast, Sharyn refused and put the breakfast burritos, my coffee, and her tea on her American Express.

"I'll get it next time, then," I told her.

"Deal."

I graced my coffee with a touch of honey and cream, just the way I like it. Then we found a table near a window that overlooked an ornate reflective pool and rock garden.

I downloaded the TypeKnot app onto my phone so I could look into it more later, then tried the coffee. My hat went off to Idris Kourye. This was the best coffee I'd had in the last month.

Sharyn had only taken a couple of bites before saying, "I guess I should just go ahead and address the elephant in the room."

"Which one is that?

"Kevin. We met right after I graduated from the Academy. He was charming and smart and finishing med school to become an emergency room doc and launch out and change the world. I fell for him right off the bat. Fell hard. But the marriage was short-lived and the only good thing to come out of us being together was Olivia—and she was born before Kevin ever proposed. He's a very good doctor and he loves Livvy, but he was not a good husband. It didn't take long after we were married before he decided he liked something else better than brunettes. Redheads."

"Ah."

"And blondes."

"Oh."

"He can be a real jackass sometimes."

It didn't feel quite right to agree with her assessment of her ex-husband or his preferences in women. "You mentioned last night that Olivia is seven?" I framed it as a question.

"Yeah. She's a real girlie girl—the three *P*s all the way."

"Three *P*s?"

"Ponies. Princesses. Pink."

"Oh. Right."

"I love her more than anything, Pat. I can't even bear the thought of losing her."

"Losing her?" Earlier she'd mentioned custody issues, but I didn't imagine that would mean losing custody altogether. "Why would you lose her?"

"Kevin's claiming that my job could put her in danger. He's trying for sole custody." She shook her head in disgust, then sighed. "I've always been a rebound girl. And what can I say? I have a weakness for a scruffy guy with haunting eyes. Hasn't always worked out well for me, though."

I didn't know about the haunting eyes part, but I self-consciously caught myself rubbing my hand across my chin. "Are you saying I need to shave?"

++++

No. I'm saying you don't, Sharyn Weist thought, but caught herself just in time, and held her tongue.

Thank God, she hadn't said what she was thinking.

Why did you tell him all that? About Kevin? He's going to think you're coming on to him.

Well, maybe I am.

You shouldn't have hugged him last night or told him you used to know him well—any of those things.

Maybe I should have. Maybe I should have done it years ago.

Ever since picking him up at the airport, Sharyn had been berating herself for not keeping her old feelings toward him in check.

When he looked into her eyes, she felt breathless.

The quickening heartbeat. The slight slipping of focus. That sweep of hot desire crowding in on her attention in ways that were distracting, but also that didn't seem to be a distraction at all, but instead the way things were really meant to be.

She hated the power he had over her.

And she loved it too.

One day last winter, she'd been talking with Julianne Springman about relationships and Julianne had said, "You know, Sharyn, many women have the fantasy of being powerless in the arms of a powerful man."

"I have to say, that sounds a tad sexist."

"It's not sexist to acknowledge our differences or desires. Come on, Sharyn. Look at the covers of romance novels—

how many of 'em show a woman losing herself in the embrace of an effeminate man?"

Actually, she did have a point.

"A woman," Julianne went on, "wants to be independent and also fawned over. It's only when she's captured that she's really set free. Romance trumps utility every time. A computer might cost a thousand times more than a rose, but if a man gives a laptop to his woman, she'll be grateful and thank him. If he gives her that one single rose, she'll melt."

Yeah.

No kidding.

Pat gave her six roses during their relationship, one at a time, and every one of them had spoken volumes to her.

A rose waiting for her on her pillow, then one beside her mirror, on her desk, next to her plate on the dinner table, awaiting her at that sushi restaurant, and then he even left one on the front seat of her car after picking the lock. Just as a surprise—not a creepy, stalkerish one, but one touched with a brand of romance that only an FBI agent who can pick locks could offer.

"Yes, she will melt." Sharyn had agreed with Julianne. "And feel loved."

"Yeah. And feel loved."

Pat made her feel weak in a way that gave her more strength than she ever knew she had, and that had helped her cope with the tragedy that still lingered in her heart, in her life, from the night she turned twenty-one and went home with that man who did those things to her.

And in her terror, she'd promised not to tell, never to tell, if only he would set her free.

And he had.

But she had told.

And then, three months later, during the trial, she'd made the most difficult decision in her life: she'd tried to erase the memory of that night and aborted that man's baby—something she'd never told anyone about, not even Pat.

But she hadn't done it because she'd been raped.

It was because of something else altogether. Something that brought her so much shame that she couldn't even bear the thought of it.

However, later, when Pat accepted her, it helped make the stain fade. He didn't look at her the way other men did. And he didn't ask her to share secrets that she didn't feel comfortable sharing.

He was the kind of man you only find once in a lifetime.

She had found him.

And lost him.

When he broke things off back at the Academy, she'd tried to turn her sense of loss into anger, or even a feeling of betrayal, but it'd never worked. The love had never been dispelled, never faded, never gone away, even when she'd been with Kevin.

So, of course, when she requested his help on this case she'd been curious if the sparks would still fly between them. And yes, she'd been hoping that they would, but she hadn't had any idea how hard it would be when they did.

Now she looked past him out the window at the courtyard and tried to regain her composure to be able to look at him without holding his gaze so long that it revealed what she was truly feeling inside.

Don't step any closer to the edge, Sharyn. It's been too long.

He's probably seeing someone. Besides, he's living in New York City. It could never work, anyway. Don't even entertain the thought!

"Are you okay?" Pat was looking at her curiously, with a hint of concern. "Did I do something wrong?"

"No. Sorry. I just got lost in my thoughts there for a minute."

She promptly veered away from the topic of what kind of men she was attracted to and asked him, "How's the coffee?"

"Very nice, actually. Mild acidity, a warm lingering finish. Uganda Bugisu is always a good breakfast choice. Especially when it was just roasted in the last two weeks."

She blinked. "You can tell all that just by drinking it?"

"Well—"

"That's amazing."

"And from that sign hanging behind the counter."

"Aha. And see? You had the chance there to really impress me and you passed it up."

"I'll save it for later," he said, clearly oblivious to how forward the words could've been taken. "By the way, I saw you jotting some notes in there. In Canyon's room."

"Just trying to track all the threads, keep them straight. Feel out if he was lying."

"You were always better at that than I was—at reading people, I mean. Do you think it's possible he sent in the previous tips regarding the victims' locations?"

"Hard to say," she told him. "And, by the way, don't sell yourself short."

"Sell myself short?"

"About reading people. You always seemed to read me well enough."

Stop it, Sharyn. Don't—

"Oh, well, you were easy to read."

"Was I?"

"As I remember." He took another sip of the Ugandan coffee. "Yes, you were."

"Read me now. What am I thinking?"

You're flirting, Sharyn. Stop!

"That you wish they had Sriracha sauce instead of just ketchup for that breakfast burrito."

"I have always been partial to—"

++++

My phone dinged: the nine thirty reminder to call Christie and find out why she'd been so upset last night.

I quieted the alarm. "Listen, Sharyn, I need to make a call."

"Sure." She rose and hastily gathered the rest of her food to go. "Should I wait outside? Would you like to follow me to the Ninth Precinct station?"

"I'll meet you there. Since the briefing isn't until this afternoon, I think it'll be worth my time to drive to the sites of the previous homicides, hopefully get a better feel for the layout of your city. It'll help me with the geoprofile."

A nod. "Alright. I'll take a closer look at the apps on the victims' phones and have the officers check their informants and contacts to see if we can find anyone fitting Igazi's description. I'll see you at the briefing."

"Wouldn't miss it for the world."

"You're not a very good liar."

"So I've been told."

She seemed to lose her bearings for a moment and then turned around and said with embarrassment, "Door's that way."

"Right."

But her sudden distractedness told me something was up.

In all the time I'd known her I'd never sensed that she was fragile. Sensitive? Yes. At times. I hoped I hadn't hurt her feelings or our friendship by something I'd said or done.

As she left for her car, I speed-dialed Christie, who answered on the fourth ring, just as I was expecting her voicemail to pick up.

29

"Hello, Pat."

"Hey." I didn't mention Tessa's concern for her, or the fact that she'd heard her crying last night. "I've been thinking about you this morning."

"That's sweet of you. What were you thinking?"

"Let's see . . . Well, first that I miss you."

"Okay."

"Second, that I should have touched base right away when I got here last night. I shouldn't have waited."

"Well, I could have just as easily called you from this end, but thanks for saying that. I'll count it as Sweet Thought Number Two. Anything else?"

"That I wish we would've had more of a chance to talk before I left."

"To talk."

"Because I want to make sure things are cool between us. Because upsetting you, making you sad, is the last thing I would ever want to do."

"It's the same for me."

I searched for where to take things but ended up just asking what she had on the docket for today.

"A few errands," she said. "I took off work for the next couple days. I had some personal time coming."

"Oh. Okay."

"So . . . how did it go last night? In your text you mentioned that you were thrown into the thick of things right after you landed."

"A woman's body was discovered." I couldn't give her case-sensitive details, but I could share as much as our OPA, or Office of Public Affairs, would have released to the media. "And an adolescent boy was stabbed—but it looks like he's going to be alright. It's not clear yet if, or how, the two instances are related to each other."

"The homicide—that's in addition to all the ones that've already occurred, that you flew out there to consult on?"

"Yes."

"I'm sorry. So much death."

"Yes."

"But you say the doctors expect the boy to recover?"

"He seems to be doing quite well—considering."

"Well, at least that's one thing to be thankful for."

"Absolutely."

I really wanted to find out what her tears last night were about, but I didn't want to be too obtrusive about it. Also, if I asked directly, she might feel self-conscious about the fact that Tessa had heard her crying.

So, a different tack.

Christie has always loved tongue twisters, so I said, "Hey, here's one that just came to mind: 'blue jewelry.' Five times fast. Let's hear it."

She went for it.

Crushed it.

"Nicely done. I am genuinely impressed. But that's not the first time you've impressed me."

"Thank you. I'm glad there have been a few others. You try."

"Alright—Blue jewelry. Blue jewelry. Brue jewely. Bue jewlery. Bool—man, I don't know how you're so good at these."

"Too much free time as a kid. Here's one for you. It's tougher than it sounds: 'lit wick.'"

"Actually, it sounds pretty tough right off the bat."

"Try it."

I only made it through once before coming up with "Licked wit."

A touch of silence spread between us.

So far, even though she seemed a tad guarded, she didn't sound as heavy-hearted as I'd anticipated, based on what Tessa had said. Maybe she'd been mistaken about what she heard last night in her mom's room.

"What's that music?" Christie asked.

"Oh. I'm here at the café—hospital—there's a coffee shop here. I was visiting the boy who was hurt last night. The one who was stabbed."

"The one who's doing well. Who's recovering."

"Yes."

Stillness again.

"Oh, hey," I said. "Thanks for sending the umbrella. There, in my suitcase. It brings back good memories."

"I'm glad to hear that."

As the words pooled off again, I said, "So, you're doing alright, then?"

"I'm fine."

One thing I've discovered over the years: when someone says she's fine, it's a bad sign.

"Hmm. But 'fine' isn't as good as 'good,' and it's nowhere near as good as 'great.' Am I right?"

"There are just some things on my mind that I need to sort out, that's all."

"From the other night? What I said?"

"It isn't that."

"If you want, I can talk now. I have a little time."

"Not over the phone."

I didn't like the sound of that.

"Pat, I need to go. We'll talk later. Tonight, maybe. Okay?"

"Sure. Alright. Talk to you tonight."

Then we were both saying good-bye and a moment later we were hanging up and I was left with an even more disconcerting feeling than I'd had when I dialed her number just a few moments ago.

Outside the hospital, shredded cirrus clouds clung to the far horizon, wispy and stretched out in long strands across the base of the sky.

High, still clouds.

Clouds made of ice.

Usually, when you see those distinctive torn streaks of cirrus clouds, you can count on pleasant weather coming your way.

Calm summer days ahead.

That's what I was thinking as I left the parking lot and directed the car toward the first of the houses where someone had posed a fresh corpse before waiting two days to notify the police that it was there.

Only when I was four blocks from the hospital did it dawn on me that Sharyn had taken off with that Glock still in her car.

30

10:34 A.M.
Dispersal in 28 hours

Ali was sitting on the hotel room bed, packed and ready to leave, when he got the call.

"Yes? Hello?"

"Mr. Saleem, I understand that there was a slight wrinkle at the airport."

Ali didn't recognize the voice. The man sounded more Western than Middle Eastern.

"Who is this?" he asked suspiciously.

"My name isn't important. I am calling on Fayed's behalf."

"How do I know that?"

"How would I have gotten this number? How would I know who you are or about the incident at the airport?"

"No, no. I need to speak with Fayed."

"Ali, I know about Yemen. About the four days in the room. About the man behind the building, the one kneeling between the two soldiers. I know it all."

That confirmed it. Ali decided that the man couldn't have gotten that information unless he really was working with Fayed. "I was afraid the border agents would arrest me or send me back to Kazakhstan. I didn't want to compromise what we are doing."

"Of course. We need you to drive up to Dearborn. We'll contact you tonight and tell you where to stay. We'll still move forward tomorrow, as planned."

Ali had not been informed about the timeline, just about the symptoms.

"And you wish for me to make the trip by car?"

"Yes. Leave your phone in the snack machine dispenser tray on the hotel's ground floor. There's another phone waiting for you in there. It's encrypted. Take it. That's the one we'll use to communicate with you from now on."

How could that phone have gotten there? Did they really visit this hotel? How many people are involved in this?

"Keep it with you at all times," the man continued. "We've installed an instant messaging app called TypeKnot. That's how we'll be in touch. Do not contact anyone else. No other calls. Do you understand?"

"Yes. And my sister?"

Ali waited for a reply.

"Is Azaliya safe?"

When no answer came, he realized that the man had hung up.

++++

The voice of Blake's pilot came through the intercom, requesting his presence in the cockpit, and he made his way past the three rows of empty seats to speak with him. "Yes?"

"I heard from my wife," the pilot said. "The authorities have been asking questions about my whereabouts. There might be a BOLO at domestic airports. I'm afraid if we land in Detroit there could be a welcoming party waiting for us on the runway."

"You think land north of the border, instead?"

"Yeah. Sarnia Chris Hadfield Airport. I've flown in there before. It's about an hour's drive from Windsor, so you can still get to Detroit easy enough. Sarnia is classified as an airport of entry. A lot of private and corporate jets use it. We won't stick out."

"That should work. You can get us in?"

"I'll close the IFR flight plan and turn off the transponder before we cross the border. We land, you two take off before the customs guys show up. I'll handle them when they do—it's nothing I haven't had to deal with in the past. I just don't want a Detroit SWAT team swarming in on my plane and finding me here with you."

It was a valid point.

"Take us to Sarnia," Blake told him.

Returning to his seat, Blake checked his messages and found that Terry Manoji had run into some snags but was confident that he would be able to access the footage for them by the middle of the afternoon.

Alright. That would work.

They could review the footage once they were back across the border in Detroit.

31

At the snack machine, Ali did as directed, retrieving the new phone and leaving behind the one he'd been using.

At last, as he walked to the rental car, he thought of the day six months ago when the pathway to this moment had begun, when he first met the man calling himself Fayed Raabi'ah Bashir.

The long, winding road to today.

At the time, because of the economic downturn in his region of Kazakhstan, fewer foreigners were traveling to the area, and that meant less translation work. As a result, money had been scarce. The conversation with Fayed had started with an inquiry about Ali's work and a possible job opportunity, but then Fayed had steered things toward Ali's family.

"Your sister, her name, it's Azaliya, yes?"

"How do you know that?"

"An associate of mine was researching you for this job. Her name came up as well. So, Azaliya?"

"Yes."

"It is a beautiful name, my brother."

"Yes. It is."

"And how old is she?"

"She just turned fourteen last week."

"Praise Allah."

"Yes."

"This can be a difficult city for girls that age."

"What do you mean?"

"Just what I have heard."

"What does that mean? What have you heard?"

"Oh, I am sure you have heard it too, my friend. The stories. Walking to school in the morning or back home in the afternoon can be dangerous. Girls are sometimes taken."

Ali felt his muscles tensing. "Are you threatening my sister?"

"By no means. I am simply saying that with both of your parents gone, I am certain you are doing all you can to provide a good life for her."

"What do you know about my parents?"

"You are a Muslim."

"What is this about? Why did you mention my parents?"

"Your sister, has she been with a man?"

"What?"

"Girls her age are at a premium."

At that, Ali grabbed him by the collar and threw him roughly against the wall. "Do not speak of my sister that way! I could kill you. I should kill you for saying those things."

Fayed seemed unfazed. "But will that ensure her safety? If you are in prison, who will care for her? Who will provide for her? Who will protect her? Ali, you must know that if I am dead, others will come. Especially if you are in jail."

"What is it you want from me?"

Then, the offer.

The promises.

The reassurances.

And the trip to Yemen. The training camp, the sand

everywhere—impossible to avoid. The heat and the sweltering, unmerciful sun. The prayers. He had grown up learning some of the teachings of the Qur'an, but in Yemen he was given detailed instructions about the *jizyah* that The People of the Book must pay if they refused to convert to Islam, the rightly guided caliphs after the death of Muhammad, Peace Be Upon Him, and the inevitable, forthcoming establishment of the worldwide Caliphate.

And through it all, Ali had his questions. Yes, of course he did.

After all, who wouldn't? To accept Fayed's version of Islam was not easy.

Executing other Muslims who just happened to be Shia? Child suicide bombers? Beating your wife if she refused to have sex with you whenever you desired? Throwing acid in the faces of women for not wearing proper head scarves? Shoving homosexuals off rooftops to their death? How could any of that be God's will? What kind of a God would put up with that? What kind of a God would honor it? What kind of a God would condone it—let alone *demand* it?

But Ali kept the questions to himself.

Throughout his entire time in Yemen he remained silent and obedient and compliant.

After all, he wasn't doing any of this for God, either out of fear of Him or out of love for Him.

He was doing it all for his sister.

Out of love for her.

He turned on the phone, opened the TypeKnot app, and positioned the screen so that he would be able to monitor it for incoming messages during the eleven-hour drive to Dearborn, Michigan.

Scarlett Farrow—II

The Tree House

In the movie, after Millie's dad died, she spent a lot of time in the tree house he'd built for her in the big *ginormous* tree just outside her window. The tree house wasn't anything super amazing, but it was from him, so it was special enough.

All throughout that part of the movie, in order to make Millie believable, to make her seem sad, Scarlett had to act sad too.

And the longer you *act* sad, the more *real* sadness seeps into you, like when your shirt gets wet and then soaks through to your skin, but this time it didn't stop at your skin. And the more pretend sadness you pile on, the deeper in the real sadness goes.

In the story, eventually, Millie's mom starts dating this guy that Millie can tell right away isn't very nice. The actor did such a good job of playing Harris's part that Scarlett didn't even want to be alone around him when they weren't filming. He was that good. That *freaky.*

That good at being bad.

But Tracy—Millie's mom—couldn't see what he was really like.

In the movie, Harris had a *terrible* temper, but Tracy just ignored it.

It was like he was gonna explode, like a bomb just waiting, waiting, waiting to go off. *Boom!*

One night, after they were done filming for the day, Scarlett was eating dinner with the woman who played Tracy's part.

They were in the tree house.

It was a good place to talk when you wanted to be alone.

When Scarlett asked her why Tracy couldn't tell what Harris was really like, she told her that love in real life is sometimes like that too: "Tracy loves you so much—Millie so much, I mean—and wants her to have a loving dad, a loving family, that it's blinding her to what Harris is really like."

"But then how come Millie can tell?"

"She doesn't love Harris. Love opens your eyes in some ways, but closes them in others."

"I don't get it."

After a small pause, the woman said, "Neither do I, sweetie."

Sometimes that lady called her that—*sweetie*—and it made Scarlett feel loved *for real*, not like when her actual mom called her those names that weren't very nice at all.

PART 3

The Idols We Gladly Embrace

The sword might be against my neck but it cannot be against the neck of us all. If I die, the world may turn its back, but if *we* die, the world will take notice and take action. And so, though today the government may target me, may kill me, they will not kill us all. What will you do with your life? Will you stand with me? Or will I die alone in this Courtyard of Blood?

—THE LAST WORDS OF SAUDI ARABIAN DISSIDENT AND SECULAR BLOGGER ASIM RASHADI BEFORE HE WAS BEHEADED FOR APOSTASY, ON JUNE 17, 2006. NO ONE IN THE CROWD OF MORE THAN TWO HUNDRED PEOPLE STEPPED FORWARD TO DIE WITH HIM. MOST CHEERED HIS DEATH.

The heart is deceitful above all things, and desperately wicked: who can know it?

—JEREMIAH 17:9, KING JAMES VERSION

32

The next few hours passed quickly as I navigated through Detroit, trying to get a feel for each of the five neighborhoods where the bodies we knew about so far had been left.

Whoever had killed those people had made sure to spread the crime scenes out over a wide geographic area.

From a place called Campus Martius at the epicenter of Detroit, the city is measured by miles, with 8 Mile being the city's official terminus.

The drive took me past Highland Park and Hamtramck, two anomalous suburbs located within Detroit's city limits, and through the crime-riddled east side to the mansion-lined streets of Grosse Pointe. So close, yet so distant. A few blocks separated them geographically, but they might have been two entirely different continents.

I passed the old Packard Plant and even hopped onto Outer Drive, which loops you around from one end of the city to the other.

Along the way, I analyzed the network of streets, took note of the residential clusters and socioeconomic state of the neighborhoods, and tried unsuccessfully to establish a causal, or at least correlational, relationship between the crime scene locations and the residences of the victims.

There weren't any traffic cameras at the intersections nearest to where the crimes occurred, so we had no footage of vehicles or individuals leaving the scenes. I imagined that cameras didn't last long out there before scrappers stole them for profit or destroyed them to assure anonymity.

But it also spoke to the meticulous care the offender had taken in avoiding leaving clues.

I visited the first four sites in the order of the crimes and did a walk-through at each of them: St. Clair Street, where Maxine Nachmanoff was found; then Worcester Place, where a young man named Gideon Flello was killed; then to the site of Dakota Sawatzy's homicide on Walton Street; and the house on Montrose where Meredith Getz was found.

Since randomness is often complexity in disguise, the apparently random distribution of the locations got me thinking, and I pulled up the Detroit Police Department's precinct map.

In many urban centers, the police department's patrol routes, workloads, and precincts aren't drawn up in response to crime types, locations, or frequency, but rather to correspond with voting districts and other arbitrary criteria that have little or nothing to do with crime prevention or suspect apprehension.

Often, politics and bureaucratic or administrative entrenchment in outdated law enforcement models and methodologies keep precincts from evolving, even as a city's demographics change. And, analyzing Detroit's precinct map, that appeared to be the case here.

However, when I overlaid the precincts with the sites of the crime scenes in this case, I discovered that each crime scene was in a different precinct and always within two blocks of that precinct's terminus.

Five bodies. All near the perimeters of the precincts in which they were found.

That couldn't simply be a coincidence.

To spread them out? To hinder the investigation?

It was likely that most people in the general population wouldn't even be aware of which police precinct they lived in, let alone be able to delineate the other precincts in the city, at least not with such pinpoint accuracy.

Obviously, the offender was familiar with the DPD's precinct map. It would be too much of a leap to assume that he would necessarily be involved in law enforcement, but I wanted to keep an open mind and follow the evidence wherever it might lead.

Since I'd already had a look at the site of Jamika Karon's homicide yesterday, I saved her street for last. Somehow, that man I'd chased into the school had eluded us. We still didn't know how. And that was something I wanted to remedy.

Based on the school's location, I figured I had just enough time to have a quick look around and still make the one thirty briefing.

Or at least make most of it.

"Oh, sorry. I didn't realize what time it was. Really? Is it that late? Huh. I never would have guessed."

Might work.

Who knows.

While I could certainly look up some of the information about the school online, all too often, public records aren't on the web or even on any law enforcement databases. Instead, they're stored in file cabinets and in boxes and drawers in back rooms and basements and would likely never be scanned in or posted online unless there was a reason that would justify the time spent doing so.

Today, I had a reason.

I contacted the city records department, and, since I figured the secretary would have done more actual filing than her boss and would probably be able to locate the information more quickly, I spoke with her instead of him. She told me her name was Starr "with two *r*'s" when I gave her my federal ID number for clearance.

"Can you pull the records for Lincoln High School?"

"I don't know. I'm pretty busy here today." She yawned, either out of actual boredom or for effect. "I need to slip out anyway at my break. I just ran out of fingernail polish."

I wasn't sure how serious she was being. "I'll send you some. You just might be able to help us solve a series of homicides."

"London Reckless."

"London Reckless?"

"That's the name of the color I use."

"That's a color?"

"Uh-huh. It's how they do it with lipstick and nail polish."

"Right. Okay. I'll order you some London Reckless."

All at once, she was all business. "Structural, architectural, mechanical, or civil prints? Site plans, floor plans, or elevation views?"

"Blueprints, building plans, permits, anything you can get your hands on."

"Give me an hour."

But Starr must have been better at her job than she gave herself credit for, because less than thirty minutes later as I was pulling into the parking lot behind Lincoln High School, she called me back.

"I don't know if this will be of any help," she said, "but it looks kind of interesting."

"Interesting is good. Go on."

"During World War Two, since Detroit was a manufacturing city, the automobile plants were retrofitted to build tanks and construct military convoy vehicles. Because of that, the city was considered a prime air strike target. So the schools—and even many of the churches—that were built in those years were constructed with bomb shelters underneath them."

Starr obviously knew what she was doing. Maybe the ditzy secretary bit was just her way of sloughing off extra work.

She continued, "In some cases, the tunnels connected with each other beneath the neighborhoods so residents could get to them easier, quicker. Basements, cellars, that sort of thing. The entrances to 'em might not always be visible, though—might not even be accessible anymore. You're talking about passageways that might not've been cracked open since half a century ago. From what it looks like, some were pretty well hidden to keep an encroaching army or invading force from finding them."

As far as I knew, none of the officers last night had searched any bomb shelters, so this was sounding promising.

"And this specific school? Lincoln High?"

"Yeah. It was one of 'em. It's got a bomb shelter under it, but I couldn't figure out how to locate the entrance—the records aren't as comprehensive as they should be. And some are missing."

"Do me a favor, scan in the plans—whatever you have—and send them to me."

"There's a bunch of 'em," she noted. "It might take a while."

"Start with any that might show how that bomb shelter can be accessed."

"Nude Velvet."

"I'm sorry?"

"Lipstick. Nude Velvet. Send me some lipstick too. With the nail polish. That's my color."

"Um. Alright. London Reckless nail polish and Nude Velvet lipstick. Not a problem."

"Thank you, Agent Bowers."

"You're welcome, Starr."

I had my flashlight, but no weapon, so I was cautious as I entered the school and traversed through the hallway I'd been in last night.

Sometimes I carry an automatic knife, but I'd been distracted thinking about how things were going with Christie and had forgotten to pack it for this trip.

Excellent foresight there.

Around me, a hush. Just like there had been when I chased the man with the hoodie through here.

Still, stagnant air.

As I swept the light in front of me, I caught a glimpse of movement at the end of the hall near one of the doorless rooms. The Maglite's beam barely reached that far, but there was enough light for me to make out that it was a dog.

I'm no expert on canines, and I couldn't tell what kind this was, but it looked big enough to do some real damage if it decided I was a threat.

It stared at me motionlessly for a long moment, its eyes catching light that didn't quite manage to illuminate the rest of its face, making it look like its eyes were glowing green in the shadows.

For a moment it reminded me of the wolf in the essay "Thinking Like a Mountain" by the conservationist Aldo Leopold when he wrote of the "fierce green fire" in the wolf's eyes fading as she died.

The dog growled at me. A challenge.

"Get!" I yelled.

But it crouched into a more aggressive stance and growled again, a deeper, more guttural warning for me to leave.

I glanced around for anything I could use to defend myself if this dog meant me any harm, but apart from the mashed ceiling tiles, the hallway had been picked clean by scrappers.

"Go on!" Instinctively, I waved my light toward it, although I wasn't sure how that was really going to help.

It took a few steps toward me, but when I hollered at it again, it finally grew disinterested, turned, and trudged off, out of sight.

Sharyn's case notes had mentioned that there were fifty thousand stray and feral dogs in this city.

That's a lot of hungry Rovers and Spots and Fidos, and from the crime scene photos from the first four homicides, I knew that human flesh was not off the menu.

The scanned-in photos from Starr with two *r*'s came through on my phone and, keeping an eye out to make sure the glowing-eyed dog didn't return, I began to study the school's blueprints and building plans, looking for a way to access its World War II bomb shelter.

33

Blake's pilot guided the Sovereign in for a smooth landing at the Sarnia Chris Hadfield Airport and as soon as they touched down, Blake and Mannie slipped away before any border agents could stop them.

In corporate circles, the Fixed Base Operator offered services to aircraft owners and passengers. So on the flight, Blake had contacted the FBO and a car was waiting for them when they touched down.

Their abrupt arrival might have raised some suspicion to the operator, but if you pay people enough, they'll keep their questions to themselves.

Blake thought momentarily about diminishing the chances of getting caught by having Mannie take care of tying off the loose end of the pilot, but decided violence in this case wasn't required or justified. The man had served them well. He was a friend. He didn't deserve to die today.

When they reached the vehicle, Blake directed Mannie to drive so that he could check his email to see if the CCTV footage that Terry was going to provide from the Atlanta airport had arrived.

++++

At the 9th Precinct, Sharyn Weist studied her notes in preparation for the briefing, which was scheduled to begin in less than ten minutes.

No usable prints on the boards over the windows. Nothing from Officer Springman about the dojos or the Type-Knot app. That avenue just might be a dead end. He was moving on with the parkour possibility.

She hadn't heard from Pat since leaving the hospital, and she wondered if she'd said something that upset him.

Probably not. Don't worry about it. He's just doing his job. Do yours.

She'd found overlap regarding the apps on the phones of the five homicide victims.

To some degree that was to be expected: Google. YouTube. Facebook. Krazle, the latest hybrid social networking/web search engine that seemed to be everywhere these days.

Just about everyone had those, so it made sense that the victims would all have those installed.

However, each of them had also downloaded the Hook'dup app, and she did not think it likely that all five people just randomly happened to use the same relatively unknown dating application.

It didn't take Sharyn long to discover that this app was pretty much just what it sounded like. You go online, post your photo and what you're looking for—a man, a woman, a threesome, whatever—and the app helps you find others who are interested and a place to hook up.

But this dating app was unique in that it was designed specifically for Detroit and listed the top five hundred hookup locations in the city: abandoned houses, churches, schools, warehouses. It included which entrances and exits to use, the best times of day to be there to avoid detection, and even which rooms were recommended for "the discreet adult recreational pursuits" that the app's users were seeking.

The app would flash green for "go." Yellow for "easy does it." Red for "keep your distance."

Whoever designed it would've needed to be intimately familiar with the abandoned buildings in the city.

A street artist?

Igazi?

She downloaded the app.

After opening it, she was able to confirm that each of the five crime scenes was listed as a potential hookup site.

The developer, Inntoit2U Designs, had an office about forty minutes outside the city.

Alright.

Good.

Rather than calling ahead to set up a time to interview people, anyone in law enforcement can tell you that, if at all possible, you should just show up to speak in person. Calling beforehand gives people a chance to rehearse what to—or what not to—say, to shred documents, or to flee. So Sharyn decided that as soon as the briefing was over she would go and have a chat with the app's designer.

Maybe Pat would be available to go with her.

Just a thought.

Just a possibility.

See how things played out.

++++

Although the architectural plans were detailed, the scanned-in files were a little blurry and difficult to read.

However, from what I could tell, the bomb shelter's entrance would be in the boys' locker room, where some sort of tunnel or stairwell along the west wall led beneath the gymnasium.

If so, I guessed that, because of the proximity of the locker room to the gym, the suspect probably would've had just enough time to slip away last night while I was descending the attic's access ladder.

Starr had mentioned that some of the entrances were well disguised. Since the briefing was about to get started, time was an issue here.

On the one hand, I hoped it would take a while to justify not attending.

On the other, I hoped this entrance wouldn't be too hidden or obscured by the years so I could get right in to see where it might lead.

At first, the locker room door resisted when I pressed against it, but with a little additional effort, it creaked open.

Cautiously, I went inside.

34

Without windows to let in any daylight, I needed my flashlight to see anything at all.

The faint sound of claws scratching across the floor caught my attention and I flicked the light over just in time to see a sewer rat that looked as thick as my thigh flattening itself into a jagged hole in the wall, its tail whipping behind it like a brownish-gray snake, slithering out of sight.

As I swept the Maglite to the side, my phone buzzed with an incoming call with Ralph's *A-Team* ringtone. In the stillness, the sound startled me so much that I jumped and I was glad no one was here to see.

"Got your text earlier," he said. "I couldn't get away. What's up? How's it going in Motor City?"

"We had another homicide." I filled him in while I scrutinized the empty wall where the lockers would've been if scrappers hadn't removed them. As far as I could see, there was no entrance to the bomb shelter. My search here reminded me of scouring the garage for the hidden room at the house in New York yesterday.

Apparently, looking for secret doorways was my new hobby.

"Where are you now?" he asked.

"In the school, trying to find a bomb shelter."

"Bomb shelter?"

"There's supposed to be one beneath the gym. I think it's possible the suspect fled through it last night."

"Speaking of fleeing, there's still no word on Blake. But we do know the Russian bioweapons researcher's name: Dr. Vladislav Kuznetsov. He dropped off the grid about six years ago. Wasn't really on anyone's radar screen—ours or the Russians'. They're still being pretty tight-lipped about what kind of projects he was involved with, but at the time he disappeared he was doing some pioneering work in synthetic biology."

"I've heard of that, but I'm not sure I know what it is."

Only a few of the sinks and urinals were intact. Most had been smashed to pieces. All of their metal fittings were gone.

"Next frontier after gene splicing," Ralph told me. "Biotech, genetic engineering. I don't know how it all works, but you can design new viruses from the ground up. Basically playing God."

"That doesn't sound good."

"No, it does not. Oh, and there weren't any rope fibers beneath his fingernails. The lab verified it: the petechial hemorrhaging and the bruising on his neck are both consistent with manual rather than ligature strangulation."

"I doubt the guy manually strangled himself."

"Yeah. That's always tough to pull off. By the way, I understand you sent in a request for a Monday meeting with Maria Aguirre, that OPR lawyer."

"Where'd you hear that?"

"Word gets around. Thing is, she left for vacation nine days ago and no one's heard from her since, but her passport was used to enter a country in the former Soviet Union: Kazakhstan. And guess how that's significant?"

I took a stab at it. “Kuznetsov?”

“Yeah. After he left the State Research Center of Virology and Biotechnology near Novosibirsk, Russia, his last known whereabouts was in Almaty, Kazakhstan.”

“The plot thickens.”

“It always does. One other thing: we traced a call to a pilot who has past ties to Blake. Went to do a knock and talk. The guy’s not home. His wife says he’s fishing in New Hampshire, but couldn’t tell us where.”

“And his plane?”

“Gone from Teterboro. We’re monitoring flight departures and arrivals at airports nationwide. Municipals. Everything. If he did take off with Blake and we catch up with him, I might have to fly out myself and have a little sit-down with the man. Eighty thousand miles so far this year, what’s one more trip? Anyway . . . It looks like we’re about to get started here again in the conference room. I should probably go in a sec. Why’d you leave a message earlier for me to call you back?”

“Man, I need some advice.”

“On?”

I gave him a quick rundown of the situation with Christie. “She’s upset and I’m afraid I might’ve had something to do with it.”

“You think?”

“Well—”

“Did you apologize?”

“Yes.”

“Really?”

“Yeah.”

Finding nothing in the rest of the locker area, I went to the shower area and began to systematically pass my light across the wall, eliminating one tiled-off portion at a time.

No private shower stalls here, just that traumatic group showering area that all the guys used to dread when I was in school.

"So," he said, "Is it 'yeah' or 'yes'?"

"What's the difference?"

If the guy did escape through here, there has to be an access door somewhere.

"'Yeah' means you're getting a little defensive with me. 'Yes' means you're still open to admitting that you've been a dick."

"Then 'yes.'"

"Good to know."

"But I haven't been a dick."

"That's still to be determined."

All four of the shower area's metal drains and all but one showerhead were gone.

"When I was growing up," Ralph said, "Mama used to tell us that the two most important things you can say to someone are 'I'm sorry' and 'I love you.' But you have to say 'em in the right order or they won't do any good."

I examined the grooves between the tiles on the walls. In some cases, they appeared deep enough to have hidden a door of some type.

That had potential.

"The right order?" I ran my hand along the wall, feeling for any trip levers or sliding tiles. "I'm not sure I know what you mean, Ralph."

"If you say, 'I'm sorry. I love you,' that's good. The apology, then the declaration of undying devotion. But if you say, 'I love you. I'm sorry,' that's bad. People use the first way to try to save a relationship, the second way when they're about to end one."

"Hmm." I wasn't completely sure I agreed with Ralph's mama, but I could at least see where she was coming from.

"Did you tell Christie you love her?" he asked.

"Not in so many words."

"Which words then?"

"Well . . . I guess, 'You too.'"

"Ouch. That's no good. Do you love her, Pat?"

"I think so."

"Bro—you did not tell her that, did you? That you *think* you love her?"

"No. Of course not."

"How long have you two been together? Since April, right?"

"We met at the end of April, had our first date on the second of May."

"Well, there you go."

"There I go?"

"Think like a woman, Pat. What's today?"

"August second. Ah. Okay, I get it. That's three months."

"You forgot your anniversary."

"But Christie and I aren't—"

"Yeah, well, maybe she thinks you are. Or she wants you to be."

I let that sink in. "I see."

"Are you messing with me here or are you really this ignorant when it comes to women?"

"Not messing."

"I was afraid of that."

There's nothing here, Pat. No bomb shelter. This isn't how he fled the school.

"Doesn't that seem a bit petty of her, though?" I said.

"And that right there is something only a guy who's being a dick would ask. The correct question is, 'How do I salvage things from here?'"

"How do I salvage things from here?"

"That's better. The next time you see Christie, you look her in the eye and tell her you're sorry and that you love her, in that order. And don't forget to pause."

"Pause? Oh—so I'm not saying that I'm sorry I love her."

"Lead with 'I'm sorry,' end with 'I love you.' Trust me. And don't put it off. Christie's special. You're not gonna do any better. You don't want to lose her."

"Agreed."

You should tell him about Sharyn.

No, that wouldn't solve anything. It would just complicate matters even more.

"Promise me you'll do it," Ralph said.

"I will."

"Promise."

"I promise. 'I'm sorry.' Pause. 'I love you.'"

"Alright. By the way, just so you know, DeYoung might be calling you this afternoon to ask about why you're wanting to meet with Maria from OPR."

"Thanks for the heads-up. And for the relationship advice."

"Thank my mama."

He hung up, and I was ready to call the search for the bomb shelter quits and just get to the briefing, when I glanced back at that sole remaining showerhead.

An incongruity.

Why is that still here? Why didn't the scrappers take that one too?

I pocketed my phone and felt around the showerhead, tried twisting it and tilting it sideways, but it didn't move.

However, when I pulled down on it as if it were a lever, I found what I was looking for.

With a faint but audible click, and then the sound of heavy gears grinding against each other, the tiling parted and an entrance just over a meter wide and slightly shorter than me appeared.

I angled the Maglite into the darkness, revealing a narrow tunnel that sloped down beneath the gym.

Since this place had been designed to withstand a bomb, the door leading into the passageway was reinforced. Considering the goal the builders had, I imagined that the seal would've also been airtight. The concrete walls certainly did look thick enough to repel—or contain—bomb blasts.

The darkness before me seemed somehow starker and more foreboding than the darkness around me did, almost like something solid that I needed to crack open. So, etching it aside with my light, I stepped into the cramped opening and started down the tunnel.

35

Someone had been through here recently.

I could tell because, although a few cobwebs hung in torn, thready clumps from the corners of the ceiling and the wall to my right, the walkway before me was clear of them.

I wasn't able to make out any sole impressions on the concrete floor.

The farther down I went, the more the temperature dropped, just like it would have if I'd been descending into a cave.

Cool.

Damp.

Mildew in the air.

After about twenty meters, the pathway leveled off and opened into a wide, low-ceilinged bomb shelter that looked large enough to hold several hundred people during an air raid.

Only one other tunnel was present, extending from the far end, about thirty meters away. As I moved toward it, I had to hunch over to avoid scraping my head on the coarse concrete ceiling.

Dust-covered boxes and crates, as well as eighteen large cylindrical drums—some of medical supplies, others of

MREs—were shoved against one wall, surrounded by stacks of canned soup, fruit, and beans.

I entered the mouth of the second tunnel, which, for some reason, was nearly two meters wide and tall enough for me to stand in.

I'd learned earlier that some of the tunnels connected to cellars throughout the city, and I wondered where this one would emerge.

I walked for a few minutes through the muzzled stillness of the tunnel and eventually saw something flat and about a foot high on the ground at the far edge of my flashlight's beam.

It only took three more steps for me to realize that it was a mattress and was positioned at a place where the passageway widened slightly, allowing space for an old wooden crate on one side of it, and four of those supply drums from the bomb shelter on the other.

The crate supported a large plastic water jug that would've looked a lot more at home in an office break room than it did here.

The mattress was squalid and filthy and topped with a snarl of ratty blankets.

Beside it, a lump of indistinguishable clothes bulged like a cancerous growth from the floor of the tunnel.

A scattering of discarded, open cans of food—some spewing contents threaded with sinewy mold—lay strewn between me and the makeshift living quarters.

When I tapped one of the cans aside with my foot, two cockroaches scuttled out. One hurried away from me, but the other came straight at me.

Instinct took over, and with my heel, I ended that roach's chances of surviving a nuclear holocaust. Christie's daughter, who is a dedicated vegan and a PETA member, would have been appalled.

Me, not so much.

I rubbed the roach's remains off the bottom of my shoe, and as I neared the mattress I thought I heard a distant click.

I paused.

Listened.

Nothing except for the metronomic dribble-drip of water somewhere out of sight.

Dribble.

Drip.

Targeting my light before me, I saw that I was still alone.

A tower of nineteen books stood balanced in a precise stack beside the mattress.

Each had its unique, uniformly handwritten Dewey Decimal numbers on the spine, and I figured it was likely they'd been brought down here from the library of the school above me.

Someone was a fan of the classics: *Pride and Prejudice*, *The Scarlet Letter*, *Sister Carrie*, and more.

Not titles that topped my list.

I go for stories with a little more suspense and a lot more testosterone.

And a twist.

I always like a good twist right there at the end.

The books must have become waterlogged at some point, or the constant humidity down here had taken its toll, because every one of them was swollen and oddly deformed.

A rectangular piece of paneling lay across the four drums, forming a makeshift table that held a dozen burned-out votive candles surrounding a painting of Jesus hanging on the cross. A clutter of trash was carefully arranged emanating out from the painting like rays from the sun.

An altar.

Someone had made an altar down here.

Together, the mattress and altar swallowed up nearly the entire width of the tunnel so that it would be tough to pass the living area without walking across the mattress.

I recalled an exchange from a book I'd read when I was in college. I wasn't sure of the author, or even the book's title, but three lines of dialogue had stuck with me over the years:

"I keep my idols in a closet."

"I keep mine on a pedestal."

"Which of us is the greater sinner?"

I guess we all offer our ultimate devotion and affection to something, whether it's a relic, an actual idol, a Porsche, a graduate degree, or the image of that person staring back at us from the mirror.

All of us have our gods, even the people who don't believe God exists.

Sharyn had mentioned that the family who'd lived in the house where Jamika was found had a painting of Jesus on the master bedroom wall.

This one looked to be about the right size.

I held my hand beside it, compared it to the photo on my phone—the one that I'd taken in that room down the block on Runyon Street.

Yes.

Same size.

But that's not what caught my attention the most.

Now I saw that Christ's face had been scratched away, and a snipped-out photo of a girl had been glued in its place. A few errant scratch marks were still visible, emanating from beneath the photo.

My heartbeat caught, then raced forward immediately into a tight beat-thumping-beat-thumping-beat when I recognized who it was.

Sharyn.

Back when she was a girl.

When we were dating, she'd always underplayed her past life as a movie star. In fact, we'd been together for nearly two months before she even told me that she was Scarlett Farrow.

I was never a big film buff and hadn't seen the movies she'd been in, but I knew this photo. It was one of the most famous pictures of her from that time, an iconic photograph of her glancing uneasily to the side as if she was aware of danger approaching. It'd been used in the promotion for the film she was best known for, the one that she was nominated for an Academy Award for best supporting actress in, a thriller named *Sanctuary.*

At the time, she was one of the youngest stars ever to be nominated for an Oscar.

And here, someone had clipped out her photo and inserted it over the place where Jesus's face would've been as he hung dying on the crucifixion hill.

Scarlett Farrow, when she was only ten years old.

Sharyn Weist, when she was still Scarlett Farrow.

Facts might be open to interpretation, but context does not lie. If nothing else, this photo revealed a connection between her and whoever had pasted it onto that picture.

I couldn't accept that her picture was here simply by coincidence.

Across the tunnel, a grimy mirror faced the altar, a lightning bolt–shaped crack splitting it through the middle.

At the base of the painting, between two of the rays of trash, lay a crumpled photo.

A young man and a boy stood in a driveway beside a palm tree–lined street. The older of the two looked maybe seventeen or eighteen and had his hand resting on the slender shoulder of the smaller boy, who might've been five or six. The iconic hillside HOLLYWOOD sign peered across Tinseltown from behind them.

The colors of the photograph were faded with the years, and the cars parked along the idyllic drive reminded me of the car my parents used to drive when I was a boy growing up in Wisconsin. I pegged the photo at maybe a quarter century old.

Both boys were wearing karate uniforms—the older of the two with a black belt sashed around his waist; the younger boy's belt was white.

Martial arts?

The man you fought in the attic?

Don't get ahead of yourself, Pat.

I studied the other items on the altar.

The trash contained the head of a doll, an Atari game cartridge, and a clown's yellow wig.

Which was next to a broken Joan Baez album.

And the cap of a laundry detergent bottle.

Oh.

Wait.

The head of a doll? It sure looked like it matched the doll that was in the master bedroom where Jamika was found.

Also, the photos from the first four crime scenes showed objects that related to the rest of these items: Atari games, record albums, detergent bottles, costumes.

This isn't just trash.

Is he leaving clues at the scenes—or is he taking mementos?

I glanced down and saw a pile of black cloth that had been deposited on the ground beside my foot. Up until now the shadow of the altar had hidden it well, but from this angle it was visible.

Prodding it with my foot, I realized it was a hoodie.

I knelt and examined it more carefully and found four drawstrings rather than two.

Not just one hoodie.

Two of them.

If there were two people, that could explain how the suspect got away from the gym after that fall—he might've had help.

Stop assuming, Pat. These could be from the same person. Analyze and evaluate, don't guess and speculate.

Some hoodies have knotted-off ends on the shoelace string that's used to tighten the hood. These had plastic-tipped ends like most shoelaces.

And that might turn out to be a lot more helpful.

Crouching beside the hoodies, I snapped several photos of them, then angled the phone to photograph the altar.

However, this time when the flash went off and illuminated the tunnel around me, it revealed something else.

A man.

Standing less than four meters away, just on the other side of the mattress.

36

I whipped the flashlight up at him.

Dirty beard, wild hair, torn clothes.

He was staring directly at me but was turned slightly to the side so that only one of his hands was visible.

He gave a labored, phlegmy cough and shambled forward a step.

"Stop." I rose to my feet. "Sir, I need you to stay where you are."

He pointed at the mattress. "My bed." His voice had that quavery, tenuous feel that so often follows years of substance abuse. "Get away from my beeeeeed."

"I'm an FBI agent. I'm not here to hurt you. Show me your hands. Both of them."

He revealed a lighter in the one hand I could see. On the side of it, even from here, I could make out the imprint of the caduceus, the intertwined snakes curling up a rod, the symbol that's often used in the medical profession.

He didn't turn, and that other hand remained hidden.

"Drop the lighter and let me see both hands."

He pointed. "Back from beeeeeed."

I edged back slightly so I wouldn't appear to be a threat. "Now, show it to me."

He did.

A bottle of lighter fluid.

"Put that on the ground."

But instead, he sloshed the fluid around inside the bottle. It sounded nearly full. "Maybe you keep telling me what to do, maybe I pour this on my head. Maybe then I light the fire."

"Easy." I decided to defuse things by asking him questions rather than giving him orders. "Tell me about these items on your altar, where did—"

"Shrine. My shrine. My shriiiiiine."

"The things on your shrine, where did you get them?"

"Found 'em."

"Where?"

"All of 'em."

"Sir, where did you find them?"

He jammed his response into one word: "Notsirnotsir." He shook his head emphatically. He jabbed a thumb toward his chest. "Anthony."

"Anthony, I'm Patrick. What can you tell me about the things you found?"

No answer.

"Did you hurt someone to get them?" I avoided the word "kill."

He took a step forward.

"No, Anthony. Stay there. Not another step."

He waved the lighter at me. "What if I light the flame? Burning, burning, burning."

He snapped open the cap to the lighter fluid bottle.

"Anthony," I said firmly. "That's enough."

"Burning." He lifted the bottle high, tilted it down toward his head.

"Anthony, stop!"

He squeezed it, raining lighter fluid onto his hair and then his shirt.

Even from where I stood, I could smell that it really was some type of gas.

He was just far enough away so that if I rushed him, I anticipated that he would have enough time to flick the lighter and ignite it before I could stop him, and I didn't want to take that chance.

He held the lighter close. "Maybe I light it."

"Easy." I held up an open hand and patted it softly against the air to signal for him to calm down. "I just want to ask you a few questions."

"Away!" He flicked the lighter to life. "From. My. Bed!"

I eased back two more steps. "There. See, Anthony? We're good."

He extinguished the flame.

"How did these hoodies get in here?" I asked him.

"Blaaaaaack hoodies."

"Did someone give them to you?"

"He was hurt."

"The man who gave them to you was hurt?"

A nod.

"Do you know who he was?"

"Traded clothes. He gave me black hoodies."

"Anthony, do you know his name?"

"Running, running, running." As he spoke, with each word he sent a stream of lighter fluid splashing out across the mattress. "Running."

I needed to stop him, but he was evidently unstable.

Be firm, but not too verbally aggressive.

"Anthony. I'm telling you," I said unequivocally. "Put down that lighter fluid. Do it now."

He paused, suddenly appearing confused. With a look of disorientation, he eyed the lighter and the bottle quizzically, as if he were trying to figure out how they'd even gotten into his hands in the first place.

"Set them down," I repeated.

Anthony shook his head emphatically. "No, no, no, no. I do not like when the dogs come. I do not like the *dogs*!"

"Do you know someone named Igazi?" I said.

"Iiiiiih . . . Gaaaaaaah . . . Zeeeeeee . . ." As he repeated the name, he stretched out the syllables, turning each one into its own word.

He said it again.

It became his mantra.

"Iiiiiih . . . Gaaaaaaah . . . Zeeeeeee . . ."

"Is that the man who was running? The man who gave you the hoodie?"

"Iiiiiih . . . Gaaaaaaah . . . Zeeeeeee . . ."

He squeezed the bottle again but this time flung the thick stream of gas at me, catching me by surprise. I leapt aside, but not quickly enough, and the gas splattered across my pants leg and the bottom part of my shirt.

"Stop it, Anthony. I need you to—"

"My home." He sprayed more at me. "Go away."

The hoodies were almost within reach, but not quite. It didn't appear that they'd been drenched yet, so if he ignited the lighter fluid, I still might be able to save them from the fire.

I bent to try to grab them, but he managed to splash more of the gas onto me as I did, and when I had to move backward to get out of the way, I came up empty-handed.

He began to indiscriminately drench the shrine, the mattress, the clothes on the ground. The pile of books.

"I need you to tell me about the man you traded clothes with," I said.

Every time I edged forward to stop him, he targeted me again and I had to step back. Though I was quick, I ended up with a lot more lighter fluid on my clothes than I was comfortable with.

"Go away!" Anthony shouted. "He can't know!"

"Who? Who can't know?"

He tapped the side of his head, and his words were a mixture of breathy confusion and more harsh coughing. "Here. He's here. Here, here, here."

I didn't know if Anthony was high or schizophrenic, or had maybe been drugged. Whatever the case, he appeared to be paranoid and hallucinating, and that's never a good combination.

"Come with me, Anthony. Let's go. We'll get you some—"

He surprised me by letting out a mad, erratic ripple of laughter and splashed the fluid wildly back and forth, back and forth across everything. "Here, here, here!" he yelled.

"Do you know who's killing these people, Anthony?"

"Killing them!"

"Who is?"

"Killing them. Iiiiiiih . . . Gaaaaaaah . . . Zeeeeeee . . ."

I pointed to the painting of Christ that was now saturated with lighter fluid. "Did you put the girl's picture on there?" I would have grabbed it if I could have gotten any closer to the shrine, but at this point, that wasn't going to be possible.

"Pretty girl. Mooooooo . . . veeeeeee . . ."

"What do you know about the movie?"

In reply, he thumbed the flame of the lighter to life, and

held it close to his face. The tongue of fire tossed nervous shadows up across his scraggly beard and weathered skin. His gaze was surprisingly clear and alert and not clouded or rheumy, like I would have guessed.

"Put it down, Anthony."

But something in his appearance changed, a sad, final look fell across his face, and I sensed that this was it.

Like dusk falling.

Like darkness crawling across the countryside.

He's going to do it. Stop him!

I dashed forward, but before I could get to him, he tossed the flame onto the mattress and a plume of fire erupted between us.

The scorching rush of heat sent me scrambling backward.

It wasn't going to be possible to save Anthony's shrine or any of the evidence on it, but maybe I could salvage the hoodies so we could test them for DNA. As far as I could tell, from where they were, they'd escaped most of the lighter fluid.

I reached for them and drew them to safety, but there was still some lighter fluid on the ground and as I moved closer, the flames decided to slither toward me at that moment and caught hold of my left pants leg, then rushed up my leg and leapt to my shirt.

I yanked the burning shirt off and tossed it aside. I was about to do the same with my pants, but I wouldn't have been able to do so with my shoes on, so I grabbed one of the hoodies and wrapped it around my leg to stifle the fire, then dropped to the ground, kicking over the crate that held the water jug.

It crashed down beside me and I grabbed it, slammed the spout fiercely against the wall to break it off, then used the gushing water to put out the rest of the fire on my pants.

I assessed myself and realized that the worst damage had been to my left side.

Between the flames on my shirt and the fire rising up from my leg, the skin was reddened and even blistering in a few spots.

It didn't appear to be severe enough to put me out of commission, but the burns were definitely deep enough for me to notice.

For now, adrenaline was masking the pain, but that wasn't going to last forever.

Anthony's outline was visible on the other side of the flames and his mantra-like words cut through the noise of the hungry, crackling fire. "Burning," he called.

I tried to identify if he'd been injured or if his clothes were on fire.

"Burning—"

But I couldn't tell.

"Burning—"

Not from where I was standing.

"Pretty girl!"

He let out a wild, half-choked cry, but in the screeching echoes of the tunnel I wasn't able to tell if it was birthed from madness or pain.

"Anthony?" I shouted. "Are you hurt?"

He said nothing as the flames coursed higher, but simply moved backward like an apparition merging with the night, and he was gone.

I didn't like that Sharyn's face had been pasted onto that image of the crucified Christ.

I didn't like that Anthony knew about the movie.

And I especially didn't like his words: "Burning . . . Pretty girl."

Whether he'd been injured or not, with the flames roiling between us, there was nothing I could do right now to check on him.

I grabbed the hoodies and my flashlight and retraced my steps to the locker room to call Sharyn and warn her that this guy knew about her movie star days.

37

"What?" Sharyn gasped. "Wait—someone tried to burn you alive?" She was at the 9th Precinct's station and the briefing had started, but when she saw that the call was from Pat, she'd excused herself and slipped into the hallway to answer it. "What are you talking about? Back up. Are you alright?"

"I'm okay. I'm not sure if he was trying to burn me alive or if it was just about what was in the tunnel. He had Scarlett Farrow's photo. He knew about the movie. Do you have any idea who that man was or why he would've had a photograph of her down there?"

Sharyn noticed how, even now, Pat was being careful not to mention that she was Scarlett, perhaps in the event that the call had somehow been compromised. "No. I don't," she told him.

But that wasn't quite true.

Maybe she did.

"Is it possible he wasn't really a homeless man?" she asked.

"It's possible. Why?"

Could it be him? Has he been released?

But how would he know I'm here in Detroit? No one knew that—

Except Simone. Whom you haven't heard from since May.

On the one hand, it seemed almost incomprehensible to her that the man who'd attacked her on her twenty-first birthday might be out of prison. He was supposed to be serving twenty-five years, but on the other hand, prison overcrowding and "good behavior" often resulted in early release.

The prison officials didn't have her new identity. Scarlett Farrow was famous enough that word might very well have leaked out about who she'd become. So, through the years, Sharyn had kept her past hidden even from the department of corrections. Consequently, the warden wouldn't have been able to call and notify her even if he'd wanted to.

But if Dylan was free, that would mean . . .

You have a new name. A new life. It's just not possible that he's behind this.

But what if it is? What if it all revolves around him?

Or around you?

"Sharyn, why did you ask if it was possible that he wasn't a homeless man?"

"I'll be there in fifteen minutes. Twenty tops. I'll explain when I see you."

"You don't need to come."

"You said you got burned. How serious is it?"

"Just a little on my side. It's nothing."

"Remember when you told me I was good at reading people?"

"Yes."

"Well, I'm reading you and you're lying. Listen, the dance studio where Olivia has her ballet camp is probably only ten or fifteen minutes from the school—you're there, right?"

"Yeah."

"If Kevin is at the studio, he can be at the school before I can, probably even before an ambulance. I'll call him, have him take a look at the burns."

Pat was slow in responding and Sharyn guessed he was trying to come up with a polite or reasonable way to decline the offer, but finally he said, "Okay. Listen, I'm heading back down to see if I can salvage any evidence, or see if the guy is still down there."

"Wait for help to arrive."

"I'll be careful. He might have been burned, and if he was, I don't want to wait before checking on him."

"If he's still there, he might—"

"Trust me. I'll be alright. And listen, watch yourself. It's not good that this guy burned up Scarlett's picture like that—or that he even had it on that shrine of his in the first place."

"I'll watch myself. I'm coming. I'll call Kevin. Don't do anything stupid."

38

Blake and Mannie didn't run into any trouble at the Windsor border crossing, and now Mannie guided the car into the parking lot at the Midtown hotel where they would be staying.

Inside the room, Blake reviewed the Atlanta airport CCTV footage and data files that Terry had accessed for him. Mannie went to the restaurant on the ground floor to get them something to eat.

From his conversations with Fayed, Blake knew that the man whom the jihadist had sent into the States was named Ali and wasn't an Arab. Fayed had also mentioned that there was some sort of glitch at the airport. So Blake was able to narrow down pretty quickly non-Arabs named Ali who passed through security in Atlanta and find the footage of the person he was looking for—the man who was given a secondary screening where he used an inhaler.

Which, from all that Blake knew, made sense.

Though the act of using the inhaler was innocent enough in itself, given what it initiated and all that would follow, Blake found it chilling to watch the scene.

Simple.

Deadly.

Game-changing.

By the time Ali was cleared, the last flight to Detroit had already departed.

Blake dialed to the footage of the baggage claim area and also the rental car desks to see who picked Ali up, or if maybe he drove away on his own.

Using the Federal Digital Database's facial recognition, he analyzed the people leaving the airport and those approaching the rental car desks.

Although he and Mannie were here in Michigan to find Fayed and repay him for what he'd done to Maria, they were also here to find and stop the man who'd been released from prison earlier that spring.

The one who'd killed that woman at the cabin in Minnesota.

The one who'd killed so many women before he was sent to prison fifteen years ago.

The one who'd most likely orchestrated the grenade attack on the Detroit police precinct and was now no doubt searching for the movie star who'd dropped out of public life all those years ago.

The object of his obsession.

Blake wasn't sure what name Dylan would be using these days, or exactly how to find him if he was in the area, but he knew it wouldn't be unheard of for him to have visited military surplus stores and perhaps karate studios or gyms if he truly had been in this area for several months.

There.

The computer identified a match.

Ali approached the Alamo desk.

Okay, yes.

So he did rent a car.

Blake thought that if Ali was driving to Michigan rather than flying, that might give him and Mannie some time to focus on the search for Dylan in the meantime before his arrival. The main meeting with Fayed wasn't scheduled to happen until tomorrow, so that meant tonight he could give his attention to finding his little brother.

Dylan Neeson.

Dylan had been adopted and thirteen years separated them, but in a certain sense that'd just served to solidify their relationship. Blake had raised Dylan from the time he joined their family when he was five until he joined the Army when he was eighteen, so he felt more like his father than his brother.

And so, just like a father feels responsible for his children, Blake felt responsible for the actions of this man.

Even from an early age, it'd been clear that Dylan was not a normal boy.

His biological father had never been in the picture and his mom had been a meth addict who was beaten to death in front of him by her dealer two months before his adoption. The man had locked the door before he left, maybe hoping that the boy would die in that apartment.

But he had not died.

Dylan had been stuck in there with her body for nearly four days before a woman in a neighboring apartment smelled something strange and sent the super to see what was wrong.

When Dylan was eight years old, Blake found out what'd happened to him and the boy's mother, so Blake had tracked the dealer down. It took almost three months to find him.

He'd just been released on parole when Blake paid him a little visit and taught him a lesson that, in his dying breaths, his dying screams, he apparently learned well.

As Blake worked on him, he said, "I didn't come here so you could beg for forgiveness or plead for your life."

"Then why did you come here?" the man gasped.

"To make sure justice gets done," Blake told him.

And then he delivered on his words.

It was what a father would've done.

Then, as he raised Dylan, he taught him about the importance of justice as well.

More than a decade had passed since Dylan had replied to any of Blake's letters, so Blake didn't know if his brother was well. Still, he'd kept writing to him, once a week, every week. More than five hundred letters and no response.

Once again, it was what a dad would do for his son.

You don't give up on family.

However, based on what Blake had seen when he was caring for Dylan all those years ago, he also knew what Dylan was capable of and how it went far beyond anything justice would require.

Once Dylan got started here in Michigan, got a taste for killing again, he wouldn't stop on his own and Blake doubted the police would be able to find him before he killed again.

And so now, if Dylan really was in Detroit, Blake needed to stop him. If he did not, innocent people would die and his brother might be killed by police during his apprehension. Dylan could not be allowed to roam the streets, and Blake did not want him dead.

Blake's options were limited and he wasn't sure exactly what he would do, even if he found his brother.

Mannie returned from getting the food. "What's the next step?" he asked.

"Karate studios and military supply stores. My brother doesn't always know when to lie low. Let's see if he poked his head up anywhere."

39

Dylan stood stoically in the shadows and watched the flames whip and wisp and curl around and through each other, intertwining in their urgent ascent to lick at the tunnel's concrete ceiling, scarring it with soot.

Sharp-tipped, flaming tongues.

Black-powdered, spreading soot.

He wasn't sure how badly the FBI agent had been burned. He wasn't even sure how the man had ended up down here this afternoon.

The timing had been impeccable.

Serendipity?

Fate?

Whatever it was, it might've been just what Dylan needed.

The agent had identified himself only by his first name: Patrick.

But it was the same guy from last night in the attic. Same name. Same voice. Same face.

He was tough. Not as well trained as he might've been, but a scrappy fighter.

Scrappy enough to win the fight.

Dylan remembered falling to the gym floor. It'd knocked the wind out of him, and if the floor hadn't been warped like it was, he might not have been able to get out of there at all.

It hadn't injured him severely. Still, the way he landed had tweaked his left leg, and he'd sustained a slight limp that wasn't easy to hide.

Sometimes in prison, you learn to act crazy. During his years behind bars, Dylan had seen plenty of men get unhinged or get high on the drugs family members or guards snuck in for them, or on the cleaning agents that they mixed together in ways that only the most desperate drug addicts will do.

The coughing and the slurred speech.

Given time, they weren't that difficult to learn.

He'd imitated those for the agent. His disguise as a vagrant had served him well over the last several months. People don't give the homeless a second thought. If you want to disappear in a city like Detroit, you don't wear a suit. You don't call attention to yourself. You hide in plain sight by walking around dressed up as one of the Invisible People.

But he wasn't dressed like that when he committed the homicides. He was dressed as himself.

Though everything on the shrine held significance to him, he was the saddest to know that the photo of him and his brother was gone. It was the only thing he'd taken with him into prison and the only thing he'd taken back out with him when he was released.

He'd left the letters there. All read. Hundreds of them. All channeled through his lawyer's office. It'd been far too long since he'd replied to his brother, but still he loved him. Still, he'd been glad to get those letters every week.

Shame had kept him from writing back.

Shame that he was not more ashamed of what he had done.

It certainly seemed that, based on what Patrick said, the FBI agent knew something about Scarlett. He'd recognized the girl in the photo and was apparently familiar with the movie.

Also, he knew the name "Igazi."

So, that meant he merited getting some of the lighter fluid squirted onto him as well.

No, today, the timing wasn't right for the Feds to find the shrine. And with the agent down here, it was necessary to use the gas he'd kept available for an emergency to destroy the evidence.

He'd learned one thing from his older brother and that'd been reiterated to him in prison: to find people who don't want to be found, you start with those most likely to know them. Then you squeeze them with a threat or offer them a promise.

How do you get someone to do something for you? Promise to give him what he wants, or threaten to take away what he loves. Bribe or extort. Almost always it boiled down to one of those two approaches.

Dylan removed the wig and fake beard and the reeking clothes he'd taken off the squatter that he'd killed with the box cutter right after arriving in Detroit.

He was thankful that the person he was working with, the one he'd promised his devotion to, had not been present when Patrick was here. It would've made things awkward. It might have required actions that Dylan wouldn't have wanted to take and might even have regretted.

He tossed the lighter-fluid-drenched disguise into the fire and stood naked before it. Eyes closed. Arms outstretched, as if he were about to be transformed into an angel.

The Angel of Light.

Or the Destroyer of Worlds.

He still wasn't sure which.

Maybe the same angel could, at times, be both.

He was only interested in justice and in righting wrongs, and sometimes that happened in the light, sometimes it happened in the darkness.

Yes, he deserved to die for the things he had done, but he had served fifteen years for his crimes. He figured that had earned him a few more years of freedom before he would need to take his own life. But Scarlett also deserved to die for what she had done. A murderer does not deserve to go free.

He would not run from his fate, but first he needed to make sure that Lady Justice visited Scarlett Farrow, whatever name she might be using today.

After a minute or so, he backed away from the fire, put on some fresh clothes, and went to clean up before meeting the person he had found it so profitable to partner with.

40

In the tunnel again, I found that the mattress was still smoldering hot enough that I wouldn't be able to get past it. The shrine and all the evidence it'd held were destroyed.

Still unsure if Anthony had been injured or not, I scanned the tunnel beyond the burned-out living quarters.

No sign of him standing there. No sign of a body.

The tunnel, although tall enough for me to stand, didn't allow me enough height to jump over the mattress, unless I managed some sort of diving roll, which my burned side and sore ankle wouldn't have accepted very well, and which I wasn't sure I could even pull off anyway.

I glanced in the mirror that was facing the burned-up shrine. As I did, I thought of those letters, the ones that the offender had carved into the victims: *WORR*.

With the backward *R*s.

Maybe it was going to spell something after all—but not forward, backward.

Would he have carved an *A* in Jamika's forehead?

ARROW.

FARROW.

Is he spelling her name out on his victims? Her full name would mean fourteen letters. Is that where all this is leading? Fourteen homicides?

After one more look around, I grabbed my ruined shirt and returned to the surface.

By the time I was walking out of the school, Dr. Kevin Gordon, Sharyn's ex-husband, had arrived.

"Sharyn called me." He was standing beside his BMW, and a young girl who I guessed was Olivia was staring out the backseat window. "You were burned?"

"That was quick," I said to Kevin. I waved at the girl and, after a brief hesitation, she waved back. "Getting here, I mean."

Kevin gestured toward my side. "I was in the area. Let me take a look."

I set my shirt on the ground beside the hoodies and, as he examined the reddened and tender skin, he said, "Was Canyon helpful to you this morning?"

"I can't really discuss those matters, Kevin. I think you know that."

"Right." As he inspected me, he took the most careful note of the areas where the skin had blistered. "You know how, in an action movie, there's always that scene where the hero takes off his shirt so the audience can see either his abs or his scars? You know what I'm talking about?"

I wasn't sure if he was mocking me or not. "I don't get to the movies as much as I'd like."

"Well, he's usually ripped or there are battle scars that tell the story of how tough he is."

"Okay."

He pointed to my left shoulder where I'd sustained a through and through years ago when I was still a homicide detective, then he indicated the more recently healed knife wound from a fight I was in earlier this year.

"Sometimes you get a little close to the action," he concluded.

"It's been known to happen."

An ambulance pulled into the parking lot.

"Whatever happened between you and Sharyn?" Kevin asked. "Why didn't it work out?"

"Different paths," I told him simply.

"Well." He finished studying my burns. "Topical antibiotics. Keep the area clean. I think you'll make it out alright this time without any more."

"Any more?"

"Scars. I'll give you a prescription for some pain meds, just in case."

"Don't worry about it. But thanks."

One of the EMTs was hurrying my way carrying a large first aid kit.

"It's going to hurt."

"I'll be alright."

"Whatever you say."

I thanked Kevin again, then asked the EMT if the CSI unit was on its way.

"There was a shooting across town. Everyone's stretched thin. Not sure when they'll get here."

To preserve the evidence as much as possible, I asked him if he had anything I could put the hoodies in. While he was looking for a couple of bags, Olivia climbed out of the BMW and Kevin called to her, "I told you to stay in the car, Olivia."

She made an unhappy face. "I'm hungry. And I like to be called *Livvy*."

"We'll get you something to eat in just a minute."

She was eyeing me carefully.

Since I didn't have a shirt on, it was easy to see the burns—and the scars. To avoid frightening or upsetting her, I put on the shirt that was half burned up.

"Hello, there." I waved again. "I'm Pat."

When she didn't reply, Kevin urged her, "Tell him your name."

"Livvy."

"Olivia," Kevin said.

She didn't correct herself.

"I'm not supposed to talk to strangers," she told me.

"Pat is one of your mom's friends," Kevin explained in a tone that was hard to read. "You can talk to him."

Knowing what to say to children has never been my strong suit, but in an attempt to be friendly, I said, "I hear you were at ballet camp this morning."

"Uh-huh." She pointed at my injured side, which was still visible through the hole in the shirt. "Does that hurt?"

"Not too much. Your daddy helped me."

"Oh."

"Pat is very brave," Kevin told her. "He's good at catching bad people."

Maybe it was simply because his daughter was here, but his entire demeanor now was strikingly different from what it'd been earlier today.

"Are you a hero?" Olivia asked me. "Daddy likes movies with heroes."

"No. I'm just—"

"Yes," Kevin said. "Pat is a real hero. Just ask your mommy. She'll tell you."

Now his tone was getting easier to read, but Olivia didn't seem to notice or care about the attitude it carried. "I like ponies," she told me.

"Your mom told me that. And princesses, huh?"

She nodded.

"Okay, Livvy," Kevin said, opting for the name she preferred. He opened the car door and guided her into the sedan. "Let's go get you some food."

41

The EMT offered to bandage my side for me, and unsure if I would be going back into the tunnel and perhaps getting soot or dirt on the burns, I agreed. Paramedics often carry extra shirts in case one gets blood on it, and one of the men gave me his from the ambulance.

It had a slew of EMT achievement patches on it.

Another type of trophy.

Idols by another name.

As the man worked on bandaging me, the smell of smoke struck me again—my mind probably just registering at last how much my clothes were still carrying the evidence of the fire.

The guy was just finishing up as Sharyn arrived, leapt out of her car, and hurried toward me. "Are you okay, Pat?" she asked urgently.

"All good."

Ever since Kevin had left with Olivia, I'd been processing what the man in the tunnel had said to me and I was ready to talk it through with Sharyn.

The paramedic tucked the end of the bandage wrap in, then stepped away, leaving the two of us alone.

"Your ex-husband was very helpful, by the way," I said, buttoning up the shirt.

"I'm glad he made it."

"He had Olivia with him. It sounded like they were on the way to lunch."

"Huh."

"Everything alright?"

"Yeah, yeah." She gestured toward the plastic bags. "The hoodie?"

"Hoodies. Two of them. Pretty much everything else was destroyed. Make sure CSI checks the tips of their drawstrings for prints. They're plastic. Last night I saw the guy I chased rolling one of them between his fingers while he was standing across the street. It might just be the break we need."

"Good eye."

"Also, there were cans of food down in the tunnel. We might get prints or DNA. The lighter will be somewhere in the remains of the mattress. It has a medical symbol on it."

"A medical symbol?"

"The caduceus. Who knows? Maybe if we find the lighter we can trace it back to the place where he bought it. And we might be in luck if the bottle of lighter fluid melted."

"Prints get melded onto it."

"So you've done this before?"

"A couple of times. Tell me about the man who was in the tunnel."

I kept my voice low to make sure no one else heard what I had to say. "He happened to show up at precisely the same time that I was in there. He had a picture of you and apparent evidence from the crime scenes—even though they were located all across the city. For instance, the head of that doll that was in the room where Jamika was found.

Then he destroyed it, burned it all up. He knew the name 'Igazi,' and that the girl in the picture was from a movie. Also, he told me he'd traded clothes with someone to get the hoodies—but that would have put him there at the time of the chase last night—too coincidental. No, I'm not thinking it was random. And I'm not convinced he was a vagrant—or at least not one who had nothing to do with these crimes."

"We're on the same page there."

"You mentioned something on the phone earlier about who this might be, that you might have an idea. What were you going to tell me?"

++++

Sharyn evaluated how much to share.

She glanced around and noticed that the paramedic who'd treated Pat's side was lingering nearby. For privacy, she took Pat's elbow and led him toward the overgrown, unkempt field beside the school.

"When I was in college," she told him, "I had a stalker. He'd seen *Sanctuary* and became obsessed with it. He attacked me, was sent to prison. On the ride over here, just a few minutes ago, I found out he was released in April."

"What? Are you serious?"

"Yes. It was so long ago that it never even occurred to me that there might be a connection until you mentioned that my photo was down there in the tunnel."

"How could he have found out what city you're in?"

"There are only four people who know who I am, or, well, who I was. You, Kevin, the agent from the Department of Justice who finalized my new identity, and a friend from my modeling days named Simone Tee." She tried to keep the tear back but felt it leak out of her eye. She quickly wiped it away.

"What is it?" Pat asked concernedly.

"She was killed in May. In an explosion. I just found that out now on the drive too. The man I knew had a thing for grenades." Another tear.

This one, he wiped away for her.

"We'd been in contact about getting together this summer," she said. "Her father was dying, she needed someone to talk to."

"I'm so sorry to hear about your friend."

"She didn't follow up with me, but until today it didn't click that any of that might be related to this case."

"You had no reason to think it was. From what we knew, there weren't any clues linking those events."

She was quiet for a moment, then sighed and collected herself. "Thank you. I'll be okay. I just . . . it's just a lot to process."

Patrick appeared to be sorting through everything she'd just told him. "What's his name? The man who attacked you?"

"Dylan Neeson."

"And no one from the warden's office contacted you when he was released," Pat concluded, "because they didn't know your name, your current identity."

"Exactly."

"Any idea on his location?"

"No." As she thought about what had happened to her fifteen years ago, she wondered if the same thing had happened to her friend and found the tears hard to hold back.

"Do you need a minute?" Patrick asked her. "Or is there anything else I can do for you right now?"

"No." She tried putting on a smile. "I'll be alright."

++++

When Sharyn hesitated, I wasn't sure if she was waiting for me to reply. "You said that Dylan had a thing for grenades?" I said.

"He tried sticking one in my mouth when he was . . . well, when he was done with me."

I had no idea what to say. "Sharyn, that's terrible. I can't even imagine what it was like to go through that. And about your friend. I'm very sorry. Really."

I knew that Sharyn cared deeply about people, and I could tell that even though she might not have been especially close to this woman and was doing her best not to let it affect her right now, the impact of Simone's death was still a fresh wound.

"Sharyn, this morning Kramer's partner mentioned something about a grenade here in Detroit. Do you know what that might have been about?"

"A couple of weeks ago, a man entered one of the precinct stations, yelled something no one was able to distinguish, tossed a grenade into the lobby, and then ran. Thank God the grenade didn't go off."

"Any clue who it was?"

"No. The security cameras at that precinct hadn't worked in months." When she went on, she returned to the topic of her friend. "The last I heard from Simone was a text from her number that said *I'm coming to see you*. Now I wonder if she was really the one who sent that text."

"Her killer might have. It might have been Dylan."

"Yes."

There was enough to justify a response. We contacted dispatch and put out a BOLO for Dylan Neeson. Then I said to Sharyn, "I'm not sure if this is too personal, and you don't have to answer it, but a moment ago you said, 'when he was done' with you. Sharyn, what did he do to you?"

She stared past me, toward the tangled underbrush. When she finally did answer, her voice was hushed, hardly above a whisper. "He raped me, Pat."

I felt that same breed of sharp anger and deep sorrow that I always felt when I saw a dead body, but in this case, it was worse, because her suffering wasn't over. By the look on her face, I could tell she still felt the pain of what'd happened all those years ago.

At this point, I knew that anything I said would not be enough, so I took her in my arms and I held her. I hugged her like a friend.

Or, maybe, just a little more.

42

2:34 P.M.
Dispersal in 24 hours

The pinging sound of gravel spitting up against the undercarriage of the rental car jarred Ali awake.

The car he was driving was on its way off the shoulder and into the ditch.

He swung it back onto the highway, but overcompensated and careened all the way into the passing lane, clipping the rear bumper of a white minivan, sending it fishtailing across the road as Ali managed to draw his car to a stop.

White-knuckled, he clenched the steering wheel, breathing rapidly, with the car half off the road, his heart racing, his arms shaking.

The driver of the minivan parked, climbed out, and studied the back of his vehicle.

Ali had heard about "road rage" in America, about how drivers sometimes shoot those who cut them off in traffic, and he worried that everything might come to an end right here, right now.

He couldn't see any damage to the minivan, but the man, who was tall and angular and brisk, must have, because he came storming toward Ali's car.

Unsure if he should get out or not—if it would be perceived as being aggressive—Ali finally decided to meet the man and offer him money.

He cannot call the police. You cannot let that happen.

Ali walked toward him.

"What the hell was that?" the man roared.

"I am so sorry," Ali said.

"You see the back of my van?"

Ali was not about to argue with him by telling him that there was no damage, and just repeated, "I am very sorry."

"You better have insurance!"

"This is a rental car," Ali said. "I do not know."

His response seemed to take the man by surprise and even calm him down somewhat. "A rental?"

"Yes."

The man cursed under his breath but then became suddenly sympathetic when he saw the dent in the front of the rental car. "You're screwed worse than I am, my man."

"What can I pay you?" Ali pulled out his wallet. He had some American money but didn't know how much of it he would need over the next twenty-four hours. "To fix the damage to your car."

The man's eyes were on the wallet.

"How much you got?"

Ali had no idea how much to offer. "May I give you three hundred dollars?"

"That won't cover it. You can give me six hundred."

Ali gave him everything. It was short of six hundred, but the man accepted it.

Ali decided he could use the credit card for gas, for food, for whatever else he needed.

"Good luck with the rental car company," the man said before he left. "You're gonna need it."

Back in the car, Ali let out a long breath.

He hadn't realized how tired he was, but the lack of sleep last night had finally caught up with him, and although his adrenaline was pumping now, he knew that wasn't going to last.

You must rest, Ali.

No, you must get to Dearborn, Michigan, as soon as possible.

Rest. You won't get there at all if you crash this car first.

He checked the map on his phone and found a rest area that was about forty-five miles, or just shy of seventy-five kilometers, farther up the road. If he could make it there, he could sleep, stretch, and take some time for Salat Al-'Asr prayer—which was not something he wanted to do at a petrol station.

After that, he would still have six hours of driving in front of him. But it was the kind of break he needed.

He waited for a gap in traffic, pulled onto the highway again, and headed for the rest stop.

++++

Sharyn and I left the edge of the field and returned to the school's parking lot.

Julianne's brother Eddie Springman and two other officers arrived to hold the scene until CSI could get here. We received word that Lieutenant Sproul was on his way. Kramer's partner, Officer Sunshine, was limping, and when Sharyn asked him about it, he said, "Bum ankle. Hurt it at the gym."

"The gym?" I said, thinking about what happened inside the school last night.

"Men my age shouldn't be playing basketball anymore, I guess," he said with an annoyed head shake.

Huh.

Naw.

Too easy.

Sharyn had stopped crying, and I was glad that I'd at least had the chance to be here for her. We called Angela Knight at Cyber to have her team work up a full background on Dylan Neeson.

"Are you going to be okay?" I asked Sharyn.

"I should be the one asking you that with your burns."

"Oh, they're alright. Losing someone you care about, that hurts a lot worse and for a lot longer."

"Thanks. It means a lot. Your concern, I mean."

I wasn't sure if I should pivot the conversation back to the case, but when at last it felt appropriate, I said, "Listen, I'm wondering if we might be looking at a modern Bluebeard here."

"A blue beard?"

"Yes. Like in the story."

"You mean the pirate?"

"Actually, that's Blackbeard. The Bluebeard designation is something the advisor in my doctoral program, Dr. Calvin Werjonic, came up with. He hasn't published his findings yet, but it's a name he's given to a killer who entices people to come to him rather than hunting them down like most serial killers do. Think of the difference between a spider and a bat. The bat goes out each night and searches for its prey. The spider weaves a web, sets a trap, and his prey walks right into it. Two completely different types of predators."

"Most serial killers are bats," she said, tracking with me. "A Bluebeard is a spider."

"Yes."

"But if he lures them into his web, why the different locations in the city?"

"I'm not sure. Most of the time it's one location, but sometimes he has more than one web."

"Why is the story called Bluebeard, though? I'm not really that familiar with the fairy tales—at least not that one."

Officer Springman informed us that an officer had located the tunnel's exit at a vacant factory two blocks away. He gave us the address, and as Sharyn and I headed toward it, I said, "There are different versions of the story, but normally it goes something like this . . ." And then, not being the most natural storyteller, I began to tell it as close as I could remember to the way Calvin had told it to me.

43

Once upon a time there was a young woman named Constance who was courted by a man with a blue beard. Her two older sisters were too troubled by his appearance to be interested in him.

Constance liked him well enough, but still—there was that beard.

However, her mother said, "If he is a good man, the color of his beard means nothing. Besides, brown or blue, it doesn't matter, all beards turn white eventually."

And so, despite the rumors that he had already been married at different times before, and that the marriages hadn't worked out well, the young woman wed him.

He held a great feast and she invited all of her friends and family, who were quite impressed by his wealth and his grand and expansive home.

But he had one room that he did not allow Constance to show to anyone. Instead, he informed her that it must always remain his, and his alone, to enter.

"Of course," she told him, knowing that all people have secrets that, for their own reasons, they feel must be kept hidden.

A few days after the feast, he had to leave for a long journey. "Here are the keys to all of the rooms in the house," he told her. "But that one key you must not use."

"To the room at the end of the hall?"

"Yes."

"Certainly," she told him.

"I will know if you open it. Please respect my wishes."

"Yes. Of course."

After he left, she enjoyed exploring the estate and all of the other rooms in the mansion, all the while making sure she avoided going toward the end of that hall so that she would not be tempted to go into that room.

But, in time, when he did not return on the appointed date, she found herself drawn to that door. She stood outside it for a long time before finally inserting the key, unlocking it, and then easing it open.

The darkness inside the room did not allow her to see much.

But it allowed her to see enough.

Bones and hair and a vat of blood, all from the other women that the man with the blue beard had brought home in the past. Seven forms hanging from hooks. Forms that she could now see were not dresses, but empty skins.

The seven wedding rings still encircling the seven severed fingers on the crimson velvet pillow all matched.

And they matched the ring that she wore on hers.

These women had been his previous brides.

Constance gasped, backed out of the room, and tried to remove the key from the lock, but it would not come out.

And it bled.

The key bled.

Dark red drops fell from it to the floor and pooled at the base of the door.

The key bled, for it had been marked with a dark magic.

Hearing the sound of hoofbeats, she rushed to the window.

A cloud of dust rose from the road as her husband galloped on his horse toward the mansion, his long blue beard whipping to the side, caught in the wind.

Desperately, she tried to think of how she might escape and stop her husband from killing her, from killing anyone again.

If only her brothers or her sisters were here to fight him for her!

But they were not. So, being alone, she had to act alone.

She hurried to the kitchen, prepared herself, and then made it to the front door just as he was walking up the steps.

"Hello, my dear," she said.

"Hello, Constance."

"How was your trip?"

"Pleasantly uneventful." He kissed her. "And did you enjoy yourself in my absence?"

"Oh, yes."

"Constance, did you go into the room I forbade you from entering?"

"My dear, all I want to do is fulfill your wishes."

He held out his hand. "May I have the keys?"

She pretended to reach for the keys, but instead drew out the kitchen knife she had hidden and brought with her.

A look of shock fell across his face and he tried to back away, but her determination made her swift and certain with the blade. She thrust it into his neck and he collapsed limply to the ground at her feet.

The dark magic of that place had seeped into her heart and she watched as he bled, watched as he struggled to breathe, watched as he died. He was a big man and strong and he did not die quickly or well.

It wasn't easy, but she managed to drag his body to the room at the end of the hall, where he would now join his previous wives.

After she had used the knife to slice the ring off his finger, the key that was still in that lock stopped bleeding and she was able to remove it.

She cleaned up the blood and cleaned up the ring and waited.

Another suitor would come by, especially when he found out she lived alone in such an exquisite home.

She slipped the keys into the top of her gown beside her left breast, where they would remain close to her. Close to her racing heart.

++++

Sharyn listened with rapt attention as he finished telling the story.

"Pat, honestly, that was creepy. You told that a little too well."

"Thanks. I guess. Mostly that's the way I heard it from my friend."

"So her innocence was corrupted? Evil won in the end?"

"In that version, yes."

"Maybe being one of the previous wives would have been better. Even though they were killed, I'd say it's better to die in innocence than to live having been conquered by evil."

"Well," Pat replied, "just like with most folktales, there are lots of variations. In some, Bluebeard is killed when the young woman's brothers arrive just in the nick of time. In others, he murders her as well and gets away with it. From what I understand, this seventeenth-century French variant is similar to a story from England called 'Mr. Fox,' which, if Calvin is right, seemed to be familiar to Shakespeare's listeners because the bard refers to it in *Much Ado About Nothing.*"

"You really know your folktales."

"Calvin does."

They arrived at the old car factory where the tunnel exited.

It opened up in a shipping area on the first level, but after looking around for a few minutes and not finding anything that appeared to be significant to the case, she suggested they return to the school so Pat could head back to the motel and change clothes.

"Honestly," he said, "that doesn't sound like such a bad idea."

As they walked, she filled him in on what they'd covered at the briefing before she left. Then, she considered his theory about the Bluebeard and how it might fit in with what she'd uncovered involving the Hook'dup app. "If we are dealing with a Bluebeard, and if it really is Dylan, I might have the connection we're looking for. You were right about the victims' phones. I found a dating app that all of them were using."

"Which one is that?"

"Hook'dup." She took a few moments to summarize how it worked, then said, "The developer's office is near the airport. I was planning to head over there. At this time of day, it's probably an hour or so drive."

"If we leave now, we can probably make it before they close."

"I'm sorry, 'we'?"

"I'll come with you."

"Pat. No. You need to go get cleaned up, get some clothes that aren't singed or covered with soot and that don't smell like smoke or lighter fluid."

They were almost back to the school.

"Sharyn, I don't like the fact that someone snipped out your face and stuck it on that painting where Jesus's face should have been. Or that the man in the tunnel knew about the movie. Or that Dylan is free and might be here in Detroit. That can't all be a coincidence."

"Did you say over the face of Jesus?"

"Yes." He gave her the details about the painting and explained that it was most likely the one from the room where Jamika's body had been found. "He set you up as an idol. He worships you."

"Maybe."

"If that was Dylan down there in the tunnel, is wearing a disguise part of his MO?"

"Not that I know of. Listen, I can tell you're worried about me. Don't be." She smiled at him. "I'm a big girl. I can take care of myself."

"I know. And I respect that. But I wouldn't respect myself if I didn't also want to protect you. I'm a guy. I can't help it."

When he said that, she thought of what Julianne had told her about how so many women fantasize about being powerless in the arms of a powerful man.

No matter how independent you are, intimacy requires you to be dependent also. And that's okay. And with Pat, that would be more than okay.

Love is the greatest liability because it leaves you with a weakness.

No. It is your greatest asset, because it gives you a reason to be strong.

Don't think about those things, Sharyn. This isn't about you and him. It's about stopping Dylan before he kills again.

"If it'll make you feel better, I'll have another agent or

officer go with me to the app developer," she told Pat. "Maybe Ted."

"Detective Schwartz?"

"Yes."

"Okay. Sounds good."

++++

Sharyn invited me over to her car to give me the Glock that she'd picked up earlier from the armory.

As she opened the hatch, the angle of the sunlight glancing across her necklace shifted and the sapphires in it gleamed.

Oh.

Blue jewelry.

Of course.

That must have been where the idea for the tongue twister that I'd told Christie when I was at the hospital came from—seeing Sharyn's earrings and necklace earlier this morning. The subconscious is acutely observant. The image of the blue jewelry must have gotten lodged somewhere in the back of my mind.

Still, I felt a pang of guilt that I'd shared with Christie a tongue twister inspired by something Sharyn was wearing.

++++

Sharyn noticed Pat noticing her, and self-consciously brushed a hand across her cheek. "What is it? Is there something wrong? Something on my face?"

"No. Everything's . . . Sorry. I was just . . . You kept the earrings and the necklace."

"Oh." She reached up to remove the left earring. "Yes. I'm sorry. I'll take them off."

He touched her arm to stop her. "No, it's okay. It's just . . . I'd say most of the time when people break up with each other, they get rid of the remnants of the relationship. Makes it easier to forget. To move on."

She'd never thought of them as remnants of their relationship.

But maybe that's what they were.

Maybe she didn't want to move on. Maybe she was clinging to something she should have let go of a long time ago.

You shouldn't have worn them! Why did you wear them today?

He must have been able to read the look on her face, because he said, "Sharyn, I didn't mean to . . . Never mind. Don't worry about it. It's fine."

++++

And when I said, "It's fine," I realized again, as I had earlier with Christie, that when people say "fine," it's most often a lie.

When others ask us how we're doing and we say "fine," or when they ask us what's wrong and we say, "nothing," we're rarely telling the truth, the whole truth, and nothing but the truth.

Saying "fine" and "nothing" are socially acceptable ways of hiding what's really going on in our lives.

I debated whether or not to tell Sharyn that I was seeing someone but decided it probably wasn't the best time to get into all that. We could talk about it later—would talk about it later. I definitely needed to clear the air at some point.

"I won't wear them," Sharyn told me. "I don't want you to feel uncomfortable."

"It's okay. I shouldn't have said anything."

A somewhat tepid, African-American man approached us and Sharyn told me softly that it was Lieutenant Sproul.

After a curt introduction, he asked me for the rundown and I filled him in on the bomb shelter, the fire, and the search for the homeless man, and the BOLO for Dylan Neeson. However, I left out anything that would lead him to know Sharyn's true identity.

I explained my observations about the locations of the sites being in different precincts. "By all accounts, the killer is familiar with the precinct map," I told him.

"Can you tell where he's going to strike next?"

"No. But I don't believe in random crime distribution. There's a pattern beneath all of this."

"And what pattern is that?"

"I'm still working that out." I summarized the possible Bluebeard connection, then Sharyn told him about the Hook'dup app, and he listened in silence until she was done.

He looked at the high school thoughtfully. "It sounds like to find Dylan, the first step is identifying the reasons the victims are showing up at those locations, and then trying to predict where the next crime will most likely occur."

Earlier, Sharyn had indicated to me that Sproul wasn't the sharpest knife in the drawer, but he seemed pretty dialed in at the moment. He echoed what she'd said about me getting changed, then went to speak with the team about the evidence recovery efforts in the tunnel.

As I filled out the paperwork Sharyn had brought along for permission to use the Glock, she assured me that she would touch base tonight and let me know what she found out from the app developer.

"I'll be waiting for your call," I told her.

"One other thing." Her voice was hushed. "Dylan was obsessed with the movie and my Academy Award nomination. That might explain him putting the photo on that painting. You've seen it, right? *Sanctuary*? You know about the ending?"

"Actually, no, I never did."

She looked at me curiously. "You never watched it? Even when we were dating?"

"No. When we were together, I just wanted to get to know you for who you were—I mean, who you are—and not who you were when you were ten: the person right in front of me, not the person you pretended to be in front of the cameras when you were a kid."

Sharyn looked stunned, as if no one had ever told her that before. This woman who could've ruled the world with her beauty seemed touched in a deeper way than I would've ever imagined by the simple fact that I'd wanted to get to know her for who she truly was regardless of her fame or her past.

"Pat, that was very thoughtful of you. Really. Maybe you should watch it—at least the end. The scene in the church. That's the one that's most famous, the one that got me the Academy Award nomination. I'm wondering if it might relate to this case."

"I'll take a look."

I figured that I could stream the movie and watch it tonight at the motel—at least the ending, if I didn't have time to watch the whole film. Maybe I didn't even need to wait. I could play it while I changed and wrote up the report of what'd happened here at the school.

She took off to meet up with Schwartz and pay

Inntoit2U Designs a visit, and I contacted the CSI team to confirm that they knew about the possibility of fingerprints on the drawstrings.

Before leaving for the motel, I went to see if the headless doll was still in the bedroom where Jamika's body had been left, but found that it was gone. I sent an officer to check the other sites for the corresponding clues that related to what had been on the shrine, but I wasn't going to hold my breath. Dylan—if that's who was behind this—had shown he was good at cleaning up after himself.

++++

Canyon had been trying to sleep, but he was just too distracted by everything that was going on to really get any rest.

Now, he was lying in his hospital bed checking his text messages when someone knocked lightly on his door.

The nurses didn't always knock—which was *completely* rude—but the doctors did, so he thought it was probably one of them coming back to check on him.

He looked up as the person opened the door and stepped into the room.

"What . . . What are you doing here?" Canyon stammered.

The figure closed the door softly. "I wanted to see how you're doing."

"Yeah, no. I'm good. All good."

Canyon had entered that lady FBI agent's number into his phone, and now scrolled to his contacts to speed-dial her, but the visitor was quick and stopped him before he could call her.

"No, no. There's no need for that."

Canyon tried to pull free to punch the button beside the bed to call a nurse, but the person's grip was too tight.

"Let me go," he exclaimed.

"I'm afraid that's no longer an option."

With one rough hand, the visitor stopped Canyon's scream.

Then stopped his breath once and for all.

It wasn't bloody, wasn't messy, and it didn't take long.

The person stood back and took a photo when it was over, then walked back into the hall and passed the nurses' station as if nothing had happened.

And because of who that person was, the nurse sitting there only looked up briefly from her work, gave a tiny smile, and then went back to her typing.

Scarlett Farrow—III

The Bedroom

Cheating.

That's the word he used.

The man that Millie's mom was seeing, the one who scared Scarlett in real life, started to think that Tracy was cheating on him and he decided to kill the guy at work.

And it was something that Scarlett didn't really get at all. Why would someone just cheating at *anything* make you want to kill them? Sure, cheating was bad, but so were lots of other things.

So, in any case, Harris went over to kill him. It was a scene she wasn't supposed to see, but she was off-set and was sneaking around a little bit and watched it all. It looked so *real.*

Mostly they tried to keep her from seeing the scary parts of the movie, but she was a kid, and kids always find a way to see stuff grown-ups don't want them to see.

It's fake blood, she told herself. But it didn't look fake at all. And it gave her nightmares for years.

Harris stabbed the man over and over and over and blood kept spurting up and splatting onto everything and

Scarlett just kept reminding herself that it was all fake, that none of it, none of it, none of it was real.

Then, not long after that, they shot the scene when Harris comes to attack Millie's mom.

Scarlett was upstairs in her bedroom and saw him walking toward the house in the moonlight.

As he came closer, he zipped up his jacket to cover up the blood.

She clung to her stuffed bunny, Snowball, the one Millie's dad had given Millie for her birthday the night before he died trying to save her from drowning. But he didn't die. He didn't drown. No one drowned.

Don't forget this is just a movie, Scarlett. Don't ever forget!

When she saw Harris, she felt a shiver, a real shiver, and called to Tracy and ran to the top of the stairs.

But Tracy was busy in the kitchen and didn't hear her.

It was just like they'd rehearsed it.

All like they'd rehearsed.

The real world began merging with the pretend one in a way that was too, too confusing.

When the doorbell rang, Millie cried out for her mom not to open the door. She even started down the steps to make sure she could hear her, but it was too late.

Her mom swung it open and greeted Harris.

"Mom!" Millie shouted, trying not to sound too scared so it wouldn't make Harris realize that she knew what was going on. "Come here, okay?"

"Just a minute, dear," Tracy said, and then let Harris into the living room and told him, "I'll be right back."

Millie called for her again, and went down a few more steps, but then stopped when she heard Harris threaten her mom.

The shouts got louder.

"What happened to Cole?" Her mom's voice was desperate. "Is that blood on your hand? Millie!"

Tracy ran toward the stairs to protect her daughter, but Harris was right behind her and just as she got to the foot of the stairs and yelled for Millie to *run!* Harris appeared, clenched a handful of her mom's hair, smashed her head against the wall, threw her to the floor, and then dragged her out of sight.

It all looked so real.

So very, very real.

And that's when Scarlett began to think that it was, at least part of her did.

Terrified, she ran back up the stairs, down the hall, and into her bedroom, where she opened the window and stared outside.

It was a long way to the ground.

The tree that her dad had built the tree house in was nearby, with branches reaching toward the window.

Stretching, stretching. So, so close.

Before they started filming the scene, the director had told her, "I want you to really make it look like Millie is thinking about jumping out the window or climbing down that tree." He patted her on the shoulder. "You do a good job at acting scared. Keep it up."

"Okay."

Now, as she stood there looking out the window, she heard grunts and screams coming from the kitchen. Her mom crying out in pain.

Millie's mom. Not yours. It's all pretend. It's not real. None of this is. She's not your real mom.

But I wish she was. I want her to be!

So Millie hugged Snowball close and leaned out the window, trying super hard to reach the closest branch.

Then there was the heavy sound of a *thud*.

A short hallway led from the house to the church, and now the lights in it went on and Millie could hear the footsteps of the man walking through it.

The man who was dragging her mom.

Then the lights in the church flicked on.

Scarlett knew what was happening. They'd rehearsed everything.

He would be ripping off the tape from the roll.

Lots of tape.

To keep her mom in the chair.

Scarlett reached for that branch and found that she really did want to get it, but couldn't.

She kept Snowball, but tossed one of the dolls in her room out the window so that it fell by the base of the tree.

It was something she just thought of, hadn't planned, something that wasn't in the script. But the director didn't stop filming. Just kept the cameras rolling. It was just something that seemed honest to what Millie would do.

Scarlett ran down the hall to her mom's bedroom and hid there in the closet, whispering a prayer that Millie's mom had taught her earlier in the movie: "Now I lay me down to sleep. I pray the Lord my soul to keep. If I should die before I wake, I pray the Lord my soul to take."

She clenched her eyes and said it over and over. And she wasn't just fake-praying. She was really trying to reach God with her words.

"Millie." Harris came stalking up the stairs calling her name. "Don't be scared, Millie. It's just me. Your mom is in the church. She needs you."

Even there in the closet, Scarlett knew what was happening in the hall. She had to know those things in order to play her part.

They would do a close-up on the knife he was carrying.

And of the blood on his hands.

"I'm not going to hurt you, Millie," he said.

Millie's prayer became more and more rushed.

She hugged Snowball.

"If I should die—"

Down the hallway.

"Before I wake—"

To her bedroom.

He would be walking in there now, and he would see the open window, stare into the night, look for her, but not find her.

"I pray the Lord my soul to take."

Later, when she watched the dailies, she saw him stare confused at the doll, maybe wondering if there was a change in the script. But then he just went with it and began down the stairs to go out into the night and find her, but suddenly he stopped.

"Clever girl," he muttered to himself. "You don't like dolls, do you?"

He retraced his steps, searched her bedroom, and then went to her mom's bedroom. "Millie? Are you in here?"

And there she was, huddled in the closet, terrified, hugging Snowball, praying, praying, praying, "If I should die . . . If I should die . . ."

No, it isn't real.

Yes, yes, it is!

Harris came to the closet, opened the door, and smiled. "There you are, Millie. Come on."

But she shook her head.

"It's going to be okay."

"What'd you do to my mom?"

"Come and see."

"Did you hurt her?"

He held out his hand. "Come and see."

She didn't want to go, she wanted to stay there, but he was holding that knife and blocking her only way out of the closet, and it made her think that if she didn't go with him, she really wasn't going to survive, wasn't going to live at all.

It's the only way to save Mom.

Millie's mom. You mean Millie's mom.

This isn't real. None of this is real. It's all a game. Just a game of pretend.

Harris took her hand and led her to the stairs.

PART 4

No, Her Cage Is Not Enough

WEATHERS: Some people have claimed that your group carries out these attacks because you envy the West. How do you respond?

BASHIR: We do not envy you. We pity you. We do not desire this democracy of yours. We decry it. We abhor it. Democracy is idolatry because it places man-made laws above God-given ones.

WEATHERS: I would counter that there are more than a billion moderate Muslims worldwide who do not share your view.

BASHIR: Do you still not understand that there is no such thing as a moderate Muslim? The phrase is nonsensical, a contradiction in terms, just like the phrase "unborn-again Christian" would be.

WEATHERS: I'm not sure I understand what you mean.

BASHIR: To be a Muslim is to be surrendered to Allah, to submit to him. Submission is not something a person can do halfheartedly, or to a moderate degree. It's not radical to submit to something wholeheartedly, it is the only way one can submit. And it's not just Muslims who understand this,

Miss Weathers. Even Søren Kierkegaard, from the Christian tradition, wrote, "In relationship to God one can not involve himself to a certain degree. God is precisely the contradiction to all that is 'to a certain degree.'"

WEATHERS: So are you also saying that there is also no such thing as radical Islam?

BASHIR: Just as with any religion, there are those who call themselves Muslims but do not live out their beliefs, those who are not devout. Muslims who follow the Qur'an are not extremists who have been radicalized. They are not the radical ones, they are simply the ones who take their religion seriously, who are faithful and obedient to its decrees. If you wish to call me radical, feel free. I will take it as a compliment, one that I will carry with me to the grave and on to paradise.

—FROM THE TRANSCRIPT OF *EXTENDED STORY LIVE*, EPISODE 46, FEATURING THE AUDIO INTERVIEW BETWEEN CABLE BROADCAST NEWS JOURNALIST JORDAN WEATHERS AND THE MAN CLAIMING TO BE FAYED RAABI'AH BASHIR, FOUNDER OF THE BRIGADE OF THE PROPHET'S SWORD

44

Back in my motel room, I cleaned up and changed.

I thought about calling Christie to tell her what was going on, but decided it might just cause her to worry more if she heard that I'd been burned, even if the injuries weren't that serious.

After dictating some notes and observations from the day, I went online, bought a digital copy of *Sanctuary*, and, unsure that I would have the time now to make my way through the whole thing, I moved the cursor to the end to watch the last twenty minutes.

While I completed the report of what'd happened at the school, I let the movie play.

I wasn't sure exactly what had happened earlier in the movie, but in reviewing the plot synopsis on IMDb, I was able to get the gist of it. A young girl's father died trying to save her from drowning. Her mother, hoping to find a positive male influence for her daughter, ended up unwittingly inviting a man who was violent and dangerous into their lives.

In the current scene, the girl that Sharyn was playing watched this man, who was covered with blood, walk up to the house after he'd just murdered one of her mother's coworkers.

Millie tried unsuccessfully to warn her mom and to send Harris on a futile search outside. However, he caught on, went upstairs, and found Sharyn in the closet of the master bedroom.

Just like the first four victims were found in the upstairs bedroom closet.

Yes. It fit.

Sharyn looked so scared, her tears so real, her prayer sounded so genuine. It was no wonder she'd been nominated for an Academy Award. The movie was clearly well directed and had superb cinematography. Even though I hadn't watched the beginning, I found myself distracted from my paperwork and engrossed in the story.

We still didn't know what had happened to her mom.

Harris was leading Sharyn down the stairs when my phone buzzed.

Assistant Director DeYoung's number came up on the screen of my cell, so I paused the movie.

"Pat," he said when I answered the call, "I heard you were injured. Burned?"

"Nothing serious, sir."

"Are you anywhere near the Field Office there in Detroit?"

"That's downtown. Not too bad. Why? What is it?"

"I need you there ASAP. We intercepted a video. You're going to need to watch it for yourself. The most secure feed is at their cyber center."

I wanted to ask for more info, more clarification, but this line wasn't encrypted, and if he wanted me to know more he would've already told me.

"I'm on my way."

"When you get there, ask for SAC Kennedy."

++++

Blake and Mannie struck out at the first two martial arts studios and military supply stores they visited. However, at the third dojo, the rather brash karate instructor and two of his students snickered when Mannie asked them about a person fitting Dylan's description.

"Yeah, I've seen him," the guy said, "but I'm not planning to tell *you* anything about him."

"And why is that?"

He was glaring at Mannie. "Don't like people of your . . . *ethnicity*."

Blake shook his head. "Oh, that was not a smart thing to say."

"Really?"

"I'll tell you what." He nodded toward Mannie. "If any of you can knock him down just once, we'll leave. If he ends up being the only one standing, you tell us everything we want to know. Or, you can just tell us now and avoid any chance of injury and embarrassment."

He scoffed. "I'm a sixth-degree black belt. These are two of my top students."

"If you must."

"If I must?"

"Call for more help. You have my permission as long as it doesn't take too long for them to get here. We're on a bit of a tight schedule."

He sneered. "Screw you. I don't need help. I don't need anyone."

"Well," Blake said, "in that case, since there are only three of you, I suggest you work together, or I can't guarantee that any of you will be walking out of here."

Mannie cracked his neck as the three men surrounded him.

Probably to save face, the instructor went first. He sent a flying kick to the side of Mannie's head, but the metal plate that Mannie had on the left side of his skull from a car accident he'd been in twenty years earlier took the brunt of the kick.

When the man's heel smacked against it, he was the one who yelled out in pain.

He attacked Mannie a second time. Another flying kick, but Mannie snatched him out of the air, spun him around, and threw him roughly at the other two students.

After that, even when the other two black belts moved in to work together, there wasn't much of a fight.

None of their kicks or punches had any consequential effect on Blake's hulking friend, and in less than thirty seconds, all three of the black belts were on the floor groaning in pain.

Blake guessed that the bone sticking through the instructor's forearm was probably going to slow down his teaching for a while.

By the time he and Mannie left, they had the information they needed.

Dylan had indeed trained here a few times earlier in the summer. Though the instructor didn't have contact information for him, he did say that Dylan had some sort of connection to the city morgue at Grandshore Medical Center.

Before he was sent to prison, back when he was still active, Dylan would often visit the morgue to see the victims. Sometimes he broke in. Once he killed the custodian, wore his clothes, grabbed a mop, and simply walked in while a family was there to identify one of his victims.

Knowing that Dylan had a connection to the morgue here made sense, and was plenty for Blake to go on.

++++

When Sharyn met up with Schwartz at the 9th Precinct, she asked him to drive so she could look into a few things on the way.

As he hopped onto I-94 toward Inntoit2U Designs' office, first, she initiated a trace on Simone's phone, but Cyber wasn't able to locate it and, according to the phone company's records, there hadn't been any data usage on her account for the last two months.

She also reviewed Dylan's background, including his stint in the Army, to see if there was anything there that would help them find him now.

Finally, she familiarized herself with the Hook'dup app and began to study the types of profiles that got the most traffic and generated the most interest, already planning what to include if she set up an account herself.

45

I parked in the garage adjoining the federal building.

A hand-printed sign notified me that the staff entrance was closed for the day and included an arrow to the public one around the other side of the building.

Christie's daughter called as I was rounding the corner.

Because of the urgency of getting into this meeting, I debated whether or not to pick up, but out of concern for Christie, I answered it. "Tessa, are you—?"

"Well? I've been waiting, like, all day. Did you call Mom?"

"She's okay. I touched base with her this morning."

"But something's on her mind, right?"

"Something. Yes. She's going to call me again tonight. Until then, don't worry about her." I grabbed the door handle. "Right now I have an important appointment that I need to—"

"Do you know where she's going?"

While opening the door, I paused in midswing. "What do you mean?"

"Going, as in leaving. As in not being here. As in sending me to stay at Cherise's house tonight after the babysitting gig and staying there until this weekend."

"Tessa, what are you talking about?"

"I'm talking about my mom asking me if I could stay with my friend Cherise—like I just said—while she goes to visit a quote *friend*. Unquote."

"What friend?"

"Um, it's pretty clear she didn't say, or else I wouldn't have just told you 'quote' and 'unquote.' She's acting weird."

"And this friend, you don't know if it's—"

"*I don't know who it is!* That's why I'm calling you!"

"Okay. Hang on a sec. Let me think."

Christie hadn't mentioned visiting a friend and, although we were dating, we weren't married or even living together and she had no obligation to tell me where she was going or what she was doing.

But still, I wasn't thrilled that she was keeping something from me.

Oh, as if you're not doing the same thing when it comes to your history with Sharyn?

That's different.

No. Actually, that's pretty much the same.

"Tessa, tell me what you know."

"I just did!"

"Alright. Is she there now?"

"She slipped out to buy some power bars or something. I don't know."

An urgent and impatient-looking woman in a business suit was exiting the building and I held the door open but stepped to the side to give her space to leave. She bristled past me. "I'll call her," I told Tessa.

"I'm worried."

"I know."

"This isn't like her. Something's going on."

"Don't worry, Raven." I opted for the Edgar Allan Poe–

inspired nickname I called her sometimes and she seemed to actually like. "It's going to be fine. In the meantime, let me know if you hear from her. Text me."

"Promise?"

"Promise?"

"Do you promise it'll be fine?"

"Yes." As I said the word, I thought again of how the word "fine" does not always mean *good*, but I didn't get into that with Tessa. Sometimes reassurance is a gift you can offer people even if you have no direct control regarding the outcome. "I promise."

"Look, I gotta get ready for this babysitting thing tonight, but let me know what you find out, okay?"

"When I reach her, I'll have her call you. Until then, don't worry."

After hanging up, I tried Christie's number but she didn't answer.

I texted, asking her to give me a call, then entered the lobby and identified myself to the two guards flanking the metal detector. "Patrick Bowers. I'm here to see SAC Kennedy."

They verified my ID, then one of them led me past the first set of elevators to another elevator bank farther down the hall, where he swiped his badge.

Inside, he punched floor 4, then 26, 2, and 12, a combination that was some sort of code.

I looked at him curiously. "Which floor are we going to?"

"The one that doesn't exist." He pointed at the floor. "Going down, Agent Bowers. Way down."

46

Ali found the rest stop, pulled into a parking spot in a deserted corner of the lot, and turned off the ignition.

He let out a sigh of relief at having made it here safely.

He was still exhausted, and the adrenaline rush he'd gotten from the near-miss traffic accident had worn off.

Sleep.

Just rest.

Then you can pray and get back on the road.

He set an alarm for thirty minutes and closed his eyes.

++++

A stout, graying man in his late fifties met me as I exited the elevator.

He had a kind face and probing eyes that held an entire weather system in them and I liked him right away.

"Charles Kennedy."

"Patrick Bowers."

His handshake was crisp, brisk, professional.

"I spoke with Assistant Director DeYoung," he said. "My team is getting everything set so that we can watch the video in the suite at the end of the hall." I caught a touch of east Texas in his voice.

Kennedy invited me to follow him, and we made our

way down the hall past four rooms that were clearly designed for suspect interviews. "Agent Bowers, do you know the story about the biting worms?"

"Biting worms? No. I don't think so."

"Two men come upon a boy who's fishing in a creek. They ask him how the fish are biting and he says, 'Not so good.' Then he holds up a coffee can with some dirt in it and adds, 'But the worms sure are.' So they think that's a strange response, and they go on their way, but when they return an hour later, they find the boy lying there dead, and when they look in the can, it's full of baby copperheads. The boy had collected them, thinking they were worms."

It sounded like it might be an urban legend, but reality can sometimes be stranger than fiction.

"Is that true?" I asked.

"It's truth."

"Assumptions can get you killed?" I said. "Is that what you're trying to say?"

"Their consequences cannot be overestimated."

We arrived at the cyber center and he placed his palm on a scanner. "From what DeYoung tells me, when we see this video it'll be tough not to assume too much. Let's both of us hold back."

"Alright."

Then he pressed the door open.

All of the workstations in the room were oriented toward the eight sprawling video screens that covered one wall.

Four other agents were present, but Kennedy excused them all and they joined the guard from the front desk who'd followed us down the hallway, leaving the two of us alone.

Kennedy password-clicked his way past three levels of

security, then logged in to a video conference call with Assistant Director DeYoung.

"Pat." DeYoung looked as grim as he'd sounded earlier on the phone.

"Assistant Director."

"You scheduled a meeting with Maria Aguirre from OPR on Monday. What were you planning to discuss?"

I couldn't help but notice his use of the past tense, and being here under these somewhat obtuse circumstances, I didn't anticipate that my meeting with Maria had simply been canceled. "What's happened, sir?"

"You don't know where she went?"

"Ralph mentioned earlier that she'd entered Kazakhstan. That's all I know."

"And so, your meeting, though, what was it concerning?"

"I had reason to believe that she might have a connection to Blake."

"Why is that?"

"Too many coincidences. Too many arrows pointing in her direction."

"Go on."

When I was done delineating the reasons I'd come up with during my workout this morning for thinking that one of our Office of Professional Responsibility lawyers might be connected to a known terrorist, he said, "And you didn't bring this up with anyone?"

"She's OPR. Who else would I bring it up to except—"

"Me. Perhaps."

"Yes."

"And did you suspect me too, Pat?"

"Not suspect, sir. But consider—yes. Briefly."

DeYoung leaned to the side and spoke for a moment to someone offscreen. They kept their voices low so I couldn't make out what they were saying. When he appeared back on the monitor again, he said, "Okay. We're ready on this end. We're sending the link now."

Kennedy entered his credentials one final time and the main screen in front of us blinked on, showing the frozen image of a cement block–walled room. On the right, the corner of a cage that looked about a meter and a half high was visible on the edge of the screen.

On the next monitor over, two faces came up. I didn't recognize either of the people, but DeYoung said, "I've asked the Bureau's Bioweapons and Counterterrorism Director Dr. Chung Qiao and Dr. Kate Ferrier, the director of the CDC, to join us."

The FBI is the responding agency in the result of a terrorist act on United States soil, but the CDC is in charge in the case of a bioweapon attack or a disease outbreak.

I didn't know much about Dr. Vladislav Kuznetsov, the man we found hanged on Wednesday, but we did know he was a Cold War bioweapons researcher.

Bringing the CDC in made sense, considering the circumstances, but it did not bode well for Maria.

But what struck me most of all was the fact that I'd even been invited to participate in this video conference at all.

Why are they reading you in on this? What does it have to do with you?

"This video was intercepted by NSA," DeYoung explained. "They were following up on some jihadist chatter. The way my counterpart over there put it to me: 'One of our analysts dipped her hand into the data stream and came up with a fish we didn't even know was swimming in those waters.' A little too metaphorical, if you ask me, but you get the gist. As far as NSA can tell, there wasn't any disruption of the transmission, so it's unlikely that the sender or the receiver knows we have a copy."

"Okay," Dr. Ferrier said.

"We'll talk more after you've seen the footage. I think it's best if you simply watch it for yourself."

"Remember the worms," Kennedy whispered to me.

Then DeYoung signaled to him, he tapped the space bar, and the video began.

47

The footage lingered briefly on that cement wall, then panned right to include the cage, which I now realized was constructed in a cube. It didn't appear large enough for an adult to actually stand in.

A woman lay inside the cage, curled in a fetal position, her clothes crumpled and stained.

Her back was to the camera so I couldn't see her face, but given DeYoung's questions regarding Maria, it wasn't too difficult to postulate who the woman was.

Beyond the cage, the room's far wall contained a wide window to an observation area. Blurred figures stood behind the tinted glass. Unrecognizable faces. Ghostly images.

A voice-over came on speaking Arabic, a language I could only identify but not understand.

However, a moment later an English voice offered what I expected was the translation: "We are ready to move forward as we've discussed. This is one of the infidels who works for the United States government. This is a demonstration of what we have succeeded in accomplishing and a promise of what is to come."

I couldn't tell if the speaker was the person filming or not, but he was obviously close to the camera's microphone.

It was clear now that Maria wasn't alone in the room. The people behind the glass were just observers. Someone else near the camera said, "When will she wake up?"

"It shouldn't be long now," another voice said. Male. A light Middle Eastern accent, but the English sounded natural, perhaps someone who'd been raised in or studied in the States.

A digital date and time marker was running in the lower right-hand corner of the screen, and flicked to approximately five minutes later, indicating that the film had been edited.

She stirred, then turned.

Yes.

Maria.

Her disheveled hair covered half of her face. The part that was visible was savagely swollen and bruised.

She'd been beaten.

Beaten badly.

The person filming her walked closer until he—or she—was only a few meters away.

More Arabic.

No translation this time.

There was no way this was going to end well.

A dog's water dish and food bowl sat inside the cage beside Maria.

Defiantly, she snatched up the food bowl and threw its contents at the person with the camera, an act that clearly couldn't harm anyone, but also, just as clearly, communicated her resolve not to be intimidated.

"Maria," the man said, "if you help me, I will help you."

"I'm not helping you with anything. No matter what you do to me."

"I'm afraid it's already been done."

He exited. Whoever was holding the camera stabilized it, setting it perhaps on some sort of stand.

Although the video was approximately fourteen minutes long, the time marker showed her rapid decline over what would have been the following five days.

It started with sores that made me think of chickenpox. They first appeared on her arms and face. Over time, they darkened and became firm, and, based on how she scratched at them, they must have itched terribly as they hardened.

As time passed, she occasionally spoke to a man in a biohazard suit who returned sporadically to watch her or refill the bowls with water or food. He wore a self-contained breathing unit, a full face mask, and a positive pressure air respirator that allowed him to have filtered air rather than breathe what was in the room.

She must have become more and more disoriented and incoherent, because her shirt was soaked with sweat when she took it off for no apparent reason and threw it toward the observation room. Her abdomen was also covered with the rash and ulcers. It felt a bit intrusive to see her crouching there in her bra, but even more so to see the intimacy of her suffering.

Toward the end, she was hemorrhaging from her nose and eyes and I couldn't even imagine how much pain she was in. Eventually, at about the ten-minute mark, I learned the reason I'd been brought in to watch this.

Maria mentioned my name.

She faced the camera, at this point barely even distinguishable as the woman I knew. "Agent Bowers." Her voice was raspy and coarse, but also somehow liquidy and wet.

"The Russian women who don't speak. Follow them. Listen to what the ladies say."

I figured the people filming this must have guessed that she was simply delusional, and that's why they didn't edit it out. If it was a code of some kind, its meaning eluded me.

DeYoung paused the video at that point. "Do you know what she's referring to, Pat?"

Dr. Ferrier answered before I could. "Probably human trafficking. Or maybe it's something related to the human rights of women in Muslim countries."

"No." I shook my head. "I don't think so. The women who don't speak—I think it has to do with the mannequins."

"Mannequins?" she said.

"Blake's. The silent ladies." I explained to them about the frequent appearances of female mannequins located in the places where he worked. "I spoke with Maria about this a couple of weeks ago in relationship to the investigation into Blake's whereabouts."

"Did anyone else know about that conversation?" DeYoung asked.

"No."

"Why Russian women?" Dr. Ferrier asked, "And what does it mean to follow them or listen to them?"

"I'm not sure," I said. "But we need to take a closer look at the mannequins we found in Dr. Kuznetsov's house. See if we can find out where they were made or shipped from—if it's Russia."

DeYoung started the video again.

Watching Maria's suffering was profoundly troubling.

As the sores spread and the hemorrhaging increased, she

became weaker and weaker, and eventually, when her suffering was the most severe, she begged the man in the biosuit to shoot her.

Rather than a gun, however, he retrieved a scimitar that had been left somewhere out of view of the camera.

"Stick your hands through the bars," he said in rough, whispery English. He must have been using some sort of mic for us to hear his words under that air mask.

"What?" she said.

"Your hands. If you want this to be over, I will help you. If you wish to die quickly, slide them through the bars."

Trembling, she complied.

He laid a board on the floor outside the cage.

Oh no.

"Lower them to the wood."

Though I wanted to turn away, I knew I needed to watch this all the way through to the end.

She knelt and placed her palms upright on the wood, in a pose that might have been that of a supplicant before her god.

Her spirit was broken. That was perhaps the hardest thing of all to see.

The man raised the sword, then whispered, "Die in your rage," a phrase I'd seen tweeted by jihadists after terror attacks, a Qur'anic saying that Islamic extremists sometimes used to mock and celebrate the death of the innocent.

Swiftly, definitively, he brought the sword down, severing both of her hands at the wrist.

48

Amid a wash of blood, Maria collapsed backward, even as her severed hands remained on the board outside the cage, creating a viscerally disturbing image that I knew I would never be able to unsee.

Blood spurted from the two stumps at the ends of her arms.

Arterial bleeding. She did not try to stop it.

Death would come swiftly.

And for her, that would be a form of mercy.

Maria shivered as she died, almost as if she were freezing to death rather than bleeding out.

The camera zoomed in on her and didn't pan away until she lay still, slumped against the bars of the cage. At last, it pivoted from her body, lingered on her hands, and then rotated to focus on a flag bearing the symbol of The Brigade of the Prophet's Sword, before the screen faded to black.

For a long moment, no one spoke.

Finally, I said, "Is that disease what I think it is? Is that smallpox?"

Dr. Ferrier replied, "To establish its etiology, we would need to confirm the presence of nucleic material of the *variola* virus in a clinical specimen."

"Clearly, we would need to do tests, Kate," said Dr. Qiao, somewhat impatiently. "Based on what you can see, what would you say?"

"If the time markers on the bottom of the screen are accurate and haven't been altered, it's not smallpox. No strain of the virus progresses that quickly after the symptoms first precipitate themselves."

"At least not in its natural form," I said. "But if it were genetically altered?"

Dr. Ferrier asked DeYoung to slide the video back to the seven-minute mark.

After he'd reset it, she told him to press play.

As we watched Maria's anguish again, Dr. Ferrier said, "With the manifestations on the skin, it appears to be an acute vesicular or pustular rash. But there are any number of those. It could be varicella, herpes simplex, or *Erythema multiforme.* Maybe an enteroviral infection or even contact dermatitis."

Dr. Qiao scoffed. "You know as well as I do, Kate, that it isn't any of those."

"It might be impetigo—"

"It's a strain of smallpox we haven't seen before," he said unequivocally.

I didn't know what their history was with each other, but obviously they were not on the same page regarding what we could and could not assume in a situation like this.

"Alright, listen," I interjected. "I understand that we can't test it or confirm anything definitively right now. Let's just work from the hypothesis that it is smallpox. What would that mean? What are the implications?"

Dr. Qiao spoke up. "It's one of the most deadly and contagious diseases the world has ever seen. In the twentieth century alone, smallpox killed over three hundred million people. The last confirmed naturally occurring smallpox death was in 1977 in Somalia. Since the disease was eradicated worldwide, the general population hasn't been vaccinated against it. Not since 1980."

Dr. Ferrier took over, almost as if they were tag-teaming the explanation. "Today, since it doesn't naturally occur anymore, even one instance of it is considered an outbreak. There is no effective treatment. There's no known cure. It's fatal about thirty-five percent of the time. However, some strains will have a ninety-eight to one hundred percent fatality rate."

"In 1980," Dr. Qiao concluded, "all of the world's remaining smallpox samples were taken to the CDC and the Russian equivalent in Moscow. Do you want the official reason or the real reason why it was those two countries?"

"Official first," Kennedy said.

"Because the U.S. and Russia could provide the most secure places to house the samples until the decision could be made about whether or not to destroy them all for good."

"And the real reason?"

"Balance of power. There wouldn't be just one superpower that would have the ability to study and perhaps weaponize it."

Kennedy processed that. "Okay. Let's say both countries did. From what you know, does this look like a strain we would have produced or they would have?"

We all directed our attention to Dr. Qiao, who was slow in replying. "This isn't anything our country has developed."

"Well, in any case, we have enough vaccine stored in our

warehouses to vaccinate the entire U.S. population," Dr. Ferrier reassured us.

"But we don't know if the vaccine would be effective against this strain, right?" I said.

She fumbled for a reply, and finally gave a qualified answer: "It's possible that it might not be as effective as we would hope. Unlikely, but possible."

"Let's get back to the genetic modification possibility. If someone were altering the virus to be used as a bioweapon, what changes would they make to it?"

"I'll let Dr. Qiao answer that," she said stiffly.

He thought for a moment. "You would want a fine-particle aerosol delivery system that would transmit and deposit the virus into the nasal, oral, or pharyngeal mucosal membranes. An inhaler, nose or throat spray, anything along those lines. You're trying to get it into the alveoli of the lungs. Once it's there . . ." He shook his head. "Well, you just saw what'll happen."

Assistant Director DeYoung clarified, "I think Patrick was wondering what specific changes you would make in how the virus is spread."

"If you were genetically modifying it, you'd want to keep the person vertical and infectious before they become bedridden and incapacitated. Ideally, make it transmissible before the symptoms appear. The longer the carriers are walking around without knowing they're contagious, the more the disease will spread. Second, increase its virulence. Third, if possible, make it contagious not just through aerosol means, but also through dermal contact."

"Excuse me," Dr. Ferrier interjected. "Let's not get ahead of ourselves. First of all, we don't know who developed this. We don't know where this event occurred. And we haven't even been able to examine a laboratory specimen. Also, this video could be a fake."

"No," I said. "No one else knew about our conversation regarding the silent ladies. It's not fake."

DeYoung glanced at his vibrating phone. "That's the Director. I need to bring this to a close. Here's what we know: Blake is free, on the run. We have a dead germ warfare specialist from the Cold War who's somehow tied to him, and now we have the threat of a smallpox outbreak related to a known terrorist group. Patrick, I want you to figure out what her message means. Kennedy, I'll keep you informed about any progress we make at this end. Kate and Chung, you two work up a timeline and an interagency response plan. We need quarantine and social distancing recommendations. I'll have my team try to identify where this video was filmed and we'll see if NSA can track down the digital fingerprints of the receiver. Are there any more questions at this time?"

"Do you want me to return to New York City?" I asked.

"No. Stay there. We don't have enough information yet to justify bringing you back. However, be ready to board a flight if I need you to. Don't share what you've seen with anyone there in Detroit. We can't risk a panic."

"Understood."

Kennedy spoke up. "Has this been posted anywhere online?"

"Not that we can tell," DeYoung replied. "But believe me, we're looking everywhere we can for it."

The Bureau's Cyber Division has been working on a new program called Bloodhound, which can search for images or videos online and delete them wherever they appear. Even if someone has downloaded the video, Bloodhound can sniff it out on their hard drive and remove it. The program cycles through sixteen thousand times per second. We knew that even though civil liberties and privacy advocacy groups would eventually be bringing lawsuits against the Bureau, for now, in a few limited cases involving national security, we'd been using Bloodhound under the radar.

I assumed that my friend Angela Knight would be sending her hound out to search for the video online—on both the Internet and the Dark Web.

"By the way, Pat," De Young said to me, "I'm reading Hawkins in on this. I'll keep you briefed."

And with that, he ended the video conference.

++++

Ali woke up from the nap feeling somewhat groggy, but refreshed enough to tackle the second half of his drive.

After his prayers.

He took a minute to stretch his legs, and then carried his prayer mat across the lawn to a quiet, shady, deserted picnic area about fifty meters from the parking lot.

A formidable-looking young man about Ali's age watched him from where he and three friends stood beside a vending machine.

Using a compass app on his phone, Ali oriented himself to Mecca. Then he laid out the mat and began his afternoon prayers.

Today, despite his best efforts, his thoughts strayed from focusing on the Mercy of Allah and drifted toward this trip to Dearborn, to the meeting he would be having tomorrow with Fayed, to the number of hours left before he would be contagious.

To how many people would be infected within the next seven days.

And to the incalculable masses that would be dead within seven more.

He begged Allah, the Beneficent, the Merciful, for a pure mind and the courage to make the right choices, and for forgiveness for being distracted even now, when he should have been focused on the One he was pledging his devotion to rather than being concerned at all about himself.

49

Even though Tessa's hair was only shoulder length, it got tangled a lot and when she didn't stay on top of things, it ended up looking like a mop dipped in India ink flopping around on top of her head, which was just plain annoying.

She yanked at the brush. It hurt. So she yanked harder.

Seriously? Her mom leaves without telling her where she's going—to see a friend, whoever that might be?

"I'll call you when I get there," her mom said right before she left.

"I can't believe you're not telling me what's going on."

"It's just something I need to take care of."

Tessa stared at her. "This doesn't have to do with my dad, does it?"

"Your dad?"

"Yeah. My. Dad. The guy who bailed on you when you were pregnant with me. The guy who's never shown up *even once* over all these years to wish me a happy birthday or tell me not to play video games so much or hassle me about my boyfriends or wait up for me when I come back late after my curfew so that he could yell at me in a way that told me he loved me even though he was mad at me. My dad."

"No. No, it doesn't. This has nothing to do with him."

So then, her mom ran through the instructions for her, told her to call Jodie, the FBI agent they were sharing the apartment with, if there were any problems, and then made sure she had enough money for a cab so she wouldn't have to take the subway to Cherise's when she was done babysitting tonight.

After picking up her purse, her mom leaned in to give her a kiss on the forehead, but Tessa stepped back before she could.

Now, Tessa went back to trying to brush her stupid, stupid hair, and *also* figure out how she was supposed to babysit those two kids without being upset about her mom the entire time.

Before leaving for Rachel's house, she remembered that the girl she would be babysitting was five, and that when she was little, hugging her teddy bear Francesca made her feel safe—okay, so maybe that still worked, but that wasn't the point.

With Jodie and her mom gone, she really didn't want to be at their apartment alone right now. Even though it was too early to head over to the lady's house where she was going to be babysitting, Tessa grabbed her stuff, brought Francesca with her, and left to get a cup of coffee before heading across town.

++++

"Take this exit," Sharyn told Detective Schwartz.

"Nope. I think it's the next one," he said.

"Trust me. Exit here."

He sighed and grudgingly made the turn.

Inntoit2U Designs would be located about a mile down the road.

"You know what you're gonna ask 'em?" he said.

"Besides why people who use their app keep showing up dead?"

"Yeah."

"I'm hoping we can get a master list of everyone who has set up a Hook'dup account."

Over the course of their drive, she'd discovered that the profiles of the first four victims had been 404'd so now there wasn't any trace of them, but Jamika's information was still accessible. Also, she heard the update that there was no DNA from the bed sheets at the scene of Jamika's homicide and nothing usable from the tunnel where the shrine had been.

"Huh," Ted said when he noticed they were passing Henry Ruff Road. "Looks like you were right after all. We should be there in a couple minutes."

50

Ali finished his prayers, returned the prayer mat to the car, and then went to use the men's toilet before resuming his trip to Dearborn.

He had just finished at the urinal and was washing his hands when the four men he'd seen earlier beside the vending machine entered the restroom.

Two of them walked toward the urinals behind him, one stayed by the door, and the other approached him and began rinsing his hands at the next sink over.

It was the young man who'd been watching him pray.

"Hey, bro."

"Hello," Ali replied.

"Saw you kneeling out there. Not feeling good?"

"I'm alright. Thank you."

"What were you doing?"

"Doing?"

"Kneeling down like that. Thought maybe you were carsick or something."

"I was praying."

"Praying."

"Yes."

The man finished at the sink and shook his hands dry

rather than using the paper towels hanging from the dispenser nearby. "To who?"

Go, Ali. This is not good.

"Have a good day," Ali told him, but as he turned toward the door, the man stepped in front of him, blocking his path.

"Whoa. Easy. We were just having a little conversation here, right? You're gonna walk off in the middle of it without answering my question? That's kind of rude, don't you think? I was just wondering who you were praying to."

"Allah. Most Gracious. Most Merciful."

"Oh, Allah most merciful. Huh. Is this the same merciful Allah who ordered his people to kill the infidels wherever they might be found? You know, Hadith 9:4?" He eyed Ali. "Yeah. You do, don't you? Or Surah 9:5. The Verse of the Sword, and its command to 'slay the idolaters wherever you find them.' That's always a good one, right?"

"I have nothing against you, sir."

He turned to his friends. "You hear that, guys? He doesn't have anything against me. That's—man—that's reassuring." He faced Ali again. "Did I say you did?"

"No. If you'll excuse me."

Ali took one step, but the man didn't move.

"Let me ask you a question—why do you people hate us?"

"I don't hate you. My people don't hate you."

"Oh, I think they do."

The men by the urinals zipped up and faced Ali.

"I'm Bill." The man shook more water from his fingertips, clearly unconcerned that some of it landed on Ali. "And you are?"

"My name is Ali."

"Ali? Like Muhammad Ali?" Bill shadowboxed, threw a couple of fake punches. "Are you a boxer?"

"No."

"Abrogation. That mean anything to you? How the later verses in the Qur'an trump the earlier ones?" He winked knowingly at Ali. "And those verses Muhammad wrote in Mecca aren't quite as peace-loving as the ones he wrote in Medina, are they? Come on. You know what I'm talking about, right?"

"I don't want any trouble. I just want to return to my car."

"I'm not making any trouble. Are we making any trouble here, guys?"

The other men told him that no, they were not. No one was making any trouble here.

Bill said, "My brother was in Maiduguri on January tenth. You recognize that?"

"I've never heard of Maiduguri."

"Oh, well, it's in Nigeria. What about Kaheesha Youssef? Do you know that name?"

"No."

"Yeah. Makes sense. It was never released to the public. With child suicide bombers, the media doesn't usually share their names. But I did some digging. I found out hers."

"I—"

"January tenth. That was the day she blew herself up. You know how old she was? Ten. She killed twenty-nine other people in the market that day. My brother was a news correspondent covering the upsurge of violence in Nigeria. The girl's bomb ripped him in half. The survivors said the girl was shouting *'Allahu Akbar,'* right before she did it."

Ali felt bile rising in his throat.

Yemen.

The scimitar.

All the hatred.

All the death.

"I am very sorry for your loss."

"Right," Bill said. "Well, but it's not just mine, though, is it? More than twenty families lost people in the market that day. Are you a jihadist, Ali?"

"Those people are extremists. They do not represent all Muslims."

"Yeah. Right. No, I get it. They're the violent ones. You follow Muhammad instead."

"I follow the Qur'an, which he introduced into the world."

"So what about Jesus? Oh wait. You call him Isa, don't you? Well, wouldn't it make more sense to follow the teachings of a man who was born of a virgin, a man who never sinned, than those of a pedophile who married a nine-year-old-girl?"

"Aisha was nineteen when she married Muhammad, Peace Be Upon Him."

"Peace be upon a pedophile, but not upon us, huh? Not upon the rest of the world? Not upon those people in the market that day?"

"Islam is a religion of peace." But even as Ali said the words, he knew it was a misleading statement. Islam is not about love or about hate, about peace or about war, it is about submission. Islam is about submitting to Allah above all else. That might result in peace. It might result in war, but neither of those mattered as much as following Allah. But that was too much to explain.

"A religion of peace. Over the last fifteen years, 99.5%

of suicide bombings in the world have been committed by Muslims. If you hear about a suicide bombing and you just happen to venture a guess that it was a Muslim who did it, you're gonna be right 99.5% of the time." He turned to his friends. "That sound like a religion of peace to you?"

They shook their heads. The one closest to the door said, "Doesn't sound peaceful to me."

"Me neither." Once again he addressed them rather than Ali. "There aren't too many things in this life that you can be 99.5% sure of, are there, guys?"

No, they agreed. There weren't too many things you could be that sure of.

The men tightened their circle around Ali.

Get out.

Now!

Ali shoved one of them aside and rushed for the door, but Bill grabbed him before he could escape, threw him against the wall, and punched him brutally in the jaw.

The force of the blow whipped Ali around, but on the way to the floor, he smacked his forehead against the sink.

A deafening *crack*.

A jolt that shot through him.

He collided with the floor.

A whirl of pain pounded against the inside of his skull, a deep, throbbing, tightening vise that seemed to grow thicker and harsher with each beat of his heart.

From somewhere in the fog descending around him, Ali heard one of the men say that they should kick him once for each of the people who died that day in the market, and they may have, he had no way to tell. He lost track of the number of times their shoes and boots slammed into his face, his stomach, his ribs.

Get up!

Fight back!

But no, he did not.

Someone deserved to be punished for the innocent people who'd died in that Nigerian marketplace, for every innocent person who'd ever died at the hands of those who claimed to follow a God, by any name.

He lost track of everything, of pain, of conscious thought, until he knew only darkness, even as he prayed for forgiveness for himself and what he was doing this week, and for the men who were now making him pay for the sins of his people.

51

Christie still hadn't called, but she did text me: I'm going to be out of town for a couple days. I'll be in touch.

I wasn't sure if I should forward the text to Tessa, but in the end, I figured I would leave the issue of communicating her plans to Christie. However, I did send Christie a message that I was here if she wanted to talk.

Regarding the case, there was a lot to process.

Rather than head back to the motel, after I'd grabbed a sandwich from the federal building's cafeteria, SAC Kennedy gave me the keys to an empty office on the twenty-third floor, and I spent some time analyzing the data in order to pull the geoprofile together, and also trying to discern what Maria's words meant.

Through it all, however, the images of her locked in that cage, the suffering she went through, and that final, brutal footage of the man with the sword hacking off her hands kept haunting me.

Why Russian women? Did she mention Russian women just because of the scientist?

Or maybe she was delusional after all?

No, I didn't buy that.

We had a portion of a shipping manifest in Dr. Kuznetsov's things. Maybe that tied in with this somehow? A shipment from Russia? Human trafficking or under-the-radar travel, but why would the mannequins matter?

"Listen to what the ladies say."

But how do the silent speak?

I followed up with DeYoung to have the team redouble their efforts at identifying the contents of the manifest, and analyzing the composition of the mannequins. "Maybe we can find a lot number or serial number that can help us track where they were before they ended up in Dr. Kuznetsov's house," I told him.

Then I checked my messages.

Three had come in.

(1) The autopsy confirmed Jamika Karon's time of death and that she'd died as a result of a single gunshot wound to the chest.

(2) Mimi's texts to Canyon were benign and fit what he'd told us.

(3) Canyon Robbins had died.

The shock of that last message hit me hard.

I tried to let it sink in. It's so hard when you see someone, speak to him, and then soon afterward, find out he's passed away. It's like a punch in the gut, a stark reminder of the brevity of life and the inevitability of death.

We live.

We die.

The ripples pass away.

And then, all too quickly, the surface becomes smooth once again.

Canyon's father was the medical examiner. I wondered

if he would do an autopsy or have his assistant take care of it. I expected that either way, they would want specific answers regarding how he'd died from complications related to that stab wound.

Assumptions are just too easy to make and too often wrong.

Kennedy's story of the biting worms came to mind.

Death often follows on the heels of not quite getting the facts straight.

++++

"Hey, buddy, you alright?"

To Ali, the words seemed to be liquid, dripping onto him, seeping into him, landing and—

Someone was nudging his shoulder now. "Buddy?"

Ali opened his eyes but immediately had to squinch them shut again because of the unyielding light staring down at him from the fluorescents on the bathroom ceiling.

Turning to the side, he tried opening them again and found that his vision was smeared, especially through his left eye, making it hard to see anything clearly.

"Yes?" he muttered in a faraway, distant voice that seemed to come from someone else, a bit like it had sounded when he first spoke to Fayed after being left in that room in Yemen for four days at the start of his training.

"You alright?" the man asked worriedly.

Ali tried to sit up, but the blazing fire in his side sent him dropping to the floor again. He'd never had a cracked rib before, but the sharp pain in his side with every breath made it pretty clear what had happened.

The man, who was obese and wore khaki shorts and flip-flops, had his phone out. "I'll call an ambulance for ya."

Ali shook his head. "No, no. I'm okay."

"What happened?"

"I slipped."

"You—?"

At last, Ali found a way to sit up, masking the pain the best he could. "I just slipped."

"You don't look so good."

"Really, I'm okay, sir. Thank you."

The man continued to insist that he help him up, and in order to avoid making a scene, Ali finally accepted his offer.

When he was on his feet at last, even though the guy continued to fret over him, Ali simply thanked him and assured him, as convincingly as possible, that he was fine.

Before turning toward the door, Ali caught sight of his reflection in the mirror.

His face was a mess of blood and bruises, his upper lip split in half, his left eye swollen nearly shut.

"You really don't look good." The man who was trying so hard to be helpful lamely handed him a crumple of damp paper towels. "Maybe this'll help?"

Ali thanked him once more, took the paper towels, and then quickly escaped out the door and made his way to the car.

The four men who'd beaten him were nowhere to be seen.

As he stumbled up to the rental, the pain in his stomach tightened, and he found himself crumpling to his knees and throwing up. Finally, he made his way into the driver's seat and locked the doors.

With his side raging against him, he used the paper towels to wipe some of the vomit out of his mouth and some of the blood off his face, but he didn't want to wait around here too long, so as soon as he could, he pulled out of the parking lot and merged onto the highway.

Thinking about Azaliya.

And about that ten-year-old girl who'd blown herself up and killed all those people.

Kaheesha Youssef.

He didn't like knowing her name. It made it harder to accept what she'd been sent into that market to do.

52

Sharyn stepped out of the car while Schwartz answered his phone.

Inntoit2U Designs was located in a strip mall that contained a sub shop, a furniture rental store with one of those tall, wobbly, blowy balloon men outside, and a yoga studio—with yin-yang symbols painted on the glass of the front window.

Schwartz said, "This call might take a few minutes. I'll be in as soon as I can."

Sharyn went inside. A blast of overly conditioned air breezed into her face from a vent directly above her head.

In the corner, a basset hound lounged near the wall and lazily tilted his head her way without bothering to lift it from his paws. A wan young man, who looked twenty-five at the oldest, smiled at her from behind a stand-up desk. His hair was short-cropped, but his Amish-style beard was not. Glasses. Jeans. A plaid shirt. He looked like he might be auditioning for the part of Quintessential Millennial Computer Geek in a sitcom.

"Can I help you?" he asked amiably.

"I'm looking for the person who developed the Hook'dup app," Sharyn told him.

"For?"

"For?"

"What are you looking for him for?" He was still smiling.

The door opened behind her and Schwartz came in. The hound gave him the once-over as well.

"I'm Agent Weist with the FBI," she told the man. "This is Detective Schwartz. We'd like to ask the developer a few questions."

"Oh." He swallowed slightly.

"What's your name?" Sharyn asked.

"Chip. But you're gonna want to talk to Tony." He leaned back and called over his shoulder, "Hey, Ton?"

When no one replied, Chip said, "'Scuse me a sec. I'll be right back." He disappeared through the hanging bead doorway behind him, but his hurried footsteps told Sharyn that he was hightailing it down the hall and wasn't trying to locate Tony—if Tony even existed.

She called for Schwartz to cover the front in case the guy doubled back, then she threw the beads aside and sprinted down the hallway, passing two empty rooms on the way.

Out the back door.

Chip disappeared around the corner of the building toward a chain-link fence encircling a thistle-filled field nearby.

Sharyn dashed after him. "Stop!"

He must have spent a lot more time behind his computer desk than on a treadmill, because she gained on him quickly and, while he was trying unsuccessfully to scramble over the relatively tame six-foot-high fence, she caught up with him.

Schwartz angled around the building about forty yards away.

Sharyn pulled Chip down from the fence and he collapsed out of breath onto the grass, cowering behind one hand as he begged Sharyn not to shoot him.

By then, Schwartz had his gun out. "Hands to the side!" he ordered. "Now!"

Sharyn patted Chip down and then told Schwartz to lower his weapon.

At this point, cuffing Chip was a judgment call, so she said, "I like to speak to people without distraction and without them running off in the middle of the conversation. Do I need to handcuff you?"

Chip shook his head urgently. "No, no, no. I won't run."

"If you do, we'll have to arrest you," Detective Schwartz said. "Understand?"

He nodded, still clearly rattled. "I didn't do anything,"

"Then why'd you run?" Sharyn asked.

"I don't know. I was scared."

"Don't you know it's not smart to run from an FBI agent or a cop?" she said. "We might be led to think that you have something to hide."

"Do you have something to hide?" Schwartz pressed him.

"Me? No."

"Your team developed the Hook'dup app. We want to know about it."

"If you mean by 'my team,' 'me,' then yes."

"You're the team?"

"I'm the only employee."

"Okay," Sharyn said. "Tell us about the app."

"It's completely legal. Seriously. I researched everything. It's not breaking any laws."

"Talk us through it."

"It's super simple. You click in, set up an account, list your preferences. Only takes a couple minutes."

"Preferences?" Schwartz asked.

"Yeah, like male/female/she-male."

"I don't even want to know what that is," he muttered disgustedly.

"What is this about, anyway?" Chip said. "I know it's all legal. Tons of people are developing dating apps."

"Yes, but not ones that encourage people to trespass."

"It's just an app to help people meet. What they do after that is up to them."

"Uh-huh."

"The app notifies them if a location is open for use or not and if there are likely any cops in the area."

Sharyn eyed him curiously. "How do you know when officers might be patrolling the neighborhood?"

"Police dispatch. It's public domain information. I analyzed the calls from the last two years, came up with an algorithm for identifying the most likely sites for different patrols on different days to work out a rudimentary work routine for different precincts. It wasn't really that hard. It's all legal, I—"

"You keep saying all this is legal," Schwartz said gruffly.

"Yeah, it is . . . It's . . . Am I in trouble?"

"That depends. Have you done anything wrong?"

"It's free. I don't get any money from this."

"That's not what I asked you."

"Okay, slow down for a second," Sharyn said to Chip. "Who pays for your time developing it? The research, the coding, the office space?"

"Angel investors. They see potential. These days, you

gotta have a track record before you start selling apps. That's what Hook'dup is for us—well, for me. I invited urban explorers, photographers, really anyone who wants to take pictures of the sites to contribute to the app. It's all wiki-based. People work together."

"We know what 'wiki' refers to." Schwartz sounded like he was really starting to lose his patience.

"Does one of your contributors go by the name 'Igazi'?" Sharyn asked.

"Yeah. How did you know that?"

"We're looking for him. Do you know how to locate him?"

"Um . . ."

"I'll take that as a yes. Tell me."

"All of our communication has been through TypeKnot, so I don't know his phone number, or address, or anything. TypeKnot doesn't keep a record of chats."

"I'm going to need the list of your investors and access to the wiki page of contributors."

"No, really, I can't give you all that. It's supposed to be confidential."

"Chip," Sharyn said firmly. "We're going to track this information down either with your help or without it. Do you really want added scrutiny by the FBI? Word gets out that you're at the heart of a federal investigation, that can't be good for business—or for instilling more trust in your investors."

"Okay, okay. I'll help you."

To Sharyn, it seemed like he gave in a little too fast there. Resisting one moment.

Then willing to help just seconds later.

"And records of everyone who has downloaded or is using the app," Schwartz added.

"What?" Chip gasped. "Why? Why do you need that?"

Back to resisting again.

"For the investigation," Schwartz said bluntly. "We have a growing body count, and every one of 'em is using this app."

"Body count?" Chip gulped. "I don't know anything about that."

"Are your files back at your office?"

He nodded.

"Well then." Sharyn gestured for him to get moving. "After you."

++++

I contacted Sharyn, and she told me that she was on the way back to the app developer's office, that he'd tried to run, but it looked like we would be able to get the information we needed.

"I didn't know if you'd heard yet," I said, "but I wanted to make sure you got word that Canyon passed away."

"What? We were just there this morning." Shock and surprise cut through every word. "He seemed to be recovering."

"I know." Words in instances like this always failed me.

It's not a coincidence, Pat. Something else happened.

Maybe not. Don't assume!

All I could think to say was, "I feel terrible for his family."

"And those kids who were with him when he was stabbed."

"Yeah."

Then we were both quiet.

DeYoung had been clear that I wasn't to mention the situation with Maria to anyone, so I didn't bring it up, but in the end just told Sharyn that I would be working at the federal building and to touch base with me later tonight.

53

Blake had been hoping that there wouldn't be much happening at the morgue today, but this was Detroit, and it did average nearly a homicide a day, so he wasn't too shocked to see the medical examiner's team transferring a body into the building for an autopsy.

He and Mannie were seated at a restaurant across the street. Even given an entire day, he wouldn't have been able to eat all the ribs that Mannie had polished off in the last fifteen minutes.

"Dylan always had a thing for drugs." Mannie wiped some of the barbeque sauce off his chin. "You want me to start poking around, see if any dealers might've seen him over the last couple months?"

"No, not yet," Blake said. "I don't want to draw any more attention to us being in the city than we need to." He tapped his phone. "I'll stay here, keep an eye on the morgue, and do some online searches for locations where the meeting might occur tomorrow between Fayed and Ali. Why don't you look for a place where we can take Dylan after we find him."

"Somewhere quiet and private?"

"Yes. You know the kind of place."

"I believe I do." Mannie rose and left the restaurant.

Using his phone and headphones, Blake watched the footage that'd been uploaded on Wednesday evening at the site of the murder of a young African-American woman and saw two people entering the house. The woman, he didn't recognize. But he did recognize the man.

Special Agent Patrick Bowers.

Hmm.

If Dylan was here, Bowers might be the answer to everything.

Working from the assumption that if Bowers was called in to work on a case in Detroit, it would be a serial homicide investigation, Blake took some time to research the details regarding the woman's death and the theories out there on different forums about how she was killed, and about others who were supposedly murdered by the same man.

And with every new murder Blake read about, he became more convinced that this had to do with his brother.

It didn't take long to figure out that the woman's autopsy had been earlier this afternoon. So the timing worked perfectly. If Dylan was going to return to the morgue to view the body this evening, as he'd done so often in Los Angeles, Blake would be waiting for him.

++++

Sharyn's car was still at the 9th Precinct parking lot, so after she and Schwartz had what they needed from Chip, they returned to the station and Schwartz dropped her off.

To save time, rather than battle traffic and drive to the fed building at this time of day, she found an empty desk at the precinct and flipped open her laptop.

First, she wrote a note of condolence to Dr. Robbins, the medical examiner, regarding the loss of his son, and offered to help him and his family out if there was anything she could do.

It wasn't much, but at least it was something. She decided to follow up later, after the initial swell of support had passed.

Then, she sorted through what was in front of her.

Three things in particular:

(1) Have the Bureau's Cyber Division analyze the information from Inntoit2U Designs to try to find a relationship between the crime site locations and user analytics.

(2) Figure out if Dylan really was behind the homicides here in Detroit.

(3) Do whatever was necessary to draw him out or provoke him to make a mistake.

She'd heard about Angela Knight and her computer, Lacey, in Cyber. Angela treated Lacey as a fellow agent and, according to what Sharyn had heard, it was best to play along if you wanted to get results. Hoping that they might be able to help, Sharyn put a voice call through to Angela, who immediately transferred her to video instead.

Angela looked weary and worried, and Sharyn had the sense that the woman hadn't slept much at all in the last couple days. Or weeks.

After introducing herself and giving a quick rundown of what was happening, Sharyn said, "Is there any way that someone on your team could review this data regarding the Hook'dup app?"

Angela glanced anxiously at her watch. "There's something big going on here, Agent Weist. I can't guarantee that we could get to this for at least the next twenty-four hours."

"This deals with five linked homicides here in Detroit," Sharyn emphasized. "From everything we know, the killer might very well strike again."

Angela bit her lip and shook her head slightly. "I'm not . . . Lacey and I are just really backed up."

"At least let me send you the analytics. Maybe if you have a break, you can take a look. We're specifically searching for a connection between the victims and other users—particularly one with a military background who might be targeting them. Dylan Neeson. I know Pat spoke with you about him earlier."

A tired sigh. "I'll tell you what. Send it to me. I'll see what I can figure out. If I can't get to it, I'll see if Lacey can get it processed."

Sharyn thanked her and, after hanging up, immediately passed the information along. Then she moved on to the search for Dylan.

Her last communication with Simone back in May was through TypeKnot. For that app she'd chosen the username Snowball4, so now she used the same name to begin setting up a profile on Hook'dup to lure the Bluebeard toward her.

To draw the spider out.

54

For the next few hours I remained sequestered in the office on the twenty-third floor working on the geoprofile, entering data, analyzing the locations of the crimes, and puzzling over Maria's "Russian women" comment.

I still hadn't heard from Christie, which also concerned me, but I could only leave so many voicemails and messages. Her secrecy in telling her daughter where she was going unsettled me. It all seemed so out of character for her. However, I finally acknowledged that until she replied, there wasn't really anything else I could do to reach her.

Putting my personal issues aside, I followed up on the timing of the crimes in relationship to the work schedules and family obligations of the victims.

The first one, Maxine Nachmanoff, left for lunch and wasn't seen again. The second, Gideon Flello, was killed during lunch as well. The remaining victims were murdered in early evening or after dark.

Patterns.

Dig deep enough, and they'll emerge and the mirage of coincidence will evaporate.

Why did the crimes occur then? Why in those locations?

Hook'dup? Did they each head out for a discreet sexual encounter?

The timing for the first three crimes fit with travel times from the victims' place of work. The other two had been killed at night and could easily have driven to the sites from their residences.

I cross-checked all of the victims' credit card transactions, the locations, the amounts, the items purchased, dates, and times, trying to identify if any of the victims were together or near each other when a purchase was made, or were buying similar things from the same retailer. However, I didn't come up with any statistically significant correlation.

Then, using the Federal Aerospace Locator and Covert Operation Network, or FALCON, I ran the geoprofile but once again didn't end up with anything specific related to the potential home base of the offender. So unless there were more victims that we didn't know about, the link we were looking for was not their residential addresses, which fit in with a Bluebeard offender.

Finally, my thoughts rotated back to the precinct map and Sproul's hope of predicting the killer's next move.

Think neighborhoods that (1) are near the edge of the precincts, (2) have abandoned homes in a similar distribution to the areas where the previous crimes occurred, and (3) are within two blocks of populated streets.

Ralph's ringtone caught my attention. When I picked up, he said, "DeYoung showed me the video, Pat. The one of Maria. It's terrible." Then he swore harshly. "It's worse when you know someone. Know what I mean?"

"Yes."

"And it's all connected to Blake somehow. You still think Maria was referencing the silent ladies?"

"I do."

"Have you figured out the connection?"

"I'm wondering if it's something with that shipping manifest we found, but I don't know. What about from your end? What else do we know about Dr. Kuznetsov?"

"Not much. Even the file the CIA has on him is pretty slim. But we do know that he worked with Colonel Alibekov in germ warfare and smallpox research."

I'd heard about Alibekov, who changed his name to Ken Alibek and wrote a book back in the nineties called *Biohazard* after he defected to the United States.

"The big news, though, is Blake's pilot landed at a Canadian airport that's about an hour from Detroit. That's one of the reasons I called. We don't have a record of anyone with Blake's name traveling back into the U.S., but we did find some footage at the border crossing into Detroit that clearly shows him and his partner driving into the States. Fake names but a legit break."

"So they're here in Detroit?"

"Looks like it. And I'm about to be. I'll be flying over first thing in the morning after I wrap up a few things here. Should arrive at nine thirty or so."

We tentatively planned on me picking him up.

After the call, I took a few minutes to stretch my legs and walk down the hall to grab some water at the drinking fountain. On the way back, Sharyn called to fill me in on what she'd been investigating. When she was done, she said, "Are you still at the fed building?"

"Yes. What about you?"

"I just left the Ninth Precinct a few minutes ago. When do you think you'll be calling it a day? I'd like to see you."

When I checked the time, I found that it was already past seven.

At this point I was admittedly a little annoyed that I hadn't heard from Christie. I was hungry. Tired. Needed to decompress. And, though I didn't really want to stop working, I could see the benefit of comparing notes with Sharyn.

"You remember how I told you last night that I'd take a rain check on dinner?" I said.

"Yes."

"How about I turn that in now?"

"I'm on my way home, actually. I'm across town from you. Should we meet somewhere? I'd offer to make you dinner but as you might recall, I'm not a very good cook and I really don't have anything on hand except for some frozen pizzas and oranges. And beer."

"You know, some frozen pizza, an orange, and a beer doesn't sound all that bad."

"I'll text you my address."

After I left the building, on my way through the parking garage to my car, I saw SAC Kennedy speaking with a man about my height of Middle Eastern descent.

Trim beard. Athletic frame. When Kennedy saw me, he signaled for me to join them.

"Agent Bowers, I'd like you to meet Idris Kourye. He runs the Ferilex Corporation and is one of our city's most generous philanthropists."

"I was at Grandshore Medical Center earlier today," I said. "It's quite a place."

Idris took a sip from a travel mug. From here, the coffee smelled Kenyan, but I couldn't pinpoint it, which kind of annoyed me.

"I can't take any credit for that," he said. False humility

is annoying. His sounded genuine. "The people who serve there, they should get all the credit in the world."

"Right. I enjoyed the Bugisu. I hear you're a bit of a connoisseur. I am as well."

"I like a good brew." He held up the travel cup. "Maybe before you leave town, we'll be able to grab a cup together. Talk the art of roasting."

"I'd be up for that."

Kennedy nodded. "It's all due to Idris's work that Ferilex got the contract for providing the state with emergency medical materials—at a very competitive rate."

"It's the least I could do for the city I love." Again, the humility did not seem feigned.

The text with Sharyn's home address came through.

I was about to head to my car, but Kennedy gestured for me to join him. "May I speak with you for a moment, Agent Bowers?"

Idris politely excused himself and left for his Tesla.

"Yes?" I asked Kennedy once we were alone.

"I need to tell you: I asked to speak with Idris for two reasons. First, he's involved with an organization, the Muslim Concern League. Are you familiar with them?"

"I've heard of them, but that's about all. It's an advocacy group?"

A nod. "We have reason to believe that some of the Muslim charities they represent . . . Well, I don't trust them."

"You don't trust them or you don't trust him?"

"He's a pillar of our community."

That's sometimes where the deepest cracks can be found, I thought, but said, "Yes. Of course."

"Secondly," Kennedy said, "I gave him a heads-up to

have his supply warehouse staff on call 24/7 until further notice."

"Did you tell him about the possible outbreak?" I asked.

"His company has the contract for emergency response supplies. Also, Grandshore is the most logical hospital to use for a base to head up a response in the city. I told him simply to make sure that his people were prepared in case we decided to run a simulation."

I wasn't sure I agreed with his decision to let Idris know anything, but I could see that with all that was at stake, it was prudent to be prepared. Detroit was Kennedy's city and it made sense that he would do all he could to protect the people here.

"Additionally," he said, "I should mention that I've been thinking about all of this, especially in regard to what's happening with the serial homicides and Blake ending up in the area. I don't think it's a coincidence that these events are triangulating here in Detroit."

"I agree with you. The timing speaks to a correlation."

"I'm wondering if someone in law enforcement might have been compromised."

"What? Why would you think that?"

"I'm not at liberty to say at the moment. In the meantime, until you hear from me, don't trust anyone."

"I'll keep my head up."

And with that, he patted my elbow, nodded, and headed to his car.

And, trying to process the implications of our conversation, I unlocked the Crown Victoria and took off for Sharyn's place.

55

Tessa set down her purse and her teddy bear, Francesca, and then listened to Rachel give her the first-time-babysitter-for-my-kids spiel. When she was finished, Tessa stared at Aja. "I've never changed a baby before."

Rachel picked her up and sniffed at her bottom. "It looks like you're in luck. Smells like she could use a change right now. Give you a little practice."

"How is that luck?"

"Come here. I'll talk you through it."

Rachel handed Aja to Tessa and went to get the changing table ready.

Tessa held Aja stiffly. "Hi."

The baby drooled onto Tessa's arm.

"I'm not smelling you."

Aja smiled mischievously, as if she actually understood the words, which sort of weirded Tessa out.

"And I do not coo."

Aja smiled again and Tessa gently laid her on her back on the changing table.

She seemed so small and fragile and also so *amazingly alive* at the same time. It was a little freaky, but also, admittedly, pretty cool.

She was waving her chubby little arms and legs back and forth like she was trying to jog vertically up through the air.

Rachel held up some powder. "You'll want to get everything ready before you take off the diaper."

"Why's that?"

"Because you're going to want to wipe her and powder her and get the fresh diaper on as quickly as you can. Sometimes she likes to send a poop stream out while you have her down."

"Poop" and "stream" were two words that just should never appear in the same sentence.

Tessa unwrapped the old diaper from Aja's bottom. Even at arm's length, it smelled yellowish and brownish and gross and looked just as bad as it smelled.

"How is it possible that something—one, someone—this small can make that much poop?" she muttered.

"Babies poop out their own weight every sixty hours," Rachel replied.

"Did not know that. Am not glad I do."

Tessa found herself calculating how much poop that would be three hours from now, when Rachel returned. But it was too unpleasant to think about, so she gave that up.

Seriously afraid of having to weather a poop stream, Tessa hurriedly wiped Aja, powdered her bottom, and snugged the new diaper onto her.

Then tugged her onesie over it. Snap. Snap. Done.

"See?" Rachel said. "You'll be a pro at it by the end of the night."

"I was kinda hoping I wouldn't have to have any more practice."

Rachel checked the time. "Aja's had some tummy problems lately. If she cries, you'll probably need to burp her. You know how to do that, don't you?"

"Who doesn't know how to burp a baby?" Tessa said, but then added, "But just, you know, you can review it for me once if you want to. Just in case there's some sort of new findings or research out there that I didn't know about."

"Right. So, hold her like this." Rachel demonstrated. "Then pat her back gently. Talk to her. Maybe sing a lullaby. Or do a little bouncy walk. She likes that. It usually calms her."

"Bouncy walk I can handle. But believe me, if I tried to sing it'd probably make her cry more."

"And you'll want to put a towel over your shoulder first, for when she spits up."

"Right."

"Got it?"

The words formed in Tessa's mind, a way to remember it all: *Pat her back. Gentle talk. Towel shoulder. Bouncy walk.*

"Got it."

"Great." Rachel laid Aja down in her crib and turned on the butterfly mobile above her. "I really need to get going."

She grabbed her purse and called to her five-year-old, "Hannah, come in here, I want you to meet your babysitter."

Hannah peeked around the corner of the hallway.

"It's okay," her mom assured her. "Come on."

Hannah edged out. She was holding a stuffed alligator.

Tessa picked up the teddy bear she'd brought over, hugged her, and smiled at Hannah to show how nice it was to hold her.

Hannah watched her carefully.

"That's a nice alligator you have there," Tessa said.

"She's not a alligator. She's a crocodile."

"Oh. Right. What's her name?"

"Toothy."

"Toothy the crocodile."

"Uh-huh."

"That's a good name for a crocodile. Does she bite?"

"No." Hannah shook her head. She was still eyeing Tessa's teddy bear.

"Do you wanna hold Francesca?" Tessa asked her.

Hannah nodded.

"Can I hold Toothy?"

"If you're nice."

"I will be. I promise."

They exchanged stuffed animals and Tessa slipped two fingers gingerly into Toothy's mouth and pretended to be seriously relieved that the crocodile didn't chomp down on her.

"Told you," Hannah said.

"Yeah. You were right. Oh, by the way, if Francesca cries, just do a little bouncy walk. She likes that. It usually calms her."

"Just like Aja," Hannah said.

"Yep, just like Aja. There's a rhyme to help you remember what to do if she gets fussy: Pat her back. Gentle talk. Towel shoulder. Bouncy walk."

Hannah nodded knowingly, then repeated the words softly to herself, accurately remembering the entire rhyme.

"Well," Rachel said to Tessa, "looks like you've found a friend."

"Yeah."

Rachel summarized the snack and bedtime routine, then finished by telling Tessa, "Feel free to call me if you have any questions at all."

"Thanks. Okay."

Then Rachel kissed both of her kids on the forehead and bustled out the door, leaving Tessa alone with them.

Hannah crossed the living room to show Francesca her dollhouse, then asked Tessa, "Does Francesca like tea parties?"

"She likes root beer best, but yeah, tea is okay."

"Do you?"

"Yeah, of course," Tessa lied. "I love tea parties more than anything." Then she carried Toothy over and had a seat beside the dollhouse, glad that the tea party wouldn't have any actual tea.

56

Sharyn's place was in a slightly run-down neighborhood at 20 Mile.

"You'll have to excuse the mess," she said self-consciously as she invited me in.

Her place had an outdoorsy vibe to it. Warm autumn colors. Somewhat austere. Not cluttered with knickknacks, but decorated simply, with stylish, framed photos of Detroit's iconic buildings and of Michigan in the fall.

"If this place is a mess, I wish my apartment was messier." I gestured toward the photos. "Did you take those?"

"Nope. Julianne did. She has a really good eye. Sells them online. I try to support her. Honestly, with her disability, she hasn't always gotten a lot of breaks at the department."

Until Sharyn mentioned it, I hadn't thought of Julianne's underdeveloped left arm, not since the first time I met her.

Rather than kitchen chairs around the table, Sharyn had three rolling office chairs.

I took one and spun it in a circle beneath my fingers.

"They were used," she explained. "They were cheap. I'm here by myself, so I only needed two—I mean the second one for when Olivia stays with me. But the used office furniture store had a buy-two-get-one-free sale."

"Gotta love a good deal."

"Olivia likes 'em better than normal chairs. She rolls all around the kitchen when she's here. Oh, and she named them." Sharyn pointed to each chair in turn as she introduced them to me. "That's Annabelle. Then you have Gracie. And here's Horace."

"Those are the three best chair names I've ever heard."

"I'll tell Olivia you said so."

I chose Annabelle.

Most office chairs are designed so that anyone over six feet tall needs to crank them up to their highest position in order to find any semblance of comfort, but when I pumped this chair's handle, the seat didn't move. So, as low as it was, when I sat down, my knees jutted off to each side.

A light smile creased Sharyn's face. "That looks comfortable."

"Just the way I like it."

"Uh-huh."

"You'd be amazed how hard it is to get most adjustable chairs into this exact position."

"I can only imagine."

She'd already set her laptop and a stack of file folders on the table. She pointed to my side. "How are the burns doing?"

"No worse than a sunburn."

She waited me out.

"Well, a little worse, but I'll be alright."

She put in a pizza, uncapped a couple of beers, and then offered me an orange.

"Thank you. Oranges and beer. A classic combination."

We worked for a while at the kitchen table, and when

the pizza was done, I watched her smother her piece with Sriracha sauce.

No surprise there.

Although I kept my phone nearby in case there was an emergency, I turned off the ringer so it wouldn't disturb us.

We ate quietly for a few minutes, then as Sharyn slathered her second piece with hot sauce, she asked me, "What did you figure out regarding the geoprofile? I'm guessing that with a Bluebeard it's more difficult to pinpoint where his home base might be."

"That's true."

"Especially with how these sites are scattered all over the city. What does that tell you? That he's trying to cover his tracks?"

"I'd say they're scattered *throughout* the city, not all over it."

"What's the difference?"

"Intention."

I took a moment to show her the precinct map and what I'd discovered earlier today.

"Hmm. It would make it harder to link the crimes at first, because they would all be in different precincts, but eventually, it would almost certainly ensure that the Feds would get involved. Maybe that's what he wanted all along. The grenade would do that too—or it might've been meant to."

"You know how we've found letters carved into the victims?"

"Yes," she said.

"Spelled backward, he has started to write 'arrow.'"

It only took her a moment to come to the same conclusion I had earlier. "Or Farrow."

"Yes. It's possible."

She considered that carefully, then said, "Why a blue beard?"

"What do you mean?"

"Why does the killer in the story have a beard that's blue? What's the significance of that?"

"The way Calvin explained it to me, both the beard and the key carry the same significance. People don't typically have blue beards, and it's certainly not natural for a key to bleed. The world of the story is an aberration from the natural order of things. It's likely that the man's crime was just so horrifying and inexplicable that the beard color was the folk teller's way of acknowledging that there was something completely foreign about an individual who would do such a thing."

"A medieval serial killer."

"Most likely. Yes."

She reflected on that for a moment. "So how do we catch him? Think like him?"

"No. Think like the victims."

"Or maybe a potential victim."

"What?"

"I think we need to draw him out. And the best way to do that might be offering him the right kind of bait."

"Bait? What are you—?"

"Me."

"No." I shook my head. "You'd be the fly landing right in his web."

"On the contrary," she said. "I'll be the bat looking for the spider. Right now, the question is: how is he keeping his identity secret and also enticing the potential victims to meet at those specific locations? And I think the answer is Hook'dup."

She told me about what she'd found so far regarding the app, then asked, "Why do you think the guy posted that footage of the house where Jamika was found onto the news feed?"

"Maybe to get a crowd there."

"Or to hide in plain sight? So he wouldn't be the only one there?"

"Interesting. Let's have an agent search through any news footage we have of the other sites, see if there's anyone who keeps showing up taking pictures or posting through the same account."

She put a call through.

"Back to the bait idea," I said, "put that on the back burner."

"Alright. For now."

We talked some more about the case, and after we'd both had our fill of pizza, we migrated into the living room with our beers and a small bowl of orange slices.

After my second slice, I said, "I started watching *Sanctuary*, but I didn't get a chance to finish it yet. What happens in the scene you were telling me about?"

"You get to see how I became a star."

"That's a killer teaser." I wasn't sure how to frame what I wanted to ask next. "Sharyn, you never really told me about Hollywood."

"About it?"

"Growing up there. Living there."

"Truthfully, it wasn't easy—especially with two parents who despised each other almost as much as they both loved the idea of me making them rich. Made for an interesting dynamic."

"That must have been tough."

"You live in a trailer half the year. Every aspect of your life is orchestrated by adults who don't necessarily have your best interests in mind. From the outside it looks glamorous, but when you're inside the fishbowl, you just want to swim away from it all."

"And that's what you did eventually."

"Yes. But that wasn't the worst of it. When I was ten, I played the role of being eight, and then when I was twelve, I played a ten-year-old. So my handlers did everything they could to make me look younger for the parts, but they made me dress like I was eighteen for the premieres. You can't begin to imagine the things grown men said to me when I was twelve and out of earshot of my parents."

"I can guess."

"Yeah, I doubt it. You're too much of a gentleman. Anyway, every woman in Hollywood tries to look twenty-five. The teens do, their moms do too." She paused. "Pat, I have a question for you. If it's too personal, just say so. I'll drop it and I won't ask about it again."

"Alright."

"Can you tell me about her?"

"About who?"

"The woman you're seeing."

Curious, I said, "What makes you think I'm seeing someone?"

"Maybe I'm assuming too much, but I have the sense that if you weren't in a relationship you would hold my gaze longer when you look at me. Am I right?"

"Possibly." I swirled my beer around for a moment in the bottle. "I have been seeing someone, yes. Since May. Her name's Christie."

"So, it's serious, then."

"That sounded more like a conclusion than a question."

"I think I know you pretty well. Even when we were together at the Academy, I got the impression that you wanted to find someone to be with long-term. The way you treated me, I could tell you weren't the type of guy to be unfaithful to your woman. Maybe I didn't appreciate it as much back then, but I do now. It makes things a lot less complicated when you know whose arms you'll be going home to at night."

"Is your life complicated?"

She pointed to one of the kitchen chairs. "Just me and ole Horace here. Seriously, though, not since the divorce. Not anything long-term." She took a slice of orange, and might have edged forward a little on the couch. "So, what does this lucky woman do? The one you've been seeing since May?"

"Graphic designer. She recently got a promotion." It seemed like a strange thing to mention, and I wasn't sure why I added that last part.

"That's nice."

"Yes."

I was about to say, *She's lovely and quirky and fun and brings out the best in me*, but didn't end up saying anything.

"Is something long-term in the cards?"

I looked at Sharyn out of the corner of my eye, as if to say, *Wasn't this going to be one question?*

"I'm sorry." She rubbed her head in a self-reprimand. "I know. It's none of my business."

"Christie has a daughter who's fifteen. That makes the cards a little hard to read."

"Oh. A teenage daughter. Wow."

"We get along okay, but I don't even pretend to understand her. She's a bright girl. Perceptive and inquisitive, but also a bit opinionated."

"Imagine that. A teenage girl with an attitude," Sharyn said lightly. "I'm glad I was never like that."

"Is that so?"

"Don't expect to understand her, Pat. Women are a timeless enigma to men. It's part of our charm. But when we're teenagers—well, then you've got an enigma wrapped in adolescent angst. Is her dad in the picture?"

"No. I don't think she's ever met him."

"That's too bad. A dad is . . . Well. It's important for a girl to have a dad in her life. There's a lot of research on it. It's pretty conclusive. It's one of the reasons I want Kevin still involved with Olivia."

A moment passed.

"I'm glad you found someone," she said. "You deserve to be happy." She raised her bottle. "Here's to finding the right person."

After a slight hesitation, I tapped my bottle against hers. "To finding the right person."

We drank to the toast.

Another moment drifted by.

I noticed for the first time that from where I was sitting I could catch the scent of her perfume. It was light and airy and inviting, and when she looked my way, I didn't avert my eyes as quickly as I had been doing.

++++

"Listen," Pat said. "Let me just say I'm sorry."

Sharyn looked at him curiously. "Why? What are you sorry for?"

"For ending things the way I did. Back when we were

dating. Back at the Academy. It was abrupt. Out of the blue. It wasn't fair to you. I shouldn't have treated you like that."

"The timing wasn't right," she said, but she wasn't really sure if she believed that was the case at all.

"There were times over the years when I thought you might call," he said.

"You asked me not to."

"Yes, you're right. That's true." He seemed to evaluate what he was going to say next. "And you never asked why I broke things off."

She felt her heartbeat quicken. It was hard sitting here with him, so close to him. She wanted so badly to pat the couch beside her leg and invite him over, but she didn't.

"I couldn't see how it would have helped," she said softly. "I had the sense that asking you to explain it would have made it tougher on you, and that was something I didn't want."

"That's why, Sharyn."

"That's why?"

"Why I broke things off—because I wanted what was best for you."

"And so you ended things?" She noted a touch of tightness in her voice. It might have sounded like anger, but it wasn't. It was more a sense of loss, of regret over what might have been. "Shouldn't that have been more of a mutual decision?"

"I thought that the longer we were together, the harder it would be when we were inevitably pulled apart."

"Pat, it's supposed to hurt when two people who love each other are pulled apart."

Yes. She said it. She meant it. She had loved him. And from every indication, he had loved her as well.

"That's part of the deal," she went on. "But that's not the kind of pain we need to be protected from. There are no guarantees in a relationship, but that's the risk of intimacy, of what it asks of you."

"Yes," he said. "I suppose it is."

"You said 'inevitably.'"

"Inevitably?"

"That we would inevitably be pulled apart. Why'd you think it would be inevitable?"

"Life. Assignments. Just the way things go for new agents after graduating from the Academy."

"It wasn't me?"

"No, no. Of course not. It wasn't you."

"Did you look for me?"

"Yes," he admitted. "A couple of times over the years. I took note of your assignments, where you were working. I was curious if our paths would cross at a conference or something. You?"

"I thought of you once or twice." And with that, she let a smile escape. "I read your book: *Understanding Crime and Space: Geospatial Investigation Theory and Techniques.*"

"So you were the one."

"The one?"

"Based on sales."

"Ha. It was good. Didn't agree with everything."

"So that means I at least got a few things right."

It was a way to spend time with you, she thought but held back from saying it. Instead, she said, "Hey, listen. About the earrings and the necklace. I can get rid of them if you'd like. I don't need to keep 'em."

"It doesn't feel right for me to tell you what to do with them, Sharyn."

Despite the fact that he was in a relationship, she didn't feel like she could just let this moment pass and drift away like she'd let things drift away eight years ago.

Do not say it, Sharyn.

Yes, you need to. You'll regret it if you don't.

Before she could argue herself into doing something sensible, she said, "Earlier today, you told me that most people get rid of the remnants of a relationship because it makes it easier to forget, easier to move on."

"I didn't mean anything by that."

"Maybe that's not what I wanted."

++++

Her stare was intense, unswerving. Unnerving.

I looked away.

And then I looked back. In that moment, I could tell that neither of us had a good sense of what to say, and that both of us probably wanted to say more than we should.

"I'll go grab us some more oranges," she said awkwardly, even though the bowl wasn't nearly empty yet.

++++

Ever since Mannie had left earlier, Blake had been keeping an eye on the morgue's entrance. He was almost ready to give up on Dylan visiting it when he saw a man agilely climb over the fence of a nearby property and head toward it.

In the shadows, Blake couldn't tell if it was Dylan or not, but then the man glanced around to make sure he was alone before pulling out a lock pick set and leaning in by the door.

Blake phoned Mannie. "How far away are you?"

"I'd say about ten minutes."

"Is the place ready?"

"Yup. Should be all set."

"Alright. Get over here. It's time for you to meet my brother."

57

While Sharyn was in the kitchen, even though my phone's ringer was off, I saw the screen flash with an incoming call from Christie with those two telling words beneath it: *Accept. Decline.*

Sharyn was rooting through the fridge in the next room over.

I picked up the phone.

For a fraction of a second my finger hovered over the wrong icon, then I tapped *Accept.*

"Hey."

++++

Sharyn felt that tingle, the subtle, rising tinge of desire, that nudge to go one more step.

Everything so far had remained pretty much on the friendship level, simply platonic, until just a few moments ago when there was the hint that this might go so much deeper.

Here he was, at her place. Here, now, at this time of night.

Along with an orange, she took out another bottle for herself and called over her shoulder, "Pat, would you like another beer?"

++++

Sharyn's voice was loud enough for Christie to hear on the other side of the line. "Who was that?" she asked me.

"The woman I'm working with. She's an agent at the Field Office here."

"You two are working late."

"Trying to make some headway on this thing."

"This thing?"

"This case."

"Right. Of course. Is that where you are, then?"

"Is what where we are?"

"The Field Office. You said a second ago that she's an agent there. Is that where you two are working?"

Sharyn stepped through the kitchen doorway holding two beers. "I didn't hear if you wanted one," she said brightly. "I figured I'd just bring a—"

I waved her off and she looked aghast, as she realized that for whoever I was talking to, hearing her voice wasn't going to be a good thing. She quickly returned to the kitchen.

"Not at the moment, no," I told Christie. "We're not at the Field Office."

"Where are you?"

"Christie, we're just looking over some files."

"But where?"

You're not a good liar. Just tell her.

"We're at her house."

"Her house."

"Yes."

"Okay."

"This isn't what it seems like."

"You're just going over some files, trying to make some progress on this case."

"Yes." And then I reiterated, "That's it. That's all."

"And having drinks."

"A couple beers, but—"

"Do you know where I am, Pat?"

"Where are you?"

"I'm at the airport."

"You're still at the airport?" This afternoon Tessa had said that her mom was flying somewhere, and all I could think of now was that her flight had been delayed. "Tessa told me you were leaving. Try Jodie if your flight was canceled, maybe she—"

"Not JFK, Pat. Detroit."

"What?" I felt the bottom drop out of the moment. "What are you talking about? You're here? Why are you here?"

"I came to see you."

"How did— I don't understand. Why didn't you tell me?"

"It was last minute. I wanted it to be a surprise."

"Booking a last-minute flight must have cost a fortune. Where did you get that kind of money?" Even as I said the words, I realized how out of place and even moronic they must have sounded, but I was still recovering, still trying to figure out what to make of all this.

"Ralph set it up," she told me. "He was worried about us after he talked to you earlier today. He called and offered to let me use his frequent flyer miles to come be here with you. I told him no, that was kind, but that we would be alright. But then he went ahead and booked the ticket anyway. He can be a bit strong-willed."

"Yeah." I winced. "Is this because of our anniversary? Three months?"

"It's because we've been having some rough spots lately. He cares about us. I care about us. I was hoping that if I was here we could smooth things out. I know you're on a case, but you're always on a case. This way I can encourage you."

My first reaction was anger. It shifted quickly from being directed at Christie for not telling me, to Ralph for not warning me, and finally to myself for being here at Sharyn's this late when I should've been just about anywhere else in the city.

It didn't make any sense to be angry at Christie or Ralph. He'd given her the miles because he was my friend, because he wanted things to work out between us, and it must've been a lot of miles for him to book a flight the same day.

"I'll come pick you up," I told Christie. "Where are you staying?"

"I was kind of thinking that I could . . . Well, it doesn't matter."

"Stay with me? Sure. Yes. Of course."

"You weren't going to stay with her tonight?"

"Sharyn? No, of course not. Why would you say that?"

"Sharyn?"

"Agent Weist."

"Is this the same Sharyn Weist you used to date back when you were at the Academy? The one you told me about that day we went to the shooting range?"

"Christie, I'm not spending the night here."

"Of course it's the same Sharyn, right? How many Agent Sharyn Weists could there be out there?"

I understood why she was upset, I just didn't know how to solve things.

"Why didn't you tell me earlier that she would be here?"

"I . . ."

"You could have told me you'd be working with a woman you used to be in a relationship with."

"Why didn't you tell me you were flying here?" I blurted out stupidly, and immediately regretted saying.

"Because I love you," she said. "And I wanted to do something special for you."

I had no idea what to say. I was striking out every time I opened my mouth.

"Listen, Christie, I'm getting my keys. I'm coming to get you. We'll talk all this through. We'll sort everything out."

"I think I need a little space right now. I'll call you in the morning."

"Where are you staying?"

But it was too late.

She was already off the line.

++++

From where Sharyn was standing in the kitchen, even though she wasn't trying to listen in on Pat's conversation, she couldn't help but hear his end of it.

A hot wash of guilt swept through her.

She waited until she was certain the phone call was over. Then, at last, when she heard Pat moving around and the sound of his jangling keys, she returned to the living room. "Pat, I'm so sorry."

"You heard that?"

"Enough of it. I shouldn't have had you over."

"It's not your fault."

"The woman you're seeing—she's here? In Detroit?"

"At the airport."

"Oh, Pat."

"Flew in to surprise me to patch things up. Looks like I might've made an even bigger rip in the fabric."

"What can I do?"

"Nothing. I need to go. I'll talk to you in the morning."

"Would you like me to call her? Assure her there's nothing going on between us?"

"I already did, and if she can't trust me, it's already too late to fix things. Hearing from you isn't going to help."

Then he gathered his papers, thanked her for dinner, and, without another word, left for his car.

58

In the basement of Grandshore Medical Center, Blake indicated for Mannie to head down the south hall to cover the other exit, then he approached one of the doors to the room where the autopsies were performed.

He'd thought that his brother was the only other one on this floor, so he was surprised to hear two voices inside the room.

Yes, one was Dylan's. The other was male as well, and sounded filled with urgency and fear. "You said no one would find out," the person exclaimed. "You said film it, upload it, and they wouldn't be able to find me."

"You shouldn't have answered the phone," Dylan told him. "You should've just stuck with the graffiti and making the calls."

"I did everything you asked me. I told the kids when to be at the house."

"They went early. They went a day early."

"Why does that matter?"

"If something didn't matter," Dylan said, "I wouldn't have asked you to do it. Do you still have the phone?"

"Yes."

"And it has that agent's number on it?"

"Yeah, but I—"

"Give it to me."

There was a slight pause. Blake edged closer to the door and eased it open just a crack, just enough to see his brother in the room standing beside that second guy: dark hair. Early thirties. The man was wearing a hospital badge on his scrubs.

"Are you going to hurt me?" the man asked Dylan.

"'Hurt' isn't exactly the right word."

With that, Blake whipped out the 1911 MC Operator .45ACP that he carried and burst through the door, aiming the gun at his brother's chest. "Dylan, this man won't tell. Let him go."

Dylan didn't move. "Brother. I was wondering how long it would take you to find me. I thought at least another month."

The man beside Dylan was trembling. "Yeah, like he said. I won't tell."

Dylan turned to him. "What did you say?"

"I promise. I won't tell anyone. Just let me—"

Without another word, Dylan drew a SIG and fired one shot through the man's left eye, and then, immediately, two more center mass. His body dropped backward, colliding awkwardly against one of the exam tables before smacking to the floor.

Blake did not shoot his brother.

Dylan turned his gun toward Blake, and the two men—the older brother and the younger one; the one who had taken the role of the father, the other, the son—stood still and quiet, aiming their guns directly at each other's chests.

"Dylan, I'm going to need you to come with me."

"That's not going to happen, brother. I have unfinished business here."

"I'm afraid it'll have to remain unfinished."

Behind Dylan, Blake saw a huge shadow move and realized that Mannie had found his way into the room through another door. Once again, Blake was impressed at how quietly someone Mannie's size could cross through space.

"Since when do you carry a SIG?" Blake asked him.

"It was a gift to me from an FBI agent. Listen, brother, I want you to lower that gun. I don't want to shoot you, but I will if I have to. And we both know you're not going to shoot me."

"You're right. I'm not."

Blake did lower his gun.

While nodding to his associate.

And with that, Mannie was on his brother.

Dylan put up a good fight—better than any of the black belts had. He even got a shot off, but it missed Mannie and ricocheted off the floor and into one of the metal shelving units nearby.

Blake had brought a sedative in a syringe with him, but Mannie used his fist instead.

"Sorry about that," Mannie apologized as he stood over Dylan's unconscious form. "I didn't want to hurt him."

"He'll be alright," Blake said. "Let's get him out of here."

He picked up the phone that Dylan and the man that he'd shot had been talking about, the one with the agent's number on it, slipped it into his pocket, and opened the door so that Mannie could carry his little brother to the car.

59

After the tea party, Tessa played with Hannah for a while, fed Aja, did a little bit of the bouncy-walk-calmy-down-thing, changed another diaper—which seemed to be an entire sixty hours' worth of poop—and got a snack for Hannah as a sort-of-maybe-partial excuse to get one for herself.

Then Tessa went through the bedtime routine with Hannah—helping her find her pajamas, brush her teeth, say her prayers, and then climb into bed.

Hannah nestled up to her, hugging Francesca in one arm and Toothy in the other.

"How did you end up with both of them?" Tessa asked her. "That's not fair."

"It is for me." Hannah beamed. "Can you tell me a story?"

"Sure. Which book do you want me to read?"

"No, I mean *tell* me one. With your mouth."

"You mean without a book?"

Hannah nodded and snuggled in closer.

"I don't really know any good stories to tell. Most of the ones I know are pretty scary."

"Uh-uh. Don't tell me one you already *know.* Tell me one that isn't there yet."

"Isn't where?"

"Anywhere."

"A made-up one?"

"They're the *best.*"

"Oh. Gotcha."

Although Tessa loved to write—poetry especially—she'd never really tried to write a story for a little girl and wasn't sure how to get started or make one up on the spot, so she launched into it with the old standby opening, then went on from there. "Once upon a time there was this place called, um, Upper Downmongo."

"That's a funny name."

"It was a funny place. It was down in the Mongo Valley but way up high in the Peaks of the Eastern Realm. But it's a special place too because all the animals there could talk and kings and queens ruled the land and princesses lived in beautiful, stately palaces."

"What's *stately*?"

"Means they were very pretty and very elegant."

"Was one of the princesses named Hannah?"

"Yeah. Huh. How did you know that?"

Hannah smiled. "I don't know."

"Have you heard this story before?"

"Uh-uh."

"Well, so near Hannah's castle, dragons lurked in the hills."

"Lurked?"

"It just means they lived there, hiding in their caves. But lurking is a sort of crawly and creepy kind of hiding."

Tessa noticed Hannah hugging Francesca and Toothy a little more closely. "Were the dragons mean?"

"Um, no, but . . . well . . . they were lonely."

"Oh."

"They just wanted a friend, but whenever they went to meet the people in the villages, everyone got scared and ran away."

"'Cause they thought they were gonna eat 'em?"

"How did you know that? You *have* heard this story before."

"No!"

"Well, the princess's name *was* Hannah. But I need to tell you about someone else for a second first. There was one girl dragon whose mommy dragon left her one day and didn't tell her where she was going. And the girl dragon got worried and kinda mad because she didn't want anything bad to happen to her mom and because she didn't like her mom having a secret."

"Did she love her?"

"You mean the girl or the mom?"

"Both."

"Yeah, they loved each other."

"So then the mommy will come back and things will be okay."

"How do you know that?"

"When you love someone, you always come back for 'em. The girl dragon just needs to wait and trust her mommy."

"What if the mother dragon doesn't ever tell her the secret?"

Hannah's answer was so quick that Tessa could tell it was something that just seemed self-evident to a five-year-old. "You can love someone even if you don't tell 'em all your secrets."

"Huh."

"What happens then?"

"Oh, Princess Hannah goes out on an adventure and meets the girl dragon, whose name is Bernice."

"Bernice?" She scrinkled up her face.

"It was a common name for dragons in that land," Tessa said, holding back the fact that it was also her middle name. "So, at first, Hannah was scared of the dragon, and Bernice was kind of scared of the princess."

Hannah seemed to find that hilarious. "Why would a dragon be scared of a *princess*?!"

"'Cause they didn't know each other too well yet. But once they started to play hopscotch they became good friends. Princess Hannah would scratch Bernice on the back of her neck, right where she liked it. And Bernice would help start campfires for Hannah so she could roast Meadomallows, which are kind of like marshmallows but don't come from a marsh but instead, a flowery mountain meadow."

Tessa hated marshmallows and justified telling Hannah they came from a marsh to keep her from ever trying them herself. Gross.

"They played catch," Tessa said, "and tag and—"

"Did Bernice tag her with her fire?"

"Uh-uh. She was super careful not to. And she kept Hannah safe from porcupines and mean beavers, and Hannah taught Bernice how to have tea parties and use her fire to make the tea not too hot, not too cold, but just right."

"Like Goldilocks!"

"Right."

"Is that the end?"

"No. It's really just the beginning. They had lots of adventures together."

Hannah smiled. "Tell me about one of 'em."

"Well, let's see . . . The one with the giant rhino who liked to smash everything, or the one with the walrus who liked to frolic in the Southern Swamp?"

"Frolic?"

"To swim playfully and happily."

"Both!"

"Both?"

"Both stories!"

"Why doesn't that surprise me."

Hannah leaned her head against Tessa's chest. "I like you."

Tessa found herself ruffling the girl's hair and then realized it was the first time in her life she'd ever done anything like that.

It was a little weird.

But nice too.

"I like you too," she said.

When the stories were over and Hannah had fallen asleep, Tessa didn't want her to be scared or to wake up alone in the dark, so she stayed there by her side and listened to the little girl's soft breathing and thought about secrets and love and what else might happen in Upper Downmongo and what other stories she might one day tell.

60

Even though I tried calling Christie three times on my way back to the motel, she didn't pick up.

Traffic was light, but still, by the time I got there, it was nearly eleven thirty.

Back in my room, I texted her to call me in the morning. I also sent her an email with the same request and messaged her through every social networking app I could think of.

After getting ready for bed, I found a text from Lieutenant Sproul that the fingerprints on the plastic tips on one of the hoodies matched a third-year resident who was currently serving as the assistant medical examiner. He'd never been arrested but had been fingerprinted as one of the security measures and background checks at the hospital. They'd sent a car to his house, but he wasn't there. They were currently looking for him.

I was thinking of watching the rest of *Sanctuary*, but with everything that was going on in regard to Christie and Sharyn, I wasn't in the mood.

Instead, I reviewed the case files, checked my messages one more time, saw nothing from Christie, and then went to bed.

++++

When Dylan woke up, he was no longer in the morgue. For the most part, the room he was in was dark, but a hint of light seeped in from the city through a shattered window to his left.

His head ached, and he found himself rubbing his forehead and finding a tender lump.

The last thing he remembered was fighting the big guy who apparently worked with his brother.

Dylan tried to push himself to his feet but found that his left wrist was chained to a sturdy pipe running down the wall. He only had six feet or so of freedom.

He tried his hardest to pull free, but it didn't take long for him to realize that the pipe wasn't going to budge. Also, despite the strength he'd gained from his workouts in prison over the last fifteen years, he was not superhuman and would not be able to pop the links.

Well, they hadn't killed him, so they weren't done with him.

Truthfully, he didn't think his brother would ever be able to kill him, even if that act of mercy ended up costing him his own life.

But the other guy, well, Dylan wasn't so sure about him.

It was too dark to see what assets might be in the room, and he wasn't going to be able to get out of here until he could get a good look around.

So, for now, he decided he needed to wait things out.

If he could get some sleep, he would be refreshed and ready to address the issue of escaping in the morning.

++++

Sharyn processed everything that'd happened tonight. It was clear that Pat really did care about Christie. But it was also clear that there were trust issues between them.

Don't get in the way. Let them work things out.

But what if they don't work out?

Sharyn chided herself for her thoughts.

She needed to move forward with tracking down Dylan.

And right now, the best way to do that was through Hook'dup.

Through offering him bait.

Earlier, she'd started creating a profile and now she updated it.

She held her phone at arm's length, tried out a couple of different smiles and poses, and eventually landed on one with her head tilted slightly to the side, a flirtatious look in her eyes, as she bit the end of a pen in a sultry way.

She listed her job as a model, her favorite animal as a rabbit, and her favorite movie as *Sanctuary.* If anything was going to attract Dylan's attention, that should do it.

Username: Snowball4.

On the app you could list your status as "Busy," "Interested," "Available," or "Hot and Ready."

She went with "Available" for now.

If necessary, tomorrow, she would move on to "Hot and Ready."

61

11:34 P.M.

Dispersal in 15 hours

On his drive up to Dearborn, Ali had found it necessary to stop numerous times to put ice on his eye to ease the swelling so he could see well enough to drive. He'd also needed to rest, since the broken rib—or ribs, he wasn't sure—made it hard to sit for long periods of time. As a result the trip had taken longer than he anticipated.

Now, he finally arrived at the address he'd been given, went to the back door, knocked twice, waited, and then knocked again just as he'd been instructed to do.

As he stood there, he heard movement inside, but at first, no one came and for a second he thought about running, trying to escape what he had done, who he was. But there was no escaping it anymore.

He did not run.

He waited.

Just as he'd been taught while he was at that compound in Yemen.

Finally, a tall yet unimposing bearded man opened the door and assessed the bruises on Ali's face.

To Ali, his eyes seemed to be filled with both curiosity and concern.

The man gazed past Ali, scanned the neighborhood, studying it for any movement or sign that Ali might have been followed, and then, without a word, gestured for him to come inside.

He put a finger to his closed lips and shook his head no. Ali wasn't sure if it was because the man was unable to speak, or perhaps if he suspected that his home had been bugged and that someone might be listening in on them.

He took out a tablet computer and typed into it: I am Abdul.

Ali nodded.

The man wrote: You are hurt. What happened?

He handed the tablet to Ali and Ali wrote: At a rest area four men attacked me simply because I am a Muslim. They knew nothing of my reason for being here. They hate Muslims.

For the rest of their conversation, they handed the tablet back and forth, typing their responses to each other.

—But Ali, are you certain they did not know?

—Yes.

—Allah will have his revenge. They will die in their rage.

—Is everything set for tomorrow?

—Yes, brother. But you are hurt.

—I am fine.

—You will be able to carry everything out as planned?

—I will.

Ali didn't want him to know the extent of his injuries, so he tried to ignore the pain in his side that caused him a hitch with every breath.

Although he thought about asking for some medicine to relieve the pain, he decided to allow his suffering to be a way of acknowledging his devotion, and said nothing to Abdul about it. A small sacrifice.

Abdul showed Ali to a room at the top of the stairs, invited him to rest, and typed on the tablet that his wife would bring up breakfast at seven.

—We leave for the restaurant at ten thirty. There, we will meet the others. Then, we will be told what happens next.

—I am looking forward to it. Do you know if my sister is okay?

—Yes, brother. She is fine. Faatina is watching her. She can be trusted.

Ali calculated that he would be contagious tomorrow in the late afternoon. Though Fridays are days of worship for Muslims, this was holy work. Surely Allah would honor that.

He knew nothing of the length of the meeting and wondered briefly if it might be cutting it close, but then realized he must trust that all would occur in due time, just as it should, and that he simply needed to go to sleep and prepare to play his part tomorrow in the bigger scope of the plan.

++++

After showing Ali to his room, Abdul went to his car and headed south on I-94 toward the warehouse.

Ever since 1980, when the remaining smallpox samples were locked away, there'd been an ongoing debate in the scientific community about whether to destroy them, with some scientists claiming that it was necessary to keep the samples for research purposes, and others claiming that it could fall into the wrong hands and be weaponized and used as a bioweapon.

But postponing a decision is making a decision.

And of course, when you lock up a beast that does not die, eventually someone will leave the door open a crack and it will nudge its way out into the daylight.

It was time for this species to return and make its long-awaited comeback.

He had his scimitar with him but left it in the car's trunk as he pulled up to the security checkpoint at the south entrance of the Ferilex Corporation distribution warehouse fifteen minutes from his home.

He did not think that his car would be inspected. It never had been before.

He had a security clearance card and showed it to the guard, who nodded, greeted him cordially, and waved him on.

The shipment had arrived. The same shipping company that'd delivered the mannequins for Blake's purposes. The same shipping company that'd brought Blake to their attention in the first place.

Here in the warehouse, there were thirty SCBA air tanks—or self-contained breathing apparatus units—currently ready to be utilized in the case of an emergency.

The preparations would take him about four minutes per tank, plus thirty to forty seconds between tanks. So, maybe five minutes with each one.

If he kept at it, he would be able to finish up in two and a half hours.

This was the part of the plan Ali did not know about, and this was the part that mattered most of all, for it would be not just a strike at the heart of the Great Satan, but a blow to America's confidence in itself.

Scarlett Farrow—IV

The Transept

In the next scene of the movie, after Harris led Millie Evans from the closet, he took her down the stairs.

She had to hold his hand.

It was in the script.

They passed through the living room and the kitchen, and then through the narrow hallway that Millie liked to run back and forth through—from the house to the church to the house.

Holy to normal.

To holy again.

They entered the back of the church, or the *narthex*. She knew the word. A real-life pastor who was there on the set to help them with the religious parts of the story had told her what it was called.

It was one of those words that wasn't naughty to say, but sounded naughty when you said it.

Narthex. Narthex. Narthex.

There in the front of the church was her mother, there on a single chair in the transept.

And that one was a good word.

Transept. Transept. Transept.

Her wrists and ankles were wrapped thick with tape around the arms and legs of the chair.

Harris had also covered her mouth with tape to keep her quiet, and now he tore it off.

"You bastard," her mom said. It was a word that really *was* a bad word, but it seemed like, in this case, it was okay for her to say it. "If you even—"

"Shh. Quiet, or I'll tape your mouth shut again." Then he turned to Scarlett. "Now, Millie, I'm going to need you to be brave. You know what a gun can do, don't you?"

She nodded.

He pulled a gun from where he'd slid it under his belt.

"Alright. Then you know it can hurt someone in ways that they can't get better from."

"They die."

"That's right."

"Just like Daddy."

"That's right, just like your daddy."

"And they go to heaven."

"Not everyone does. Not everyone goes to heaven, Millie."

"Daddy did. He's in heaven."

"Well, your mommy won't go there. She's been very bad."

"No, she *hasn't*! Don't hurt my mommy!" The fire in Scarlett's words was real. The tight, angry threat they carried was not scripted. She was supposed to play the scene as if Millie were scared, *just* scared, but she knew Millie. After all this time, she knew how Millie would really act, and even though she would be scared, of course, that wasn't all. Mostly she would be mad, because she loved her mom more than she loved herself.

Mad, mad, mad, *mad*!

"Well," Harris said, "I have a gun, and if you try to run away, I'm going to hurt your mommy with it. Do you understand?"

"Yes."

Her mom yelled at her to go, to run, but she didn't.

No, instead, she stayed right there and tried to figure out how to save her from Harris.

He pointed the gun toward one of the church pews. "Millie, I want you to go over there and get that pair of scissors. You know how to use them, don't you?"

"Of *course*."

"Alright. Go on."

"What are you doing, Harris?" her mom shouted desperately. "Do not hurt her!"

"I'll let you choose how things play out," he said.

Scarlett found the scissors. Picked them up.

Her mom kept crying out, "Please don't hurt my daughter. I'll do anything, please. I won't tell. Please, just let her go."

"You'll do anything?"

"Yes, yes. You can do whatever you want to me. Just let her go."

Millie loved her mom.

She didn't want anything bad to happen to her. And she wasn't going to let her die.

No.

Matter.

What.

PART 5

Decreed Stones

In the name of Allah, the Beneficent, the Merciful
Hast thou not seen how the Lord dealt with the
possessors of the elephant
[Abraha arrived mounted on a white elephant]
Did He now cause their wars to end in confusion?
And send against them birds in flocks?
Casting at them decreed stones—
So He rendered them like straw eaten up?

—FROM THE HOLY QUR'AN, 105. SURAH AL-FIL

It's incredibly ironic that the great public health triumph of eradicating smallpox in the 1970s and the discontinuation of worldwide vaccination have opened the door for this virus to be once again used as a weapon.

—FROM THE TRANSCRIPTION OF *HISTORY OF BIOTERRORISM: SMALLPOX*, CREATED 11/23/2003, BY CDC BIOTERRORISM PREPAREDNESS AND RESPONSE PROGRAM. DATE RELEASED: 7/31/2006.

62

Friday, August 3

6:34 A.M.

Dispersal in 8 hours

Sleep was not my friend.

Christie was on my mind, of course, so every time I woke up during the night, I checked my messages to see if she'd replied to me.

And found that she had not.

Now, I finally rolled out of bed, tired, frustrated, and distracted.

No workout this morning.

Burned side too sore.

I kept thinking of the video of Maria's death and the fact that Canyon had passed away from the injuries he'd sustained, and of all of those previous victims who'd been killed by a man who, if we were correct, was the same one who had raped Sharyn.

Why did Igazi want the kids there on that night? To set up one of them or one of their parents? To lure Sharyn out? But why would that night have done it? Because of Canyon's dad?

The case here was definitely taking turns I hadn't

anticipated, branching out like a tree that for some reason was seeking a patch of shade rather than sunlight.

Ralph would be flying in this morning at around nine thirty to pursue the possible connection with Blake and to see if that had anything to do with Maria's death. If it did, we could be looking at a pandemic that would dwarf anything our country has seen in the last century.

I confirmed that I would pick him up at the airport. We would head to the federal building for a briefing immediately afterward.

As I was eating breakfast, I received the bad news.

Another branch reaching into the darkness.

"Pat," Detective Schwartz said, "I'm calling from Grandshore Medical Center. I'm down here in the morgue, and we have a body—one that's not supposed to be here. You know how we were looking for the resident whose fingerprints matched those found on the hoodie?"

"It's him?"

"Yeah. Name's Geoff Dryer. He was shot once in the face, twice in the chest. Close range."

If he worked in the medical examiner's office, he would've been familiar with the map delineating the police precincts. He also would've known how to present a clean crime scene without leaving trace evidence.

If this man was Igazi, what about Dylan? Was he still involved? Was he the man who shot him?

Don't assume, Pat. Keep your perspective. Avoid the static of preconceptions.

"The reason I called," Detective Schwartz said, "isn't just because of the body. It's because of what we found lying next to it."

I put two and two together, anticipating that the dead resident was Igazi. "Let me guess. My SIG."

"The one registered under your name, yeah. And from our initial assessments, it appears to have been the murder weapon."

Why would Dylan have left it behind? Just to taunt us? It seems sloppy. He's never done that before.

"See if the prints match those of Dylan Neeson. He's a felon. He was released this spring from prison, where he was serving time for sexual assault."

"Gotcha. Will do."

"Alright, I'm on my way. I can be there in half an hour."

I grabbed my things and went for the door, but my room phone rang. Although I wasn't sure how many people had this number, I realized it was possible that Sharyn or Christie might be calling that line, since the call waiting on my cell didn't always behave and I'd been tied up on it talking with Schwartz.

I picked up and a nervous voice with a catch in it said, "I need you to come down to the lobby, sir. There's someone here who needs to speak to you."

"Who is it?"

"He says he's an old friend, and he says that if you're not here in thirty seconds, I won't be either."

63

Unholstering the Glock, I sprinted to the motel office.

Since we weren't exactly in the best neighborhood in Detroit, a bulletproof glass window with a small slide-out drawer for transactions separated me from the front desk at the check-in window.

The clerk who stood on the other side of the glass looked petrified. His hands shook noticeably and his eyes flicked to the side.

I followed them, and that's when I saw the second man, the one standing in the corner of that room, holding a 1911 MC Operator directed at the young clerk's head.

"Blake," I said. "It's been too long."

"Put your gun in the tray, Patrick," he replied evenly. "Then slide it through. Your phone too. Do it or he dies."

I evaluated the situation. Though I wanted to make a move, I did believe that Blake would take this man's life and there wasn't anything I could do at the moment to stop him. Even if I were able to somehow break through the glass or get around to the office door in time to stop Blake, it wasn't worth chancing this guy's life.

"Okay." Blake was probably too clever for games and too coldhearted to care, but I needed to at least give it a try. "I'll send the gun through, but first I need you to let him go."

"I think I'll let him stay here until we're done having our conversation. But—" He pulled out a syringe. "I can't have him listening in on what we're talking about."

The guy saw the needle and cried out, "No, don't! I'll—"

But Blake injected him before he could finish.

Whatever was in the syringe was fast-acting and within seconds, the clerk was out, slumping to the floor.

"Don't worry," Blake assured me. "If I wanted him dead, he'd be dead. This is just to give us a chance to chat confidentially, but if you make a move, I will put a bullet between his eyes. Now, the gun and your phone."

I turned my hand so he could see that my finger wasn't on the trigger, then slowly set the Glock in the tray. "My phone's in my room," I said, hoping he wouldn't call my bluff.

But he did: "So if I dial the number I won't hear it ring?"

I debated what to do. Somehow, he'd found out I was here at this motel. He had access to the Federal Digital Database, so that could explain how he'd found me. It could also mean that he very likely did have my number.

I placed my cell in the tray beside the gun, then sent both of them through to the other side, where Blake removed them and placed them on the counter.

"Lock the door to the lobby," he told me. "I don't want us to be interrupted by anyone passing through."

After I'd locked it, he told me to hold up my hands where he could see them.

"The Federal Digital Database," I said. "Is that how you found me?"

"It is. After I realized it was you in the video that was uploaded from the site of Jamika's murder, it didn't take long to locate the transfer order from the New York City

Field Office for you to come and consult on this case. From there, this motel was easy to find. They're skimping on your travel allowance, I have to say."

"What do you want?"

"I have an offer for you."

"I'm glad you've finally decided to turn yourself in. It's the right thing to do."

"Actually, I want to turn someone else in."

"Who's that?"

"The man you're looking for. My brother."

I eyed him. "What did you say?"

"It's about time you knew who I really am. As careful as I've been over the years, at this point, the more you learn about him, the more you'll find out about me. I'm certain that by the end of the day you would've been able to figure out that he's my adopted brother. But there really isn't time to get into all of that right now."

"I saw the photo of you two, from back when he was a kid. Karate."

"Ah. I know the one."

"He torched it when he tried to burn me alive."

Blake was quiet for a moment. "The group that killed Maria is planning to kill more people, many more. I can help you stop them. But I will need something from you in return."

I shook my head. "No deals."

"Listen. I have a name. I can get the location. You have the resources to bring in the man who infected Maria, but right now, here in this city, I do not. You can get him. I want him. You can apprehend him without excessive and unnecessary civilian casualties. If I go in, it won't be pretty and it won't be surgical. It'll be big and blunt and messy.

Neither you nor I want that. Give me that man and I'll give you Dylan."

"That's not going to happen."

"We both want the same thing here, Pat."

"And what is that?"

"Justice. We want the guilty to be punished and the innocent to be protected. I have Dylan and I know how to stop Fayed. If you don't work with me, both will go free and thousands, if not millions of people will die."

Fayed. Follow up on that name.

"I'm not here to barter with you, Blake."

"Think about it, Patrick: how could you not? You'll get everything you want: justice for both Dylan and Fayed. This is the only way that will happen, and it won't cost you anything."

"I also want justice for you, Blake."

"Well, that's one thing I can't promise you today."

I took what he had to say to heart. "You have Dylan?"

"I do. We can't have my brother out on the streets. You know that. You've seen what he's capable of."

"So why not just turn him in?"

"Because if I do, Fayed will get away with what he has planned."

"Then just give us the beta on Fayed—wait, you want him to yourself."

I thought of the connection between Blake and Maria, of how both of them had ties to L.A., and at last it struck me how all of this was tied together. "You loved her."

"They told me it would be quick. It was not quick."

"No," I agreed. "It was not."

"I'm not going to kill my brother. I raised him. I don't kill—can't kill—people I love. And I don't want him killed in a shootout with some trigger-happy police officers. He needs to be locked up. It's the safest place for him and for everyone around him."

I was getting a little irritated by Blake's talk of love—all of this coming from a man who was involved in human trafficking, who smuggled cocaine into the States to sell to minors, who had his fingers in the illegal arms trade.

"And to you," I said, "what does that mean, to love someone?" Partly I was interested; partly I was stalling. The longer I kept Blake talking, the longer the clerk stayed alive.

"To serve without feeling that it's a sacrifice," Blake replied, without even giving it much thought. "As soon as you want someone to reciprocate your affection, it ceases to be love and becomes an exercise in solipsism. Love is not a mutually beneficial exchange. It is much more than that, or it is nothing at all."

I needed to give it some more thought, but at least for the moment his definition of love struck me as surprisingly profound. Maybe he really did understand what it was like to love Maria and Dylan.

"What do you gain from all this?" I asked. "How does it benefit you? If you give us Dylan and we give you Fayed, what happens then?"

"Then you keep looking for me. The chase goes on. You know I'm not going to turn myself in, and I know you're not going to give up the search, so that chapter of our story will still have to play out."

I knew that my supervisors would never go for a deal like this, but I also knew that sometimes protocol needs to slide to the backseat. It needs to remain a means to an end, not an end in itself.

"If you don't agree to this," Blake told me, "I'll be forced to let Dylan go free, and both he and Fayed will be on the streets. Either lose them both or stop them both. The choice is up to you."

"If our team catches Fayed, we question him first, find out about his network, and the current threat. Only after we have what we need. Only then do we make the trade."

"Agreed."

"How do you propose we make this exchange?"

"We'll deal with the details later. I just want the commitment now. Give me your word, and I'll give you mine."

"And Fayed?"

He read my intent.

"I guarantee you that justice will be meted out for what he did to Maria."

I shuddered to think of how much he was going to make Fayed suffer, but then recalling what Fayed and his people had done to Maria, and evidently had planned for others, I didn't shudder for long.

The bat.

The spider.

The fly.

I wasn't even sure which role I was playing anymore.

From all that our team had been able to figure out so far, it seemed evident that this group had access to weaponized smallpox and the resolve to use it.

The stakes were simply too high right now to chance that we would indeed catch Fayed on our own in time to stop whatever he had planned. We needed to act. We needed to move on this.

And that meant I needed to trust Blake.

"Alright. I'll do it."

"I'll be in touch." He held up a cell phone. "I have your number. I'll call you." He backed up, easing toward the exit. "I'm leaving. I can either shoot this man to make you stay behind and help him, or you can assure me that you're not going to follow me. Say the word and I don't shoot. Your call."

"I won't follow you," I told him. "For now. But I am going to catch you, Blake. This justice you're so interested in pursuing . . . well, I'm going to hand it to you, man to man."

"I wouldn't expect any less." He pressed the door open. "Don't tell anyone you've spoken with me. You do, I'll find out, and our deal is off."

Then he slipped outside.

I waited until the door closed, then bolted around the side of the building to get into the office, retrieve my gun and my phone, and check on the condition of the desk clerk.

64

The man was fine and woke up less than five minutes later. In the meantime, I'd called the paramedics and they were on their way.

I spoke on the phone with Schwartz and explained simply that I'd gotten held up, but that I could still come to Grandshore if he thought it would be helpful.

"Honestly," he said, "Kramer's here and so are Julianne and the other CSI techs. Everything's being processed. There really wouldn't be anything for you to do at this point. Let me check. I'll shoot you a text if we need you."

I contacted Angela and told her that I needed everything she could pull up on Dylan Neeson's adopted family. "Cross-reference it all with what we already know about Blake."

"Blake?"

"If my information is correct, Dylan is his adopted brother."

"Where does this information come from?" she said, somewhat skeptically.

"A confidential informant."

"Okay. I also got a call from one of your associates there, Sharyn Weist. Lacey's doing some work for her on the connection with the Hook'dup app."

"Sharyn mentioned that. Any progress?"

"Not on that, but I have a lot number for you regarding the mannequins. They did originate in Russia and came to New York City via Toronto."

"Toronto? Huh. Good work. Let's take a closer look at the shipping company and their other clients."

"On it."

"By the way, does Sharyn know that Lacey isn't quite, well, a carbon-based life form?"

"Pat, just because someone isn't born biologically doesn't mean she can't think."

"I'll have to get back to you on that." Lacey's AI was as strong as just about any computer's on the planet, so I could certainly see where Angela was coming from. "Alright. Tell Lacey I need everything we can get on those Neeson brothers. And I need it ASAP."

"When have you ever *not* needed something ASAP?"

"There've been times. Occasionally."

"Uh-huh."

"Oh, also, someone named Fayed—run the name with connections between him and Blake, and also him and Dr. Kuznetsov. Anything and everything. Take it deep. It's all related to Maria's death. Make this case priority one."

"I always do."

Angela ended the call and I took a look around the motel to see if there was any evidence that Blake might have left behind, but finding nothing, my thoughts circled back to what Schwartz had told me about Geoff Dryer, the young resident in the morgue.

He'd been shot with my gun, so the SIG would almost certainly be taken into evidence. Although it would likely be released back to me eventually, I was definitely going to be without it for a while.

Did not make me happy. But right now that was insignificant compared to everything else that was going on.

Dylan.

Fayed.

The Bluebeard.

The terrorist.

The nexus between them: Blake. He stood at the crossroads of his brother's obsession and his lover's suffering.

When I was a kid, my older brother Sean would sometimes gross out our mom by mixing all of the food on his plate together into one indiscriminate pile.

I was never sure why it bothered her so much, since in a few minutes it would all be mixing together inside him, but she would always cringe and he would always smile. "It tastes better this way."

"Mm-hmm," she would say.

Well, now, my plate was full and, although there were different piles of food for each different aspect of the intertwined cases, they were getting swirled together in a way that made it increasingly more difficult to tell where one ended and another began.

65

Now in the daylight, Dylan could see his surroundings.

He was in some type of old industrial warehouse. Although he couldn't view much outside the window, it appeared that he was in a decrepit and run-down part of the city—which, from what he'd seen of Detroit so far, didn't narrow things down too much.

Somehow at the same time the air smelled dabbed with decay, and also fresh, sweeping in from the nearby lakes.

The water-damaged ceiling had rotted through in several places and, based on the perspective out the window and the view up through the holes in the ceiling, he could tell he was on the first of three floors.

Although someone had removed whatever furniture might have once been there and the file cabinets were all gone, he figured he was in the office. The papers that'd been dumped onto the floor now lay, mildew-speckled, near the window.

He tried again to free the end of the chain from the pipe but soon realized there wasn't any way he would be able to get loose or break the pipe without some sort of tool.

Earlier he'd heard Blake in the other room speaking with his associate. "Mannie, I want you to stay here. I have to go speak to someone across town. You know who it is."

"Yes."

"I'm going to ask him for his help."

"It may take some convincing."

"I plan to offer him the thing he wants most."

"You?"

"Close. Justice."

As far as Dylan knew, Mannie was still in the warehouse, perhaps in the next room over, perhaps outside. Neither he nor Blake had shown their face yet this morning.

Dylan thought of Scarlett.

From his history with her, he knew about her interest in law enforcement.

During the trial, she'd changed her major to criminal justice and, if she indeed had gone that route, it might very well have meant a federal job rather than work as a patrol officer—especially in Detroit where, it didn't take him long to discover, the department paid their officers an average of ten thousand dollars less than the departments across the street in the suburbs.

Scarlett was used to having money and was smart, and considering her criminal justice studies, he figured he would start with local law enforcement and then move on, as needed, to the FBI.

One precinct at a time.

One victim, one letter at a time.

Draw out the officers, have someone film them, and, eventually the FBI would get involved.

Meanwhile, he would be searching online for any clues as to where she was.

One search.

And another.

Without assuming too much, he had to admit that all the signs were pointing toward the FBI.

But he realized he needed time to make it work.

Well, prison had taught him patience.

He would do it body by body until he found her.

Dylan had been in prison for fifteen years and technology had taken off exponentially in that time. Although he could navigate his way around online, he was by no means a hacker.

So he went about it old-school.

Scarlett Farrow had disappeared, and with all the ways to search for someone today, that wasn't an easy task, so she likely had help.

The Department of Justice? The Witness Protection Program?

Maybe.

If Simone was right and Scarlett was in Detroit, he might be able to get her to show her hand.

And so, that's what he had tried to do.

Now, extending the chain as far as it would go, he searched for any assets he could use.

He had on his clothes. There was a drain by his foot.

Other than that, nothing useful was within reach.

However, on the other side of the room, a crowbar lay forgotten in the corner, obscured by the shadows until now, as the sunlight angled through the window and revealed the top of it.

The crowbar was about twelve feet from him.

It looked like whoever had been in here scavenging had tried unsuccessfully to pry out a wall safe and left the bar behind, perhaps accidentally, or perhaps with the intention of returning later.

Dylan reasoned that he might be able to use it to pry the pipe loose from the wall or, if he got the angle and torque right, maybe even crank open one of the chain's links.

Calculating how much distance he could get by using his pants, shoelaces, and belt to create some sort of retrieval system, he figured it would be close—close enough to at least justify giving it a shot.

He snaked his belt free from its loops and slipped off his pants to tie them into a makeshift rope.

++++

Sharyn's phone vibrated and she checked the screen to find her first three requests for hookups through the app.

Scrolling to the first profile page, she saw the photo of a male twenty-two-year-old graduate student from Thailand now studying here in Detroit. *I've never done this before. Wanting to study international AFFAIRS. Git it?*

Um. No.

That was definitely not Dylan.

The second profile picture showed a graying man in his sixties posing behind the wheel of his convertible. *Looking for someone to take a ride with me.*

Oh, this could not seriously be what the singles scene in Detroit was like these days.

The third message was from a middle-aged Hispanic woman who must not have looked carefully at Sharyn's profile preferences of F looking for M.

She declined all of the hookups but kept her profile active and kept her status as "Available."

As she went to take a shower, her thoughts kept replaying what had happened last night: having Pat over. Their conversation regarding relationships. His apology concerning the way he'd broken things off when they were at the Academy.

Then, Christie's phone call right before he left.

And what it might mean for the three of them.

66

7:34 A.M.

Dispersal in 7 hours

As I was finishing up at the motel and collecting my laptop and notes, my phone rang and Christie's face appeared on the screen.

I said a small prayer that things would be okay. Praying isn't in my wheelhouse, so I wasn't sure of the right words to use, but I figured God in all his wisdom didn't need me to figure them all out. He knew what I was getting at.

Help me save this.

Help me say the right things for once.

Please.

Please.

"Good morning, Pat."

"Good morning."

Bypassing small talk, she cut to the chase. "So, you're working with a woman that you used to date?"

Careful now. Don't get defensive.

"Yes."

I was going to say more. I was going to explain helpfully that our relationship ended eight years ago, that that's a long time, that I hadn't seen her since then, that I was over her, but said nothing. Which was probably for the best.

"Why didn't you tell me about her, though?" Christie asked. "That she would be here?"

"I couldn't see how telling you would've helped us stay us."

"Us stay us?"

"Yes."

"And what does that mean to you, Pat? 'Us staying us'?"

"I know what I want it to mean."

"What's that?"

"A future together."

I didn't elaborate on the specifics of what that might entail, and she didn't ask me to.

"Pat, did you take this case so you could see her again? Did that influence your decision?"

Motives.

Roots, interlaced and impossible to trace.

When I was slow in replying, she said, "I see."

"Christie, don't read too much into my silence. I want to be honest. I've never been the best at sharing my feelings."

She was quiet.

"Look," I said. "I'm sorry. I want to figure this out. We should meet, talk things through."

"You're right. We should. But before that, I need to speak with Sharyn."

Sharyn still had feelings for me so I didn't like the thought of that, but I had to admit that it would probably be good for them to talk—and the sooner, the better.

If things were ever going to work long-term with Christie, I needed to make sure she could trust me—and that she knew I trusted her.

"I'll call her, see when she can meet with you."

"If you give me her number, I can call her myself."

Last night Sharyn had offered to do whatever she could to help resolve things, so I gave Christie both her mobile and work numbers. Then I said, "Let me know when you're available to talk with me. Whatever I'm doing here, I'll drop it so we can meet."

"Alright."

After we hung up, I texted Sharyn to tell her to be on the lookout for a message from Christie, and passed along Christie's number so her phone would identify the call when it came in.

++++

The nightmares were a noose around Ali's neck. Dark, sinewy cords that tightened the longer he was asleep and that only let go when he was finally awake, heart hammering, hands clinging to his sheets, the shirt he'd slept in drenched in sweat.

The pillow was smeared with blood from his split lip and fluid from his swollen, leaking eye.

So, the dreams.

Blood on blood on blood.

Splattering across his clothes and onto the sand around him, all during the night as he slept.

It was easier to believe that it was all a dream rather than a memory. Some nightmares are like that—we think they're real until we wake up.

Only to find out we're still asleep and that we need to wake up again.

Wake up, Ali.

He recalled an old saying that his mother used to tell

him when he was a boy: *"A man may outrun his past but he cannot outrun the person it has led him to become."*

So, now that he was awake, Ali had a different kind of terror, a different kind of pain: he was who he had become. There was no running from that. No hiding from the truth.

Nightmares came at him from two directions—what he had done and what he was doing. The past and the present, squeezing any possible joy out of what was to come.

He tried futilely to find comfort by reminding himself that the pathway he was on would serve Allah.

Ever since he'd been recruited and given this assignment, Ali had wondered why Fayed and his group didn't just infect him beforehand, before he flew to the United States. Why wait? Why was the timing important? And why hadn't he been told about others who were going to martyr themselves? Were there others, or was he alone? And if he was alone, why?

If there was a way that he could put an end to what he'd become a part of, if he could stop Fayed, protect his sister, and save innocent lives, he would do it. He *had* to do it, no matter what that might mean, or how great a sacrifice it might require.

Last night Abdul had told him that his wife would bring breakfast up at seven, and checking the time, Ali realized he had overslept.

After slipping on a loose-fitting shirt that could hide a suicide vest if necessary, he opened the door to head downstairs and ask her to forgive him and saw the meal waiting for him on a tray beside his door.

Taking it back into the room, he went online as he ate.

Fayed had instructed him to read up on the city, but

since he'd had to drive up rather than fly, he hadn't had the chance yet to do so.

Now he studied the materials and links he'd been sent, and as he clicked through from one site to another, he discovered that over the last one hundred and twenty years a lot had gone on underneath the city of Detroit.

In an online article titled, "It's Not What You See That Counts," the author, Gwyneth Leroy, a woman who'd extensively explored the bomb shelters beneath churches and schools, wrote about all that existed beneath the city's surface.

The article covered the airtight bomb shelters as well as a tunnel that led from the Packard Plant to vast underground salt mines, and an Underground Railroad system that was used to secretly transport slaves to Canada during the times of oppression and the Civil War.

As Ali was sorting through the implications, someone knocked on his door.

Expecting that it might be Abdul, who didn't speak, Ali simply said, "I'm coming," rather than asking who was there.

At the door, Abdul greeted him silently, then handed him the tablet with the words already typed in: Good morning, brother. How are your wounds today?

Ali tapped in his response: I am recovering well. Thank you.

—I am sorry I could not meet you for breakfast. Will you join me for prayers?

—Yes. Of course.

—Forgive me if I must pray silently.

—There is nothing to forgive.

—See you downstairs.

—I will be right there.

++++

Tessa was asleep when she heard her mom's ringtone and, even though it usually took her like an hour to wake up, she somehow found herself immediately alert as she answered the phone.

"Mom, where are you?"

"I'll explain everything when I get home—which I think will be tonight."

"I thought you were gonna be gone for a couple days."

"I'm hoping to change my flights, and if everything works out, I should be landing at JFK right around seven thirty."

Tessa could tell by her mom's tone of voice that she was upset, but when she asked what was going on, her mother simply said, "It's fine."

"So, you're done seeing whoever it was you flew out to see?"

"Yes. It looks like we're done."

67

8:34 A.M.
Dispersal in 6 hours

Sharyn entered the tea and pastry shop where she and Christie had agreed to meet.

An attractive, yet clearly heavy-hearted woman was seated by the window and rose when Sharyn entered.

"Hello." She had a to-go cup in her hand. "Sharyn?"

"Hi, Christie. Can I buy you breakfast?"

"No. Thank you. But if you'd like something . . ." Christie gestured toward the glass counter. "Please."

"I'm okay."

"No doughnut? Croissant?"

"No thanks."

"Alright. Um . . . I was wondering if you'd like to take a walk along the river?"

"Sure," Sharyn said. "The path just outside is actually quite a popular trail for runners. Dog walkers."

"Okay."

So far it was one of those conversations where you edit everything carefully before you speak and say only the safe things. But Sharyn didn't expect it to stay that way for long.

Christie retrieved her purse, and Sharyn led her to the walking path along the bank of the Detroit River.

A group of four joggers who were taking advantage of the cool morning were huffing toward them.

Sharyn stepped to the side to allow them to pass. When they had, she said to Christie, "First of all, I'd like to apologize for the misunderstanding last night, and also assure you: there was nothing going on between Pat and me."

"Okay."

It was a response that was too quick and too polite: *Oh, well, now that we've cleared that up, I can rest easy.*

Christie's next words took Sharyn by surprise. "You are quite beautiful." Christie's voice was soft. Almost reverent. "I have to admit, I was wondering."

Sharyn searched for an appropriate response. Thanking Christie for the compliment didn't feel right, and neither did reciprocating and telling her how pretty she was as well, so in the end she didn't address the comment at all, but instead said, "What do you want to know? I'll tell you anything that would help."

"You're the one who requested Pat for this case?"

"Yes."

"Why did you?"

"His geospatial specialty. He's the best at what he does, and I thought he could help us save innocent people by catching the guy who's doing this."

That sounded prepared. Too planned out.

Sharyn hesitated slightly, then went on, "And because I wanted to see him. Full disclosure: I knew he wasn't married. I didn't know if he was seeing anyone, and I wanted to find out if there would still be chemistry between us."

"And?"

"And?"

"Was there? Or maybe I should say, 'Is there?'"

"Yes."

"Do you still love him?" Christie asked.

Water rippled toward them, a gentle morning breeze whispered past, but the calm morning belied the tension Sharyn was feeling here with Pat's girlfriend.

"It's been a long time since we were together," she said.

"That's not what I asked you, Sharyn."

"No. No, of course not . . . I mean, I don't."

"You were doing better a minute ago when you were telling me the truth. I have to say, you lie about as badly as Pat does."

"Okay, you're right. I don't know that I ever stopped loving him."

"Thank you."

"For?"

"The truth. Have you told him that? I mean, that you still love him?"

"No." Sharyn stopped on the path and Christie stood beside her. "Listen, I know that last night looked . . . Well, I can understand why you'd be upset. I'd be upset too if I were you. But Pat and I didn't do anything. Please, don't let me get in the way of you two being happy."

Christie sighed lightly. "I was hoping it would be easy to hate you."

"Well, I'm glad it's easy to like you."

"Why?"

Because I want what's best for Pat, and in a few days, he'll be heading back to New York City and you'll be there and I won't.

"He cares about you," Sharyn said. "He cares about you a lot."

"How do you know that?"

"By how upset he was after he got off the phone with you, thinking that he'd hurt you."

Neither woman said anything.

But they didn't start walking again either.

"Now what?" Sharyn asked at last. "Where do we go from here?"

"I need to decide if I should stay for another day like I was planning to, or change my flight and head back to the city today."

"Which way are you leaning?"

"I'm not sure. The earliest flight I could get on leaves at five. It doesn't look full, so I have a couple of hours yet to figure that out."

Honestly, Sharyn didn't know what would be best for Pat and his relationship with Christie—if she returned home now, or if she stayed in Detroit and tried to work things out here.

And, as much as she'd been telling the truth about wanting Pat to be happy, it hadn't been the whole truth—she really wished she would be the one waiting for him in New York City.

And so, she was torn.

Yes, she liked Christie, but she didn't like her enough to quell the love she still had for Pat.

"Let me know if there's anything else I can do," she said to Christie. "I promise not to get between you two."

"Because you still love him?"

"Because I want what's best for him." She could have said more. Maybe she should have, but she left it at that.

68

I went to the airport to pick up Ralph.

While I was walking into the terminal, I recalled that yesterday I'd promised Starr, the secretary at the city records department, that I would buy her lipstick and nail polish in exchange for her help locating the records for Lincoln High School.

Pausing near baggage claim, I went online and found the makeup products on Amazon—and they were each at least five times what I'd expected, but I didn't want to go back on my word, so I put the order through.

Nude Velvet.

London Reckless.

Ninety dollars for the lipstick? Sixty-five for nail polish?

I wish I'd heard about this on career day in high school.

For the shipping address I listed the city records department "Attn. Starr."

Then I placed a second order and typed in Christie's address in New York City. It seemed to me that Starr probably had good taste and that it couldn't hurt to have a little something special waiting for Christie back at her apartment.

On Wednesday night, I'd been reminded that my friend Calvin Werjonic had consulted with the city on environmental crime reduction strategies, and now that I suspected that we were looking for a Bluebeard and I had a few minutes to myself, I thought it might be the ideal time to give him a call.

For privacy, I found a quiet corner near the security checkpoint where I could wait for Ralph's plane, which was scheduled to land in about fifteen minutes.

Calvin travels a lot and I wasn't sure what time zone he was in, but I also knew him well enough to realize that he was an early riser—as a distinguished Englishman, he loved those brisk early-morning walks—and for him it was never the wrong time to consult on a case. And even though everyone except for Supreme Court justices and school cafeteria workers would have retired by the time they were his age, he was going as strong as ever.

When I was studying for my doctorate, there'd been no question in my mind about my first choice for an advisor.

Dr. Werjonic was a legend in the field of environmental criminology. His groundbreaking research on serial offenders had given legs to the entire field of geospatial investigation as it stands today.

An ardent student of human nature, Calvin always opted for video calls rather than simply audio ones. As he commented to me once, "So much of communication is nonverbal—we know this from reams of research. So, why would we eliminate all of that from our important conversations when we have the technology to utilize it to the fullest?"

I texted him to see if he'd be up for a video call and within minutes my phone was notifying me of an incoming call through the video app he preferred using.

"Patrick, my boy," he said in his distinct and endearing English accent.

"Calvin, it's good to see your face."

"Yours as well."

After quickly catching up with each other, I got right to the matter at hand.

Without stating specifics that might undermine the confidentiality of the investigation, I told him what I could about the case, sending him select information to review.

He listened carefully, asking an occasional question for clarification, but mostly he just sipped the Earl Grey tea that he appreciated almost as much as I did my coffee.

After he'd had a chance to look over the files I sent, he said, "I'm certain you've plowed the obvious fields: looking into parents, teachers, friends of the victims."

"Yes. No links that we can see. However, we have strong reason to believe that the offender is the man I told you about a moment ago, Dylan Neeson."

"The one who attacked your coworker."

"Yes."

Coworker. Yes. That's who she is. That's all she is.

No—

Yes. That's all.

"Why that one male victim?" Calvin interrupted my thoughts. "An outlier, you think?"

"I'm not sure. I was wondering about that as well."

"Hmm. Well, we must focus on victimology." He often spoke in this way, as if he were part of the investigation. He'd been involved in so many hundreds of cases that the approach just came second nature to him. "The epicenter of his crimes will correspond to the movement patterns of the victims. That's the key. With a Bluebeard, establishing the link between him and the victims is more important than establishing the links between the victims themselves."

"I've been looking into that, but coming up short."

"In some cases, victims will travel several hours to come to the Bluebeard's home base."

"These were all regional."

"The ones that you know of."

A slight pause. "Yes."

"Do not assume, Patrick, that all of the victims have been recovered. Think now, what attracts them to the Bluebeard?"

"The promise of pleasure—however they might define that."

"Indeed." He nodded. "The one motive, the only motive that matters. If you find out what the victims were seeking, or how they viewed or pursued pleasure, it'll help you discover how he was luring them. The solution might very well hinge upon identifying the nature of the invitation because, with a Bluebeard, it's always one place, but that place is not always the same location."

"I don't follow."

"I tracked one Bluebeard a number of years ago who drove a delivery truck. He'd constructed a torture chamber in the back of it. The location was always moving, but the place was always the same."

"A peripatetic offender," I said. "But honestly, in this case, the locations and timing of the crimes don't speak to a killer who's traveling through the area. And, if it is Neeson, he might be here specifically to target Sharyn."

"The question isn't so much one of significance as one of attribution—not how much the detail mattered to the completion of the crime—"

"But how much it mattered to him to commit the crime in this way."

"Yes. Let's go back to the male victim for a moment." He consulted his notes. "Gideon Flello. Was he gay?"

"Not as far as I know. Why would that matter?"

"The attraction factor: pleasure, as you just pointed out. What desire precipitated the act of the victims traveling to meet the killer? How is the Bluebeard allowing his victims to choose him?"

"Don't you mean how he's choosing his victims?"

"Perhaps it's both."

"I don't understand. You're saying they want to die?"

"By no means. And yet, they might have all come to him for the same reason. Thus, this mobile dating application you were telling me about."

"Sex."

"Perhaps."

"So, if Gideon was looking for that, it might not have been that the killer was looking for him."

"We have far too many 'mights' right now, Patrick. At this point I would advise discovering all that you can about the Hook'dup connection."

"Sharyn is looking into that."

"I think that perhaps you might need to look into Sharyn."

"What? Why?"

"According to what you told me, the killer is, to a certain degree, obsessed with her, and obsessions are not birthed in vacuums. The more you understand her past, the more you'll understand his choices here, in the present."

I hadn't told Calvin that Sharyn was Scarlett Farrow, but I had told him that her photo appeared on the painting of the crucified Christ.

"Alright."

The flight monitor registered that Ralph's plane had landed.

If Blake had been telling me the truth, then he had Dylan and he was willing to turn him over to us—but I wasn't going to bank on any of that. At this point, we clearly needed to pursue as many investigative routes as possible.

Calvin closed up by saying, "Call me at the weekend, let me know what you found out."

"I will. And thanks."

"Don't thank me yet. Find him. Stop him. Then we'll meet for a pint."

A few moments after wrapping up the video call with Calvin, I got a text from Ralph that he was deboarding, and I walked over to the TSA checkpoint to catch up with him.

69

9:34 A.M.

Dispersal in 5 hours

"How was the flight?" I asked Ralph.

"Not great. I am not a small man, but the woman sitting next to—well, I didn't have any room. How can I say this . . . She was a venti woman."

"A venti woman?"

"Starbucks. Think about it. The next size up from a grande."

"Ralph, you can't call a woman 'venti.' You say she's . . . well, um . . . substantial. Or, like with a car, you might have compact, sedan, or full-size."

"Okay, then, she's a Winnebago," he muttered. "What do we know about the case?"

I updated him as much as possible without mentioning the meeting with Blake or the deal I had agreed to.

Ralph didn't have any checked bags, so we walked directly to my car, but before we climbed in, he chugged my shoulder. "So, Christie made it here, right? You two have a good night?"

"I have to say, that was very generous of you to give her

your frequent flyer miles." It wasn't really an answer, but my best attempt at a pivot.

"All for a good cause. Were you surprised?"

"Yes, I was."

A smile. "And? How'd it go?"

"Maybe not as well as it could have."

"Okay. And what does that mean?"

"Um . . ."

"Did you tell her?"

"Tell her?"

"What you promised me you were gonna tell her as soon as you saw her. Remember what you said yesterday? That you're sorry and that you love her—with a pause."

"Yeah, I didn't exactly get to that."

He looked at me sternly. "Go on."

"It's sort of a long story."

"Edit it."

"I wasn't at my motel when she called."

"I've known you for a long time, Pat. I can tell when you're being evasive, and you're being evasive. What happened?"

"I was working late at the house of another agent when Christie arrived."

"Ah. A female agent."

"Yes, as a matter of fact."

"Name?"

"Sharyn Weist."

"And?"

"And what?"

"Where you working or playing?"

"Working. I'm telling you, nothing happened."

"Then why do you sound so defensive?"

"Well . . ."

Just tell him, Pat. Go on.

"She's someone I used to date, back when we were at the Academy."

He eyed me coolly without saying a word.

"I'm not here in Detroit to see her, Ralph."

"I never said you were."

"I'm here to help solve this case."

"That's right."

"I want things to be right with Christie."

"Uh-huh."

"You don't have to agree with me every time I say something."

"I know."

"Ralph, I'm—"

"You didn't tell Christie about Sharyn before yesterday, did you?"

"Well, she knew I used to date someone back at Quantico."

"Bro, you know that's not what I'm asking."

"No, I didn't tell her that Sharyn would be here."

"Or that you'd be at her house working late on a case."

His tone might have put quotes around the word "working," but I wasn't sure.

"Why didn't you tell her?" he pressed me.

"Openness and honesty aren't always the same thing."

"Yeah, well, how many times has someone been less than open with you and you've been thankful later when you found out the whole truth?"

"I was trying to do the right thing."

"Well, you did it the wrong way." He put his beefy hand on my shoulder like a big brother might have done. "Dude, there's never a time when you're gonna be as tempted to contact an old girlfriend as when you're going through a rough spot in a new relationship. But that's the worst time to do it. It's bad for you. It's bad for both of the women. You gotta wait, man. If things don't work out with Christie—and they'd better, but if they don't—give it a little time, then call Sharyn. But right now, every moment you spend thinking about her is gonna be chopping away what you're trying to accomplish with Christie."

He angled his hand and hit me with the edge of his palm to accentuate his point as he repeated the word. "Chop. Chop."

"Okay, I get it."

"Chop."

"Alright, alright. It's good advice."

"Comes from experience. Don't ask me which one."

"Gotcha. Let's get to the federal building. SAC Kennedy and the team have been pursuing all the leads related to Maria's death. I also have Angela from Cyber looking into who Fayed might be."

"Fayed?"

"A lead from a confidential informant."

"This Fayed, he a Muslim?"

"I believe so."

"Just like in the video."

"Yeah."

"That's not good." He cussed under his breath. "The OPA is going to try to keep everything quiet, and that might not be what we need. The head of Office of Public Affairs, Darlene Licata, she can be a real something-that-I-don't-want-to-spell-out-that-rhymes-with-witch sometimes."

"Yeah. I hear you."

He was right. In our culture today, the Bureau's Office of Public Affairs bends over backward to avoid offending any group, especially Muslim-Americans, and sometimes it bends too far.

Ralph and I were on the same page here. We had nothing against being careful not to propagate stereotypes or hurt people's feelings, as long as it didn't get in the way of speaking or pursuing the truth. And every year far more Muslims are killed in hate crimes against them by other Muslims than by adherents to all other religions combined.

It's a fact. It's a hard fact for some people to accept, but it's a fact. Yet the Muslim Concern League makes more of an issue over a little graffiti on a mosque or some name-calling than they do about the weekly—if not daily—suicide attacks by Muslims targeting other Muslims. When it comes to hate crimes, Muslims should be the most upset at people of their own faith.

Lately the OPA had even been inviting the Muslim Concern League into meetings so they could review press releases before they go to the public. It was unprecedented, but these were unusual times.

I didn't know Kennedy well, but he didn't seem like the kind of guy who would bow down at the altar of political correctness.

"I think we'll be fine. The SAC here seems like he's more interested in solving cases than in group hugs."

"I'll make some calls on the way. See what HQ has on Fayed."

We climbed into the car and took off for the federal building.

70

It was taking Dylan longer than he thought it would to get the crowbar, and he wondered briefly if his brother had positioned it just out of reach, as a way of testing him.

But he abandoned that thought. Whatever else was true about Blake, he was not the kind of person to make someone that he cared about suffer indiscriminately.

By now, Dylan was using his shoe tied to his belt and his pants and was flipping it across the room.

He'd managed to hit the crowbar a few times, once even knocking it over, but because of its weight, he hadn't been able to drag it any closer, and it'd just lain there beside the wall, mocking him.

He still didn't know why Blake had brought him here or why he'd chained him up.

Yeah, he knew that his brother loved him too much to kill him, but the big guy just might be less apt to show compassion and restraint than Blake would.

If it came down to it, would you kill your brother so that you could remain free? Do you love him more than your freedom? Would you chance going back to prison, or take the ultimate step to make sure you don't?

Tough questions.

Ones he didn't want to answer.

And, if he could get free now, he wouldn't have to.

Dylan didn't want to make too much noise or draw too much attention to what he was doing, so he needed to find something that would be heavy enough to drag the crowbar toward him, but not so loud that it would bring Mannie in to check on him.

He studied that drain on the floor.

It looked substantial enough to do the trick—even when he spread out his fingers, he wasn't able to span its width. Also, it would be easier to throw, but although it would probably be enough weight, it would also clang when it landed.

Unless you cover it with something soft.

First, though, he needed to get it out of the floor.

He bent and was preparing to use the belt buckle to pry it loose when he heard footsteps approaching outside the room.

Hastily, he tugged on his pants, stuffed the shoelaces and belt into his shoes, and then slid them aside and turned, barefoot, toward the door.

It opened.

And Mannie and his brother stepped into the room.

"Hello, Dylan," Blake said.

"Hello, brother." Dylan held up his fettered wrist. "Why this? Can't we trust each other?"

"Just a precaution. You aimed a gun at my chest last night."

"Only after you aimed one at me."

"True." Blake acknowledged that with a nod. "Let's see how much of this I have right. Before killing Simone Tee, you made her tell you the location of that actress, Scarlett Farrow. That led you here, to Detroit. Then you began at the karate studio, located a young man who worked at the morgue who could do your bidding. How am I doing?"

"Close. When I arrived, I discovered an app called Hook'dup. It's one where they have people contribute locations for encounters of a romantic bent. So, I first found a photographer that I liked, and she led me to Geoff—the resident. He stole Oxycodone from the hospital and sold it to the medical examiner's son. His graffiti art took him all over the city. It was a bit serendipitous that he worked with the medical examiner. Turned out to be a profitable partnership."

"Until you shot him dead."

"Yes. Until then. And I hadn't gone to the dojo until after I met him."

"He videotaped the scenes and posted them to that news site to see if Scarlett Farrow would show up." Blake might have been guessing or deducing. Dylan wasn't certain how much his brother knew. "Is she a cop?" Blake asked.

"I'm not sure," Dylan replied. "Possibly FBI."

"Why the grenade in the Ninth Precinct? Just to draw attention?"

"I wouldn't include the word 'just.'"

"And now you're trying to find Scarlett so you can have revenge on her for turning you in?" Blake approached him. "That seems beneath you, Dylan."

"I'm not interested in vengeance, brother, only justice. I don't want to find her because she got me arrested—I deserved that for my crimes. I want to find her because she murdered my son."

"What?"

"Or, I suppose I should say 'our son.'"

Blake was standing within reach of Dylan, but neither made a move to go after the other. "She got pregnant when you sexually assaulted her?"

A nod. "She killed him," Dylan said. "Before I could ever see him or hold him or hug him. That's why I want to find her."

Now, for the first time, Mannie spoke. "Was your son born?"

"No."

"An abortion?"

"Yes."

"How do you know that?"

"My lawyer had her followed. Long story. When I was in prison, I met a man named Bryan. He was a pro-life activist and was serving an eight-year sentence."

"Did he attack an abortion doctor?" Blake asked.

"No. He never harmed another human being. He simply did to puppies what abortionists do to babies. He would jam a knife into the back of their skulls, then insert a vacuum tube and suck out their brains while their hearts were still beating. Sometimes he would crush their skulls or cut off their legs. Over the course of a month he killed more than a hundred puppies—the same number of babies that the abortion clinic down the road killed during that same time. He was convicted of animal cruelty and inhumane treatment of animal charges, all while the abortion doctors got paid to do the same things to humans. And still continue to."

"That's because abortion is legal and torturing and killing puppies is not."

Dylan shook his head. "Brother, we both know that

you're too smart for a sophomoric retort like that. Legality and morality are two distinctly different things. The former does not require the latter, and the latter does not depend on the former. Do to a stray dog what an abortionist does to a human baby and you'll go to jail. How is that, in any universe, right?"

"You raped a woman, she had an abortion, and now you want to kill her. How is that, in any universe, right?"

Mannie spoke up again, his voice rumbling and low and firm. "A womb should be the safest place in the world for a baby, not the most dangerous one. But that does not make it right, what you did. You dishonored a woman."

Dylan eyed him. Once again he was reminded that this guy, Mannie, was a wild card. Dylan had no idea what he was capable of if someone got on his wrong side.

But based on the man's size, demeanor, and fighting ability, he could guess.

"Do you know where Scarlett is?" Blake asked. "Did you find her?"

"Perhaps that is one thing I'm not yet ready to share."

"Well." Blake backed up. "It'll be over soon. You're going back to prison, brother. We'll let God deal with Scarlett and her choice."

Dylan said nothing.

Blake and Mannie left, and Dylan waited a few minutes after their voices faded away and a door clanged shut, and then he used the prong of the belt to pry the drain cover loose.

It popped out on the fourth try.

Nice.

He attached the drain to the end of one of the shoelaces. He needed padding, so, since his wrist was chained, he had to rip his shirt to get it off. Then, he wrapped it around the drain to dampen the sound, just in case Mannie or his brother returned or were working out of sight somewhere. Finally, he gave his attention to the crowbar once again.

He needed to get out of here before they came back for him or called in the police.

Holding the drain like a Frisbee, he slung it toward the far side of the room.

71

10:34 A.M.

Dispersal in 4 hours

The federal building's staff entrance was open today, and Ralph and I were able to get into the building directly from the parking garage. We'd just walked into the lobby when Christie called. I signaled for Ralph to go on ahead, told him I'd be right there, and answered my cell.

"Hey," I said to Christie, "How are you?"

"Good. I was able to meet with Sharyn."

I tried to keep the worry out of my voice. "And how did that go?"

"It went well."

"Good. That's good to hear."

"Can I see you?"

"Yes, of course."

"Where are you?"

"I'm at the federal building, but honestly, now is not a good time." As I said the words, I thought about the promise I'd made earlier, that I would drop everything and come to see her. "But I can come soon."

"When do you think?"

I rubbed my head. "Actually, Christie, I don't know. There's a lot going down right now."

"I understand. And I'm sorry I interrupted your work. I am. That was never my intention, I just thought that . . . It doesn't matter. Listen, I'm flying back home tonight. I was just hoping we could connect before then."

"No, Christie. That's not necessary, heading home I mean. Listen, can you come by here? I'll meet with you as soon as our briefing is over, that, or I'll find an excuse to slip out so we can talk."

"I can be there in an hour. Will that work?"

"Perfect. We're going to make this happen." I didn't specify if I meant seeing each other now or working things out long-term. "Text me when you get here. I'll meet you at the front doors."

After we hung up, I joined Ralph at the elevator bay.

"I just got word." He was pocketing his cell. "Dr. Qiao and Dr. Ferrier won't be arriving in Detroit until after one."

I was still a little caught up thinking about my conversation with Christie. "Alright," I said.

"That Christie a minute ago?"

"Yeah."

"Well?"

"She spoke with Sharyn. We're going to talk in an hour."

"Stay focused," he said. "Eyes on the prize."

"Right."

"I don't mean just her, I mean the case."

"I know."

We got a clearance badge, took the elevator down to the floor that didn't exist, and headed to the briefing.

++++

The more Sharyn thought about it, the more she came to believe that the meeting with Christie had gone exceptionally well, considering the circumstances.

Patrick's girlfriend seemed like a good person, and Sharyn hated the idea that she might be in any way responsible for their problems.

But she also did not hate it all that much either.

She wanted them together, and she didn't. She was human. It was natural. But still, it was hard. For now, though, she needed to focus on finding the Bluebeard, who, by all accounts, was most likely Dylan Neeson, the man who'd attacked her, who'd raped her. The man whose child she had aborted.

She realized that, because of her past with Dylan, Kennedy would never clear her to use herself as bait. If he found out about what she'd put it into play, he would almost certainly call it off.

Pat was busy at the fed building with the other case, but if she was going after Dylan, she really did need a partner, and it needed to be someone she could trust. She decided on Detective Schwartz and gave him a call.

"Ted, I think I might know how we can catch the Bluebeard, and I think I might know who it is. I need your help."

"I was reading the files about what Pat posted last night on his Bluebeard theory. It's interesting. And you think it's this Neeson character that you noted in the case file?"

"Yes. I'll fill you in on everything, but I don't want to do it over the phone."

"Tell me where to meet you and I'll be right there."

"No one can know about this."

"Got it. Mum's the word."

++++

After morning prayers and before he left the house, Abdul had given Ali directions on how to reach Aisha's Halal Restaurant. Now, Ali was en route and his phone told him he would arrive in twenty minutes.

72

By the time we entered the briefing room, Kennedy had already pulled up the video chat with Assistant Director DeYoung. Ralph and I took a seat beside Lieutenant Sproul, who'd no doubt been called in to coordinate local law enforcement with the FBI in the case of a bioweapon attack in the city.

Kennedy said to me, "FYI, I spoke with Agent Weist. I informed her that I would be needing you for the next few hours. She said that was fine, that she and Detective Schwartz were following up on some leads regarding the search for the Bluebeard. I'm not quite sure what that referred to."

"It's our working theory about who the serial killer is. We're thinking it might be a convicted felon named Dylan Neeson."

"Gotcha. She told me she'd be in touch with you later."

I didn't bring up my conversation with Blake at the motel. It was going to be hard, if not impossible, keeping that to myself until I heard back from him about Fayed's location.

"Alright, then," DeYoung said. "Let's get things rolling here. In my office I have our OPA Director, Darlene Licata. Since this threat deals with Islamic extremists, I've asked her to join us."

"First of all." Darlene cleared her throat authoritatively. "Let's avoid that term, 'Islamic extremists,' and go with 'militants' or 'violent extremists.'" Her face was all angles and bones, and so was the tight, shrill clamor of her voice.

"Oh, this is BS." Ralph cut in. "If we're gonna tackle this situation, let's at least have the balls to call it what it is. These people are not just violent and extreme, they belong to a certain religion. Their actions are the direct result of their beliefs. They're not just 'militants.' What do you think, they're Amish militants? Or maybe we have some Buddhist militants out there trying to chant us to death? Or atheist militants trying to debate us into submission? Look as hard as you want, you're not gonna find Shinto militants or Presbyterian militants or Jehovah's Witness militants, or Mormon militants who're trying to start a potluck Caliphate in the church basement or run us over with their bikes. No. Like it or not, they're Muslims. You can be as politically correct as you want as long as you still tell the truth, but when people's lives are at stake, it's time to stop singing 'Kumbaya' around the campfire and start solving problems. 'Militants' is a term that's reserved for one religion. It's code for Muslims. So let's just say Muslims."

"Are you done, Agent Hawkins?" Darlene asked stiffly.

"No, I can go on if you want."

She narrowed her eyes. "That won't be necessary."

"Lose the scowl, Darlene. It's about as intimidating as the siren of a French police car. We've been through this before. Let's respect whatever religion people are, but let's not play games with words."

"Alright." DeYoung cut in. "We all know where we're coming from here. We'll just say 'terrorists.' And I'll work with Darlene to figure out the exact wording of any press releases we send out. Let's move forward. We're not in a war against Islam, but, yes, the people we're talking about here do consider themselves to be Muslims. Whether or not they're true Muslims, or are actually living out what that religion teaches, they believe they're on a mission from God, and they're not afraid to die for their cause."

But that wasn't good enough for Darlene. "Muslims have a public perception problem, and I do not want us to have any part in fueling the flame against them."

"I wonder why that is?" Lieutenant Sproul interjected, apparently taking Ralph's side in the discussion, but with an even sharper tone than Ralph had used. "This public perception problem of theirs."

"I do not appreciate sarcasm," Darlene said.

"Google 'honor killings in Pakistan,' or 'capital offenses in Iran,' or 'Islamic guidelines on how to beat your wife.' Or maybe 'acid attacks in the Middle East.' Or even worse, try, 'Die in your rage,' and watch the videos that come up—if you can stomach 'em. If you really care to watch people get beheaded and drowned and burned alive and run over with a steamroller in the name of God, go ahead."

"That was completely uncalled for!" Darlene exclaimed.

But Sproul wasn't done. "One percent of the U.S. population is Muslim, right?"

"Yes." She did not sound happy to be agreeing with him. "Approximately."

"But they're responsible for more than ninety percent of the deaths caused by terrorism on American soil since 9/11. You do the math."

"More people are killed in school shootings than—"

"Alright, alright. That's enough." DeYoung signaled for everyone to be quiet but let out a heavy sigh himself. "Let's just figure out the next step here. Ralph, tell us what you know about Blake and his connection to what's going on."

"He passed through the border crossing at Windsor yesterday. His brother, Dylan, is very likely the one responsible for these murders here over the past few months. And then, of course, we have the video of Maria's death and her association with Blake. A video that, even though no one is admitting it, might've been sent with the intention that we would intercept it but yet believe that the sender and receiver didn't know we had it."

"True," Kennedy acknowledged. "Can we confirm that Blake is in the area?"

"He is," I said.

Once again, I struggled with whether to share anything about the encounter I'd had with him at the motel earlier. If Blake really did have Dylan, he might be our best bet to finding Fayed, but he wouldn't help us at all if I mentioned our meeting and he found out about it. And I had the feeling that he had enough connections that even in this room, even on this call, he could do that.

"You sound pretty certain of that, Agent Bowers," Sproul said. "How do you know he's here?"

"Based on all of our current intel, it's the most logical hypothesis to work from."

"Pat also has a confidential informant," Ralph explained. "We'll let him work his sources and give us the information as he gets it. Oh, one more thing—Blake has connections to someone named Fayed Raabi'ah Bashir."

"What do we know about him?" Kennedy asked.

"He's the real deal. CIA and military intelligence have been looking for this asshole for three years. From what they can tell, he's behind numerous suicide attacks in

Yemen and Nigeria and a bombing last year in Brussels. Homeland suspects that he's involved in helping plan, fund, or carry out at least eight other attacks, but his group is too good to leave their signature in too many places. Releasing the smallpox virus here in the States? Yeah. That's right up his alley. And they usually don't do just one attack. They like the pile-on approach."

Blake had mentioned that he could get me the information I would need to find Fayed. If that was true, it was even more important than I'd realized that we stop him.

DeYoung said, "We'll be sending out everything we have on Fayed, although it's not much. We don't have any clear photos of him. At least three different people have all claimed to be him in the last year, but we don't know which of them, if any, is really him."

"The Dread Pirate Roberts," Kennedy muttered. "Like in *The Princess Bride*."

"What do you mean?"

"Same role, different men. Live off the reputation of the one who came before you."

Darlene, who'd been taking notes as we spoke, said, "I'll work on a press release. Is there anything that absolutely cannot be released to the public?"

DeYoung listed a few of the details of the case, then gave out assignments for everyone to work on and was wrapping up the meeting when Sproul said, "Look, we have the most concentrated population of Muslims in the country living just down the street in Dearborn. The most likely people to have any information about a potential terrorist attack by this group would be those who attend a mosque. I propose we get undercover officers in all the mosques and

Islamic educational centers in the area so we can see what kind of information is floating around out there."

"Absolutely not," Darlene said. "If word gets out that we're profiling Muslims—"

"It's not profiling, it's logic and—"

"I'll take it under consideration," DeYoung said, cutting them off.

Then, point by point, we began to analyze everything that we knew about the situation and what kind of response might be called for if there really was a terrorist attack here in Detroit.

73

Ali arrived at the restaurant and checked the time. They had told him not to be early, but to go in at exactly eleven thirty. That gave him almost half an hour.

He didn't want to draw any attention to himself, so he wondered if he should drive around the surface streets rather than stay here, but there was uncertainty if he left, so instead, he simply parked at the back of a nearby lot and locked his doors to wait there for the meeting.

++++

Dylan was getting frustrated by his lack of progress. He tossed the drain repeatedly, as low as he could to avoid it making too much noise, and though sometimes it landed on the other side of the crowbar, he was having trouble dragging it any closer.

However, in time, little by little, it began to slide toward him. Sometimes it twisted to the side, but even if it came only an inch or two closer, it gave him hope that this actually might work.

A few more throws, a few more slides and turns, and finally it was almost within reach. He drew it closer with the drain, and managed to press down on it with his toe and drag it the rest of the way in.

Quickly, he put his clothes on again and got started trying to pry the pipe loose from the wall.

++++

Blake and Mannie were outside the warehouse where Dylan was being kept. When Blake's phone rang, he expected that it would be Fayed, but another voice came on when he answered.

"Mr. Neeson, I understand that you are looking for the location of a meeting."

"What meeting is that?"

"It involves an old friend of yours named Fayed and a young man who just arrived in the States."

Blake was about to ask him where he'd gotten his name or number, but for the moment the fact that he had the information mattered more than the means through which he had obtained it. "Go on."

"Be at Aisha's Halal Restaurant at eleven thirty. You'll find what you're looking for there."

"Why are you telling me this?"

"Because we share a common interest."

"And that is?"

"Dissemination."

"Of?"

Blake waited, but the man didn't reply.

After he'd hung up, Mannie asked him, "Who was that?"

"I'm not sure. He gave me a time and a place to find Fayed. But something else is up here. I don't trust him."

"What do we do with the information?"

"We pass it along. If it's a trap, we won't be the ones caught in it. Stay here. I'm leaving to keep tabs on how things play out at the restaurant."

++++

I got the text from Christie that she'd arrived at the federal building. The meeting was almost finished, so I told her I'd be out in five minutes.

We wrapped things up at the briefing. I took the elevator to the ground floor, found my way through the maze-like halls to the public entrance, and saw her waiting for me on the sidewalk outside the front doors.

"Hey there," I said, as lightly as I could.

She took a deep breath. "Listen, Pat, I trust you that nothing happened between you and Sharyn, but if we're going to have a relationship, you'll need to trust me as well."

"I understand. What do you want to know? I'll tell you everything, whatever it is. I don't want to lose you over a misunderstanding."

"Maybe it's not a misunderstanding, Pat. It may be that the timing isn't right for us. Did you ever see the movie *Final Rendezvous*?"

"No, I don't think so."

"Well, I get that. It's a chick flick. Anyway, there's this one scene where the woman says, 'If you say you love me but yet keep your distance, keep your heart back where it's safe, you're not in love with me at all. You're just playing games with my heart. You can only claim to be my lover when you give away enough of yourself to feel, deep inside of you, the sting of my wounds and the throb of my own aching heart.'"

I was about to tell her how impressed I was that she'd memorized those lines, but I had the sense that if I did, she might infer that I hadn't really been taking to heart what she was trying to tell me.

But she seemed to read my mind, and smiled furtively. "I know. Let's just say I've seen the movie more than once."

"The last thing I want to do is play games with your heart."

"Then don't make me compete with a fantasy. And you can't be infatuated with what you used to have. If you want to be with me, be with me and don't hold back. If you pit a real person against a fantasy, the fantasy will always win. If you think of Sharyn as your plan B if your plan A doesn't work out, I don't want to be your plan A. There can't be another woman in the picture, in the background. But if you're hoping to make your plan A work no matter what it means or how much it costs, then I can't think of anything I'd want more than to be your plan A."

"I'm not going to pit anyone against you. No plan B. I won't let the past intrude on what we have. I promise."

Tell her you're sorry. Tell her that you love her. Just like you promised Ralph you would do.

But before I could say a word, she leaned in and gave me a kiss. As I was replying in kind, my phone rang. It was from an unidentified caller, but I knew that Blake had been intending to contact me.

I excused myself from the kiss before I wanted to and told Christie, "I need to take this. I really do."

"I know."

I tapped the *Accept* icon. "Yes?"

"Eleven thirty." It was Blake. "Aisha's Halal Restaurant. Use your team however you need to, just make sure Fayed doesn't get away. Once you have him and have obtained the information that you need, we'll make the trade."

End call.

An entire SWAT team could be too obtrusive. Additionally, earlier, Kennedy had warned me about who to trust, but we couldn't take any chances that Fayed would get away, so even though I wasn't completely sold on the idea, I called Sproul, told him what was happening, and said, "We'll need SWAT."

"You'll have it," he replied.

Alright, priority number one: bring Fayed in. Priority number two: get him alone so that we could find out everything about the smallpox virus, and then three: figure out the logistics of making an exchange—or break my promise to Blake.

I wasn't sure yet which way I was going to go with that.

I texted Ralph: I need your help with something.

After checking on the location of the restaurant, I realized that getting there in time was going to be tight. Very tight.

I sent him a second text: We need to leave right away.

I said good-bye to Christie and told her I'd contact her later. "Are you still flying out today?" I asked.

"Yes," she said. "But not because of you. Because of Tessa. I haven't been up front with her and I need to clear the air."

++++

No matter how hard Dylan wrenched against the pipe with the crowbar, it didn't budge. He tried cranking open one of the links in the chain, but that didn't work either.

He stared at his hand. The problem of pulling it through the shackle was the bone in his thumb. If his thumb weren't there, or if the bone were dislocated or broken, he could probably get his hand through.

He looked at the beveled end of the crowbar.

Yes, it appeared to be sharp enough. With enough force, it would do the trick.

He bit down on his belt so he wouldn't cry out. Then he laid his hand flat on the concrete, positioned the crowbar at the place where the bones of his thumb attached to his wrist, closed his eyes, and with all of his strength, thrust the crowbar down.

74

The pain in his hand was bad, but it didn't compare to some of the beatings he'd endured in prison. If there's one thing being behind bars teaches you, it's how to deal with pain.

Manageable.

Barely so, but manageable.

It took a lot of effort to dislocate and then pry the bones loose from the base of his thumb, and when he was done, he needed to yank the thumb forward to pull it completely out of its socket. He considered using the crowbar to remove his thumb altogether, but the bleeding would have been inconvenient and would've left too much of a blood trail.

Holding his left forearm in his right hand, he stretched the chain to its end, leaned backward, and yanked his hand through the shackle.

Although his left thumb was now useless and there was some blood because the metal shaved off the skin on the back of his hand and because of what he'd done with the crowbar, he was able to tie a sock around his hand to quiet the bleeding and, carrying the crowbar, he left the room to make his way out of the building.

++++

Christie felt disappointed with herself about the way she'd treated Tessa.

All this time while she'd been trying to get Pat to trust her, she hadn't been trusting her daughter. For all these years it'd been just the two of them. They hadn't always gotten along perfectly, but they had always trusted each other, and right now, Christie felt like she'd been holding back too much from her.

She decided that she would call her and tell her that she'd come here to Detroit to see Pat.

When her daughter didn't pick up, she sent a text for her to give her a call. Since Tessa never listened to her voicemail anyway, it wouldn't have done any good to leave a voice message. But she was a prompt text replier, so Christie expected a call back soon.

++++

Blake wasn't in sight, but Mannie was standing near the only exit door that Dylan could see.

Mannie looked only momentarily surprised when he saw Dylan, but then worked his shoulders back and forth and popped his knuckles, ready for a fight.

"Set that crowbar down," Mannie said.

"Take it from me."

The big guy had surprised him the other night at the morgue, but now Dylan was ready and he was armed. When he was a kid, his brother had taught him martial arts and he'd continued practicing his form during all those years in prison.

He strode toward Mannie, feigned a punch, and kicked

at the side of the man's knee with enough force to take most people down, but Mannie didn't even flinch.

Instead, he reached for Dylan's arm, but Dylan pivoted so he would grab his weaker left arm, then he spun, swinging the crowbar directly at the Goliath's forehead.

To Dylan, it sounded like the clank of metal on metal, and Mannie grinned slightly, then tapped his head. "Metal plate. Car accident."

"Well, that's handy." But instead of hitting him there again, Dylan swiveled around and smacked the bar against the back of Mannie's head.

There's that one spot back there that's ideal for knocking people out. All martial artists learn about it, but not all guys who are the size of a city.

Mannie's eyes rolled up, and the giant collapsed onto the floor.

For a moment, Dylan thought about using the crowbar to make sure Mannie never stood up again, but decided that since this guy was his brother's friend, he would let him live.

On a shelf below the window, Dylan noticed the box cutter they'd taken from him yesterday. After retrieving it, he stepped outside into the daylight to find Snowball4.

75

11:34 A.M.

Dispersal in 3 hours

Ali sat at a long table in a hidden room behind the kitchen at the back of the restaurant.

Fayed and one of his associates were there with him.

A man that Ali did not recognize walked through the door and greeted him in *Arabic*: "As-salaamu 'alaykum." *Peace be upon you.*

Ali replied, "Wa 'alaykum salaam." *Upon you be peace.*

The man smiled and switched to English. "I am Fayed," he said. "I understand that you were detained at the airport in Atlanta."

"Wait, you are Fayed?" Ali glanced at the man who'd identified himself earlier as Fayed Raabi'ah Bashir, and who Ali had thought was the mastermind behind all of this, ever since their first meeting in Kazakhstan. "I thought he was."

The man who was now claiming to be Fayed said, "Some secrets must be kept for the greater good. His name is Turhan. I understand you took the inhaler during your secondary screening."

Now as he thought about it, Ali recognized this man's

voice as one that he'd heard speaking outside his room while he was waiting on the bed at the compound in Yemen.

"Yes," he said. "I was afraid they would take it from me. I wanted to make sure nothing got in the way of our plans."

"Of course. Alright—water that has flowed past us down the river cannot be drunk. So do you know when you'll be contagious?"

"Later this afternoon. Probably sometime between three and five."

Fayed took a seat at the far end of the table, then said to Ali, "I understand you work as a translator?"

"Yes."

"So then you know that some English words should not mean the same thing, but yet do."

"Do you mean, for example, like 'flammable' and 'inflammable'? Or 'surge' and 'upsurge'?"

"Well done. Or 'void' and 'devoid.' And then, of course, there's 'biweekly,' which can mean twice a week or once every two weeks. That's a tough one. And some words mean the opposite of themselves, like *cleave*, which means both 'to hold close' and 'to separate.'"

"Yes," said Ali.

"And today, brother, you must cleave to your mission and also cleave your ties to this world."

"I understand."

++++

Ralph and I arrived at the restaurant even before the SWAT team did.

SWAT was going to have snipers nearby and would be covering both entrances, but when Ralph and I drove up, we saw three men wearing ski masks entering the back of the restaurant.

One of them had an AK. The others carried sidearms.

"Well, that's not suspicious," Ralph said.

"Not at all."

"With civilians in there, I'm not gonna wait. I'm going in. Are you with me?"

"I'm with you."

"I'll get the back, you take the front, low-key at first. Let SWAT do their job when they get here, but I'm not gonna sit out here on my ass until they do."

As we stepped out of the car, I was hit by the humid, asphalty smell of summer heat rising off the pavement.

"It could get messy in there," I said.

"Just the way I like it."

"I thought you liked it 'fast and clean'?"

"I'm less particular about that than I used to be. Come on. Let's go."

I walked to the front, while he headed around toward the alley that ran along the back of the building. My senses were ratcheted up and I felt the swift rush of adrenaline.

I pressed open the front door.

The restaurant smelled of Mediterranean food, and even though I was pretty sure smoking hadn't been legal in restaurants for a long time, the air was stained with the smell of recent cigarette smoke.

Quickly, I scanned the place. No apparent threats, no disturbances. The restaurant was relatively high-end and looked nearly full.

A genteel male greeter who was dressed to the nines smiled at me politely and picked up a menu. "One?"

"Yes. It'll just be me today."

“Alright, sir. Follow me, please.”

“Can I have a seat near the back—I’m going to do a little work while I’m in here. Don’t want to disturb the other patrons.”

“Of course. That’s kind of you.”

“Don’t mention it.”

++++

Fayed smiled and said to Ali, “I am reminded of a great man of faith, a warrior who fought pagans and infidels with unparalleled rage, with unequaled ferocity. In the end he was caught through the deceit and treachery of a woman he trusted, and then he prayed, and the Great Lord, the Powerful, the Irresistible God answered his prayers. And so, that faithful martyr gave his own life in order to take the lives of thousands of heretics and idolaters as he died.”

Ali considered Fayed’s words. “Are you talking about one of the 9/11 hijackers?”

Fayed shook his head. “This was long before airplanes or skyscrapers.”

“Who then?”

“The man I’m speaking about was named Samson. His story is told in the Holy Bible.”

“He fought the idolatrous Philistines.”

“Yes. Christians, Jews, Muslims, all the People of the Book, remember his story and acknowledge his valor and his willingness to martyr himself in the service of the All Merciful.”

Fayed nodded toward the men who’d entered the room a few moments ago, shedding their ski masks when they did. One was Abdul. He went to the back door to guard it. One man walked into the kitchen. The third readied an assault rifle in front of his chest.

Ali knew Samson's story and realized that there would be some people who would claim the opposite, that Samson had been motivated to act out of vengeance for the wrongs done to him rather than because of his love for God, but Ali held back from pointing that out.

Elbows on the table, Fayed leaned forward toward Ali. "You are Samson, my friend. And do you know the secret?"

"What?"

"He had to be captured to kill the enemies of the Truth that day."

"Captured?"

"You're going to be caught, arrested, taken by the FBI."

"What?"

"Our sources tell us that they don't yet know that you've been infected."

"What then?"

"Wrongs must be righted. Courage will prevail. Paradise awaits. Strike terror in the hearts of others. Do not succumb to it yourself." Fayed laid a twenty-dollar bill on the table. Numbers were written on it. "Memorize this phone number. Call it when the time comes."

"What time is that?"

"You'll know."

"Alright."

"We'll have a suicide vest available, if necessary."

"I understand."

++++

After the host who'd led me to the table stepped away, I studied the restaurant again. Most of the people appeared to be Arab or of Middle Eastern descent. I saw no evidence of any armed men, so I rose and walked toward the kitchen, which I guessed opened to the alley for deliveries.

As I passed a table that hadn't yet been bussed, I picked up the plates, unholstered the Glock, and hid it beneath them. It would at least give me a way to enter the kitchen without immediately attracting too much attention.

++++

Fayed said, "The Federal Bureau of Investigation has monitored and spied on our mosques, infiltrated our educational centers, and harassed and profiled Muslims for far too long. To strike at the heart of the FBI is to strike at the very heart of the infidels."

When his phone buzzed, he glanced at the screen.

"What is it, brother?" Turhan asked.

"There is a sniper getting into position across the street."

"A sniper?"

"Police, FBI, it's unclear who. We must leave."

++++

As I entered the kitchen, the three cooks, who were all too short to have been any of the men wearing ski masks, glanced my direction, but when they saw I was carrying the plates, they seemed more curious than alarmed.

I set the plates down, held a finger to my lips to signal for the cooks to be quiet, then waved my gun to indicate for them to get out of the room. They fled around the stove and into the restaurant rather than through the exit door.

Where's Ralph?

Where are those three armed men?

A sizable pot of boiling soup was on the stove, but the

walkway beside it was cramped and I needed to turn the handle to the side to keep from knocking it off the burner as I edged past it.

A man appeared and started shouting at me in Arabic.

He was holding a handgun, but by the angle, I couldn't tell what kind it was or how many rounds it might hold.

Glock raised at him, I identified myself as FBI, told him to *drop the weapon!*

But he targeted my chest. I spun as he fired, and he barely missed me. From a crouched position, I returned fire, three shots, center mass. Dropped him. As the report of the gunshots echoed through the kitchen, I heard shouting in a back room and screams coming from the restaurant behind me.

This was going down.

It was going down now.

Movement on my right caught my attention, and as I turned, I realized it was one of the cooks who'd returned to the kitchen. He shoved me violently toward the stove, and when I was off balance, he came at me with a kitchen knife, but I managed to grab his right arm, and using his momentum to keep him moving forward, I pivoted toward the stove and drove the knife as well as his hand into the boiling soup. As he screamed, I punched him in the face and he went down.

Gunshots in the back room.

Get back there, Pat!

Though I wasn't about to kill this guy, I couldn't just leave him here either. I quickly patted him down and cuffed his uninjured wrist to a pipe under the sink, then, Glock out, I rushed toward the back room.

76

I tossed the door open.

Assessed the scene.

Two men were down. The AK lay beside one of them. Ralph was standing over a third man who was on his knees with his hands behind his head. The guy's face was covered with bruises and he had a black eye. Ralph yelled, "Three of 'em are outside. Go!"

I threw my hip against the door's pressure bar as I cranked it open with my elbow, keeping both hands on the Glock in ready position.

Except for a dumpster on the left, the alley was empty.

Before sprinting toward the street, I checked behind the dumpster and inside it.

Nothing.

I took off down the alley.

By now, I could hear sirens.

When I reached the street, I scanned both directions. Fifty meters from me, a dark sedan was flaring around the corner. Hoping to get a look at the license plate, I darted toward it, tugging out my phone as I ran.

I made it to the corner as the car was disappearing farther down the block, but managed to click two photographs. Maybe Angela would be able to pull something from them.

I called dispatch and told them where the car was heading to see if we could get an eye on it from traffic cams or businesses that it was passing.

SWAT guys were pouring out of a van, detaining the people who were fleeing the restaurant.

Impeccable timing.

I turned toward the alley again to go back and make sure Ralph was alright.

++++

Ali lay on the floor, his hands cuffed behind him, his cracked rib creasing his side with pain.

The agent who'd stormed into the room and taken out two men, including Turhan, before they could even get off a shot had pushed him down, cuffed him, and checked him for weapons. Ali begged him not to shoot him. Not to kill him.

"Tell me, where did they go?" the agent demanded. "Where did those men head to?"

"Please—"

"Where?" he yelled.

"I don't know," Ali stammered.

The agent removed everything from Ali's pockets, including his car keys and the twenty-dollar bill with the numbers on it. They'd been written in different places on the bill to disguise the fact that they formed a phone number, with half a dozen extra numbers to further hide the truth of what it was.

Fayed had told him just moments ago that he was going

to be captured just as Samson was, in order to strike at the heart of the FBI.

Ali doubted, however, that having Turhan and one of the other men here in the room get killed was part of the plan.

A team of heavily armed police stormed in, and in less than a minute, they'd hustled Ali to a van and locked him inside with two officers in tactical gear. He heard one of them mention the federal building, and he wondered if, perhaps, this had been exactly what Fayed had in mind after all.

++++

From his vantage point a block away, and using his phone to zoom in and study what was happening, Blake watched the SWAT van drive away with one of the men. He didn't know if it was Fayed or not, so he called Mannie to have him prepare Dylan for the transfer, but Mannie did not pick up.

That wasn't like him, and Blake couldn't help but think of the ingenuity and resourcefulness of his brother. If Dylan had gotten away, the exchange for Fayed wouldn't happen, and justice for Maria's death would never occur.

Blake quickly headed to his car to get back to the factory and check on Mannie to see if he was alright.

++++

I met up with Ralph inside the restaurant.

"The guy's injured," my friend told me. "They're taking him to the Detroit Detention Center, then, if he can be transferred, to the federal building. You and I know more about this investigation than anyone else in the city, so I contacted Kennedy. Guess who gets to do the interview with our man?"

"Excellent," I said.

"Yeah," he replied. "As soon as we fill out the paperwork for what just went down here."

"I don't think we can wait until next week to speak with him."

"Ha."

As we left, I said, "Looks like you Hawkinsed those guys in that back room."

"You did some Hawkinsing yourself there in the kitchen."

"Learned from the best."

It used to be that if you were involved in a shooting while on duty, the law enforcement agency you worked for wouldn't take your gun away because they wanted to indicate to you and to the rest of the department that they still trusted you. However, with the public outcry over police shootings of unarmed civilians over the last few years, that's all changed.

Now, typically, you'd be put on paid administrative leave until the agency could investigate the shooting, but here today we were dealing with extraordinary circumstances. Ralph got clearance from the Bureau's Director himself to allow us to remain active and armed so we could respond to the "potentially imminent and catastrophic threat" and resolve this as quickly as possible without any civilian casualties—or especially without the release of a biological weapon in a major U.S. city.

I said, "I propose we dictate our reports on the way to the federal building so we can have a chat with our friend right away."

"I accept. Just don't tell Brineesha you proposed to me."

"Right."

++++

Sharyn parked at the 9th Precinct and waited for Detective Schwartz to join her.

Outside the door, Julianne was speaking with three officers: her brother, Kramer, and Kramer's partner—a man Sharyn didn't know. Pat had told her he was the man who'd mentioned the grenade.

Schwartz walked past them and joined Sharyn at her car. When he got there, he asked, "So what do you have in mind?"

"I'm trying to find Dylan, and I'm getting notifications on my phone. If we get one that looks like it might be from him, I want you to back me up."

"Notifications? The guy's gonna let you know where he is?"

She realized she hadn't updated him on what she was doing regarding the Hook'dup app. "In a sense, yes."

As she explained things, in order to lure out the Bluebeard, Sharyn changed her status on Hook'dup to "Hot and Ready."

++++

Blake shook Mannie, and the huge man groaned twice before finally stirring and opening his eyes. "What happened?" Blake said.

"He had a crowbar," Mannie replied, fierce anger in his voice.

"He must've hit you hard."

"Yeah. He did."

"Concussion?"

"I'm fine." And then, before Blake could stop him, Mannie pushed himself to his feet. "Let's go find your brother."

Scarlett Farrow—V

Heaven's Gates

In the church.

In the night.

Her mom duct-taped to that chair.

Harris told Millie, "I want you to take those scissors and cut the tape that's holding your mommy's left arm to the chair. Go ahead. Her left arm. You know left from right, don't you?"

She nodded.

Obediently, Millie cut the tape and freed her mom's left hand. Immediately, her mom drew her close and hugged her. And at that moment, Scarlett could no longer remember what anyone there was supposed to say or do. She just knew what was happening was happening, and that she needed to make the right choices, do the right thing.

"Run away now," Millie's mom whispered in her ear.

"I can't. I have to help you, Mommy."

Scarlett was no longer ten and a half.

Now she was eight.

She was no longer the daughter of the man who made her touch that huge dead doll, she was the daughter of the man who died rescuing her from drowning.

She was no longer the daughter of the woman who fussed over her just so that she could make more money, the woman who called her stupid and worthless and disgusting and all those other mean, mean things, especially after she was drinking too much, but she was *this* woman's daughter, the lady tied up in the chair who loved her and called her sweetie and meant it.

Millie.

She was Millie.

And this was real.

Harris took a bottle of pills out of his pocket and said to her, "Okay, now, I want you to hand this to your mother."

Millie took it to her mom.

"Alright, Tracy," Harris said. "It's time to make a decision. You can end your life or watch me take hers. Send her to heaven to be with her daddy, or head to the grave yourself."

"What?"

"One of you is going to die, here, now, tonight. The other gets to watch. Which would you prefer, that your daughter lives with the memory of seeing you die, or would you rather save her from all those nightmares, all that sorrow, all that pain? Will you choose to live with the suffering yourself or make her suffer? Those pills in your hand, that's the choice waiting to be made."

"Go, Millie!" she screamed. "Get out!"

Harris fired a shot toward the ceiling.

It was loud, loud, *so loud* there in the empty church.

And at that point, in that moment, Scarlett stopped saying the lines she was supposed to say, stopped acting the way she was supposed to act.

But they kept filming.

And that was the footage they used in the movie, the footage that earned them—her—an Academy Award nomination.

Millie knew she needed to help her mom. Needed to save her.

The words of the prayer came to her again: *Now I lay me down to sleep. I pray the Lord my soul to keep. If I should die before I wake, I pray the Lord my soul to take.*

"I'll do it, Mommy." Then she asked Harris, "Only one of us will die?"

He looked at her strangely.

She faintly remembered living through this before, practicing what to say and when to say it, but they were all ghostly images, soft, whispery words that might not have even been real.

"Does only one of us have to die?!" she yelled.

"Yes."

They kept filming.

She turned to her mom. "I'll get to see Daddy again. I'll be in heaven. I'll give him a hug for you."

And before anyone could stop her, she grabbed the bottle of pills and tipped them into her mouth. She nearly gagged on them, but made herself swallow them.

As many as she could.

To save her mom.

To die, to really die, so her mom could live.

Then Harris was rushing toward her and she was feeling dizzy and her mom was screaming and trying helplessly to yank herself free from the chair.

And Millie coughed and gagged and found herself collapsing and falling asleep in a forever way that she never had before.

"Now I lay me down to sleep."

—At least now Mommy is safe.

"I pray the Lord my soul to keep."

—Safe, safe, safe and I'll be with Daddy.

"If I should die before I wake."

—You won't wake up here.

"I pray the Lord my soul to take."

—You get to wake up in heaven.

Afterward, she had to go to the hospital. Someone had made a mistake. The pills weren't supposed to be real, but they were. It was the wrong bottle. The doctors did something weird with her tummy to help her get better. All she really knew was that it hurt a lot and she didn't get to go to heaven after all.

Later, they kept asking her if she understood what was real and what wasn't, what was for the movie and what was happening in real life.

And she told them she did. Of course, she did. But that night, there when they were filming in the church, she really *had* thought that the woman was going to die, she really had wanted to die in her place, and she really had thought that taking those pills would make that happen.

Her mom and dad signed a bunch of papers to make sure no one was going to get in trouble after they used the footage.

They got a ton of extra money from the director, her dad spent more and more time with that young actress, and Scarlett found her mom—her real-life mom—passed out more and more often in their trailer from all the drinking she did whenever she was in there alone.

And everyone started talking about how great an actress she was.

The day when Scarlett thought she would die was the day a star was born.

77

12:34 P.M.

Dispersal in 2 hours

Back at the federal building, Ralph and I headed toward the interview room. One of the agents had picked up some burgers for us for lunch.

Ralph shook his head as he showed me the printing on his shake's cup. "For some reason, marketers must think that if they tell us something is handcrafted, we'll be more interested in buying it. I mean, I've seen signs for handcrafted steaks, handcrafted beer. This is a handcrafted shake. How do you handcraft a shake? I've even seen ads for handcrafted biscuits. I just have one thing to say about that—keep your hands off my biscuits."

"I'm not sure you really want to say that."

"That's probably true."

The injuries of the man we'd apprehended weren't severe enough to keep him from being interviewed. The three men who'd escaped were still on the run.

Our team had located the suspect's passport in an Alamo rental car near the restaurant.

His name: Ali Mahmoud Saleem. He was a translator from Kazakhstan and had entered the country Wednesday night on a flight from Frankfurt. We were waiting to see what Homeland could dig up with the Kazakhstan government regarding his past and his possible association with any known extremists or terrorist groups, but the country's intelligence agencies weren't being as cooperative as they could have been.

On the ride over here, TSA had provided us with footage and a transcript of Ali's encounter with the border agents in Atlanta.

Angela and Lacey were still processing the photos I'd taken of the car disappearing down the street but were only able to grab two digits from my picture. They were analyzing makes, models, and plate numbers now.

Before starting the suspect's interview, while Ralph and I had a minute here, I called Sharyn to touch base with her.

She told me she was working with Schwartz to try to get the Bluebeard to make a move.

Bait.

I wasn't happy about that.

But at least she had a partner with her to try and stop this guy.

But does Blake have him?

I couldn't be sure either way.

I mentioned to Sharyn my conversation with Calvin about Bluebeards, and some of the observations he'd given me. "Flello was gay, by the way," she said. "I'm not sure that made it into the case files."

"So, the Bluebeard was more interested in where than in who," I muttered. Then I added, somewhat offhandedly, "It looks like right now we have a whole lot of geese flying overhead."

"What do you mean?"

"Goes back to the first time I went goose hunting with my dad when I was twelve. As you know, we lived near Horicon Marsh in Wisconsin, and basically, millions of Canada Geese would settle there in the marsh before moving on with their migration south."

"Millions?"

"Yes. My dad knew a farmer who owned a cornfield on the edge of the marsh. One morning, Dad and I went out there before dawn and set up a blind. So we were huddled behind this tangled mesh of camouflage fabric held up by chicken wire in those rows of old cornstalks. And then they came. This huge flock of geese. Thousands and thousands of them, rising up across the horizon and coming toward us. The sky was dark with geese. All honking and flapping overhead."

"Did you get one?"

"Not quite. I aimed my shotgun and started firing, and you'd think that with that many geese, I would've at least hit one."

"You missed them all?" She sounded slightly amused.

"Yeah, I didn't hit a single goose. Not a single feather fell to the ground. So I looked at my dad and said, 'How did I miss? There were so many geese!' And he told me, 'You aimed at the flock, son, you didn't aim at a goose.'"

She caught on. "Right now we have to be careful not to aim at the flock. There are too many things going on in both of our cases. We need to zero in on them one at a time and pick them off."

"Precisely. I'll take the Blake goose for now," I said. "You stay on the Bluebeard one."

"Aim carefully."

"I will."

Talking about hunting with Sharyn felt a little strange since it was something I more typically spoke with Christie about—she'd grown up in Minnesota and also learned to hunt with her dad, just as I had.

A common experience.

A shared past.

They can bring you together.

Sometimes they're one of the only things that can.

I hoped her talk with Tessa had gone well.

++++

Christie's phone buzzed with a call.

Tessa's ringtone.

Finally.

She picked up and Tessa said, "Yeah? What is it?"

Christie told her that she had gone to Detroit to see Patrick, and that she was coming back to New York City tonight.

"Don't lose him, Mom. Seriously. He makes you happy. He's right for you. When you're with him, you have this lightness around you that I've never seen before. And, okay, he can be pretty annoying and obsessive with his work sometimes, but what guy isn't a pain in the butt—I almost said 'ass,' but okay, 'butt'—once in a while? You wanna do what's best for me, do what's best for you. I never had a dad around. Things can be different now."

"I never knew how strongly you felt about all this before."

"Well, I do. But don't tell him. I don't want it to go to his head."

After the call, Christie decided that there was one thing she wanted to do before leaving Detroit.

See Sharyn Weist one last time and make sure, in person, that things were where they needed to be between them.

++++

After 9/11, each of the Bureau's Field Offices was equipped with a Hazardous Materials Response Unit, or HMRU. It was a designated floor or suite with enhanced cyber capabilities, interview rooms, portable and flyaway instrument packages to allow for on-site chemical and biological analyses, several dozen HAZMAT suits with air tanks and N95 fitted respirators, and other emergency communication and response equipment for dealing with a domestic terror attack. Most people aren't aware of the HMRUs. It's not something we typically advertise. Sometimes the less open you are about things like this, the better.

Now, Ralph and I touched base about how we wanted to tackle the interview.

The standby good cop/bad cop routine has its advantages, but neither one of us really pulls off the good cop part all that well.

"Wing it," he said.

"Right."

The interview room was across the hall from the HMRU's armory and the storage area for the biosuits. A bathroom lay just beyond them.

A few offices were located along the hallway, so we downed the rest of our food, Ralph scarfed his handcrafted shake, and just after we'd deposited the trash in one of the rooms, SAC Kennedy met up with us and said, "I just got word. DeYoung wants Saleem transferred out before anyone here talks with him."

"What?" Ralph exclaimed. "That doesn't sound like DeYoung at all."

"Apparently, it's coming down the pipe from the Pentagon. They want to take him to an undisclosed location for his interview."

"An undisclosed location, huh."

"Yeah."

"Once that happens," I said, "we won't get another chance to talk with him."

If we're going to get Dylan from Blake, we at least need Fayed in order to negotiate an exchange. Even if we don't go through with it, if Fayed's gone, we lose our bargaining chip. And this guy Ali is our ticket to Fayed.

Unless he is Fayed.

Is that even possible?

"No, we need to interview Ali now," I told Kennedy. "Today. And with my history with Blake and with Ralph's experience in the military, it needs to be the two of us."

"When is this transfer supposed to happen?" Ralph asked him.

"As soon as Dr. Qiao's plane lands. Two o'clock at the latest."

"Listen," I said to him. "Remember how you told me that story about the copperheads? About assumptions?"

"Yes."

"Well, if those men in your story hadn't stayed away from the boy so long, they could have saved him. Sometimes it isn't assumptions that are deadly. It's hesitation. It's not taking action when you have the chance."

Kennedy chewed on that for a moment. "It's too bad I didn't run into you guys to tell you not to start the interview. I'll be in my office, but you didn't hear me say that either." He eyed Ralph briefly. "No excessive force."

"Do I look like the kind of guy who would use excessive force?"

"I have a feeling that if I Googled 'excessive force' your picture would come up."

Yeah. I liked this guy.

"I'll take that as a compliment," Ralph said.

"You don't have much time. Make it count."

Kennedy left.

I grabbed a stack of manila file folders from the inbox of whoever worked in the closest office. I had no idea what the files contained, but their contents didn't matter.

Sometimes props can be invaluable in an interview.

Ralph entered first, and after I was in the room as well, I locked the door behind us.

++++

A Hook'dup notification came through on Sharyn's phone from someone with the username *lonelydad*.

The man's photograph showed him standing in a church with a black hoodie shading his face. A nice photo. A little foreboding, but well oriented and not like the typical selfies of most of the profiles.

The message read: Snowball4. I'd like to meet you. Simone told me you'd be in the area.

Sharyn's heart began to race.

This was him.

When? she typed.

Now. Using TypeKnot, he sent a residential address about fifteen minutes from where she was. Come alone. I'll know if you don't.

On my way.

After the exchange, she said to Schwartz, "He told me to come alone."

"Of course he did. Don't worry about me. I'm not gonna bail on you when we're this close. Trust me when I say this: I'm here for you, Sharyn."

78

A lot of psychology goes into preparing for and carrying out an interview.

For example, just setting up the room: you don't put the table in the middle like they do in crime shows on TV. Instead, you slide it against one wall and position the suspect's chair so he's in a sense trapped between the far side of the table and the wall behind him.

Not so blatant that he gets defensive, but just far enough so he subconsciously feels trapped.

So yes, we put him in a corner with his back against the wall.

Both literally and figuratively.

What makes people talk? Either pain or promises. In an interview you need to discern what'll motivate this person more—suffering or relief, either for themselves or for someone else.

And through it all, empathy is usually much more effective than threats.

You become whatever the person needs. If it's a father figure, you step into that role. If it's a lover, you flirt with him. If it's a confidant, you allow him to confess and get things off his chest. And often people do want to confess, they just don't know how. Or they don't know how it'll benefit them if they do, because, literally, telling the truth could cause them to spend the rest of their lives behind bars. So what's in it for them? That's what you need to figure out.

Often, it's effective to tell the suspect, "A lot of people out there are saying terrible things about you. That you're a monster, that you don't care about innocent life. I'm here for the truth. I need you to tell me what happened. I'd like to get your story out there. I'd like to set the record straight. What do you need to tell me?"

It's amazing how concerned people can be about their reputation and about making sure the public doesn't think that they're evil.

Sometimes interviewers are so committed to getting a confession that they manipulate the conversation toward that end, but the goal should never be making a suspect confess. Rather, it always needs to be about, and only be about, uncovering the truth, whatever that is. If you leave an interview believing something other than the truth, you'll also be on the pathway toward something other than justice.

I walked toward the suspect as Ralph stood to the side.

Ali was cuffed and his ankles were shackled. The handcuffs were also locked to a bolt in the steel table.

He was nervously eyeing the video camera in the corner of the room.

Most people try their best to act calm in a situation like this. I saw no acting here. This guy was rattled.

"I'm Agent Bowers," I said. "This is Agent Hawkins. First of all, you were injured. Those bruises on your face—are you okay?"

He said nothing.

"Can I get you anything? Coffee? Coke? Water?"

Silence.

"The men who fled thc restaurant—where did they go?"

No reply.

"We're here to find out what you know about Fayed and about the potential release of the virus."

++++

Ali debated his options.

If he simply stalled, he would be able to carry out his mission, and that would mean all of these people would die.

However, if he could trust these two men, maybe he could figure out a way to save his sister, save innocent lives, and also take out the true Fayed Raabi'ah Bashir. The man had lied about who he was, lied from the start, and Ali thought he might also have lied while guaranteeing the safety of his sister.

He'd memorized the phone number.

Fayed had mentioned a suicide vest.

He needed to play this smart, and he needed to make every word he said count.

++++

"We know all about your work back home. Your work as a translator." I was thumbing through the pages in the top file folder. They were simply timesheets and work rosters and had nothing to do with this case. I pretended to study them, hoping he wouldn't call my bluff. "Why are you in this country, Ali?"

"To see relatives."

There's something deep within the human psyche that

knows it's wrong to deceive—and even when another part of your brain tries to convince you that in this instance it's okay to lie for your best interests, or for someone else's—there's inner dissonance that plays itself out in microexpressions that you aren't even aware you're making, and other people aren't even consciously aware of seeing.

Unless you start to look for them.

They're best noticed on video recordings, but a trained eye can start to pick them up as they happen. And in this case, they happened. The flick of his eye. The quiver of his cheek. Since we already knew he wasn't here to see relatives, it gave me a baseline to discern when he was lying.

Ralph shook his head. "Yeah, you know, we have a record of your conversation with the border control agents in Atlanta and we looked into your 'relatives'—Gregor and Tatiana, wasn't it? They don't live here in Michigan, do they? They don't even exist."

Ali was silent.

I held up the file folders. "Do you have any idea how much information we have on you already?" Even though we're not required by law to tell the truth during an interview, personally I default back to it, as I did now. "I'm holding three file folders full of papers."

Ali remained quiet and sat staring past us, occasionally glancing up toward the camera in the corner.

I closed the folder. "Ali, we know about the tests. We know about what happened in Kazakhstan." I was stepping out on a little bit of a limb here, but I wanted to at least get a response out of him one way or the other.

At the mention of the country, his eyes moved toward me, and he said, in remarkably good English, "What do you know about Kazakhstan?"

Think, Pat. Say the right thing, but not too much.

"We know about the bioweapons scientist, about Fayed, about Maria. Dr. Kuznetsov is dead. Murdered. Did you hear about that?"

Now Ali began to rub two fingers together and his tongue came out to wet his lips, both signs of nervousness. I took them as an indication that he was getting closer to telling us something we could use.

I flopped the pile of manila folders onto the table out of his reach. I was about to mention something about Blake, but before I could, Ralph said to Ali, "You're looking at conspiracy to commit terrorist acts, a list of charges as long as my arm." Ralph tapped the files and let out a long, slow whistle. "Man, I can't see you getting out of here for at least fifty years. We're probably talking life without the possibility of parole. You *will* be charged. And you will be convicted."

"I don't want a lawyer."

"You don't?"

"No. I don't want anyone else to hear what I have to say."

"Go on."

"Turn off the camera."

"I'm afraid in here, everything is recorded."

"What time is it?"

"One thirty. Why?"

"I have something to tell you, but I won't do it unless that camera is turned off. And believe me, this is something you'll want to hear. And you need to hear it now. There is no time to waste."

I glanced at Ralph and then, when he nodded, I walked

over to the camera and clicked off. The operating light went dark.

"Okay," I said to Ali. "What's so important that you need to talk to us without the camera on?"

++++

Ali wasn't sure if he should trust these men, but at this point he didn't have much of a choice.

"There were girls taken from a village," he said. "In Nigeria. There were tests done. That doctor that you mentioned, he was in charge of everything, and Fayed . . . well, the man who called himself Fayed, I understand now that his name was really Turhan, he and the doctor gave me something to take."

I thought back to the footage that we'd reviewed of Ali at the Atlanta airport.

"You don't have asthma, do you?" I said, anticipating where this was going. "It was the inhaler."

"Yes."

"Where's the inhaler now?"

"It is gone. After it was empty, I put it in the sharps container in the airport's bathroom."

"The video of Maria," said Ralph. "Did you shoot it?"

"I don't know anything about a Maria. Was she one of the girls?"

"No. She was one of us. FBI."

"I want someone protected. If you can assure me that she's okay, if you can give her a new life, a new identity, I can help you."

"Who do you want protected?" I asked.

"My sister."

"I don't know." Ralph shook his head. "If we protect her, what will you give us in return?"

"It's what I won't give you," Ali said.

I looked at him curiously. "What's that?"

"Smallpox."

79

1:34 P.M.

Dispersal in 1 hour

I stared at him. "Are you contagious?"

"I will be later this afternoon, and when I am, and when this virus gets out, there will not be any way to stop it. It's too late for me."

"The director of the CDC is on her way here. There might be a treatment strategy that—"

"No. I was told there is no treatment. Not for this strain of the virus. We need to take action and we need to do it now before I become contagious, and before Fayed gets out of the city. I can give him to you, the real Fayed Raabi'ah Bashir, but only if you guarantee me that my sister is going to be safe."

"Where is she now?"

He told us an address in the city of Ust-Kamenogorsk in eastern Kazakhstan.

"I'll put some calls through," Ralph said. "CIA. Military intelligence. A few people owe me favors. We can make it happen."

"No one there must know," Ali told him.

"No one will."

"Also, there's a woman named Faatina who is with my sister, who is watching her. Faatina is sympathetic to their cause. She's a member of The Brigade of the Prophet's Sword."

"Look," I said, "we can help your sister. We can get her to a safe place. Bring her to America, if you want. Protect her. Everything. But you have to tell us what you know about this attack and where we can find Fayed."

"Get her to safety, make sure she's okay, and then I will tell you what you need to know. But only when she is safe."

"That's gonna take time," Ralph said impatiently. "And that's something neither one of us has right now."

"Then you both should move quickly," Ali replied.

++++

Sharyn and Detective Schwartz were about ten minutes from the house where she was anticipating that Dylan would meet her. Hopefully they would arrive early enough for Ted to get into position without being seen.

A text came in from Christie asking if she could meet up one more time if possible. Sharyn was glad to talk things through some more if necessary, but replied that it probably wouldn't work today. Maybe they could talk on the phone tonight.

++++

For the last five minutes, while Ralph was reaching out to his contacts in the military and the CIA to see if they could locate the girl, Ali had been filling me in on his mission and what he'd been sent here to do.

"So," I said, "you don't know what happened to Maria Aguirre? You really don't?"

"No." He looked at me introspectively. "Are you a man of faith, Agent Bowers?"

"I'm a man of science. But I do believe in some things that I can't prove. I suppose that counts as faith."

"What are those?"

"That justice will win in the end, that truth matters more than anything, and that love is more than just a biological response to certain environmental cues."

"What about God?"

"That's a hard one. When I look at the pain in the world, I can't understand how a loving God could allow it, but when I look at the glory of the world, I can't imagine how it all could've developed by chance, from nothing. Our universe both shouts out that it has no meaning and also that it has unimaginable meaning at the same time, every moment."

"So for you, existence points to God, but suffering makes it hard for you to see Him? The mist of the world's agony obscures your view of the Almighty?"

"Look," I said, "I'm not here to argue about religion. I'm just here to stop innocent people from dying. That's all I care about right now."

"It is not my religion that brought me here. It is my beliefs."

"What do you mean?"

"Religion is how we pursue God. But sometimes, because of our beliefs, we will pursue something better than being with God."

"What's better than being with God?"

"Sacrificing for the ones we love."

"The woman I'm seeing would say that that's what God did for us: sacrifice for those he loves so that we could be with him."

"So, she is Christian."

"You say that with a lot of certainty."

"By what you just said, it sounds like what a Christian would believe."

I didn't feel comfortable discussing Christie's faith. He didn't seem to be judging her, or speaking derisively, and I wasn't sure where he was coming from. "A lot of Muslim extremists still blame Christians for the Crusades."

"I was taught to do so as well," he replied, "but I do not believe that the Crusaders were Christian."

"Why would you say that?"

"They didn't follow the teachings of Isa, Peace Be Upon Him. They didn't emulate his life. They didn't pursue his ways. They were not taught the true tenets of Christianity. They were compelled by those in power to pursue power, not by an adherence to the Scriptures to seek meekness. They had not read the Holy Bible for themselves or been taught it in their own language. Christians aren't told to conquer the world, but to deny themselves and serve others. And the way of Isa, Peace Be Upon Him, is not to kill in the name of God, but to die in the name of love."

80

Ali watched Agent Bowers carefully throughout the conversation.

The man appeared to have striking resolve as well as deep convictions, but Ali wasn't sure how much faith had to do with it, and how much it was simply a pursuit of the truth and belief in compassion. But then again, Ali wasn't even sure about his own faith in God.

"Why smallpox?" Agent Bowers asked him.

"Surah Al-Fil."

"I don't know what that means."

"It is from the Holy Qur'an."

"Go on."

"In 570 BCE, in what some people refer to as the War of the Elephants, an army from Ethiopia, it was called Abyssinia at the time, surrounded Mecca. They hoped to enslave the people and destroy a shrine that was sacred to them."

"What does it have to do with elephants?"

"The king of Abyssinia, Abraha, had some of his soldiers ride on elephants when he led his army to besiege Mecca. According to the Qur'an, Allah sent a flock of birds. They carried small rocks in their talons and their beaks and dropped them onto the invaders. The rocks stuck to the soldiers' skin and soon killed them off one by one, saving the Holy City."

"Rocks?"

"Yes. The decreed stones."

++++

I thought of the photos Ralph and I had found in Dr. Kuznetsov's house and the sores that were visible on those people, as well as the dark pustules that appeared on Maria. Yes, they did look like small black rocks stuck to her skin.

"So was it an outbreak of smallpox that killed the soldiers?" I asked.

"Perhaps the rocks in the story were metaphorical, or perhaps they were real. From what I understand, scientists and those who study the history of disease . . . um, what would be the English word?"

"You just mean historians?" I suggested. "Or epidemiologists maybe?"

"Yes, I believe so. Some epidemiologists do believe it was smallpox. Then, later that year, Muhammad, Peace Be Upon Him, was born in Mecca. According to some Ulamas, Allah saved the city through that disease so that His Prophet could be born there."

"So, in essence," I said, "they believe that God delivered his people from the hand of an infidel army by sending a plague of smallpox."

Ali nodded. "And now The Brigade of the Prophet's Sword wishes to once again fulfill the will of Allah by destroying the infidels through the same disease He used fourteen centuries ago against those who would attack the land of His coming Prophet."

As I was considering his words, I heard a single rap at the door and Ralph pressed it open, returning to the room.

"Alright, listen," he said to Ali. "We have an extraction team that's gonna go and rescue your sister. They're on choppers now, they're heading to the city, but we won't know for sure that we have her for at least twenty minutes. You gotta trust me on this. I'm on your side. Help us out here. Our superiors want to transfer you to a black site. If that happens, you might never see the light of day again and I can almost guarantee you that you won't ever see your sister. We only have a few minutes. We need to make a decision and we need to move. Where's Fayed? Are there more people infected with smallpox?"

"As far as I know, I am the only one."

"But why?" I said. "That doesn't make any sense. If their goal is spreading smallpox, why have only one martyr? If they have the capability to pull this off, why wouldn't they go all the way?"

"They are planning to go all the way."

"What's the endgame, then?" Ralph pressed him.

"I do not know it all. I only know that it was part of the plan for me to get arrested."

++++

Ali tried to anticipate how this could work, what he would need to do in order to make sure that the smallpox did not spread and that Fayed would face justice for what he had done.

But you must also make sure Azaliya is safe. You cannot reveal all until you are certain.

But there isn't time! Of course it will take an American team a while to get into the city and find her. The only way to save her, to help her, is trusting these men now.

"Alright," Ali said to them. "I will give you his location, but it must be only you two. I will tell you as soon as we are out of this building, and I will trust that you will protect my sister."

"So, the deal is you give us Fayed, you tell us about the virus, we rescue your sister, and we get you into quarantine. Then prison," Ralph said. "You understand that, right?"

Ali knew he would not be spending very long in prison. He would be dead within the next five days. But he didn't say that. "I understand," he told the agent instead. "We should go now."

"Hang on one sec."

Agent Hawkins indicated for Agent Bowers to join him in the hall, and Ali wasn't sure if they were going to agree to his offer or not.

81

Sharyn parked just down the block from the abandoned house near Palmer Park, the property that the man on Hook'dup, who she believed to be Dylan, had given her as the location.

From what she could tell right now, no one was in the area.

The walls of the house were sagging, almost as if they weren't made out of wood but some other, more pliable material. The windows, rather than being broken, were all in various states of being opened—some halfway, others a quarter of the way.

It reminded Sharyn of the teeth of a boxer, a weird flat-faced, tooth-slatted thing grinning at her in this deserted corner of the city.

As they got out of the car, Schwartz pointed to a thickly overgrown field behind the house. "I'll go around back. That way, if he's here, he won't see me. Also, if he has a partner, I don't want to take the chance of anyone slipping out the back while you go in the front."

"Sounds good," she said. She kept her gun low and ready as she approached the porch.

++++

“So, what do you think?” I asked Ralph.

“I’m going back and forth. Pros and cons. Taking him out of here, cutting this sort of deal will cost us our jobs, probably result in jail time. But I’m willing to do it if it means stopping this virus from being spread. You saw what happened to Maria. Now try to imagine that happening to millions of people around the world. Operation Dark Winter was a military war game that was played out back in 2001. It simulated the outbreak and spread of a smallpox bioweapon attack in Oklahoma City.”

“What happened?”

“Things did not end well. Even with a quarantine, within two weeks the virus had spread to half of the U.S., as well as fifteen other countries. Tens of millions of people infected.”

“And that was just a war game.”

“Yeah. And they weren’t even dealing with something this deadly.”

“So,” I said. “We help Ali.”

“Yeah. We help Ali. And we just hope we don’t get infected in the process.”

++++

Sharyn opened the door and stepped into the house.

When people abandon a place, they rarely take the time to tidy up after themselves, and that was the case here.

Dust, dirt, grunge, and debris littered the floor, knee-deep in some places.

However, she wasn’t focused so much on the state of the house but instead on the reason she was there: if Dylan showed up and they caught him, this could all end today.

Although it was a memory that she normally tried to

keep in check, being here now, thinking about him, brought to mind that night in the bar on her twenty-first birthday when they met.

"So what are you doing tonight?" he said.

"I'm here to drink myself into a bad decision."

"Hmm. Would you like any help with that, or is this something you're hoping to do all on your own?"

She assessed him. "Depends."

"On?"

"Who's offering. And the type of bad decision I might be lured into making."

"Lured?"

"It's just a word."

"Are some better than others?"

"Do you mean decisions or lures?"

"Decisions," he said.

"Oh, yes."

"Well then, I promise to do all I can to make it a really bad one."

"In that case." She gestured toward the empty bar stool beside her. "Have a seat."

Sharyn passed through the kitchen, saw no one, then glanced at the stairs that led to the second floor. Now, since she suspected that Dylan was involved, it was hard for her to look at the staircase without feeling a chill.

It'd happened upstairs, at his place.

Upstairs in the bedroom.

She'd been a little tipsy that night when they left the bar—too tipsy.

As he led her into his house, it was one of those moments

when she knew she wasn't making a smart choice, not by any stretch of the imagination, but she also didn't care.

Her twenty-first birthday was supposed to be the day when she received her trust fund. It was supposed to be the day when things finally turned her way.

But instead, her parents had nearly bankrupted themselves—and her in the process—and she really wasn't sure what she wanted to do with her life.

All she'd ever wanted was to be loved. Loved by a parent, loved by a man, loved by someone. But, growing up in Hollywood, that'd always meant she needed to be rich and beautiful. With the workouts, the dieting, the creams, the makeup, she was doing everything she knew to remain young and nubile and attractive, but she was terrified of the thought that she would grow old having never experienced the love that she wanted so desperately to find.

"Drink?" he offered, gesturing toward the liquor cabinet.

"Sure," she said. "Why not."

One drink led to another, until finally they were upstairs, finally they were in his bedroom, finally he was pulling out the handcuffs and the box cutter and she was begging for her life.

After it was over, she stood in the shower in her condo, trying to wash away all that had happened, trying to make it all go down the drain. All disappear forever.

She needed to clean away the memories, from both her body and her mind, and replace them with something else—something positive and good and pure and right.

Act and act and make believe and don't let real life get in the way.

But it did get in the way.

There in the shower, she glanced at the red marks on her

wrists where the handcuffs had been, and she shook and cried and tried to pretend none of this had happened.

But it had.

It had.

It could never be undone. It could never be washed away.

Now and forever, it was part of who Scarlett Farrow was.

After clearing the first floor, Sharyn went upstairs to the master bedroom.

As she stared out the window at the neighborhood, she searched for movement in the bushes and also any cars coming down the street. But everything was still, everything was quiet, except for the sound of two agitated dogs barking at each other in a house two units down.

Then she allowed herself one final foray into the past. One final set of memories from that night grabbed hold of her and wouldn't let her go.

In the shower, as the water splashed across her, she drew her hands up to her face and wept, then lifted her head and screamed and screamed. But even the screaming did nothing to dispel her pain.

After he raped her and had the box cutter pressed against her throat, she'd begged for her life, she'd promised she would never tell, if only he would let her go. But then, after the shower, all she could think of was what if he did this to someone else? What if he did this again? And she realized that almost certainly, someone that well-prepared, someone that coldhearted, either had killed in the past or would do so in the future. And even if he didn't kill, he would almost certainly attack other women.

Even though she'd given him her word, she realized that

sometimes there are things more important than keeping your promises.

So she went to the police and told them everything. She knew where he lived, and when she showed the officer her wounds, the woman believed her. They found him, they stopped him, they put him away. After that, she decided to enter law enforcement herself, to catch people like this, and maybe make the world just a little bit better place.

She switched from majoring in journalism to criminal justice.

And so.

She'd grown up being taught that an abortion stops a beating heart. In Hollywood, that was not a popular view, and her convictions about abortion only brought her more guilt. She believed that in the case of rape, abortion could be used as a last resort. However, in her case, she hadn't gotten the abortion because she'd been raped. She'd gotten it for another reason altogether. One that she was ashamed of.

And that shame had never gone away.

No shower, no amount of time could ever make it go away.

++++

Detective Ted Schwartz heard someone moving through the underbrush nearby and shouted, "Detroit Police! Hands up!"

"It's me," came the reply.

He lowered his gun slightly as the person came into view. "What are you doing here?"

"I should be asking you the same question."

++++

Sharyn waited and watched but saw nothing, heard nothing unusual in the neighborhood.

Her phone vibrated, and when she checked the screen, she found a TypeKnot notification from the man she was here to meet: I told you to come alone, Scarlett. You'll find that detective's body around back in the weeds.

A chill shot through her.

She rushed downstairs, ran outside, and called for Ted.

Nothing.

She tried again: "Ted!"

Gun out, she began picking her way through the overgrown field.

"Detective Schwartz, are you here?"

Up ahead through a tangle of thorns, she could see a body lying in the grass. She wasn't sure if it was him, but it did look like it was wearing his clothes.

"Ted?"

As quickly as she could, while also trying to remain cautious in case it was some sort of trap, she approached the body and found that it was the same size as Detective Schwartz and did indeed have on his clothes, but she couldn't immediately identify if it was him. A spreading pool of fresh, crimson blood was seeping into the earth where his head should have been. No murder weapon visible.

No sign of his head.

Despite the horror in front of her, she found herself thinking with clinical objectivity, all federal agent rather than coworker or friend.

It takes time to cut off someone's head. Was there really enough time for him to do that? Is this really Ted's body? If not, then—

A phone had been placed in his hand and as she stood there, it rang.

Tucking her sleeve around her fingers so she wouldn't leave prints, she answered it.

"It's me," a voice said, but it was electronically disguised, so she couldn't tell who it was—male or female, if it was Dylan or someone else.

"What have you done?"

"It ends now, Scarlett. It ends today. There's a church I want you to visit. You remember what happened at the end of *Sanctuary*? Well, the time has come to make the final sacrifice."

"Tell me where you are."

"St. Gerard's Church. What happened to Schwartz will happen to anyone else you bring along. Do not call in his death or contact dispatch. Come alone."

"Oh, I'll come alone." She knew the location, had driven past it, had a photo of it hanging in her living room. She felt her hand tighten around the phone. "And only one of us is going to walk out of there alive."

"That may be true. Leave your cell there. Bring the one I left for you."

End call.

She knelt and laid a soft hand on the dead person's arm.

"I'm sorry. I'll find him," she whispered. A hot tear fell. She wiped the second away before it could find its way down her cheek. "I'll stop him."

She left her own phone beside the body, rose, and headed for her car, fists tight with rage as she did.

++++

Agents Hawkins and Bowers agreed to Ali's proposal and came back into the room to lay out the plan.

Ali didn't know where Fayed would be at this moment, but he could predict where he would be if he could set up a meeting.

At first, Agent Hawkins suggested staging an escape, but then they realized that Fayed would most likely suspect that it was faked since he'd been there when Ali was arrested and knew he was in custody.

In the end, Ali offered to simply tell Fayed the truth: that he had been arrested, that the FBI was looking for a way to use him to locate the other cell members, and that if he didn't reach out, the agents were going to isolate him because of the virus so that it wouldn't spread to anyone.

But he didn't tell Hawkins and Bowers the whole truth of what he had in mind.

He didn't tell them about his plan regarding the suicide vest. He didn't tell them that the only way he would be able to convince Fayed to meet would be if Fayed would get him the vest. He didn't explain that he was going to offer to blow himself up while in custody after being recaptured in order to spread the virus through the explosion to everyone in the federal building through the aerosolized particles in the air vents.

Ali asked if either of the men knew Arabic, and when they told him they did not, he said, "Alright, then after I call Fayed, I'll tell you exactly what he said."

But that was a lie.

Right now, Ali needed to play both sides. He needed the agents to trust him and he needed Fayed to trust him. If he could do this, if he could pull this off, he would be able to both save his sister and stop the spread of the virus.

Just enough of the truth, but not too much.

"There are too many ears in here," Agent Hawkins said softly. "We need to get you out before you make the call."

From his research on the city earlier concerning the tunnels beneath Detroit, Ali knew that only a few of the bomb shelters were still airtight. He would need one of them for what he had in mind.

82

2:04 P.M.

Dispersal in 30 minutes

It wasn't going to be easy for us to get Ali out of the building without anyone trying to stop us. I confirmed the hallway was clear, then uncuffed Ali's ankles and wrists and quickly led him into the bathroom just down the hall.

We waited inside until Ralph called to the agents near the elevator. "Get down here now! We need you in the interview room!"

I waited until I heard their footsteps. Waited until I heard Ralph shouting for them to come into the room. Waited until I heard him slam the door, locking them inside.

Then I quickly hustled Ali out of the bathroom, down the hall, and to the elevator. "How long do you think we have until those agents get out of there?" I asked Ralph.

As the elevator doors were closing, I saw the interrogation room door crash open.

"Not long," Ralph said.

The guys inside must've been as good as Ralph was at kicking through doors.

They Hawkinsed it.

The doors to the elevator shut before the agents could get any shots off, and we ascended to ground level. As we exited the elevator, Ralph unholstered his weapon, stuck it beneath his belt, and jammed the holster into the elevator transom. The stiff leather was thick enough to keep the doors from closing, and if they couldn't close, the agents couldn't get to this level.

A temporary stall.

They would no doubt get here soon enough.

After changing the settings on our phones so they couldn't be traced, we took a back hallway to the parking garage, leading Ali, whose hands I'd drawn back behind him, and telling the two people we met to step back. "Prisoner transfer," Ralph announced authoritatively and quite convincingly.

We made it outside just as the alarms were going off. If the building was in lockdown, there was no way we would be able to drive a car out of the garage, but now that we were this far, there was no turning back.

We rushed to the street and located a BMW sedan parked along the curb, but Ralph shook his head. "Too hard to hot-wire."

Two cars down, he found one that he did know how to get started. He wasn't subtle about it at all, but punched through the backseat window on the driver's side, shattering the glass.

Once in the car, he took the driver's seat and began working on the wires beneath the dashboard. I brushed the glass aside and sat in the back and recuffed Ali to stop him from making a run for it, in case everything he'd told us was a lie.

++++

A million things were racing through Sharyn's mind as she drove to St. Gerard's Church, the old, abandoned cathedral-esque church where the Bluebeard would be meeting her.

As she thought of the body lying there in the thick grass behind the house she'd just left, a tight coil of anger and revulsion wrapped around her, twisted through her. Was that really Ted back there in the undergrowth? If not, who was it?

Anger and revulsion, yes.

And grief.

Had that really been Dylan on the phone? If so, why did he disguise his voice? If it wasn't Dylan, who could it have been?

Sharyn thought of Pat's conclusions regarding the killer's familiarity with the city and the layout of the police precincts.

She couldn't shake the thought that Dylan—or the killer, if it was someone else—knew an awful lot about leaving a clean crime scene, about the precinct map, about what the team would be looking for at each site. While it made sense that the resident, Geoff Dryer, would be familiar with those things by working in the medical examiner's office, it was also possible someone in law enforcement was involved.

Also, as far as she knew, Dylan had never decapitated any of his previous victims. She reminded herself that he might have a partner other than the man who'd been killed in the morgue—if that was even Igazi after all.

She glanced at the time.

Twenty minutes to the church.

++++

While Ralph drove, I sat in the back, keeping an eye on Ali.

I put a call through to the Nude-Velvet-London-Reckless office maven, and she helped me locate a building with a bomb shelter about fifteen minutes from here. There weren't many that fit the description of what Ali required, and although not ideal, this one seemed adequate.

"Can you confirm if your people have found my sister yet?" Ali asked us.

"I'll put the call through," Ralph said, "as soon as you contact Fayed."

He gave me his encrypted phone and I passed it to Ali.

++++

Ali knew that if Fayed suspected that he was truly working with the FBI to stop the smallpox release, he would almost certainly contact Faatina to have her kill or sell Azaliya. So he needed to be convincing. Not only did his life depend on it, but so did his sister's.

He called the number he'd memorized, the one on the twenty-dollar bill Fayed had given him at the restaurant.

The ringing stopped as someone answered but said nothing.

"This is Ali," he said in Arabic. "They are letting me call this number thinking that I will be able to get you to enter a trap, but they do not realize my resolve. They do not realize that it is already too late, that they are all already dead."

Whoever had picked up the phone continued to remain silent.

"They know about the virus," Ali went on, "and they were planning to isolate me, but in order to avoid that, I told them that I would hand you over to them. If they do quarantine me, no one will get infected. They will distribute their stockpiles of smallpox vaccine and inoculate the population. I need to see you, and I need for you to give me a suicide vest. It is the only way. I will put it on, and when they recapture me, I will martyr myself with it. There are only two of them with me, you and your men can kill them if you need to, then I will allow myself to get caught once again. By myself, I can only spread the virus to a few people at a time. If I use the vest, we can infect the entire FBI building at once."

A voice on the other end of the line, one that did not sound like Fayed, said, "We will get you a vest."

"I have a place in mind." Ali told them the site of the abandoned factory that Agent Bowers had located on the east side of the city.

"Why there?"

"Isolated."

Silence.

"When can you be there?" Ali said.

"Soon."

"I will be in the basement on the southeast corner."

Without any further response, the person hung up.

"Well?" Agent Hawkins asked Ali gruffly.

"It is all set," he said, even though he wasn't sure that was the case at all. "He will meet us there."

"How did you get Fayed to trust you?" Agent Bowers asked. "What did you tell him?"

"I told him that I wanted to kill you, and I asked if he would help."

++++

As Blake was trying to figure out where his brother might have gone, he got a call from the man who'd tipped him off about the meeting at the restaurant. "Who are you?" Blake asked roughly.

"My name is inconsequential."

"It's consequential to me."

"Discretion is paramount."

"You're not Fayed. I heard on the news that he was killed at the restaurant."

"That was Turhan. Someone in my position can never be too careful."

"So . . . why did you tell me about the restaurant?"

"You have your reasons for what you do. I have mine. If you want to find the man who ordered Maria dead, get to Jefferson Avenue as soon as possible. I'll send you the address."

83

2:19 P.M.
Dispersal in 15 minutes

I took over driving so Ralph could be in touch with the black ops team that'd gone in to rescue Ali's sister. He pulled up a live feed to prove to Ali that the girl was alright.

They'd had to take out Faatina, the jihadist who was guarding her. Now they were in the back of a van rocketing through the streets of Ust-Kamenogorsk on their way to an exfil.

Before handing the phone to Ali, Ralph showed me the screen, and I saw the image of a teenage Kazakh girl who looked terrified.

Azaliya.

++++

Ali could hardly believe that after all these months he was seeing her again.

He spoke to her in Russian.

"How are you, Azaliya?"

"What's happening? Who are these men? Where are they taking me?"

"They're there to help you. They're there to save you. I was

wrong when I left, but I did it for you. You'll be alright. They'll take care of you. They'll help you."

"Where are you?"

"I can't tell you that right now."

"They killed Faatina."

"She would have killed you."

"I don't understand."

"You will."

"But when will I see you again?"

"When the time is right, I promise we will be together."

"I love you, Ali."

"I love you too, Azaliya. Good-bye."

++++

When Ali was off the line, I said to him, "Okay, so one more time, here's what's happening. You go in, Ralph and I cover from both sides. If there's more than one person, as soon as you speak with Fayed, I want you to scratch your chin. That's how we'll know which one is him. When you do, we move in and this ends. Do you understand?"

"Yes."

"If you try anything," I said, "if this goes south, we will put you down if we have to."

"Yes, I—"

Ralph cursed, interrupting him. He was staring at a notification on his phone.

"What is it?" I asked.

"The video of Maria. Those pricks released it. It's all over the web. Looks like Bloodhound couldn't keep up."

I tried not to think about how much chaos and panic a video like that could create.

As Ralph was contacting Cyber to see what else they

could do, I got a call from DeYoung. "Pat, what is going on there in Detroit? Dr. Qiao tells me that the suspect is gone, that you broke him out of the Field Office." I'd heard the Assistant Director exasperated before, but never this angry. "And now we've got hundreds of thousands of people around the world watching that video of Maria dying. Where are you?"

"Sir, I can't tell you that." I was thankful that Ralph and I had disabled the GPS tracking in our phones earlier. DeYoung pressed me, but I only said, "I'll know more in a few minutes. I'll call you back."

After I hung up, I asked Ralph how much farther it was to the warehouse.

"Not far." Then he said to Ali, "Are you sure you aren't contagious yet?"

"As sure as I can be."

And that did not exactly reassure me.

84

2:24 P.M.

Dispersal in 10 minutes

The place where we were supposed to meet Fayed was a vast, abandoned two-story factory that sprawled across an entire city block. Part of the building was gutted. At least half of it was burned out.

I thought briefly of how this place represented someone's dream, just as I had the other day when I saw the abandoned businesses near the motel. The owner here had this building designed, watched the foundations get poured, the walls rise, the rooms take shape. Then he'd paid those thousands of employees who'd worked here over the years.

And then he had not.

The business folded. The jobs were gone. The dream was gutted, just like this building. Razed and blackened and burned to the ground.

From the material that Starr had sent us, it appeared that the factory's bomb shelter would be accessible in a stairwell on the building's southeast corner.

Ralph offered to clear the first floor while I kept an eye on Ali and the stairwell.

"Do you know which way he'll be coming from?" I asked Ali.

"He would not tell me. It is possible he is already here."

"And how many people will be with him?"

"I do not know that either."

"Well." Ralph drew his gun. "Let's find out."

++++

A few minutes from St. Gerard's Church, Sharyn noticed a car that looked just like her ex-husband's parked along the road.

A slice of fear as she passed it.

No. It didn't just look like his.

It was his.

Why is he here? Did Dylan trick him, get him to come?

She wanted to call Kevin, to warn him or to find out if he was alright, but feared using this phone that she'd been given. Dylan might discover that she'd called him, and if that happened, it would put Kevin and possibly Olivia in even more danger than they might already be in.

Sharyn prayed that everything would work out, and resolved to do whatever it took to make sure they were safe, just like she'd resolved so many years ago when she was on the set of *Sanctuary* and took those pills to save the woman she wished was her mom from dying in a movie that she'd started to believe was real.

++++

Ralph left us while I led Ali toward the stairwell.

Although wide swaths of the building were charred, the cement-block walls making up the majority of the structure remained mostly intact. Where the roof had collapsed, a bent web of rusted rebar sliced the faraway sky into irregular rectangles.

A few scraggly weeds tried to poke through the debris in those places where the ceiling had caved in and sunlight actually managed to reach the ground, but for the most part, nothing was growing in here.

The walls were blackened from the fire, but colorful graffiti had been spray-painted across many of them just as it was ever-present on so many of the walls in the other abandoned buildings in the city.

With no other lights and the walls coated with soot, the corridor before us looked pitch black, apart from the slats of light every ten meters or so where empty doorways interrupted the darkness.

We were walking through a zebra's stripes, shadow to light.

Shadow to light.

We came to the stairwell.

"I'll go in first and make sure he's not down there yet," I said to Ali. "I want you to walk right behind me. Put one hand on my shoulder and don't try anything."

We started down the steps.

++++

Blake and Mannie arrived at the old factory that the man on the phone had told them about.

Blake had no real idea what to expect inside. Maybe Fayed was in there, maybe it was a trick.

"Stay alert," he said to Mannie.

"You as well."

85

The entrance to the bomb shelter wasn't disguised like the one in Lincoln High School had been, but was clearly visible and had a spinning steering-wheel-type lock, similar to what you might find on the hatch of a submarine.

I opened it and checked inside to make sure no one was there.

This shelter was slightly smaller than the one at the high school, and it appeared to be self-contained since no other tunnels led out from it.

++++

After Agent Bowers cleared the shelter, Ali asked if he could keep the pair of handcuffs with him.

"Why?" the agent asked him.

"It might help me if Fayed gets close enough."

"What are you thinking?"

"I was trained in Yemen," he said somewhat evasively. "Trust me."

After a slight hesitation, Agent Bowers handed them over and allowed Ali to remain at the base of the stairs with a flashlight to await Fayed's arrival.

As he waited, Ali thought of his time in the desert, of

his training at that compound, and of the man kneeling in the sand, the one who just happened to have been raised Shia instead of Sunni.

So the images returned, and as they did, the memories he'd tried so hard to bury forever came crawling to the surface again.

After passing his first test of being left alone in the room for four days, Turhan, the man Ali knew at the time as Fayed, had led him around the back of the building to the kneeling man.

Hands bound behind him.

A black cloth hood cinched over his head.

Then Turhan pointed to the scimitar that the ski-mask-wearing soldier beside him carried.

"Do you wish to watch or to act?"

And Ali wondered if it was another test.

Turhan and his men had killed all those who'd moved from their cots, all those who'd failed the first test.

Ali studied the eyes of Turhan and those of the sword-carrying soldier by his side.

And he knew.

They will kill you if you do not kill this man with the hood. They will kill both of you. Two dead rather than one.

And Azaliya will be sold and will suffer as a result. And her suffering will be harsh and it will be long.

"This man has rejected the ways of true Islam," Turhan said to Ali. "He is Shia. What do you think should happen to him?"

Better to suffer yourself than to bring suffering to your sister. Better to live and bring relief than die and usher in more pain.

Ali knew that if he took the sword, his conscience would

suffer, part of his soul would be lost forever, but only one person would die.

And Azaliya would be safe.

Better your suffering than hers.

"What should happen to him?" Turhan repeated.

"He should be given one more chance to find the true path," Ali replied.

Turhan's look was hard to read.

But in the end, he offered the man one last chance, words whispered in Arabic, words that were rebuffed as the man gave a defiant reply.

Turhan stood and said to Ali. "Will you act?"

"Yes."

It was horrifying that his choice was being determined by the grim arithmetic of death, but in the service of what was good, Ali did what was not right.

He accepted the scimitar that was offered to him. The glint of the indifferent sun worked its way along the rim of the wicked blade, accentuating its edge, the killing edge.

The man who knelt on the ground shook as he whispered prayers to the same God that those who stood around him vowed their allegiance to. Ali knew the words. They were not words of hatred or condemnation, but pleas for forgiveness—but not forgiveness for deeds that he himself had done, but for the forgiveness of the men who were doing this to him. For Turhan and for the soldier. And for Ali.

Prayers.

Ali raised the blade.

Death was in his hands.

The answer.

Suffering would follow.

Birds and stones and bodies in the sand.

He swung the sword fiercely down, cutting through the air and the sunlight and the stark desert day.

But his strength was sapped from all that time in the room, and he was too weak to complete the task on the first try.

"It is alright, brother. Swing again. Allah be praised."

The muscle and bone in the man's neck resisted the work of the blade, but in the end they lost to the scimitar.

They lost to Ali.

As he stood there splattered in his fellow Muslim's blood, Ali's hands shook as the terror and finality of what he had done gripped him.

Yes, he had killed this man. It was him and not someone else.

He was the one who had beheaded him.

You are a terrorist.

You are a murderer.

Dropping the scimitar, he stumbled backward and fell to his knees.

"You have done well, brother." Turhan smiled. "You are now one of us."

The man with the black ski mask took the blade and wiped it clean, and Ali prayed for mercy rather than justice, for justice would have crushed him and mercy was his soul's only hope.

86

2:29 P.M.

Dispersal in 5 minutes

Sharyn parked beside St. Gerard's Church.

She'd never been in it before but was familiar with the church from the photograph on her wall. Julianne's photo didn't do it justice, though. Before falling into disrepair, St. Gerard's must have been quite an impressive sight.

Anticipating that, even though the day was bright outside, inside, the church would be infested with shadows, she took a compact flashlight with her as she left the car.

A text came in: Do not call for backup, Scarlett. If you do, I will know.

She didn't call dispatch.

She would take care of this on her own.

Just like Constance did when she killed the Bluebeard in the folktale that Pat told her: "So, being alone, she had to act alone."

But she ended up consumed by evil.

No. That won't happen to me.

First Simone, then five victims here, then Ted.

Dylan needed to be stopped before he killed again.

++++

As Ali remembered that day in the desert, he felt a shiver run through him. Yes, he deserved to die for what he had done. And he would die. The smallpox would've been a fitting sentence, but he would be carrying out a more prompt one here today in just a few minutes. And hopefully, if this chamber held up, the virus would not spread throughout the city.

But what if it's not airtight? What if some of the particles escape? Certainly after all this time, you cannot trust the seal.

The article said it would be airtight. You have to trust it. You don't have another choice.

Ali would tell Bowers what he was going to do immediately beforehand so the agent could bring in a team to somehow clean up the mess.

All of that infected blood.

++++

To enter the church, Sharyn first had to slip through a slit in the rusted wire mesh fence that encircled the property.

She made her way across the brushy grass toward the church.

The front door was padlocked shut, but a cellar was located nearby, so, warily, she creaked its door open and as she descended the steps, she heard soft, coarse grunting sounds.

Clicking on the flashlight, she angled it into the darkness and saw Kevin standing in the corner.

A stout, rough-hewn joist ran above his head, and his hands were handcuffed around it. There was something in his mouth. At first, she couldn't tell what it was, but as she came closer, she could see that it was a grenade. She hurried over, but he shook his head frantically.

"If I remove it, will it go off?" she said.

He nodded.

"Is Livvy here?"

He nodded.

"Where—wait, is she hurt?"

He shook his head. It looked like he'd been crying.

She pointed up. "In the sanctuary?"

He nodded once again.

"I'll be back for you."

Twenty feet past him, she found the stairs that led up to the church itself.

++++

I heard movement twenty or thirty meters to my right and went to check it out but only found a stray dog, mangy and lean. It wore a collar. Likely, it'd been someone's pet and was then left behind when its owners moved away, and was driven by its circumstances to become what it was now.

A stray dog is one raised in captivity.

A feral one grows up wild.

Ali, Fayed, Blake, Dylan—I wondered which type each of them was.

Angela contacted me that Pack-a-derm Shipping, the company that brought the mannequins to Toronto, also shipped to Detroit.

Pack-a-derm.

Pachyderm.

Elephants.

The War of the Elephants.

Everything was starting to come together.

++++

Sharyn entered through the back—the *narthex*—of St. Gerard's Church.

This wasn't anything like the small chapel they used when they filmed the movie *Sanctuary*, the church where Millie's dad had been the minister. That was a much smaller clapboard building. This was more of a cathedral.

The high, vaulted ceiling had crumbled through in half a dozen places and uncertain sunlight oozed in as if it were wary of the consequences of entering the decrepit sanctuary.

Surprisingly, most of the windows were still intact and the ones that were made of stained glass distorted and twisted the light as it came through so that nothing looked quite natural in the old church.

Vile, sacrilegious graffiti marked the west wall up front near the transept.

In addition to words mocking religion and faith, someone had drawn the snake in the Garden of Eden encircling a naked Eve, its fangs embedded in her neck, a trickle of blood and yellow venom dripping down and across her chest as her face was contorted in pain.

Many of the brick supports for the building were crumbling under the weight of the years. However, the sturdy wooden beams above Sharyn's head looked surprisingly resistant to time and decay.

"Hello?" she called anxiously. "Livvy, are you here?"

The cavernous room played with her words in a way that

seemed to both swallow them and amplify them at the same time, creating a hollow, eerie echo.

"Are you here . . . here . . . here?"

++++

Only because of Ralph's military training did he hear the soft padding of movement around the edge of one of the crumbled walls.

He eyed down his Glock's barrel. "I'm FBI. Step out with your hands up."

A man did step out. A man who dwarfed even Ralph.

"Hands up!" Ralph said.

The giant raised his hands.

"Now turn around."

The man didn't move.

Ralph had never met this man, had only seen him in the footage of Blake driving over the border from Windsor—he was Blake's associate.

"I said turn around."

But the man just stared at him. Didn't reply. Still didn't move.

"Maybe you don't speak English. *Sprechen Sie Deutsch*? Wait, you don't look German. No lederhosen."

No response.

Ralph evaluated things. In his entire life, he couldn't recall ever being outmatched in a fight, but this guy looked like he could pick him up and break him in half.

The man finally said, "You're gonna need backup."

"Ah. So you do speak English. I don't like calling in backup when there's only one person. Waste of resources."

"I don't want to hurt you."

"I don't think that needs to be your primary concern right now."

"I'm giving you the chance to walk away." The man's voice reminded Ralph of the sound of a concrete mixer.

"I'm the one with the gun."

"Yes."

Ralph smiled slightly. "Alright, big guy. Easy way or hard way?"

"Let's go with the hard way."

"I'm not entirely disappointed you said that."

++++

Rather than come at me, the dog snarled briefly, then stared past my shoulder, gave two raspy yaps, and backed away.

Someone or something was behind me.

Fayed?

I spun, Glock in hand.

Blake stood between me and the wall.

Beyond him lay the stairwell to the bomb shelter.

He dropped his gun and kicked it aside. "You wouldn't shoot an unarmed man, would you, Patrick?"

"I might," I said. "Get on your knees."

++++

Footsteps echoed lightly from the stairwell that descended into the bomb shelter, and Ali tilted up the flashlight.

Fayed appeared. "How many agents came with you, Ali?"

"Two."

"And will they return you to the federal building?"

"Yes," Ali said. "And I'll do it when I get there."

The vests that The Brigade of the Prophet's Sword used were slim and easily concealed under a person's shirt, or sometimes just around his or her waist. Some were even sculpted to avoid detection in a pat-down. During Ali's training in Yemen, he'd learned how to use them efficiently.

Fayed aimed a handgun at Ali and set the suicide vest down before backing up two steps.

"Go ahead and put it on."

"Why a gun? Do you not trust me? Would you shoot me after we have made it this far?"

"This gun isn't meant for you, brother. It is meant for the agents."

Ali brushed one hand lightly across the back of his pants, to make sure that the handcuffs were ready, and then walked toward the vest.

++++

As Ralph approached the big guy to cuff him, the man barreled forward, hands still in the air, still raised to the side.

He must have guessed that since he wasn't reaching for a weapon, Ralph wouldn't shoot.

And Ralph didn't.

He wasn't about to have his conscience trouble him for dropping someone who might not be armed. If the guy had a weapon, sure. No problem. But as it was, it looked like he was going to have to take care of this a different way.

Since his holster was still back at the federal building, Ralph tossed his gun out of reach and readied himself to take the full force of the freight train.

At impact, they both went crashing heavily to the floor.

++++

"We had a deal," Blake said to me.

"Deal's off. Besides, you didn't deliver Dylan. Where is he?"

"Is Fayed here?"

"Get on your knees, Blake, and tell me where Dylan is."

Cuff him, Pat, then get back to the stairwell.

++++

Trying not to cringe from the pain from his injured rib, Ali pulled his shirt on over the suicide vest.

"It looks good," Fayed told him. "I can't even tell that you're wearing it."

++++

As Sharyn moved forward, the dampened light that sank through the stained glass merged into an odd smear of translucent colors. One of her hands looked reddish brown, the other a muted orange. As she turned to scan the area, the colors rotated, shifting, sliding across her skin.

"Dylan?"

"Over here."

The voice came from the front of the church. Male, but, with the odd acoustics of the building, she couldn't tell if she'd ever heard that voice before. She expected that it was him, but wasn't certain. Also, it'd been fifteen years since she'd heard Dylan speak.

He must have entered through the room near the front where the priests would change.

She couldn't see his face. He was backlit from a window that would've looked down on the altar if it were still there.

From where she stood, her flashlight beam wouldn't have reached him, so she slipped it into her back pocket thinking that, if necessary, she could use it as a weapon later. Pat had told her that the man he'd fought in the attic had used his light as a distraction. Maybe she could do that here.

"Are you alone?" the man asked.

"Yes. Where's my daughter?"

"Set your gun on the floor. Any knives. Anything else you have."

"First tell me where my daughter is."

"Safe. Close. You'll see her soon enough. Put your weapons down."

"And why would I do that?"

"Because even though you're alone, it doesn't mean that I am."

She looked down and saw a red dot on her chest. It wavered back and forth for a moment and then established itself right over her heart. When she gazed up, she could see a dark form crouched on the balcony, but it was impossible to identify who it might be.

Slowly, she knelt and laid her gun down, but kept the flashlight in her pocket.

"It's good to see you again, Scarlett."

"No one has called me that name in a long time."

"That's too bad. It's a beautiful name. Come here."

The floor was covered with layers of grit and dust. The broken ceiling panels that had long ago cratered in and crumbled to pieces now littered the floor. The pews were gone, leaving the vast space vacant: a shell encasing nothing but forgotten prayers and hymns lost to the past.

++++

Ali heard Agent Bowers shout to him, "Ali? Are you there?"

The sound distracted Fayed momentarily and Ali rushed him. Fayed got off a shot, but it only went into Ali's leg and it wasn't enough to stop him.

They struggled for a moment, and finally Ali was able

to grab the gun and throw it toward the wall. He snapped one end of the handcuffs around Fayed's wrist, and the other cuff around his own.

"I have a vest," he hollered to Bowers. "I will blow it! I do not want it to spread! I have Fayed! Close the door now!"

87

2:34 P.M.
Dispersal

I heard Ali shouting that he had a vest and to shut the door and finally all that he had in mind became clear to me. It'd never been about capturing Fayed.

If you don't close the door and he kills himself, the particles in the air could infect this entire block. You can't let that happen. He's close enough to being contagious. It could spread through the whole city.

Blake said to me, "So you do have Fayed here."

"Go down and meet him."

"Think I'll pass." Blake backed up. "It looks like you have a choice, Agent Bowers. Chase me, or seal up that shelter."

"How about both?" I said, and darted toward the bomb shelter as Blake ran in the opposite direction.

++++

Fayed yanked harshly at the handcuff, then with his free hand he punched Ali in his injured face, and while Ali was off balance, he dragged him to the side, reaching for the gun.

"Close it now, Agent Bowers!" Ali shouted. He didn't want to blow the vest until the seal was complete.

He couldn't!

But he also couldn't wait.

++++

I scrambled down the steps to the bomb shelter door, saw a man aiming a gun at Ali.

"Tell my sister I love her." Ali hollered, "Close it. Now!"

I slammed the door and spun the lock.

++++

As the door closed, Ali said, "You deserve this, Fayed."

"Brother," the man gasped. "I—"

And in his final moments, Ali did not pledge his love to God, but whispered the name of his sister instead.

This is for you, Azaliya, he thought.

"—am not—"

Ali closed his eyes—

"Fay—"

Ali depressed the trigger.

88

Even from this side of the bomb shelter, I could hear the explosion and feel the rumble through the floor. I could only pray that after all these years the seal would be enough to keep the aerosolized particles in.

Ali was dead. Fayed was dead. Blake was here, was close by.

The only one we didn't know about was Dylan.

Blake. Find him. Stop him.

Go.

So I did, sprinting in the direction he'd gone.

++++

As Sharyn's eyes became accustomed to the dim light, she was able to more clearly see the outline of the man, but still could not tell for certain if it was Dylan.

A simple wooden chair sat beside him where the altar would have been.

Just like in the climax of *Sanctuary.*

He rested one hand on top of the chair. "Have you been to this church before?"

"No."

"Neither have I, but I read up on it. They have weddings here."

"Who does?"

"Goth kids mostly. The space is free. It's memorable. Unique. And illegal—which I'm guessing adds to the thrill. They sweep it out, tweet last-minute invites so the police don't show up, and voilà! Good to go, as long as the church doesn't fall in on your head and crush everyone to death."

Hearing him speak that much, she was finally able to identify that it was Dylan's voice.

Yes, it was him.

"I thought this place would be appropriate."

"For what?"

"Us," he said. "Come closer."

She'd taken four steps and dipped into the shadows again when she heard the soft brush of a light footfall behind her, just to her left.

Sharyn spun to face the threat, but was a breath of a second too late and saw only the blurring sweep of the pipe swinging toward her head.

++++

Dylan nodded toward the person who'd helped him, the one who'd given him advice on how to leave a clean crime scene, the one who'd led him to the graffiti artist who called himself Igazi.

"Are you ready?" Dylan said.

"Yes," came the reply.

"Well then, I guess it's time to get started."

"I'll go get the girl."

++++

The big guy could take a punch.

No matter how hard Ralph pummeled him in the jaw,

the man shook it off. And when Ralph hit him in the stomach, it was like punching a tree trunk.

But Ralph could take a punch as well.

Neither of them backed down.

Ralph gathered his strength, balled up his fist, and hauled off a punch to the guy's stomach as hard as he'd ever hit anyone. This time, finally, it had an effect. The behemoth stumbled backward, but when Ralph swung again, he deftly avoided the punch, grabbed Ralph, and threw him face-first into the cement-block wall.

Okay, so that was a bad idea executed poorly.

Ralph turned and faced him, worked his jaw back and forth, and then glanced at the soot now smeared across his chest. "And see, I really liked this shirt. Now you've made me mad."

++++

A stretch of greasy water lay before me. Shallow. At least four meters wide.

Blake had stepped into it, and the wet footprints led south, away from the far edge of the puddle.

Judging by the stride length and partial sole impressions, I could tell he'd been running, probably full-out.

I crossed the water.

His wet footprints disappeared back into the gloom.

++++

Christie parked behind a Yaris that she assumed was Sharyn's car, and once again checked the text she'd received from Sharyn's number, an urgent request for her to get to this church as quickly as possible. We can talk in private here, it read.

Sharyn had told her earlier that she wouldn't have time to get together today, so it all seemed strange to Christie. But since the flight didn't leave for another couple of hours, it worked out. She left her car and went looking for a way to get into the church.

++++

As I ran through the old factory looking for Blake, I thought of the case, of everything that'd occurred this week.

The mannequins in the house. The unmelted ice in the whiskey glass in the dead scientist's garage. The timing of what happened there as Blake got away, and I realized that it didn't fit. That it couldn't fit.

There were no ice trays in that house.

This went deeper than we thought.

Yes. And why Detroit? Why not another city?

Because location matters. There's something here that isn't anywhere else, and that makes it the ideal place for this.

Pack-a-derm.

Ferilex.

Die in your rage.

Then a thought, and if I was right, it would turn everything on its head.

I couldn't take time now to put a call through to DeYoung or Kennedy, but I would as soon as I'd apprehended Blake.

89

Sharyn heard voices, but they were faint.

One was her daughter's, but the sound seemed to be coming from a faraway place, disguised and forgotten, finding its way to her not through the air but through some sort of thick liquid.

"Mooommmmy? Are you okaaaaaay, Mommy?"

Sharyn wasn't even sure if she was awake or dreaming.

Awake. You're awake, Sharyn.

But that's what you would tell yourself while you were dreaming.

Open your eyes.

They're closed. Open your—

She opened them, winced, and tried to gather her bearings. She could tell that she was lying on her side on something hard. Although her head throbbed, she didn't seem to be hurt anywhere else, and when she tried moving her arms and legs, she found that she wasn't tied up or restrained.

"Mommy!"

"I think she's waking up."

"Is she okay?"

"She's—"

As Sharyn blinked, the inside of St. Gerard's Church came into focus again. She could see the altar area, and there in the transept, sitting in the chair, with her ankles and wrists duct-taped to it, was her daughter, Olivia. The serial murderer Dylan Neeson stood beside her.

While Sharyn was pushing herself to her feet, she found that she was still dizzy and had to pause to reorient herself.

Finally she managed to stand, trying her best to mask how uncertain her balance was.

Obviously, Dylan wasn't here alone. Someone else had knocked her out. Someone else had targeted her chest with the laser sight. However, as she looked around the church, no one else was in sight.

When she directed her attention onto Dylan, she noticed that his left hand was wrapped with a bloody cloth, evidently injured.

"Let my daughter go. This has nothing to do with my family. It's just between you and me."

"Oh, it's not just between you and me. It has to do with *our* family."

"What are you talking about?"

"It has to do with our son. The one you aborted."

Livvy, who was crying, called out, "Mommy!"

"It's alright, sweetheart," Sharyn assured her. "Trust me. Everything's going to be okay."

"Nothing can excuse what you did," Dylan told Sharyn.

"You raped me," she replied. "Nothing can excuse that."

"But you took a life, Scarlett."

"My name is Sharyn."

"You can change your name, but you can't change what you've done. You can't undo the past, only face up to it."

The abortion had been kept under the radar. Sharyn hadn't told anyone about it over the years except for Kevin, and, this week, Pat. So it was a mystery to her how Dylan had found out about it. She hadn't even known the baby's sex and yet here he was, saying that it was their son.

"How do you know all this?" she said, partly trying to stall, partly trying to get answers. *You need to take him down. You need to get Olivia out of here.*

"My attorney had you followed," Dylan said. "He was thorough. As you remember, it was during the trial. We were trying to get as much information as we could. After you left the abortion clinic, he went in—snuck in the back, found the remains of the fetus."

Sharyn was speechless.

"We were able to do a DNA test. He was mine. He was ours. Why did you do it?"

"Because you raped me," she repeated.

"Was that the reason?"

"Mommy, please help me!" Olivia said before Sharyn could answer Dylan.

"I will in a minute," she replied. "Livvy, I love you. I'm going to get you out of here."

"I love you too, Mommy."

"Close your eyes."

She doesn't need to hear any of this!

Over the past fifteen years, Sharyn had tried to deny the real reason she'd gotten the abortion, but now she realized that if she didn't tell Dylan the truth, he might very well kill her daughter.

It was time for it all to come out.

++++

Christie entered the back of the church.

She could hear Sharyn speaking with a man up front. A girl sat bound to a chair next to him.

A handgun lay in the middle of the expansive sanctuary.

Christie didn't know what was going on here, but she could tell for certain that Sharyn and the girl were in immediate danger. She didn't consider herself an expert with a gun, but growing up in Minnesota, she'd gone hunting as a girl. She certainly knew how to use one.

Actually, she knew pretty well.

You're not a hero.

But you can't let that man hurt them! That's Sharyn. That's a little girl! You have to do something!

She kicked off her shoes to remain quiet and stayed in the shadows as she made her way toward the gun.

++++

This side of the factory had a basement, not a bomb shelter, at the bottom of the stairwell.

"This way, Patrick," a voice called.

Blake.

He's taunting you!

Alright, well let him.

It was just going to make it easier for me to catch him.

I scrambled over a tumbled clutter of concrete slabs, avoided the broken glass and rusted rebar stabbing through the concrete, and approached the steps.

Below me, at the base of the stairwell, water filled the basement, and bloated, waterlogged furniture floated by.

Water was gushing from one of the pipes that'd been broken off and perhaps sold as scrap metal. Apparently, the city had never shut off the water here. Hundreds of thousands of gallons must have already poured into the basement.

When Blake spoke again, his voice echoed up from below: "I'm waiting, Agent Bowers."

The steps were steel, but weren't grooved, and the water dripping down from the few pipes that remained nearby left them slick, so as I descended I had to watch my step or my feet would have shot out from under me.

At the water's edge, I swept the flashlight beam before me, but saw no one.

The bottom steps were submerged and I couldn't tell exactly how many were covered by the water, so I took each one carefully, feeling my way with my foot until I located the floor.

The water reached my waist.

A city that shuts off water to those who don't pay for it, but doesn't shut it off in old factories, even when it fills up the basements—crazy. But then again, how do you check tens of thousands of old buildings?

The basement was a broad, sweeping space interspersed with imposing concrete support pillars. A webbed network of cracks crisscrossed the cement ceiling. Amazingly, some type of stalactites had formed from chemical-rich water seeping through the concrete and leaving sediment behind as it dripped down.

"Blake," I called. "Turn yourself in. Don't make me shoot you."

"I'm over here," he said from behind a cement pillar thirty meters away.

I saw no one, but started making my way toward the voice.

90

Sharyn debated how much to tell Dylan, especially in front of her daughter. But right now Olivia's safety was all that mattered.

You have to tell him. You have to do this.

She felt a hot rush of shame. The shame that she'd tried to bury for all these years. No, she hadn't aborted her baby simply because of who its father was. Or even because of the way it was conceived. She'd aborted her baby because she'd thought only of herself.

Only herself.

Tell him.

No.

Yes. For Olivia. The truth for her life!

"I did it because of my weight. My figure," Sharyn said. "I grew up in Hollywood. I thought I might want to model some more. When I got pregnant, I didn't want it to show. That's it. That's the truth. Now let my daughter go."

"You killed our child"—Dylan's voice was cold steel—"because you didn't want to get fat?"

He produced a box cutter from his pocket and slid out the blade, then pressed it against Olivia's throat.

"No!" Sharyn shouted. "Stop!"

"When it comes to abortions," he said, "liberals will try

to use the gotcha question, 'So what about in cases of rape or incest, or when the life of the mother is at risk?' What would you say?"

"What do you mean?"

"Would you say abortion is wrong in those cases?"

"No."

"So what about when there is no rape, no incest, and no one's life is in danger? What about cases where the parents just don't like the sex of their child, or the eye color, or find the idea of raising a child inconvenient or a setback to their careers? Or the mother just doesn't want to get fat? Would you say it's wrong then?"

"Yes." Her voice was hushed, but she repeated it to make sure he could hear. "Yes, I would. Now put down the blade." Then she said to her daughter, "Livvy, it's all pretend. Keep your eyes closed. It's all pretend," she lied. "It's all just a game."

But it's not just pretend. It's real. It's—

"I'll give you a choice," Dylan said to Sharyn. "Just like in *Sanctuary*. The same choice that mother had in the movie."

Sharyn was about thirty feet from him. He tossed an automatic knife to her. It skidded to a stop near her foot.

She picked it up. "What's this for?"

"You get to decide how this ends. Either you cut your own throat, or I cut hers. If you come toward me, she dies. If you don't take your life, I take hers. Who will die for your sin and who will suffer for it? I'll give you ten seconds to decide."

There's a second person here. Where is he?

"Ten."

You can't do this, Sharyn.

You have to!

"Nine."

She flicked out the blade and stared at it.

"Eight."

Lifted it to her neck.

"Seven."

You deserve this. You were selfish. You would've had a son.

"Six."

You took his life. It wasn't right.

"Five."

"No, Mommy!" Olivia screamed. "Don't do it!"

"Four."

All she needed to do was press and slide to save her daughter. Press it in, swipe it to the side, and—

"Three."

I pray the Lord my soul—

"Two—"

As she was about to carry out the sentence on herself, she heard a gunshot, and then Christie's voice: "Don't move!"

But Dylan did. Leaving Olivia there, he bolted awkwardly, favoring one leg, to the side of the church as another gunshot rang out.

As he escaped into the priests' changing room, Sharyn ran forward to free her daughter from the chair.

"Christie," she shouted, "get over here. Hurry!"

She slit the duct tape and was helping Olivia stand when Christie arrived.

Christie offered her the gun, but Sharyn asked, "You know how to use that?"

"Grew up hunting."

"Alright. There's someone else here. Protect my daughter. Get her out of here. Do you have a phone?"

Christie handed her cell over and Sharyn called dispatch to get backup en route as she flew toward the room after Dylan, tightening her grip on the knife's handle as she did.

++++

The water in this part of the building flowed into a tunnel that led toward the Detroit River, and I imagined that it probably emptied into the river at some point.

The tunnel must have been part of the original plant, and although I was curious how that related to the flooded basement, right now I didn't have time to concern myself with any of that.

I tried the phone to call for backup, but here beneath the concrete and steel, I didn't get any reception. Then, maybe twenty meters ahead of me, near where the basement narrowed, I saw Blake.

I had the Glock aimed at him but I didn't trust myself to take the shot from here.

"You didn't leave the ice, did you?" I said.

"The ice?"

"In the whiskey glass, back at the Russian scientist's house. Gaviola left it."

"How do you know?"

"There weren't any ice trays in the house, yet somehow the ice in that glass wasn't melted. Someone brought it in. And that's how you were able to get away, isn't it? How long has he been working with you?"

"Why do you think it was him?"

"He was the first one in the garage. After that, there

wouldn't have been any opportunity to plant the ice. Also, he's the one who got the anonymous tip. It was a distraction, right? Something to keep us searching in that neighborhood while you slipped away? It's a little thing, but little things point to the big ones: whoever brought the ice in didn't know that there were no ice trays."

"Tell Gaviola, 'Hi,' from me when you arrest him."

"You can tell him yourself after I bring you in."

I edged toward him through the water. To my right, the current picked up. As a kid in Wisconsin, I'd always feared falling through the ice and drowning. No ice here, but I could still end up trapped, sealed underwater. I didn't even want to entertain the thought of being swept down that tunnel.

"If you want me"—Blake smiled—"come and get me." And then he ducked into the rushing water.

I waited for a moment to see if he would come back up, or if it'd all been a ploy.

91

Dylan was waiting for Sharyn in the priests' room.

He grabbed her by the shirt and threw her forward. She tumbled down a short flight of stairs and he was right behind her.

The small room at the base of the stairs was thick with shadows, and when he came at her, he kicked her hard against the place on her skull where his partner had bashed her earlier.

The force of the blow spun her around and brought a flash of stars and the same dizziness she'd had when she first woke up.

++++

It wasn't a ploy.

Blake was gone.

I cursed to myself, studied the amount of space between the top of the water and the tunnel. It looked like there would be just enough air to grab a breath inside there as long as the current wasn't too swift.

I holstered the weapon, rushed forward, took a deep breath, and dove into the water.

++++

That bloody fabric that was wrapped around Dylan's left hand was her ticket. Sharyn decided to attack him where he was weakest. Still on the ground, she struck, spearing the automatic knife at him. Her timing was spot-on and the blade embedded through his palm.

But instead of stopping him, he curled his hand to lock the blade in place and then swiped it at her.

Pain didn't seem to bother him.

At least not yet.

But she would make sure that it did soon enough.

Fights in the movies can last a long time, but most fights in real life are quick. A couple of punches, a couple of kicks, someone goes down, and then it's over.

Alright, it was time to end this one.

She got to her feet and stared at him. He had the box cutter in one hand, the knife embedded through the other.

From what Pat had said Wednesday night, this guy was an expert at close-quarters combat.

The flashlight.

She reached behind her for it, swept it forward, flicked it on, glared it in his face, and then threw it at him. Taking advantage of the distraction, she rushed forward, grabbed the wrist of the hand that still had the knife through it, and smacked his elbow to cause the arm to snap up toward his chest, driving the knife in.

He managed to use the box cutter to slice into her shoulder as he slumped against the wall and began to sink toward the floor.

Yeah, there was pain on his face now.

Good.

He tried to pull his hand away from his chest, but she pushed the blade in farther and held it firmly in place until he was on the floor and he was no longer moving.

She stood back, heart hammering, shoulder bleeding, arms shaking.

"That's for Simone and Ted," Sharyn said. She went back into the sanctuary, found it empty, and called for Christie, but heard nothing.

Running outside, she finally located Christie and Olivia. "Are you two okay?"

"Yeah," Christie said.

Olivia hurried to the arms of her mother.

"Any sign of his partner?" Sharyn asked.

Christie shook her head.

"Thank you," Sharyn said.

"Of course." Christie looked shaken and pale.

"You sure you're alright?"

"I'm just not used to this type of thing. It's more Pat's specialty than mine."

"You looked pretty good in there to me."

The sirens told Sharyn that backup was coming. She made sure they had a bomb squad en route as well to rescue Kevin, who, as far as she knew, was still in the basement.

++++

It was harder than I thought to grab air in the tunnel.

If I tried swimming forward, there wasn't enough room to get my head up for a breath, so I had to float on my back. I still had my flashlight, but in the swift and turbid water, I couldn't see much.

Without warning, the space at the top of the tunnel

disappeared, and the current became faster, tumbling me against the rough sides of the tunnel and spitting me out into the Detroit River.

I kicked my way to the surface, snatched a lungful of air, and looked around. There was no sign of Blake on shore. No sign of him in the river.

As I was scanning the bank again, all at once, I felt a hand on my ankle. Instinctively, I gasped but he tugged me down before I could draw in a fresh mouthful of air.

Blake climbed up my body until his hands were on my shoulders, then he kicked me down deeper into the water.

I stroked upward toward air, but he kicked at me again, this time hitting me in the side of the jaw. The little air that I did have burst out of my mouth, and I had to struggle to get back to the surface. Just as I did, he was on me again. But instead of going for my face, he went for my gun—the holstered Glock.

While I struggled to keep it from him, it slipped away into the river, but I managed to land a solid punch to the side of his face.

Then, all at once, he took a breath and did a surface dive into the river.

I waited for him to come up. Treading water, I turned in a circle but saw no sign of him.

92

I gave it three minutes or so but still didn't see Blake resurface. Frustrated, I smacked the water, swam to shore, and went to find Ralph.

++++

The person who'd worked with Dylan stood among the law enforcement personnel responding to the scene. No one suspected anything.

It was safe here. Here, in the open. Two weeks after Dylan had moved to Detroit, the two of them had connected. Now, even though he was gone, at least one of them could live on and continue their work.

++++

When I saw Ralph, his shirt was soot-covered and torn. His face was swollen on the left side, and he had a split lip. The knuckles of both hands were bloodied.

"What happened to you?" Ralph said, indicating my wet clothes.

"Detroit River. Long story. Blake got away. I need your phone, mine's gone in the water."

"I already made the call. Backup's on the way."

"We're gonna need a HAZMAT team. Ali blew himself

up. He was in the bomb shelter and who knows how contagious he was. I'll give you the rundown in a sec. Let me call it in."

While he was pulling out his cell, I asked, "How many of them were there?"

"Just one. But he was big enough to count as three."

"Did you Hawkins him?"

"In this case, he kind of Hawkinsed me." Ralph gave me his phone. "I'd say it was a draw, but he got away—so I guess that means he won. This time."

"I've never known that to happen."

"It won't happen again." He tapped his head. "That guy had one hard melon."

I called for the response team to bring biosuits.

After I hung up, I took a minute to tell Ralph about Gaviola.

"So you think he's dirty?"

"I think it's worth having a conversation with him."

"SWAT wears body cameras. I'll have Torres check the footage, see what Gaviola's reveals."

"Good."

Then I remembered what Ralph had said earlier about how Fayed Raabi'ah Bashir's group didn't like to carry out a single event, but liked to pile them on one another.

Just one martyr?

Unlikely.

Ali was supposed to be apprehended. That was part of their plan to infect us. But what else?

What—

Kennedy had said that Idris was the one responsible for

getting the contract for Ferilex to provide medical supplies to the government in the case of an emergency.

Oh.

I quickly dialed Angela's number at Cyber.

"Any word on the plates from the car at the restaurant?" I asked her.

"Narrowed it down to two hundred and fifty-two possibles."

"Are any registered in the name of Idris Kourye?"

"Can you spell that?"

I did.

"No."

"What about his company, Ferilex?"

"Did you say Ferilex?"

"Yes."

"It doesn't look like it, no. But I do recall that name. They also received shipments from Pack-a-derm Shipping."

"What?"

My mind was spinning.

"Have we identified the original sender or receiver of Maria's video?"

"No. What is this about?"

Russian women who don't speak.

Detroit ports.

Dr. Kuznetsov's shipping manifest.

Follow them. Listen to what the ladies say.

"Angela, see if Ferilex has received any supplies recently through Pack-a-derm Shipping from Russia or Kazakhstan."

These guys go for multiple attacks, not a single one. No. It's not about one martyr. It never was. It's about what happens after he's caught.

Vans of first responders were pulling up and they started to lay out their equipment to put on their biosuits and respirators.

"I've got it," Angela said. "They shipped SCBAs."

Self-contained breathing apparatus. It's the same shipping company. Follow the women who don't speak. That's what Maria was trying to tell you.

Ferilex distributes medical supplies.

They recently got the contract.

Air tanks. Respirators.

A Tesla drove up.

Idris Kourye was here.

I ran toward him and called to Ralph, "Stop those guys. Don't let them breathe through the respirators!"

93

It's aerosol-based.

That's the second attack.

Avoid assumptions, Pat.

Yeah, but don't ignore the evidence.

Just hit the FBI, then when the first responders show up, infect them. They'll unknowingly spread it to everyone they're trying to rescue.

I wanted to call Kennedy and ask him how long the SCBAs in the Hazardous Materials Response Unit had been there to see if we could use those, but there was no time at the moment.

You want a fine-particle aerosol delivery system like an inhaler.

What could be better than a respirator and an air tank?

Idris stepped out of his car. As I rushed toward him he held his hand up. "Agent Bowers, keep back. No face-to-face contact. Two meters. You might have been exposed."

"How'd you get here so fast, Idris?"

"Kennedy. I wanted to help the first responders with the units."

"Do not put on those suits," I shouted to the people nearby. "Do not touch the respirators!"

"What is it? What's wrong?"

I faced Idris. "Do you know who Dr. Kuznetsov is?"

"Who? No."

"You know what the terrorists say about rage?" I was still holding Ralph's phone in my hand.

"Rage?"

"Yes." I tapped the cell's screen.

"Let them die in their rage, I think," he said. "Something like that. I don't know. I'm no terrorist. What's going on?"

I held up the phone and replayed the recording of what he'd just said. "Yeah, that's a match."

"What are you talking about? What are you doing?" He was backing up toward his trunk. "Did you just record me?"

"You were the one in the video with Maria," I said. "You were the one with the scimitar. Were you at the restaurant as well? Wearing a ski mask, maybe?"

"You're not making any sense."

"You cut off Maria's hands with a sword."

He pressed the trunk release button on his key fob and was going for something in it when I tackled him.

We slammed hard onto the pavement and he wrestled to get free, but then Ralph was beside me, helping to cuff Idris, who just whispered, "The appeals will last for years. I'll have the best lawyers in the country, and I'll play the court of public opinion. No evidence, just you targeting, stereotyping, profiling Muslims."

"I wouldn't bet on that." I was patting him down, making sure he wasn't wearing a suicide vest.

The first responders stood nearby frozen, aghast.

"I'll get free," Idris told us. "Killing me is the only way to stop us."

"No. That's the only way to keep your ideology alive,"

Ralph said. "Sorry to disappoint you, but you don't get to be a martyr and be remembered, you get to die forgotten in prison."

"How many have there been?" I asked Idris.

"How many?"

"Surrogates. Body doubles. Whatever term you want to use." It was like what Kennedy said regarding the Dread Pirate Roberts from *The Princess Bride*: Fayed Raabi'ah Bashir was a role, not necessarily a specific individual.

"More than you'll ever know."

"But why?" I said. "Why do this? Any of this?"

"Obedience is its own justification."

"Obedience? Obedience to what?"

"What my religion requires of me."

"I thought Islam was more about faith, prayer, and charity? Aren't those the first three Pillars? And the last two don't mention anything about maiming and killing innocent people either. Or do I have that wrong?"

He spit at me.

Ralph hauled him to his feet.

Idris began to speak in Arabic and I couldn't understand any of it.

But the guy did not seem happy.

Oh well.

It looked like we would need to postpone our tête-à-tête on the art of coffee roasting.

"How did you know to record him saying that?" Ralph asked me after backup had taken Idris in.

"I didn't."

"What do you mean?"

"I didn't have access to Maria's video, so I had to, well . . ."

"You bluffed."

"Maybe."

"Based on what?"

"Call it a whim."

"You don't follow whims."

"Okay, how about an 'as-of-yet-unproven hypothesis.'"

"Works for me."

I got through to Christie, and she quickly gave me the rundown of what'd happened at St. Gerard's Church. She sounded rattled but assured me that she was fine, and so were Sharyn, Olivia, and Sharyn's ex-husband.

"Remember how you said you wanted us to stay us?" she said.

"Yes."

"And I asked you what that meant?"

"Yes."

"And how we were talking about being ships passing in the night?"

"Uh-huh."

"Well, I think for us to stay us we need to make sure we take the time to keep aiming for the same shore."

"I'm up for that."

"So am I."

"I'll get there as soon as I can," I told her, "but it might be a little while."

"Why is that?"

"I might need to be quarantined."

PART 6

Under My Umbrella

PARAMOUR

Endless wind
clutching at promises
unspoken and woven with
the subtext of hearts on fire.
A tryst, subtly dancing
across my face,
fingering my hair,
and either tangling
or untangling my life
depending on your perspective.

UNTITLED 1

When I walk in the ways of the night
I breathe in gasps of ragged
darkness that throw lethal tendrils
down deep into my soul.
But when I walk in the footsteps of light,
I start to glow. And the shadows
inside of me begin to recede
at last.

—FROM *DOLLHOUSE IN MY HEART: POEMS OF FRAGILE GLASS* BY ALEXI MARËNCHIVEK (TRANS. BY BRIANNA SAULE), 1999, PAGES 61 AND 143.

94

Three weeks later

New York City

Dusk

The rain came soft at first, gentle and calming, and the damp scent of the evening reminded me of growing up in Wisconsin—that touch of spring that came as the snow melted in March. Tonight seemed a lot more like a spring evening in the Midwest than a summer one in the city.

I pointed to the stuffed alligator that Tessa had set on the couch right before joining Christie and me at the table in their apartment. I'd never seen it before. "Who's that?"

"Toothy."

"Toothy the alligator?"

She rolled her eyes. "She's a crocodile."

"Oh. Well, where's Francesca?"

"On a sleepover. Hannah and I traded for now. I'm gonna get Francesca the next time I go over to babysit."

"I'm glad you've connected with her and Aja," Christie said. "Rachel says they love having you there."

"I still can't stand the stupid diapers, though. Did you know that babies poop out their own body weight every sixty hours? I'm just glad I don't."

"So am I."

"I think we're all on the same page there," I said.

Christie snabbed another piece of the vegan chocolate torte that Tessa had helped her make. I didn't exactly know how they'd pulled it off, making it vegan enough for Tessa to eat and tasty enough for me, but they had.

As a group, we'd agreed to eat dessert first tonight.

And, just for good measure, we were already moving on to seconds.

Christie had the window slightly open rather than putting the air conditioner on. Outside, night was settling over the city and the rain was washing the grime of the day away.

Tessa had pressured her mom to let her have some of the wine we were sipping with the torte, but Christie had stood firm and Tessa grumbled, but settled for root beer.

"So, is she awake yet?" Christie asked her.

"No, she's still sleeping in the other room. It was a long day. A lot to take in."

"You're not being too hard on her, are you?"

"No. Just trying to teach her to walk in my footsteps."

"That is slightly frightening."

"Thank you."

I asked Tessa what they were up to tomorrow.

"The two of us are gonna go see Dr. Flossguilt."

"Dr. Flossguilt?"

"Yeah, that's my name for him. Mr. Oh-you-haven't-been-flossing-enough-have-you? Seriously? Who flosses enough? You go to the dentist and it's like going to confession, only he isn't there to absolve you but only make you feel guiltier. No matter how much you floss, it'll never be enough for Dr. Flossguilt and his ilk. And yes, I did just say 'ilk.' I'll bet you a hundred bucks not even he flosses enough."

"I hope it goes well," I said. "No cavities."

"Course this torte's probably not helping anything." She took another bite. "Screw it. And I am *not* gonna floss tonight. Let's see how he likes that." Then she said, "Let's eat the tempeh before it gets cold."

A voice came from the hallway, thick with a Russian accent, "I do not know what is that. Tempeh."

Azaliya's English was surprisingly good, but word order can be an issue for people who don't learn English as their first language.

We would work on it.

Tessa did her best to explain the meat substitute to her, but by the look on Azaliya's face, she wasn't too excited about the idea of dining on deep-fried fermented soybeans.

It'd taken some arm-pulling, but the social services department here in the city had far more foster children that needed homes than they had families willing to take them in—especially when it came to teenagers—so they'd expedited things so that Ali's sister could have a place to stay.

Azaliya Saleem was fourteen, Tessa fifteen.

Christie hadn't applied to adopt her, but had simply offered to provide foster care until a more permanent arrangement could be made. So, until then, Azaliya was staying here in Tessa's room on the top bunk of the bed I'd built for them.

Tessa was doing her best to introduce her to screamer bands, tofu, and Edgar Allan Poe. They talked boys and clothes and complained about having too many rules and played the video game "Exo-Skel IV" until three in the morning and I was glad that Tessa, even though she didn't have many friends, at least had this one. And that she could help her navigate through mourning the loss of her brother.

++++

Five years ago.

British Columbia, Canada

The woman let him take her hand and help her over the log. "Thank you."

"You're welcome."

"So where are we going?"

"It's a surprise."

"I like surprises," she said.

"I know."

"When I asked if you'd go on a hike with me this afternoon, I didn't know we would be coming out this far."

"You can see the gorge a lot better from the overlook."

"We were there once."

"Yes," he said. "I remember. It was our second date."

Actually, she'd suspected that he might be leading her there, but she didn't tell him that. Better to please him by acting surprised.

And, truthfully, she'd been hoping they would go back to that overlook. It would be perfect. She fingered the ring in her pocket. "You're not a girl who likes to do things the traditional way," he'd told her a few months ago. "That's one of the things I like about you."

He didn't know she had the ring.

It would be better this way.

++++

For the last few weeks Dr. Ferrier and her team at the CDC had been busy.

They instituted their most stringent protocols, closed

down the Detroit Metropolitan Airport, brought in the National Guard, vaccinated everyone they could in the city, and then isolated and sealed off the building where Ali had blown himself up. According to what he'd told us, he hadn't been contagious yet, but they didn't want to take any chances.

However, that bomb shelter did present a problem. As far as I knew, they still didn't know how they were going to deal with it long-term.

The CIA's code breakers were finally able to decipher Dr. Kuznetsov's notes well enough to discover that he had come up with a treatment strategy for dealing with this strain of smallpox. He and his people had lied to Ali Saleem. There was a way to help people survive it.

It wasn't perfect, it wasn't a hundred percent effective, but in the end, seven first responders ended up infected and, although the virus hit them hard, and two of them nearly died, they managed to pull through.

We didn't find Blake's body.

Although part of me wanted to believe that he wouldn't have survived that long underwater, I couldn't afford to make assumptions like that.

But there was one assumption, as well as one promise, I was willing to make: I assumed he would be back. And I promised not to let him slip away next time.

As far as Sharyn, the world now knew that she was the long-lost Scarlett Farrow. It was a veritable revelation in Hollywood and the modeling industry. She'd already been offered some major contracts, roles, and a substantial book deal. Her story was dominating the tabloids.

Yes, she was in her midthirties, but she hadn't lost her midtwenties beauty. I wasn't sure what all of this was going to mean for her, but the last time we spoke she'd said that she couldn't afford to put the life of her daughter at risk. I didn't know if that meant staying with the FBI, or leaving it—since it was her previous life as an actress that'd influenced Dylan when he targeted her and her family.

When we spoke on the phone the other day, I'd asked her if Olivia's nightmares had stopped.

"She's doing well. Obviously, that was quite a traumatic experience there in St. Gerard's Church, but children are amazingly resilient. I'm proud of her."

Then, after some updates about the case and the ongoing search for Dylan's partner, we got talking about the next steps in our lives. She told me that if she cut back her work at the Bureau, it might help her avoid the sole custody battle with Kevin. "I might do some modeling to pay the bills. I'm still trying to sort all that out." Then she said softly, "Also, the shame I felt all these years about the abortion—it's finally beginning to go away. Maybe confessing it all in a church wasn't such a bad idea after all."

"I'm glad to hear that."

After a short hesitation, she said, "Pat, honestly, I wish you and Christie all the best. You have good taste. And so does she. If, someday, things don't work out with her, you can always—"

"No. I can't have a plan B. It wouldn't be fair to either of you."

"Right." A pause. "Good-bye, Pat."

"Good-bye, Sharyn."

++++

"Sit down," the young man told her.

"Why?"

He held up his camera. "I want to get a picture with the valley behind us."

She positioned herself on the railing. The wind whipped up over the edge and tossed her hair around her in a tiny, elegant swirl.

Right up until they'd arrived a few minutes ago, she hadn't been certain that she was going to bring out the ring, but they were alone. The spot was perfect, and the moment felt right.

He sat beside her, she placed her head on his shoulder and, arm outstretched, he snapped the photo of the two of them.

"Careful," he said. "Don't lean back. It's a long way down."

++++

When Gaviola was confronted with the footage from his body camera, he confessed to helping Blake. He was currently in custody trying to negotiate a plea deal.

The identity of the person who'd been working with Dylan at St. Gerard's Church and of Detective Ted Schwartz's killer remained a mystery.

Considering the mitigating circumstances, Ralph and I were reprimanded but not prosecuted.

I told Ali's sister that he had died a hero while killing a terrorist.

Of course, the media spread the news about his role in the attempted attack, and that was fine. It was their job, but I made sure that Azaliya also knew how much he loved her, that he'd been trying to find a way to protect her, and that his last thoughts had been of her.

"Whatever else he was, he was your brother," I said to her. "And anyone who would go to the lengths that he did to protect someone he loves deserves to be honored for that devotion, not simply reviled because he lost his way."

++++

She realized that she needed to do it now or she might lose the nerve.

Carefully, she scootched herself forward off the railing and knelt on one knee before him.

"What are you doing?" he asked.

"You told me once that I wasn't a girl who liked to do things the traditional way."

"Oh." The shock about what was happening was clear in his voice.

She didn't know what he would say, but she couldn't stop now.

"Listen," he said. "I don't think—"

"I have something to tell you, something I need to ask you."

"Babe, I—"

"Shh. Please." She reached into her pocket and drew out the ring, but kept it in her closed hand. "I've wanted to marry you since the first day I met you."

His eyes widened.

She wasn't a girl who did things the traditional way.

No.

No, she was not.

She looked up at him. "Did you sleep with Celia?"

"What?"

"Celia. My friend. Did you sleep with her?"

"What are you talking about?"

"You need to be honest with me."

"I am. No, of course not. I didn't sleep with Celia."

"I want our relationship to be based on trust."

"I know, Jules. You can trust me. I didn't. I would never cheat on you."

She peered up at him sadly, then opened her hand. Showed him the ring.

"Julianne, I—"

"She told me all about it, Kyle. About what you did. How you like it." Now tears were forming in her eyes. She hadn't wanted it to go like this. Hadn't wanted any of it to go like this.

"Come here." He began to stand, but she signaled for him to stop.

"No. Don't." She hesitated. "It needs to be like this. Celia told me everything before she died."

"What? Dead? How do you—"

She dropped the ring beside her.

"I'm sorry it had to end like this." Then she grabbed his ankle. Since her left arm had never formed properly, she had only one hand to use, but her grip was resolute and unforgiving. "A relationship needs to be based on trust."

She drew her arm up swiftly even as she rose to her feet, flipping him backward off the railing. His gasp became a scream, long and thin and final, as he plummeted backward, his body bouncing off the rocks on its descent to the base of the cliff.

She stepped forward and watched him fall. She was far enough away so that the sound of impact traveled up to her after he hit the ground.

Then Julianne picked up the ring. Celia's ring. The one she'd slid off her friend's limp finger right after she killed her.

++++

Yesterday, Idris had escaped from prison during a transfer. Thankfully, no officers were killed, but it looked like he'd had help. Who it was or where they'd taken him remained a mystery.

However, admittedly, I wondered if it might've been Blake, perhaps calling on someone in his network of underground contacts to assist him. If so, I could only imagine the kind of punishment Blake would give Idris for killing Maria in the manner that he had.

Another case. Another day.

But this moment belonged to us.

"Looks like the rain's picking up," I said to Christie. "Might be a perfect night for a walk."

"A walk?"

"Sure, under my umbrella."

"Ah. I can think of a few other things that could happen under your umbrella."

"So can I."

She took my hand, and together we headed toward the elevator.

++++

So, it had been five years now since Julianne Springman had killed the boyfriend who'd cheated on her as well as the woman he'd slept with.

She still had Celia's ring. Still wore it.

Three weeks ago she'd quit her job as a CSI tech at the Detroit Police Department, ostensibly to pursue her photography full-time.

The man she'd been working with, killing with, Dylan Neeson, was dead, but she couldn't take any chances that the ongoing investigation into who his partner had been would reveal her identity.

Yes, she was the one who'd killed Detective Schwartz. She

was the one who'd sent the text to Christie Ellis using Sharyn's phone, inviting her to St. Gerard's Church. Julianne hadn't known the nature of their relationship, but she'd wanted someone else there as a witness, or perhaps as another victim, depending on how things turned out. Julianne was also the person who'd killed Canyon in his hospital room.

And Julianne Springman was not done killing, not by any means, and she had a whole new type of photography in mind to pursue.

++++

No, there's nothing certain about love. It centers you by unbalancing you.

Logic doesn't usher in attraction, it follows it—often as the prelude to breakups, separations, divorces.

Passion and desire lead to intimacy. Logic leads to justification and paves the way to loneliness. No one argues himself into falling in love, but he might analyze his way out of it.

Reason comes late to the party, if it shows up at all, and that's not what I wanted to happen with Christie and me. I would let my feelings inform me.

And I would let my choices lead us closer to that mutual shore, no matter how illogical it might seem.

++++

Tessa watched out the window as her mom scooted under the umbrella with Patrick, and they passed down the street.

"You are thinking they are happy?" Azaliya asked her.

"Yeah. I'm thinking that," she said.

And just maybe I am too.

"Hey, Az, my mom's got this new nail polish and lipstick

that Patrick gave her: London Reckless and Nude Velvet. Weird, I know. I prefer black, but the nail polish is actually pretty cool."

"Then can we play 'Exo-Skel IV'?"

"Absolutely. And I'm seriously gonna beat you this time."

"*Nyet.* You will not."

"You're speaking Russian again, girlfriend. You do that and I'll have to bust out the Latin."

"That is a dead language."

"Part of the reason I'm learning it. C'mon. Let's go do our nails and then kill some bad guys."

++++

Life is messy.

And beautiful.

Sometimes it's easy to see the first part and miss the second.

But it's vital that we don't.

As Christie and I walked along the New York City sidewalk listening to the raindrops tap-splatter on the top of the umbrella, I said, "There's something I need to tell you."

"What's that?"

"It's a promise I made to Ralph earlier this month. Actually it's two things. An apology and a confession."

"Okay." She sounded slightly worried.

Tell her you're sorry and you love her.

And don't forget to pause.

And so that's what I did.

Epilogue

Blake stared out across Lake Michigan. The exquisite home he was renting for the week sat perched in a small alcove overlooking the water.

Losing his brother had been hard, but there was some poetic justice in the fact that he had died at the hand of the woman he'd raped. So Blake did not seek revenge against her. In Dylan's case, he counted the scales balanced.

In the case of Fayed Raabi'ah Bashir, however, they still needed some adjustment.

Behind him, he heard the sizzling hiss of Mannie heating up the knife over the open flame of the gas stove.

Blake turned. Idris Kourye, otherwise known as Abdul Rashid, lay tied up on the floor, eyes wide, a gag in his mouth.

"How's it coming, Mannie?" Blake said.

"Almost ready."

Breaking Idris out of the prison transport had required Blake to call in just about all the favors he was owed, especially since he'd requested that no police officers or U.S. Marshals be killed during the operation.

Idris hadn't seemed surprised when Blake showed up to deliver him from the prison van that lay crashed and smoking along the side of the road.

"You're here because of what we did to Maria," Idris had said to him calmly. "Correct?"

"Yes. And I'm here because of what I'm going to do to you."

Now Blake told him not to worry. "Be assured, Idris, we'll cauterize the wounds so you won't bleed out. We'll start with the fingers on the right hand, move to the left. Then on to the toes. Work our way in from there."

"Ready," Mannie announced. He turned off the gas and approached Fayed with the red-hot blade, but before he could get started, the doorbell rang.

Blake and Mannie looked at each other curiously, then Blake drew his 1911, started toward the door, and peered out the window.

A young Middle Eastern man was standing on the porch, whistling.

He rang the doorbell again.

Blake eased over, then all at once threw the door open, drew the man inside, and pressed the barrel of the gun against the back of his head. "Think carefully about what you're going to say. I want to know your name and who sent you."

"I sent myself. I'm the one who gave you the restaurant. I'm the one who told you that Fayed would be at that factory on Jefferson Avenue. I'm the one who escaped from the restaurant with this man you have tied up on the floor here. Surely, you can recognize my voice. We spoke on the phone."

Blake said, "Oh, and don't tell me—you're the *real* Fayed Raabi'ah Bashir."

"No." He eyed the man who was gagged and lying on the carpet. Then the young man smiled, faintly but visibly.

"No, I am not Fayed. But when you're done with that knife, I'm ready to be. If you're willing to work with me."

"What can you give me that I don't have?"

"My allegiance."

Blake closed the door. "Would you like to watch?"

"I'd much rather have a knife in my hand."

"How about that. So would I."

Then Blake shot the man in the back of the head, and his body slumped clumsily to the floor.

"Tell me my new name," Blake said to Mannie.

"It looks like it's Fayed Raabi'ah Bashir," his friend replied, and then reheated the blade.

"Yeah. I kind of like the sound of that. I think I could get used to it."

When Mannie was ready, Blake accepted the knife from him.

Then, Mannie held Idris down with a firm hand as the most recently ordained Fayed Raabi'ah Bashir got to work balancing the scales on the man who was his namesake.

THANKS AND ACKNOWLEDGMENTS

While some of my sources must remain confidential, I would like to thank everyone who assisted me in researching this book for their insights and encouragement.

For my research and fact checking, thanks to Jill, Betsy, Allan, Tracey, Michael, Timothy, Jesse, Ed, Donald, Tim, Luba, Mark, Shikina, Chris, Kim, and Werner.

Thanks to my readers and editors, Brent, Ashley, Pam, Bill, Eden, Trinity, Liesl, Lori, Daniel, JP, and Sonya.

Thanks to Dan Conaway, my agent, who believed in me from the start.

A special thanks to the Detroit Police Department and the FBI's Public Affairs Office at the Detroit Field Office. Thank you for your assistance in my research and for all you do in protecting and serving an iconic American city as it regroups and reenvisions its future.

Thanks to the team at Berkley for working so hard to bring this book together.

And finally, thanks to my brother, Todd, whose interest in viruses is at the same time very helpful and very troubling. Brainstorming with you is always a gift, and your knowledge of the War of the Elephants gave me the premise for this book. I love you, brother, even if you frighten me sometimes by how quickly you answer me when I ask you for a good way to dispose of a body.